ELOISE AND THE QUEEN

A NOVEL OF ELIZABETH I

LADIES OF TUDOR ENGLAND
BOOK ONE

JENNIFER ASHLEY

JA / AG PUBLISHING

PART I
PRINCESS

1547 - 1553

CHAPTER 1

I was born in the same year as my Lady Elizabeth, in the year of our lord 1533. My mother found this auspicious—she, like Dr. Dee, put much faith in the stars and the dance of the heavens, and predicted that my life would be filled with wealth and happiness.

My grandmother skeptically observed that I was a sickly child and that arriving in the world five days before the Lady Elizabeth gave me no benefit.

However, Grandmother acknowledged that I had some skill with a needle and thought it would be advantageous for me to live with my Aunt Kat Champernowne and be useful to the very young Princess Elizabeth.

And so, at four years of age, I was sent to Hatfield, where Aunt Kat had already been installed as Elizabeth's governess. There I assisted Aunt Kat and learned to sew the sumptuous garments that would robe the ladies of the court in later days, which would have many consequences for me and the entire kingdom.

At that time, I knew only that my Aunt Kat was a much preferable guardian to my feckless mother, who'd remarried soon after my actor father had died. Her new husband wanted nothing to do with me, and so I was bundled off, with my grandmother's assistance, to Elizabeth's household. There I learned that Elizabeth was also gifted with the needle and that I was happiest surrounded by fabrics and trim, creating whole ensembles from nothing.

Elizabeth and I sewed together in the dappled sunlight of the house at Hatfield, or Enfield, or at Ashridge Priory, which Elizabeth's father eventually bequeathed her.

Princess Mary, the daughter of Henry's first queen, lived with us all as well, but she was older and a bitter young woman. I came to feel sorry for her, having been forced by her father to become a lady-in-waiting to the daughter of her mother's rival, but I could never grow to like the prickly Mary. On occasion, Lady Jane, the princess's cousin, joined us, though truth to tell, I found Jane, though quite book-learned, dull company compared to the radiant Elizabeth.

Being young Elizabeth's companion was not always an honor, I was quick to discover, as her status fell, rose, and fell again. When Henry executed Queen Anne, Elizabeth's mother, and married his next queen appallingly swiftly, Elizabeth was declared illegitimate and stripped of her title. Mary rejoiced, but she was not restored to his good graces either, until Henry married his final queen, Catherine Parr, in 1543.

Queen Catherine managed to reconcile the king with his two daughters, but even so, they were only women, and King Henry's attention and adoration went for his son, Edward.

The princess Elizabeth—Lady Elizabeth, after her star had fallen—formed a friendship with me, though I never forgot how lowly I was compared to her. We sewed together, she read to me from books I didn't much understand, and I patiently listened to her rant when she was in a fit of pique.

Our life did not begin to take shape, carved into the sharp

patterns it would become, until the day in 1547 when we learned that old King Henry was dead.

Elizabeth and I were both nearly fourteen. Her recent portrait showed her in a gown of scarlet damask over a sumptuous gold underskirt, with a pearl-studded French hood pinning back her beautiful red hair—every piece designed and sewn by me.

My talent as a seamstress, my only talent thus far, had grown as I'd experimented and practiced the art through the years. I'd begun sewing gowns for Aunt Kat and other ladies of the household, including ones for myself with leftover fabric. Elizabeth praised my work and began to request—then demand—that I create gowns exclusively for her.

The day our lives changed dawned like many others in January: crisp and cold, clouds from the previous day's rain fleeing before a fresh wind. We were at Enfield, north of London, lodging in Elsyng Palace, a lovely house from which King Henry often went hunting.

I was in the Lady Elizabeth's chamber after her lessons with her tutor and Aunt Kat, sketching an idea for a new gown. I wanted to try something in the recent French fashion—sleeve caps puffed above the shoulders and stuffed with wool. I was not certain the style would become Elizabeth, who had slim shoulders that looked well in the gowns where the sleeves slipped the slightest bit to show her modest bosom.

Aunt Kat was with us, having set her plump form before the fire, her feet on a stool, a book in her lap.

"My brother has come," Elizabeth announced abruptly from where she stood in a window embrasure. She peered out into the afternoon, which was already clouding over for more rain. Her red-gold hair hung long from her high forehead, parted in the middle to reveal a straight white streak of scalp.

Her lips thinned, and her brows drew together in disapproval. "His uncle has accompanied him," she continued.

I left my unsatisfactory drawing and came to the window. I noted as I drew close to her that Elizabeth's milk-pale skin smelled of lemons.

"Aunt Kat, come and see," I called over my shoulder.

Aunt Kat threw me an irritated glance. Had it been only myself in the room, she'd have remained seated, but Elizabeth frowned at the courtyard, impatient and curious.

My aunt heaved herself up and joined us at the window, her wide skirts pressing mine.

"Whatever does Hertford want here?" Aunt Kat demanded over Elizabeth's shoulder, her disparagement as heavy as Elizabeth's.

Edward Seymour, the Earl of Hertford, was the older brother of the late Queen Jane—Jane, who'd caused Elizabeth's mother to be sacrificed so that she could bear Henry a son.

Aunt Kat had never met Anne Boleyn, but her love for Elizabeth extended to animosity to those who had harmed her charge, even indirectly. Jane's hold over Henry had caused him not only to label Anne an adulteress but proclaim Elizabeth a bastard and no heir to the throne. Aunt Kat had become Elizabeth's stalwart defender against all who'd tried to brush her aside.

Prince Edward traveling to Enfield from Hertford Castle, where he'd been staying with his uncle, was not strange. Edward and Elizabeth sometimes shared a house, either here or at Ashridge, combining his entourage as a royal prince with hers, Mary's, and often that of Jane Grey, crowding us all dreadfully.

Also not strange for young Edward to be with Lord Hertford. Still, there was something sinister in the way the banners closed around the small prince on his horse, surrounding him and cutting him off from the world. Elizabeth scowled down at the party then turned cooly away.

Something was terribly wrong. I sensed it, Aunt Kat sensed

it, and the gentlewomen who came to assist me in dressing Elizabeth to receive her brother, sensed it as well.

While a servant lit candles, we slid Elizabeth into a kirtle of deep blue and helped her fasten on her bodice and sleeves. I sewed a small tear in the blue satin sleeve, passing the silk thread through my mouth to make it slick. I turned Elizabeth toward the window so I would have more light, and continued stitching. Blossoming candlelight reflected her in the glass, clear as a mirror.

Elizabeth had a long, rather narrow face, a small nose, which was slightly hooked, and pale lips. Her eyes, intelligent and alert, flicked over the men and horses below as she stroked one long finger along her smooth sleeve.

In the reflection, I saw myself and Aunt Kat standing to either side of her, robust contrasts to Elizabeth's aristocratic slenderness. Aunt Kat was a large woman in a stiffened bodice that pressed her belly into a narrow line, and a skirt that belled from her ample hips.

I took after Aunt Kat, being a bit plump and not much taller than Lady Elizabeth. While I appeared as though I had a healthy appetite, Elizabeth was always thin.

Elizabeth's hair held the red of her father's, while mine was a dull, dark brown. Aunt Kat and I had the same eyes, round and blue, both of us gazing at the world with frank interest.

Aunt Kat had much book learning, and the pair of us shared a curiosity that everyone but we two found unusual. Aunt Kat assuaged hers by reading widely and learning languages, and I assuaged mine by poking into things that did not concern me.

I helped the gentlewomen drape on Elizabeth's overdress, encasing her in folds of velvet, soft as lamb's wool. Despite Elizabeth's preoccupation with her brother and his arrival, she scrutinized every inch of the gown and inspected the tear I had mended.

"My thanks, Eloise," she said, as though I'd done her a great favor.

I did not follow Elizabeth and her train of ladies for the meeting with Edward, but as soon as they had descended, Aunt Kat caught my hand and pulled me along the gallery that encircled the upper floor of the house. Silent as conspirators, we hurried along to another set of stairs and down to the ground floor, where we approached the great hall through a rear door.

On the hall's dais, where the high table would sit if needed, stood a tall screen. This provided a place to keep food warm before serving, and now Aunt Kat and I used it for the purpose of spying on those in the hall. We peered through the screen's slats as Elizabeth and her retinue entered.

I had not seen Prince Edward for many months. I'd always thought him a lackluster boy, even at only nine years old, and I did not change my opinion now. Fair-haired and ruddy-faced, Edward had a short chin and a cruel twist to his mouth.

He was quite robust, liking to ride and hunt, easily keeping up with his father and uncles. He wore riding clothes now, and he eyed Elizabeth's gown, sleek hair, and pearl-studded hood with some aspersion.

Elizabeth gave her brother a deep curtsy that did not lack affection. Edward politely bowed in return before his gaze moved to his uncle.

Tall and bearded, the Earl of Hertford emanated agitation. Even from behind the screen I saw that he held his mouth straight with effort while his fingers twitched.

Elizabeth waited for Hertford to acknowledge her. She was a king's daughter, he merely the brother to a deceased queen. Hertford bowed to Elizabeth almost as an afterthought, which I could see displeased her.

Before Elizabeth could speak, Hertford dropped to one knee before Edward.

"Your Grace," he said to the boy. "The king, your father . . ."
He faltered.

I pressed my face to the screen's bars. Hertford kept his mouth turned down, presenting sorrow, but I sensed that he was acting. His shoulders quivered and his dark eyes sparkled when he forgot to shield them.

Hertford took Edward's hand and pressed it to his lips. "Your Grace ... My Lord of England."

Edward gasped, his eyes widening.

Elizabeth moved to them, skirts swishing on the stone floor. "What are you saying?" she demanded. "What about our father?" Her sharp voice held none of the hysteria of childhood but only a command for information.

"My lady." Hertford forced his face once more into grim lines. "Your royal father is dead. I am the first to call His Grace king."

Two thoughts knocked through my head. First, shock that King Henry, who'd seemed stubborn enough to live forever, had gone. It was unbelievable.

Second, Hertford hadn't told Edward right away. He'd waited until the boy was with his sister, not that traveling across England's rough roads made serious conversation easy.

Why had he waited? Not out of kindness, I suspected. Hertford's expression when he regarded his nephew held no compassion. The earl was a man who liked to control all situations and all information. He'd have wanted the pieces in place to secure his own power before he revealed Henry's death, even to the king's own children, one of whom had just inherited the throne.

Hertford hid his obvious glee by bowing low over Edward's hand. "I swear to protect Your Grace, from this moment, with my life," he announced in a rolling voice. "I will give you my wisdom as though you were my own son."

Beside me, Aunt Kat gave a loud, decided sniff.

None in the tableau heard. The three of them were frozen in place: Elizabeth upright, her back straight, her face hard as marble. Edward, small, thin, and vulnerable. Hertford crouched between the two, his back a blank plane to Elizabeth, his face squashed against Edward's hand.

Edward, the new monarch of England and Ireland, began to cry.

LATER THAT NIGHT, JOHN ASHLEY, MY AUNT KAT'S BELOVED husband, sloshed a stream of purple hock into a cup and pushed it across the boards to me.

"Not too much, John," Aunt Kat admonished. "You'll make her tipsy."

Uncle John smiled at his wife with a benevolence that hadn't dimmed in their more than two years of marriage. Elizabeth liked Uncle John as well. While she often proclaimed she wished for her ladies to remain unmarried, Uncle John had been accepted. Not only did Elizabeth find him congenial but he was a cousin on the Boleyn side of her family.

"Let me indulge our Eloise," Uncle John said. "'Tis not every day a childhood playmate becomes a king."

"Edward never thought of *me*," I mused, idly twirling the cup. I'd never been much interested in Edward, in any case, who could be rather monstrous at times. Elizabeth was much more fascinating. Despite her young age, she did nothing without calculation, even in a temper.

"It was touching," Aunt Kat said. "To see Elizabeth and his young majesty weep together. My lady has tender feelings for her brother and for her father."

"Lord Hertford was certainly pleased," I said. Both Aunt Kat and Uncle John switched their attention to me as I sipped the hock, liking its sour bite on my tongue. "He pretended to be sorrowful, but he is not."

"You should not gossip about your betters," Aunt Kat said quickly, though the words lacked true admonishment.

I sent her an innocent glance. "Everyone is my better here, Auntie. Who am I to gossip about?"

"Mind your tongue, miss." Uncle John chuckled at me, drained his cup, and reached for the flask. "You are not wrong, Eloise. I foresee that Hertford will enmesh himself with young Edward so much that Edward will mouth his words. Queen Catherine hoped to be regent, as she reigned in the king's stead so well when Henry rode off to war with France, but I fear she will be disappointed."

I recalled, some months before Aunt Kat and Uncle John married, how I'd accompanied Elizabeth to Hampton Court to follow Queen Catherine and the court on their progress. It was a heady summer, Elizabeth happily basking in her return to favor with her father, which was very much her stepmother Catherine's doing.

My mind drifted as Uncle John and Aunt Kat speculated on this change in England's fate, and what Hertford meant to do. My interest in politics was negligible, unless it was something directly related to Elizabeth.

On the other hand, the arrival of a trade ship from Amsterdam or Spain enraptured me, because a ship might bring silks, velvet brocades, and other fabrics that Elizabeth would buy or be given, and then transfer to me to work.

My greatest joy was rubbing my fingers over the exquisite cloths, even burying my nose in them to inhale their dyed scent. My grasp of Latin and French might be crude, that of Greek nonexistent, but with a needle in my hand I could do anything.

The azure ensemble we'd dressed her in today had been made of satin from Milan, silk woven in a far-off city in the Chinese empire, and lace knitted by the young ladies of Liege. I understood that the satin shimmered because the warp threads were green while the weft was blue, making the skirts appear as liquid light when the princess moved.

Lady Elizabeth would need new gowns, I thought with excitement. First, for mourning her father, then later for her appearances in Edward's court. I had no doubt that Edward would ask her to attend him soon, because the brother and sister were close. Ball gowns, dresses for dining with ambassadors, ones for hawking and hunting, gowns for traveling, and plainer garb for quiet study.

My imagination spun, putting Lady Elizabeth in ermine-trimmed robes, dresses of cloth of gold and silver tissue—silk with silver thread woven through it—bodices with intricate embroidery, and skirts of damask, velvet, or silk. Sleeves of gold brocade could fold back to reveal an underlining of scarlet silk ...

I itched for my drawing paper and chalk. After the meal, I'd seek my chamber and begin sketching the designs that flashed through me like lightning on a dry summer's night.

"... his head on the block." Uncle John's rising voice cut through my whirling thoughts.

I jumped, emitting a squeak of distress. Aunt Kat shot a disapproving glance at me, knowing I'd not been listening. She'd instructed me to accord Uncle John the attention and respect I'd give a father, which meant attending to his every word.

"Forgive me," I croaked. "What on earth are you talking about, Uncle?"

"The Earl of Surrey." John's eyes held a twinkle, understanding I cared little for the world outside my comfortable sphere. "The Duke of Norfolk and his son, Surrey, tried to take over Edward's regency before old Henry was even dead, which is why the Seymours have pushed in. Surrey stuck his nose in the air and said that such power was his due. So, his head was parted from his body. Poets!" My uncle shrugged, as though writing couplets had led to the demise of the Earl of Surrey.

"His father is still in the Tower?" Aunt Kat asked him.

"For now," Uncle John answered. "Norfolk will win his freedom, I vow. The wily old man has been in and out of favor so often that turning coat is second nature to him. He knows exactly what to say to boost himself from the muck. King Henry was to have signed Norfolk's execution order the very day he conveniently died. So, Norfolk has escaped the chop once again." Uncle John shook his head, though I could see he had little use for the Duke of Norfolk and his scheming ways.

I agreed with Uncle John. I was a gentle soul and hated violence of any kind—I would catch bees in a cup and put them out of the window rather than smash them—and I disliked hearing of executions.

I also had little patience with impatient men. The Duke of Norfolk and his son Surrey had surged forward to take what they wanted. Because of their haste, they'd let a rival family, the Seymours, swoop down and seize Edward instead.

The Seymours had quite literally seized him, as I'd seen from our hiding place in the hall. After his announcement that Edward was now king, Lord Hertford had grasped the lad by the shoulders and hastened him out of the house. He'd come here to make the announcement to Edward and Elizabeth for the theatrics of it, I suspected.

I assumed they were returning to London where Edward would be prepared for his coronation. Edward, barely given time to say goodbye to his sister, had dashed tears from his eyes and obeyed his uncle.

The games will begin in earnest now, I told myself.

Prince Edward was a Seymour, but Lady Elizabeth had descended from the Howards—she was the wayward Duke of Norfolk's grandniece. Princess Mary, daughter of Henry's first wife, carried the blood of the Spanish royal families.

Even I, not astute at politics in any way, realized what a boiling mixture that would be.

I DID HELP MAKE ELIZABETH'S NEW CLOTHES, TO MY DELIGHT, BUT none for a funeral. Elizabeth did not attend King Henry's burial and neither did Edward. Nor did Elizabeth attend the new king's coronation.

As it turned out, the first sumptuous clothes I made for Elizabeth were for a wedding. Her stepmother, Catherine, the widowed queen, wed none other than Lord Hertford's younger brother, Thomas Seymour.

Thomas had, with the ease of a dancer, stepped into the position of Lord High Admiral. He'd proposed to Queen Catherine, and Catherine, in love like a starry-eyed girl, had quickly accepted.

The boiling had begun.

CHAPTER 2

April 1547

I fell in love with Thomas Seymour, now Baron Seymour of Sudeley, the moment I saw him. How I fell out of love with him again transformed me from naïve child to wary woman.

Thomas Seymour was tall, strong, and athletic, with a full red beard and dark eyes that caught and held whomever he decided to turn his gaze to. When he smiled, or better still, laughed, whatever chamber he stood in warmed.

Aunt Kat and my Lady Elizabeth fell in love with him too, I saw in the softening of their faces whenever they beheld at him. Catherine Parr had been in love with him well before she'd married Henry, and only a few short months after the former king's funeral, she became Thomas Seymour's lawfully wedded wife.

Seymour's older brother, Hertford, who'd announced Henry's death to Edward and then elevated himself to Duke of Somerset, was furious at the marriage. He excluded Catherine from court, making his own wife the first lady in England, although Catherine, stepmother to the boy-king Edward and widow of Henry, should have had that right.

Looking back, I do not believe Catherine cared a farthing about losing her lofty position. Court formality and playing nursemaid to a wretched, gouty, and aging man were now in her past. Catherine had landed the gentleman she'd loved for years, and now she divided her time between their large home in Chelsea and his castle in Sudeley.

Catherine invited Elizabeth to reside with her, to Elizabeth's joy, as she was very fond of her stepmother. And so, the ladies of Elizabeth's household, including myself and Aunt Kat, moved with her to Chelsea Manor.

In my eyes, the house was beautiful, with its many windows lighting the interior and its gardens stretching to the river, whose waters ran clean this far west and south of London. The property belonged to Catherine, bestowed on her by Henry at his death.

While I assisted Catherine's ladies and Seymour's gentlemen in waiting on the family at supper each night, I feared my bold gaze at Seymour would gain me dismissal. I need not have worried. All the ladies' eyes were fixed on the queen's new husband, and no one noticed my wanton stare.

Seymour was a man to be admired. After Edward's coronation, he'd been made Lord High Admiral of England, which I was told meant he commanded the navy and the seas.

Seymour and his older brother, Somerset, ran the kingdom between them. Somerset, who was now Lord High Protector and flaunting it, gripped most of the power. Thomas Seymour was left to bedazzle this household of ladies, and he succeeded admirably.

Seated near him, Catherine smiled, pleased with her lot. At thirty-five, she was still stately and pretty. She drank wine, laughed, and made merry, ready to let happiness enter her life.

Uncle John had made it clear to Aunt Kat and me that he was one who did *not* admire Seymour. "That man is trouble," he said darkly one night after we'd been in Chelsea a few weeks. The three of us had gathered as usual after the household's supper, in a chamber high in the house, to partake of our own meal.

"Nonsense," Aunt Kat answered. "See how fond the Admiral is of the queen. She deserves to marry for love. He is a breath of fresh air."

"Fox in a hen house," Uncle John muttered, then said no more of it.

Later that same night, I carried a pile of new cloth to Queen Catherine's chambers. Catherine liked my work and had asked me to assist her lady of the wardrobe in constructing new gowns for her as Lady Sudeley. Catherine, for all she was a modest woman of the reformed religion, dressed well, and I looked forward to creating ensembles for her.

I had a love affair with fabric. Nothing else on earth, not even the eyes of a handsome gentleman, could make my blood sing and my skin tingle like a finely woven piece of cloth. The moment I'd touched this velvet, I'd envisioned the perfect gown it would make for Catherine—a soft overskirt paired with a bodice of cloth of silver over an underdress of blue satin.

So infatuated was I with my velvet, that I never noticed Seymour until he was in front of me, filling the dark passage to the queen's antechamber and blocking my way.

I started, and then warmed with pleasurable heat. First the velvet, then encountering the very handsome Admiral by himself, thrilled my girl's heart.

I'd never stood so close to him and now realized how very tall he was. I had to tilt my head a long way back so I could take in all of him.

"Is that a pile of clothes with legs?" Seymour's voice was muted but as rich as the velvet I held.

I curtsied, trembling, and nearly overbalanced my load. A

broad hand landed on top of the pile, steadying it, then Seymour's dark eyes danced as he peered down at me. His wide smile showed white but crooked teeth.

"What are you?" he demanded.

"A girl," I stammered in surprise. A foolish answer, but I couldn't stop my tongue.

"I see 'tis so. But you have the bosom of a woman. Where is your husband?"

My cheeks grew uncomfortably hot. "I am not married, my lord."

"Ah, poor mite." Seymour leaned over the fabric, his handsome face coming close to mine. "Would you like to be?"

I was thoroughly bewildered. Why such a highborn gentleman would even notice me—a seamstress and a governess' niece—let alone speak to me so familiarly, was puzzling.

"I am too young to wed," I said shakily.

"Indeed, you are not."

Seymour moved a bit closer to me, and I backed a step. My retreat seemed to amuse him, because his smile broadened as he took another stride forward.

I repeated my glide backward. He likewise continued forward, and we moved on and on across the passageway until my heel connected with the stone wall.

"You *are* a woman." Seymour's voice dropped to a low rumble. "What is your name, lady?"

"Eloise," I said faintly. "Rousell."

"*Es-tu français?*" he asked in curiosity.

"*Non, mon seigneur.*" I resumed speaking in English, as my French was sparse, though I was fluent enough to know he addressed me familiarly, or as a superior would an inferior. "My father had a French name, is all."

My grandmother had vowed that the man's name had been Russell, plain and simple, but he, a strolling player who'd seduced my mother with his charm, had changed it to the French spelling to make himself seem more important. This was the story my grandmother told me after my father's untimely death and my mother's second marriage had caused her to lose interest in me.

"Ah, better still, a good English girl," Seymour said. "The king, he is a good English lad, son of my English sister and the very English King Harry."

"Yes, my lord." At that moment, I think I'd agree if he'd said his sister had been a mad Amazon from Saracen lands.

"Where are you taking all those clothes, Eloise of England?"

Seymour's breath smelled heavily of wine, and another smell clung to him that I could not identify—warm, sweet, and cloying. He was not drunk, but his eyes were heavy, his cheekbones flushed.

"To the queen's chamber," I managed.

"She is no longer the queen, you know. She is plain Lady Sudeley, my wife." His eyes took on a strange glow. "Do you find her plain?"

"Of course not, my lord." My eyes widened in astonishment. "My lady Catherine is most beautiful."

"For her age, I suppose." Seymour smiled as he said the disparaging words, as though it was a joke between us.

"She is no longer young, but . . ." Catherine had a dignified beauty that I admired. She was also kind, with a courteous manner she extended to all.

I could not decide how to express this while her new husband had me backed against the wall, smiling at me in an odd manner. I feared to offend him and be punished, so I kept silent. Gentle Catherine might grow angry at me for displeasing her beloved Admiral.

"Young, that is the thing," Seymour was saying. "I like a young lady. What is your age?"

"Fourteen in September," I managed.

"An excellent year. Ripe for marriage. The Lady Elizabeth, how young is she?"

"She will be fourteen as well, my lord. We were born five days apart."

Seymour's teeth gleamed in the half-light. "Now, there is a fact. I will remember it."

"Will you, my lord?"

"I will. Fourteen is a woman, Eloise of England."

Seymour reached for me. Before I understood what he was about, he slammed his palm to my left breast where it surged over my bodice and squeezed hard with his strong fingers.

In that instant, my childhood ended.

I saw myself, Seymour, the passage, and the velvet in my arms in new and brutal clarity. Lord Seymour was no longer a handsome gentleman to admire from afar. He was a man of licentious tastes, who thought nothing of accosting a girl of the household not ten feet from his wife's chamber door.

I, small, innocent, and sheltered, faced him on quavering legs. I'd encountered no other gentlemen in my life beyond servants, save my Uncle John and Master Grindal, Elizabeth's tutor. The conversations these two men had were serious and quiet, punctuated with discussions on philosophy and the scriptures, in which my Aunt Kat and Elizabeth took full part.

At Hatfield and in other houses where Elizabeth had resided, we'd never had the presence of a full-blooded male such as Seymour, a man who wanted life, power, desire.

A breath of fresh air, Aunt Kat had called him. I now knew him for a hurricane, a gale to flatten the unwary.

If Seymour forced himself upon me, he'd walk away without censure, but I'd be blamed for being loose and lascivious. Catherine would grow furious and turn me out of her house.

Even if I made Aunt Kat and Uncle John understand exactly what had happened, they likely could do nothing to help me, and I'd have nowhere to go. My mother and my stepfather, a man called Sir Philip Baldwin, did not want me in their home, and my grandmother would express her disappointment in me.

Seymour had me flat against the wall, his hand still upon me. I could not twist away. Screaming would only bring the queen from her chamber to see me beguiling her husband in the passage.

As I could go neither backward nor forward, I dropped straight down to the floor. I bumped my nose on Seymour's hard thigh, my forehead on the crease of his tall boot. The cloths fell from my hands as I went, flowing across the stones like streams of dark water.

Seymour stepped back with a startled grunt and tripped on a piece of velvet, then he snarled and lunged for me.

I scuttled out of his reach, snatched up what cloths I could, and started to run, trailing fabric. The beautiful blue velvet snaked around my ankles, and I tumbled to the floor again. Heart racing, I rolled to right myself, my hands scraping on the cold, rough stone.

Seymour stood in the middle of the passageway behind me, his lips curled in rage. Then his swift smile returned, as did the gleam in his eyes that terrified me.

I scrambled to my feet. Abandoning my precious cloth, I fled.

Seymour's laughter followed me down the cold corridor. "Scamper, little kitten. One day, come back and find your Tomcat."

He continued laughing, a sound that carried down the passageway and up the stairs as I sprinted for the safety of my rooms.

The next morning Aunt Kat seized me by the ear as I

emerged from my tiny chamber and pulled me to the middle of our eating room.

"Whatever came over you, Eloise?" Aunt Kat demanded. "Leaving costly fabric lying on the floor?" She pointed at the pile that now reposed haphazardly on a bench. A servant must have retrieved it and returned it here. "That velvet is as good as ruined. What were you thinking?"

I hesitated. If I told Aunt Kat the truth, I knew she'd never believe it of Seymour, as she thought him the nearest thing to perfection. To add to this, she always took the word of a higher-born person over mine.

I feared she'd blame *me* for enticing Seymour and perhaps even force me to relate the entire episode to Catherine. Best that nobody knew what happened but me.

"I saw a ghost," I said in a near whisper. "It frightened me."

Aunt Kat released her hold and darted a superstitious glance upward. "What ghost?"

"I could not see," I extemporized madly. "I heard her screams."

Aunt Kat shook herself. "Nonsense."

"No, Aunt Kat. It is the truth. It came from the upper gallery. I heard her wailing and shrieking."

I closed my mouth before I could over-embellish. I did not actually believe in ghosts, being much too hard-headed for such things, but Aunt Kat was convinced that sorcery was real and there were ghosts a-plenty. Besides which, the upper gallery of this house, dark and windowless, could be unnerving.

"Mention none of your ghosts to our Lady Elizabeth," Aunt Kat said in a severe tone. "She sometimes has bad dreams, and I do not wish to worry her."

"'Tis the ghosts that send her the bad dreams," I murmured.

"Enough, you silly girl." Aunt Kat waved me away. "Go on with you."

I curtsied and fled, relieved I'd diverted her attention from the torn fabric and speculation on why I, of all people, had let it be ruined.

FROM THAT DAY FORWARD, I TOOK CARE NEVER TO BE CAUGHT IN the halls alone. If I had to travel to dark corners of the house, I trotted in the footsteps of a housekeeper or other maids. When I sewed, I did so in the presence of Aunt Kat and Elizabeth, or Catherine and her entourage.

Always being in company was made easier for me, because the Chelsea house was quite full. Catherine had her ladies, at least a hundred of them, and Elizabeth's own ladies and gentlemen were there to wait upon *her*. We began to be rather cramped, which suited me, because I could hide within a crowd and avoid Thomas Seymour.

Once he caught sight of me in the great hall during an evening's revelry and shot me a smile. Though my heart pounded in panic, I pretended not to notice. Seymour mimed a cat with claws, his grin widening.

After that distant encounter, he said not a word to me, nor even looked my way when we were in the same chamber. He seemed, to my relief, to forget all about me.

I could not avoid Seymour altogether, try as I might. As the man of the house, he had his own retinue, which crowded us further, and he expected his orders to be obeyed before his wife's.

The servants, fiercely loyal to whatever master or mistress they served, fought among themselves. I'd often overhear snatches of their conversations.

"That wine is for Her Grace Elizabeth," one would declare.

"No," another would growl. "'Tis to go to the queen dowager."

"Her Grace Elizabeth always has *this* wine."

"It is the queen dowager's private stock."

"Nay, sir, it was purchased by Her Grace Elizabeth's household."

"His lordship commands the wine be brought to *him*," would come a male servant's inevitable reply. "It will be given to his lady the queen or Her Grace Elizabeth at his pleasure."

Thus endeth the argument.

IN FINE WEATHER, ELIZABETH TOOK EXTENSIVE WALKS IN THE gardens that Catherine adored and had her gardeners tend with care. I often accompanied Elizabeth, being one of the few women her age in the household. She'd also long ago professed me a favorite, her liking for me heightened by her affection for Aunt Kat.

I never made the mistake in believing that Elizabeth thought me anything more than a useful companion. I was not as high-born as the baronets' wives and daughters who comprised her gentlewomen, but she liked to confide in me things she would not the others. Harmless Eloise the seamstress did not tell tales.

One particular morning, when the sky was as blue as the kirtle I was sewing for her, my lady Elizabeth and I wandered the gardens in an aimless fashion. We walked arm-in-arm, she in silks, I in serviceable linen and wool.

Our meandering surprised me, because Elizabeth usually laid out her plans for walks like a general heading into battle.

"Where are we going, Your Grace?" I asked after a time.

"I do not know. Where shall we stroll, Eloise?" Elizabeth slanted me a half-smile, an odd light in her eyes.

"The gardeners have arranged geraniums in the front walk," I offered. "They are quite beautiful, scarlet against the green."

"No." Elizabeth gripped my arm and half dragged me toward the far end of the garden, beyond which the river flowed. The water's scent was fresh, as it flowed from the heart of the countryside. "I would like to walk among the hedges."

"As you wish, Your Grace."

I acquiesced, first because I would never disobey one of her orders, and secondly because it was clear that Elizabeth would tow me with her to wherever she wanted to go. She propelled the pair of us to the long hedges at a rapid march, no more ambling.

"What think you of this gown, Eloise?" she asked as we went. "Does it suit me?"

"Of course, Your Grace." My answer was breathless as I struggled to keep up with her. "I made certain of it."

The gown in question was black and gold silk with a fine woolen overskirt, good for brisk walks in the garden. The bodice bared a small bit of Elizabeth's pale bosom, flattering her slender frame. The gown was quite modest, because Aunt Kat would allow Elizabeth to wear nothing but decorous attire, but her exposed throat, shoulders, and chest made it alluring.

An enticing young lady, the ensemble announced. Within whom first longings had begun to stir. Untouched, untried, waiting.

Elizabeth's lips twitched at my answer. "Your talent is formidable, Eloise, as is your pride. Guard against pride, my dear, or it will be your downfall."

"Aye," I answered glumly. "Aunt Kat says the same."

"Cunning is always better. Remember that."

I did not understand her, but I murmured, "Yes, Your Grace."

Elizabeth halted so suddenly that my momentum propelled me forward a few steps before her fierce grip on me hauled me back.

"Is someone there?" Elizabeth demanded, peering into the opening between tall, carefully pruned bay trees. She spoke to me, but I sensed she'd called her question into the dark walk that awaited us.

I fancied I spied movement beyond the hedges, and my skin began to prickle. "A gardener?" was my faint suggestion.

Elizabeth's eyes glittered, but not with fear. "Let us catch him, whoever he is."

"Take care, Your Grace," I said in alarm. "It might be a robber."

Elizabeth laughed. "Not in my stepmother's gardens. They would not dare."

They would indeed dare, I knew for a fact. I'd heard of gentlemen and ladies set upon at the edges of their own estates. Some bandits did not care how highborn their victims, only wanting the riches they'd carry away. That Elizabeth hurried to confront such a thief with no more weapon between us than the scissors in my pocket horrified me.

"Your Grace," I tried.

Elizabeth's breath quickened with our pace. She pulled me relentlessly between the hedges into the shadowed walk.

Let it be a gardener, I prayed. *Or a rabbit. Even a rat.*

Our quarry sprang from the shadows, roaring and growling and waving his arms like a madman. Elizabeth screamed, but it was the squeal of an excited girl. My own cry tore from my throat in genuine terror.

"Run, Your Grace!" I shouted, and we wheeled about to flee.

CHAPTER 3

Elizabeth shrieked in the high-pitched bursts of a lady pretending to be afraid and pulled me down a side path. Not back toward the house, I noted to my dismay, and she did not run very quickly.

"Your Grace …"

"Let us hurry, Eloise," Elizabeth said in merriment. "Or he will be upon us."

The man pursued us. Did he curtail his steps, or was that my imagination? Elizabeth jogged along more slowly still. I wanted to rip my hand from hers and race to my chamber high under the eaves, but Elizabeth held me so fast I'd need ten armed soldiers to pry myself from her.

We rounded a corner to another long trail, this one lined with yews. I saw ahead of us, unbelievably, Queen Catherine, who bobbed up and down on her toes, laughing.

"This way, my dears," she called. "Come, come, else he catches us."

And what shall he do if he does? I wondered as we scampered after her. Surely, with Catherine there, Seymour, our pursuer, could do nothing.

Two weeks ago, I would have believed this a harmless game. But I remembered the dark, cold passageway, the soft cloth in my arms, and the sour taste of fear as Thomas Seymour's hand covered my breast. I felt again his fingers squeezing, the startling pain of it, the curling disgust deep inside me.

There are three of us, I told myself. *We can hold him off.*

"Come along," Catherine shouted. "Hurry, do."

We ran after her, skirts fluttering, Elizabeth laughing.

Catherine led us down a path and around a corner to a dead end. A high green hedge faced us, the boundary of the park. Here a stone bench offered the passer-by a place of peace.

For us, it was a trap.

I shrieked. "The other way!"

Too late. Seymour charged in behind us, penning us like calves herded for slaughter. I faced him, mouth dry and eyes wide, while Catherine and Elizabeth collapsed into each other in laughter.

Seymour came forward, growling and lurching in bearlike fervor. Catherine flung her arms around Elizabeth from behind.

"I've caught her, darling," she said breathlessly. "I've caught her!"

Elizabeth continued to laugh. Her long hair came free from her hood and spilled down her shoulders in a cloud of red gold.

Seymour ignored me completely, intent on Elizabeth in his wife's arms, a feral light in his eyes.

"You've caught us a lovely fawn, my dear." He swatted playfully at Elizabeth, fingers barely brushing her bodice. "Naughty fawn, to run away."

Elizabeth gazed at him in enjoyment. Seymour caught a lock of her loose hair and wound it around his fist. "What shall we do to punish our pet, my dear?" he asked his wife.

The love in Catherine's eyes for him was painful to behold. "Naughty girl," she said, hugging Elizabeth. "Naughty child."

I stood in a daze, realizing with a cold jolt that three games were being played out before me.

One was Catherine's—she happy to be lighthearted and jubilant with her husband.

The second game was Elizabeth's. Catherine, behind her, did not catch the admiration in her stepdaughter's eyes for Seymour. Elizabeth had wanted him to chase her, and she liked, better still, that he'd caught her.

The third game belonged to Seymour. He had exactly what he'd planned—Elizabeth cornered, with his wife's help. I in his play, only Seymour knew all the parts.

Seymour's gaze slid sideways to me. "You, Needlewoman. You must go nowhere without your needle and thread, eh?"

"Yes, my lord." The words were a bare whisper from my dry mouth.

"And your scissors? What needlewoman is without scissors?" Before I could answer, Seymour held out his hand. "Give them to me."

I froze in astonishment, but Catherine's face lit. "Yes, dear Mistress Rousell, give them over."

Elizabeth struggled in some earnest, though she laughed through her words. "No, no, Eloise, do not let them cut off my hair."

"Give them." Seymour's command seared like ice.

Quickly I dipped my hand into my pocket and drew out the scissors. Seymour snatched them from me.

He rearranged his expression as he turned back to Elizabeth and Catherine, becoming the teasing gentleman once more. "Hold her, my love."

"No." Elizabeth squirmed against Catherine. "I beg of you, not my hair."

"Very well," Seymour said, pretending to concede the point. "Your hair is safe."

He snatched up a handful of her skirt and began to snip it instead.

I cried out in anguish. I had labored over that skirt and knew every stitch of it. The intricate gold and silver pattern had been difficult to match, the black overskirt so fine it was like gossamer. I was very proud of that gown, which I'd designed to be beautiful for Elizabeth. I watched, my heart sick, as Seymour proceeded to ruin weeks of my work.

Snip, snip went the scissors. Catherine and Elizabeth shrieked in delight. Seymour concentrated on his task, his breath coming fast, his gaze fixed.

I stood against a hedge, the twigs prickling my back and poking through my hood. Pieces of skirt fluttered to the earth to lay like fallen flowers.

Seymour continued cutting like a man obsessed. In the end, the ground was carpeted with silk scraps, which swirled up on the breeze to be caught in the yew's branches.

When Seymour finished and tossed the scissors aside, Elizabeth had nothing to cover her loosened stomacher and chemise but her stepmother's cloak.

"FOR SHAME," AUNT KAT ADMONISHED ELIZABETH LATER THAT evening.

Elizabeth, in a dressing gown in her bedchamber with a cup of sweet herbal tea, at last looked stricken.

Only Aunt Kat could scold Elizabeth. She'd outgrown listening to her nurses, save Mistress Parry, long ago, but Aunt Kat held a special place in Elizabeth's heart. Aunt Kat alone was allowed to speak her mind.

"The shame of it," Aunt Kat continued. "Every lady and gentleman agog when you returned to the house." Aunt Kat lifted her hands in the despairing way she often took with me.

"Thank the Lord the queen was with you, though *she* ought to have known better. Why that wise lady, who held the kingdom safe through months of war by herself, would throw away her dignity on a silly romp in the garden … I ask you."

"'Twas only a game." Elizabeth sipped tea, her slim shoulders drooping. She'd become a guilt-stricken girl again, the young woman who'd wanted a man's attentions faded and gone.

"You might have thought so, but there are others who do not," Aunt Kat said. "As his majesty's sister, you must jealously guard your reputation. His Grace the king will likely make a good marriage for you, but if your reputation is in shreds, you will have to make do with the dregs."

A defiant gleam entered Elizabeth's eyes. "I could not prevail against both my stepmother and my Lord Sudeley."

"Mind that you learn to." Aunt Kat let out a sigh, her stern expression softening. She could never remain angry at Elizabeth for long. "He is a fine-mannered gentleman, is his lordship, and used to flirtations at court. You are *not* used to it, but Lord Sudeley does not understand this. Most young ladies your age have been married off already and know how to comport themselves. His lordship is not used to a simple household and does not understand."

I, my mouth full of pins and my lap piled with Parisian silver netting, did not agree. Seymour knew exactly what he was doing and exactly how far to push his wife to obtain what he wanted.

At that moment, I assumed Seymour simply longed for a dalliance with Elizabeth. I could understand why—she was a beautiful young woman, with her red hair and beguiling eyes. She'd inherited the best of her father and mother.

I'd never seen Anne Boleyn, but I'd heard gentlemen who'd known her fall into eloquence about her. Dark hair, pale face, not really much to look at, they admitted, until she turned her smile upon one. Anne's eyes had been starred with silver lights, and she could hold a gentleman with her gaze—or so they claimed—and have him in her thrall.

She'd also had a strength of character, intelligence and wit, combined with the polished manners of the French court, where she'd been sent at an early age. That wit had been her power, but also her downfall, used by her enemies against her.

Old King Henry had been robust and handsome in his youth, I'd seen in portraits, with hair Elizabeth's shade and a physique envied by gentlemen in England and beyond its shores. Henry had been strong, loud, restless, arbitrarily cruel or generous, devoted to his own passions, and unforgiving of those passions in others.

The king had been attractive and fiery, and Anne had been as well. Together they'd produced a daughter with grace, a sense of elegance, a calculating mind, and a presence like a whiplash.

Aunt Kat had a fond belief that she controlled this girl, and it was true that Elizabeth listened to Aunt Kat. But only to a point.

Seymour had designs upon Elizabeth, and I could see that Elizabeth was not unhappy with those designs. Elizabeth loved her stepmother, of course, but a handsome gentleman intensely interested in a young woman could cloud that young woman's senses. Well I knew this.

I prayed that Elizabeth would not go so far as to betray Catherine. I burned inside with my secret knowledge of Seymour's character, but I did not want to confess it in the presence of Elizabeth.

I waited until later, after Elizabeth had gone to bed, and Aunt Kat was alone in her chamber, nodding off over a book. I knelt at Aunt Kat's feet and told her of my encounter with Seymour. I bowed my head, afraid and ashamed as only a girl of fourteen can be.

Aunt Kat closed her book with a snap. "And what were you doing traipsing about the galleries at that time of night, my girl?"

"Carrying cloth to the queen's antechamber," I explained. "I was anxious to begin on her gowns."

Aunt Kat regarded me for a long moment then her usually canny eyes went deliberately blank. "You must have mistaken his intentions, Eloise."

"No, Aunt." I remembered the pressure of Seymour's hand on my breast, the unclean feeling in my belly, and the startled shock that a man had dared touch me so familiarly.

"You were mistaken," Aunt Kat repeated, stressing each word. "Lord Sudeley is a rogue, and he smiled at you. It excited you."

I shook my head. "Disgusted me, rather."

"Please do not say such things about your betters, Eloise. People will believe I have raised you with no manners."

I gazed at her, my heart beating faster. "Please listen to me, Auntie."

"No, Eloise. You were mistaken. Say nothing more of it."

Anger wound through my fears. "I thought you would wish to keep our lady Elizabeth safe."

"I do. I want that beyond everything." The shrewdness returned to Aunt Kat's tone. "There is more to this than what you understand. Say *nothing,* for dear Jesus' sake, or you will bring disaster upon us all."

"But, poor Queen Catherine," I began.

Aunt Kat's mouth turned down. "Eloise, to whom are you loyal?"

"To you, Aunt," I answered, bewildered.

"And?"

"Uncle John, of course."

"And?"

I swallowed. "Her Grace Elizabeth."

Aunt Kat nodded, satisfied, and plied me with no more *ands.* "Keep your thoughts to yourself and your mouth closed," she said. "Close your eyes as well, if need be."

I deflated, something inside me curling into a small, tight ball. "I understand nothing of this."

Aunt Kat resumed her book. "I suppose your lack of astuteness comes of your mother marrying low. I'd at first expected you to grow up to be a bearer of false tales, like your actor father. Instead, God has gifted you with a straightforward tongue and shining honesty. Unfortunately, these gifts are not always useful in the world of the court."

"You would rather I learned to lie?" I asked in amazement.

Aunt Kat patted my cheek. "Of course not, dear. But I would like you to discover the meaning of the word *discretion* and apply it well."

"Discretion," I repeated.

"Yes, dear." My aunt returned to her reading while I struggled to comprehend.

"Are you saying that the occurrence today was political?" I asked.

"I am saying nothing, you silly girl. I already know how to apply discretion."

I stared at her. "But Queen Catherine is married to Lord Sudeley."

"Yes, Eloise, I know that," Aunt Kat said patiently. "But my first loyalty is to Elizabeth. What is best for her is best for me, and for you."

I closed my gaping mouth, my jaw aching. "Perhaps you ought to send me home to Grandmama."

I winced as I suggested this, because I had no desire to come under control of that sharp-tongued lady. She was a bit kinder to me than she was to my mother, but her bluntness could be unsettling.

Aunt Kat patted my cheek once more. "Nonsense, dear. I want you here with me. I'd miss you terribly."

"Would you?" I asked in genuine surprise.

Aunt Kat was an affectionate woman, but she'd never once

told me she was pleased to have me about. I'd thought of myself as rather a nuisance, except when there were gowns to be made.

"Indeed." Aunt Kat quieted. "I need you, Eloise. Be my eyes and ears. I want to know every word Lord Sudeley speaks to our Elizabeth in my absence. Every word. Do you understand?"

"Yes, Aunt Kat," I said meekly.

"Good girl. Now off to bed with you."

I kissed Aunt Kat and departed her chamber for my own chilled room, where I sat up far into the night.

I'd gone to Aunt Kat supposing she would listen to my tale, grow horrified, and insist that Elizabeth, with herself, me, and Uncle John, leave the house immediately. Instead, she'd behaved as though the event between myself and Seymour in the passage had been simply bothersome. An unlooked-for incident to be suppressed at all costs.

You are slow, Eloise, Aunt Kat had been saying. *You comprehend neither Greek nor Latin nor the subtleties of the court.*

I wondered, as I blew out the candle, into what troubles those subtleties were rushing us.

In the morning, I was a wary creature. I performed the same rituals as I did every day—washing my face, brushing my unruly dark hair, cleaning the grime from under my fingernails. I rinsed my mouth, chewing a bit of anise to make my breath pleasant, then turned to the breakfast a maidservant had delivered to the outer chamber.

I ate bread smeared with thick, sweet butter and took a few bites of the porridge that Aunt Kat had regularly forced upon me since the age of four.

After I'd eaten, the maid helped me don a dark blue undergown, lacing my bodice in the back. Over this went a robe of plain brown, the sleeves the maid helped me fasten on pinned back to reveal the white linen of my chemise. The pointed edge of my stomacher was tied to a skirt that flared from tucks that I had taken pains to make exactly even. The maid adjusted what we called a French hood, which was a wide band that pushed my hair from my forehead, with a fine cloth to cover its length in back.

One ring, plain and silver, adorned my finger. My mother had given me the ring, telling me it had been my father's. The band was thin, beaten, and worn, without much value, but it was my only link to a man I'd never see again, and I wore it every day.

Attired and fed, I gathered my sewing basket and made my way downstairs to Elizabeth's chamber. All as usual.

However, I could not put the previous day's events out of my head. I recalled the almost savage look on Seymour's face as he cut up Elizabeth's dress. I remembered Catherine's taut laughter as she abetted her husband in dallying with another woman. And then Elizabeth, glaring at Aunt Kat and insisting she had done nothing wrong.

When I reached Elizabeth's rooms, I took my place on a bench near an open window. Soft late-April air slid around me, bathing me in pleasant scents.

From my basket, I lifted out the bodice the Parisian netting I'd begun the day before and laid it across my lap. I had already stitched in the boning and now needed to sew the side seams. My work must be carefully done, or the points in front would not match, and I'd have to start all over again.

The chamber was filled with Elizabeth's gentlewomen, young and middle-aged, pretty and plain, highborn and gentry. Elizabeth had already been dressed and was seated near the fire, but two ladies hovered around her, one settling her hood, the other shaking her skirt so it would lie straight.

Elizabeth was in a sunny mood, jesting with her ladies as she chewed on red strawberries, bright as jewels, an open book in her lap. She seemed content, but I could not be.

I worried for her, and I worried I would say the wrong thing to her about Seymour. I feared Elizabeth would ask me of him, and I'd not be able to say a word in case I spoke unwise ones.

I made one last stitch and beckoned to a lady. "Please, tell Her Grace that we must have a fitting."

The gentlewoman nodded and returned to her mistress. I saw Elizabeth brighten, which relieved me. Sometimes, she did not like to leave her books for any reason, but she did like to try on clothes.

Elizabeth rose from her seat, letting the lady's maid loosen her gown and pull it from her shoulders. I left my bench, smoothing out the half-made bodice I'd just stitched.

At that exact moment, Seymour strode into the chamber. He was dressed for hunting, in riding boots, plain doublet, and trunk hose, a half-cloak swirled over his formidable shoulders. Elizabeth, caught in dishabille, sent Seymour one startled glance before rushing to a standing screen across the room and ducking behind it.

"How now?" Seymour demanded. "Is the lady so modest? Must you hide from your step-papa?"

Only I seemed alarmed. The gentlewomen giggled or shot Seymour coquettish glances as they banded together. They formed a tittering mass before the screen so that Seymour could not get at the half-dressed Elizabeth.

"You challenge me, my lovelies." Seymour laid a firm hand on the arm of a younger lady. "I have touched you, my dear. Now, you may not sit down until you have touched me. But you must catch me, first."

The lady, instead of being indignant or frightened, responded to the game with glee. She dove for Seymour, who easily evaded her. The others joined in as Seymour dodged about the large chamber, a trail of ladies chasing him.

I remained in my corner, watching the proceedings in trepidation. Elizabeth remained behind the screen, but I heard her excited laughter.

It was a bizarre scene, this grown man chasing and being chased by ladies, their skirts rippling. The gentlewomen screeched and ran here and there, while I hovered near the window, Elizabeth's half-made bodice clutched to my chest.

Seymour dodged past me and tore the bodice from my grip. I desperately lunged for it, but he held the bodice above his head, smiling playfully. A cold light lurked in his eyes, as though this foolery meant something deeper and more dangerous.

"Tell your mistress to come out," Seymour commanded me. "Else I'll rip it to shreds."

"Your lordship." My voice was a gasp. "No, please."

Seymour's eyes narrowed in dislike as he waved the bodice over his head. "Come and get it, kitten."

He knew I could only reach the garment by climbing him, and also that I would never do such a thing. He'd read my character when I'd fled from him in the passageway many nights ago. I'd seen through his vile flirtations and rejected him.

"Tell her," he repeated, voice hard.

Mutely, I shook my head.

Seymour clutched the bodice, and then he tore it in two, a heartbreaking sound. I could only clasp my hands in despair as Seymour rent the fabric again and again, tearing out the painstaking seams I'd spent the morning making. I had to watch my hard work ruined beyond repair by a man who valued it not.

Elizabeth did not emerge. She was enjoying the game, if the laughter that recurred meant anything, but fortunately, she'd decided to be prudent this time. Perhaps she'd taken Aunt Kat's admonition to heart.

Seymour tossed the pieces of bodice to the floor, where they lay unmourned by all but me. The ladies continued the romp, but Seymour was growing weary of it.

I believe he'd simply have shoved the screen aside to reveal Elizabeth, had not Aunt Kat burst into the chamber. Despite her lecture the night before that she and I should let Seymour do as he pleased, she gazed about in horror.

"Ladies!"

Her stentorian tones cut through the melee, and the chase ground to a halt. A few of the ladies appeared chagrined, though not much so. They seemed more sorry Aunt Kat had interrupted their fun than ashamed they'd been doing it at all.

"Mistress Ashley, you do spoil our entertainment," Seymour snapped.

Aunt Kat lifted her chin. "Perhaps best 'twere left for another day, my lord."

I realized then what Aunt Kat had meant when she'd said there was more to this charade than a man wanting a young woman. He was plotting, though exactly what, I could not say.

Seymour was menacing, but Aunt Kat stood resolutely before him like a hen before a wild boar.

Aunt Kat was always brave—too much so, I believed at times, and Uncle John agreed with me. But she loved Elizabeth like a daughter and would fight for her with bright fierceness.

"Mistress Ashley, shall we step out?" Seymour gestured to the chamber door. Aunt Kat gave him one frigid nod of her head and stalked solemnly past him into the antechamber.

Seymour followed. Fearing he'd raise his fist to my aunt once they were out of sight, I snatched up the shreds of the bodice and scuttled after them.

Aunt Kat and Seymour stood together in the small wood-paneled antechamber, Aunt Kat in no wise worried. I closed the door to the bedchamber and retreated to a window embrasure to listen.

"I seek only to protect my Lady Elizabeth's reputation, my lord," Aunt Kat was saying. "You charge too quickly for her."

"I mean no harm by it," Seymour growled. "Can a man not romp with his own daughter?"

Not in the way you wish, I thought, my fingers curling around the torn fabric.

Aunt Kat regarded him squarely. "I only give advice, my lord."

Seymour's lip curled. "I'll not be ruled by a pack of women." He shot a glare at me, though I'd said nothing, and stormed from the room, the heavy door slamming in his wake.

I reflected that in this household, Seymour would not be able to escape the pack of women. The women here were family, and he was the stranger.

Aunt Kat instructed me soon after that to watch Seymour closely and tell her of his behavior. I was a dutiful spy and reported to her the day I saw him slip the key from Elizabeth's bedchamber door into his pocket.

"Should you warn Queen Catherine?" I whispered.

"The queen has much to occupy her," Aunt Kat said after a moment's consideration. "She believes herself with child, and that a son will seal Seymour's affections for her forever. Let her think her marriage idyllic for now."

I did not see how she could. Seymour stalked Elizabeth with the single-mindedness of a hunter after a prize hart, while claiming that all he did was play.

Aunt Kat at least took the precaution of having me sleep in Elizabeth's chamber with her. I did not believe my presence would keep Seymour at bay, but he did not appear in the weeks I stayed with Elizabeth, lying awake to listen to her soft breathing and the call of night birds.

Early one morning, I heard the key scrape the lock of the bedchamber door. I sprang from my cot, knocking my foot against the bed railing and stifling a cry of pain. Behind the thick curtains of Elizabeth's tester bed, she stirred and muttered a cross word.

As I hopped, clutching my hurt foot, Seymour, wearing only a nightshirt and slippers, strolled into the room. His nightshirt dropped from muscular shoulders, his strong legs bare from the knee down. He ignored me and my struggles, fixing his gaze on the closed curtains of Lady Elizabeth's bed.

Catherine entered behind him, she clad in nightgown and robe. I relaxed, but not entirely, remembering the scene in the garden when Catherine had held Elizabeth for her husband's games.

Seymour abruptly yanked open the bed curtains and put one knee on the thick mattress. "Sleepyhead," he called. "Is our precious daughter awake?"

Elizabeth, who was obviously now wide awake, scrambled to the opposite side of the bed and pulled the bedclothes to her chin. She peered over the top of the covers, her eyes sparkling with anticipation.

Catherine climbed upon the bed beside Seymour, and he held himself back, letting his wife reach Elizabeth first.

"Tickle," Catherine said. "Our daughter is most ticklish."

Elizabeth squeaked and tried to roll from her, but Catherine pounced, tickling Elizabeth until she began to giggle. Before my appalled eyes, Seymour's closed his brawny hands around Elizabeth's waist.

Elizabeth shouted with laughter. I set my weight gingerly on my hurt foot, pondering whether to run for my aunt. What could she do if the queen teased right alongside Seymour?

Elizabeth finally squirmed away from them and scrambled out of the bed. Both stepmother and stepfather pursued her, and Elizabeth dodged behind me, using my small body as a shield. My weight came down on my injured foot, and tears sprang to my eyes.

Seymour danced around the both of us, slapping Elizabeth on the hip as though trying to spank a naughty child. I attempted to block his blows, but Elizabeth swung me away, which allowed him to reach her more easily.

Catherine pushed loose hair from her eyes. "My dears, we must run in the garden. 'Tis a fine day."

"A splendid idea," Seymour said. "You," he barked at me. "Ready her. We will return."

Elizabeth stood shoulder to shoulder with me, out of breath, but flushed and pleased. Seymour reached around us and gave her one final swat, his hand half-landing on my buttocks in the process. I flinched, but Elizabeth giggled.

Catherine sashayed out the door, Seymour following. Before I could move to Elizabeth's dressing room and find her a gown suitable for a garden frolic, Seymour returned.

"Leave us," he shot at me.

I did not dare. I remembered Aunt Kat facing him down and stood my ground.

But Aunt Kat had a far more formidable presence than I. She had the weight of years, wisdom, and respect to bolster her. I was a fourteen-year-old waif, the product of a bad marriage, living here on Aunt Kat's charity.

Seymour moved to Elizabeth, who backed from him until she rested against the high bed.

"Daughter," he said, giving the word an ironic twist. Seymour laid his hands on either side of Elizabeth, resting them on the mattress behind her.

Elizabeth half-closed her eyes. She relaxed against the bed and did not fight when Lord Seymour eased his leg between hers. Before my astonished gaze, he cupped her face in one hand, leaned to her, and kissed her lips.

I could not decide whether to beat Seymour with a bolster or run for Aunt Kat. If I struck Seymour, an earl, I could be flogged, or much worse. If I hobbled for Aunt Kat, he might ravish Elizabeth several times over before I could return.

Seymour kissed Elizabeth again, a brief touch, but then it turned deeper.

The decision of what to do was taken from me. A small sound came from the doorway, and I turned to see Catherine, still in her bed attire, on the threshold, returning with Aunt Kat.

Both women stared in shock at Elizabeth lolling contentedly in Seymour's arms, Catherine's happiness draining swiftly from her.

Seymour sprang away from Elizabeth, any glib words dying on his lips.

There was no denying what Catherine had seen. I watched all belief that Seymour's attentions to Elizabeth were light-hearted fade from her eyes. With it went hope that after three tedious marriages she'd at last wed a man with whom she could find happiness.

Seymour had been fairly caught, but I read no shame in him. His expression held only annoyance that his wife had chosen to enter at the wrong moment.

Catherine turned and strode from the room.

Later that morning, I helped Aunt Kat pack all of Elizabeth's things. Catherine had decided that Elizabeth could no longer stay in her household.

That afternoon, we left for Cheshunt in Hertfordshire, to the home of Aunt Kat's sister and her husband, joining Elizabeth in her first exile.

CHAPTER 4

Cheshunt. I liked the lilt of the name and hummed it often to myself, although I knew to Elizabeth it meant humiliation.

Whatever our reason for the sojourn, those June days in 1548, in the soft air of Hertfordshire were golden to me, with quiet afternoons and serene nights. No more dangerous games, no more fear of Thomas Seymour coming upon me in the dark, no more watching with worried eyes while he plotted and schemed.

I had little doubt that Seymour *continued* to plot and scheme —he was that sort of man. But perhaps with the absence of Elizabeth and bathed in his wife's sorrow, he would grow remorseful, or at least be more cautious.

For me, existence returned to the simple pleasures of everyday living. Lady Denny, Aunt Kat's sister and known to me as Aunt Joan, became Elizabeth's appointed governess, much to Elizabeth's dismay.

Aunt Kat was in disgrace for not stopping Seymour's pursuit of her charge, and Lord Protector Somerset had demanded Aunt Kat's replacement. Elizabeth, however, would not hear of

Aunt Kat being sent away entirely, so she, Uncle John, and I lived cozily with Aunt Joan and Sir Anthony Denny—I called him Uncle Denny—and continued a quiet life.

The red brick house, built in a square around a plain courtyard, was far less ostentatious than the enormous one we'd just left. It was also mercifully less crowded. I had a tiny chamber adjacent to Aunt Kat's, high on an upper floor, with a window that looked across a field to a wood. Aunt Kat said the whole place was murky and bleak, but I found the open air and multitude of birdsong refreshing.

"Jealousy," Aunt Kat said one evening after Elizabeth had retired. She, Aunt Joan, and I sat in Aunt Kat's chamber, I sewing busily, while Aunt Joan read. Aunt Kat pretended to write letters, using a large book on her lap as a desk.

"What *do* you mean?" Aunt Joan asked, turning her thin nose in Kat's direction.

"I was there, you know, when the queen told Elizabeth why she had to depart," Aunt Kat explained, as I could see she was dying to. "She instructed me *not* to leave Elizabeth's side, no matter that I was no longer her governess."

Aunt Joan pursed her lips. She was as book-learned as Kat and as pleased to condemn my mother for her silliness in marrying my actor father, and again when she took her second husband, a Catholic, which was not much better, in her eyes.

The Champernowne women were as unalike as they could be. Aunt Joan enjoyed educated conversation more than anything, while my mother, Margaret, couldn't be bothered with books. Aunt Kat wavered somewhere between the two, reading Latin and philosophy but also adoring gossip.

Aunt Kat and Elizabeth's cofferer, Thomas Parry, nattered like women in a market, which Uncle John did not like and tried to stop. I could have told him he might as well have tried to push back the tide with a broom.

What Aunt Kat and Aunt Joan did have in common was their

love of the reformed religion. They could go on about the subject to the point of tedium.

My mother had believed that if her husband told her she must return to the old religion, she should do so without a murmur—though, I do not believe she cared one whit, truth to tell. Aunt Kat and Aunt Joan, however, plainly stated their views on the new religion versus the old. King Edward had embraced the reformed church, they said, and we could openly speak about it these days.

Today, however, the topic of Elizabeth and Seymour, while frowned upon by Uncle John, was the only thing on Aunt Kat's lips.

"The queen explained that my Lady Elizabeth must guard her reputation as she would guard the most precious of jewels," Aunt Kat continued. "How she presents herself to the people of England is of vast importance. She might be queen herself someday."

I believed this only a remote possibility, though Elizabeth had been restored to the succession by Henry's will.

Edward was a young man who would, in a few years, marry and produce an heir. After Edward and any sons came Mary, who was also young enough to wed and bear children herself, pushing Elizabeth even further down the line of succession.

I kept my focus on the gold satin sleeve I was stitching, knowing it was not my place to render an opinion, though I had them aplenty.

Most likely, Elizabeth would be married off to a prince of some faraway land. Then Aunt Kat and I would travel to France or a cold place in the north of Europe to serve her—that is, if we weren't forsaken and left behind in England altogether.

Thoughts of either prospect cut into my contented existence, so I pushed them aside.

Aunt Kat leaned to Aunt Joan, continuing her story. "Her Grace Elizabeth's fondness for Queen Catherine is unrivaled, and they embraced most affectionately before they parted. However, I saw the queen's jealousy. Queen Catherine must realize that her husband once thought to marry Elizabeth, changing his mind only when the king's privy council forbade him. Mark my words, it is still my Lady Elizabeth that the Lord Admiral prefers."

"Good heavens, you sound as though you condone this," Aunt Joan said in disapproval.

"Well, of course not." Aunt Kat sat back in her chair with a thump, as though reversing her position both in words and physically. "Never would I advise my Lady Elizabeth to marry against the wishes of the king's council. Such a thing would be tantamount to treason, wouldn't it?" She laughed shakily. "Lord Sudeley married Queen Catherine in the end, and that is that." Aunt Kat picked up her pen and scratched another word or two on her paper.

"And should remain so," Aunt Joan said, her tones cold. "'Tis dangerous and wrong to suggest otherwise."

Aunt Kat lifted her head again, eyes wide. "Think you I would stand against the wishes of the King of England? Even if those wishes come out of the head of the Lord Protector?"

"Do guard your tongue, Kat." Aunt Joan cast a furtive glance about the room. "It will be the death of you."

I shivered at the words. I had a sudden vision of Aunt Kat being dragged off in chains to a dank stone room, tears trickling through the grime on her face as she faced her interrogators. I pictured Uncle John in despair that his wife's busy tongue had taken her from him so swiftly.

I gasped out loud, and the images spun away.

The scenario was all too possible, unfortunately. King Henry had arrested and confined any who'd even hinted at thwarting his wishes, he always fearing the power of the families that surrounded him. One poor gentlewoman who'd waited on Elizabeth's sister, Mary, had gone to the Tower for absentmindedly calling Mary "princess" after Henry had stripped that title from her. The lady had been interrogated about a possibly conspiracy to restore Henry's first queen, and only the frantic intervention of her family had saved the woman's life.

"Yes, do take care, Aunt Kat, for heaven's sake," I begged.

Aunt Kat regarded me in surprise. "Gracious, I speak only to my family, and I'd say not a word of this to Elizabeth. 'Tis only a bit of harmless gossip, Eloise. Master Parry says the same, and he assures me he'd be torn asunder if he repeated aught I said to him."

I shuddered and could not warm myself. "It might come to that," I murmured darkly.

AUNT JOAN, NOT LONG AFTER THAT CONVERSATION, HAD CAUSE to travel to Sudeley Castle, where Queen Catherine had moved to begin her lying in. Catherine had taken Jane Grey and her household with her, to continue that young woman's education. Aunt Joan, instructed by Aunt Kat, sent back word of everything that happened there.

Catherine made ready for the birth of her child, which would come in September, and spoke with much hope of it being a son. A son would please Seymour and provide him an heir, and perhaps assuage his ambitious interest in Elizabeth.

Catherine's anger at Elizabeth had faded quickly, Aunt Joan informed us. Catherine missed the girl very much and planned to send for Elizabeth after the birth of her child. The scandal would have blown over then, and the two could be reconciled.

Elizabeth, for her part, never spoke about what had happened with Seymour. I knew, however, that she thought of it a great deal. When twilight came, and she could no longer see the words in her books, she would lift her head and stare out the window of her chamber, her dark eyes betraying chagrin and unhappiness.

She wrote letters of affection to Catherine and sent her small gifts, taking time throughout the day to pray for her stepmother and coming child. I was certain that Elizabeth had much remorse for hurting the queen, though I could not decide whether Elizabeth's contrition was for letting the flirtation go too far or for being caught at it.

"What think you of marriage, Eloise?" Elizabeth asked me one day toward the end of August as I sewed in her sitting room.

Summer had passed its height, and the last days of August had cooled into balmy softness. Late flowers ran riot among the hedges at Cheshunt, bleeding their last color before autumn would send them into dormancy.

I blinked in surprise. "Marriage, Your Grace? I try to think of it as little as possible."

I was not certain whether Elizabeth was in one of her whimsical moods—when she'd skewer anyone within earshot with her wit and expect their answers to be equally as witty. Or she might have asked me in all seriousness, wishing to provoke a philosophical discussion.

"I believe I shall never marry," Elizabeth said firmly. "It seems to me a dangerous endeavor."

"Aunt Kat likes it." So far, she and Uncle John, despite their occasional disagreement, were happy together.

"Mistress Kat married for love and was allowed to." Elizabeth turned to me with the air of a lecturer, but I saw her wistfulness as she spoke. "A lady of a high family marries for connections or monetary gain and usually not by her choice."

"I agree that highborn ladies do marry for duty," I said. "Perhaps sometimes duty and love can be found together?"

Elizabeth sent me a pitying glance. We might be the same

age, but she looked upon the world with eyes that were older and wiser than mine.

"Such things *can* happen," she answered. "But not very often. This time, my stepmother married for love, but from my observation, when she married her first two husbands and then my father, all for duty, she was much more contented."

I was not certain I agreed. I remembered Catherine as Henry's wife, a patient woman keeping her emotions in check.

I imagined she'd been the same in her first marriages, one to the young Sir Edward Burgh, and the second to Baron Latimer, who at least had given her a title and left her with some wealth. When Catherine had married Seymour, with whom she'd shared a close friendship before her marriage to Henry, she'd dared to be happy, laughing and enjoying herself. Her serious demeanor, which Henry had praised, had vanished.

Henry had married Catherine for her beauty, so the tales went, which had been unmarred by her two widowhoods. Catherine's attractiveness remained, and I do not believe Seymour was immune to it.

I'd come to highly suspect that Seymour's interest in Elizabeth had more to do with the fact that she was now second in line to the throne than anything else, though I did not discount her charms for him. I'd learned that Seymour was plenty lecherous enough to want Elizabeth for her young beauty as well.

"I shall not marry at all," I said with conviction, suppressing a shudder at the memory of Seymour's hands on me in the dark hall. "A gentleman is expected to rule his wife, and I dislike that notion. It is natural for a woman to obey a mother and father, and even an aunt and uncle, but most husbands, in my opinion, take advantage of their power."

Elizabeth listened to me thoughtfully. She never dismissed my words out of hand when we had these sorts of conversations, a consideration I was grateful for.

"Would the husband take such advantage, think you, if the wife was a queen?"

"I am afraid so," I answered. "There is not much that will stop husbands wanting mastery."

"The husband would be the queen's subject, though, would he not?" Elizabeth had a strangely persistent note in her voice. "If she ruled England herself?"

"But a woman has not ruled England," I pointed out. "Not for centuries. There has always been a male heir, who marries and produces at least one son, unless there is a war and another king takes over." At least, this was my somewhat muddled view of our history.

"True, but if my brother does not sire a son, my sister, Mary, will be queen." Elizabeth flicked a page of her book, as though the conversation was only of partial interest. "My father willed it thus."

Elizabeth did not continue that train of thought, but her implication was clear. If Edward left no heirs, and neither did Mary, Elizabeth would step into the role of monarch, as Aunt Kat had suggested.

I studied Elizabeth's firm jaw, her no-nonsense eyes, the tilt of her head that suggested arrogance.

Arrogance could become a detriment if taken too far. But it could also be an asset, an air that set a person apart from others and forced awe from those who beheld them.

"Mary will surely take a husband," I argued. "One that will benefit the kingdom. I would think a queen has less freedom than any other woman when it comes to choosing her life's mate."

Elizabeth lifted her head, the late summer light making her eyes gray like uncut diamonds. "But she would be queen. All must obey her then."

She challenged me, awaiting my response. I should bow my

head meekly and say she knew best, but my honest tongue rattled on.

"From what I understand, Your Grace, the people of England do not swallow things readily. It is not like the Saracen lands, where the people live in absolute terror of their kings."

I could not claim complete knowledge of the Saracen lands —or even where they lay—but I believed that in those places, the common subjects would never dream of criticizing their ruler, for fear of being put to death.

I did not remind her that when Henry had put aside his beloved first wife to marry Elizabeth's mother, rebellion had boiled under the waters of the then-placid pond of our kingdom.

Henry had executed plenty of gentlemen who would not support his divorce with Catherine of Aragon or the acts that had made Henry head of the Church of England and proclaimed Anne Boleyn's issue first in line for the throne.

Anne had been reviled, Aunt Kat had told me, openly hissed at in the streets and in danger of the mob whenever she went out. A monarch marrying badly carried dire consequences in England.

"That is true," Elizabeth conceded. "The people here have affection for their queens, and for their princesses."

"They do cheer most heartily when you ride out." Indeed, any time we ventured from the house, the villagers lined up to wave and shout for their Lady Elizabeth.

"That is not an affection one should take for granted," Elizabeth said, her voice softening. "A reputation must be guarded."

I thought back on Aunt Kat relaying Catherine's almost exact words to Elizabeth. Her admonishment seemed to have had impact.

This was the closest Elizabeth had ever come to discussing the reason she'd been sent from Catherine's household, and I feared to upset her by remarking on it.

"You are wise, Your Grace," I murmured.

Elizabeth sent me a sharp look, sensing I could say more about her situation if I dared, but she let the matter drop.

August ended on a brisk wind, and the trees began turning lovely shades of orange, red, and gold. Also, with the end of August came word from Sudeley Castle that Queen Catherine had delivered to Thomas Seymour a girl, who was called Mary.

We rejoiced in Catherine's good fortune, and Elizabeth's hope grew that Catherine would send for her soon.

But the rejoicing was short-lived. Another message came from Sudeley hard on the heels of the first, that while the daughter survived, Queen Catherine had died of child-bed fever.

CHAPTER 5

Catherine's death plunged Elizabeth into illness so severe that Lord Protector Somerset had to send a physician to attend her at Cheshunt.

In those dark days, Elizabeth liked me to sit beside her while she lay abed in her chamber. Her illness made her thinner, but the lines around her mouth had been etched there by wariness and grief. She grew quiet and watchful, as though she knew some terrible fate approached her.

Catherine was buried at Sudeley Castle, with all honors. Seymour attended, appropriately grieving, from what Aunt Joan told us. But reports servants gave of Catherine's last illness dismayed me.

Catherine, in her delirium, had apparently raved that the love she bore her husband had been ruined, that he was false and had used her for his own ambition. Seymour had pursued Elizabeth under her nose and had wished Catherine to die—indeed, had he poisoned her?

Then Catherine would come to herself and say that no, she was only dreaming, and declare she loved her Thomas dearly.

In the end, Catherine had willed Seymour everything she

owned, including the lovely Chelsea Manor, and had died with words of forgiveness on her lips.

The stories alarmed me not a little. Catherine's fevers had brought to the surface ugly truths that had been kept buried in her troubled household.

DESPITE OUR SORROW AT THE QUEEN'S DEATH, I WAS HAPPY WHEN King Edward sent word that Elizabeth was allowed to move to Hatfield again, where she would set up her own household. I was sorry to leave Cheshunt, a peaceful place, but Hatfield had many possibilities.

At Hatfield, Elizabeth would be a princess in truth, with her own entourage and gentlemen at arms, and she would begin managing the estates willed to her by her father. Despite whispers that Seymour was once again trying to gain more power at court, I hoped happier times approached.

Hatfield was a fine red brick house north and west of Cheshunt and twenty or so miles directly north of London. The estate had long country lanes for rambling and good hunting in the forests nearby. We were isolated from the rigorous pace and stink of London but close enough for an easy visit to Whitehall or Greenwich. Elizabeth professed to be fond of the property where she and I had spent our innocent days of childhood, before we'd understood what a frightening place the world could be.

"The Lord Admiral will no doubt seek permission to marry her now," Aunt Kat said to me a few weeks after we'd settled Elizabeth into the house. "Mark my words."

I was in our rooms, laying out fabrics for one of Elizabeth's new gowns, which she'd wear on upcoming visits to her brother. Elizabeth was fifteen, an adult by royal standards, and she'd need to be arrayed in finery.

My entire body thrummed as I brushed my fingers over the brocade, dreaming of the gowns that would take shape. It was an exciting time, and I'd have the opportunity to show the entire court what I could do.

An arranged marriage for Elizabeth would likely not be long in coming, I reasoned as I listened to Aunt Kat. Given Thomas Seymour's rivalry with his brother, the Lord Protector, I doubted the Protector would allow Seymour to extend his hand to Elizabeth.

"I thought you disapproved of Seymour's schemes," I returned.

Aunt Kat shrugged. "If he offers to take Elizabeth respectably to wife, what can there be to disapprove of? The Admiral is a handsome man, wealthy, and intelligent. I'd rather our lady marry him than any other man in the kingdom."

"He has spoken of it to you?" I asked in concern.

"Nay, why should he speak to me?" Aunt Kat's eyes went wide. "I hear of his wishes from my dear friend, Master Parry. I told my Lady Elizabeth she ought to write a consoling letter to the Admiral, and do you know what she said?" Aunt Kat hesitated long enough for me to give her a curious glance then trundled on. "She told me she did not dare write, for people might believe she meant to woo him." Aunt Kat nodded wisely. "She knows the lay of the land better than most."

I thought back to Elizabeth's speculations on marriage she'd shared with me at Cheshunt before Catherine's death. She'd been most adamant then to remain free of wedlock, but that was before Seymour became eligible again.

"So, she will *not* write to him?" I asked.

"No." Aunt Kat beamed me a happy smile. "Which will make him pine for her all the more."

"She is much younger than he is," I pointed out with some displeasure.

"Nonsense, that is no matter. Our Elizabeth is at a ripe age to marry, and Seymour is not so old that he has lost his looks and prowess."

I began pinning together the layers of velvet and brocade that would become sleeves fastened back to reveal gold silk beneath them.

"I believe Lord Sudeley has charmed you," I said warningly. "He seems to have pulled you firmly on his side. Perhaps more than is prudent."

Aunt Kat flushed. "Do not be silly. He has said naught to me about it, not one word."

She mercifully ceased chattering, but I felt a twinge of disquiet. I had become inured to Seymour's charms after my encounter with him at Chelsea, but I continued to witness the fascination he held for others.

My aunt's speech implied that Seymour was also busily beguiling Thomas Parry, treasurer of Elizabeth's household. The man was likely pumping Master Parry for knowledge of Elizabeth's finances, as well as Aunt Kat for knowledge of her person.

The combination spelled trouble, well I knew. But I, the seamstress, who should remain sewing in the corner, could not do much but watch and worry.

As our sojourn at Hatfield continued, Elizabeth's health gradually improved. She resumed lessons in Greek and Latin under a new tutor, Roger Ascham, after her previous instructor, Master Grindal, had sadly passed away.

Elizabeth penned affectionate letters to her brother, walked in the growing chill of Hatfield's gardens, and never spoke one word about Thomas Seymour, to my great relief.

November skies grew gray and bleak. I soon was happy to

stay indoors near the fire as I sewed, peering through thick windows at the bare trees against a pale blue sky.

Aunt Kat spent more and more time in seclusion with Master Parry, and when Master Parry took a journey to London, Aunt Kat shot bold hints at me that things would change for Elizabeth once he returned.

"What is your aunt conspiring?"

I jumped in the darkness of my chamber as Uncle John paused in the doorway and fixed keen eyes upon me. The chill had made my fingers ache, and I set down my needle, rubbing my fingertips on the velvet I'd been stitching.

"Is Aunt Kat conspiring?" I asked, trying to sound innocent.

Uncle John shut the door against the draft and drew the hearth stool close to my wooden chair. The window had gone dark, cold air seeping to us that the smoldering fire could not quite disperse. I was lucky to warrant a fire in my tiny chamber, as Elizabeth had declared I must be kept fit to sew her gowns.

Uncle John heaved a long sigh as he stretched his feet toward the flames. "My wife is a good woman, but she cannot leave well enough alone. She loves Elizabeth as she would a daughter, and like a mother with a daughter, she would do anything to advance Elizabeth's position. Even if she goes to the block for it."

"The block?" I squeaked in sudden agitation. "Why on earth do you say that?"

Uncle John sent me a tired look. "Because Seymour is ruthless, niece. He will overreach himself, and my Kat might be caught in his betwixt and between. And he will catch Elizabeth with her."

My heart sped as I realized that Uncle John was right. Aunt Kat loved Elizabeth mightily and easily blinded herself to danger because of that love.

"It may come to nothing where Aunt Kat is concerned," I ventured, hoping I was right. I recalled my alarming vision of

Aunt Kat in a prison cell, and hoped that had been caused by a bad vegetable at supper, not a premonition. "Elizabeth is indifferent to him, and would refuse even if his lordship offered."

"Eloise." Uncle John's tone sharpened. "You have more intelligence than that. Look at me again and declare there is nothing to this. That Her Grace Elizabeth does not blush when Seymour's name is spoken, that she does not smile at any who speak highly of him. Tell me this."

I glumly shook my head, because I knew I could not. "What can we do, Uncle?"

"We extract your aunt from danger, and we warn Elizabeth to take care. I have much affection for Kat, and she has a good heart, but sometimes … "

"Yes," I agreed, clutching my fabric. "Sometimes … "

Sometimes a good heart led to a downfall. Seymour's sojourn in Catherine's household and all that followed had forced my eyes open to a new world.

I could not remain an innocent child forever—I had to keep my wits about me in this whirlpool that ever surrounded the royal court. Theirs was a world of gentlemen who'd not hesitate to use a very young woman to achieve what they wished, no matter who they injured irreparably.

Perhaps Aunt Kat had such ambition as well, so that one day she could point to Elizabeth's rise and proclaim, "I did that."

A new world, and a dangerous one.

"Durham house was to have been *mine*," Elizabeth snapped at Master Parry a few days later, her brows drawn into a scowl. She'd turned from the window where she'd been conversing with a few of her ladies, consciously moving so a beam from the winter sun touched her unbound hair. "I was promised it. Does His Grace the Lord Protector not remember this?"

Master Parry betrayed as much agitation about this new state of affairs as did his mistress. He twisted the gold chain that hung from his neck, his round face a bright red.

Elizabeth had just learned that Lord Protector Somerset had procured Durham Place, Elizabeth's London residence, for his own purposes. Master Parry's recent mission in London—the one Aunt Kat had hinted to me meant more than it appeared—had been to look into the matter.

"He claims he needs it, Your Grace," Parry said with resentment. "He plans to set up a mint. There he squats, coining more money to spend in the name of your brother the king."

Elizabeth's nostrils flared, her mouth white and pinched. "He presumes."

"He does indeed, Your Grace." Parry bent his head, but I did not miss the satisfied glint in his eyes. "I spoke with Lord Admiral Seymour about it, and he was most sympathetic."

"The Lord Admiral." Elizabeth's gaze grew fixed. She moved slightly out of the sunshine, her studied pose vanishing. "Does he apologize for his brother?"

"He does indeed. He also very kindly offered you the use of his own residence when you come to London, so that you will not be inconvenienced."

"Very kind." A hint of frost touched Elizabeth's voice, but her dark eyes fixed intently on Parry. "What else did he say?"

"The Lord Admiral is quite interested in all your properties, Your Grace," Master Parry rattled on. "He asked me whether the king's council had yet bestowed all your father's bequests on you. He declared it shameful when I told him they had not. He said he would be happy to offer advice on how you might make some savings, since you have not been given everything you should."

"Did he?" The frost increased. "And what did he suggest?"

"That you look over your books yourself," Parry said. "That … " He lowered his voice almost to a whisper, his eyes as hard and focused as Elizabeth's own. "That you might make savings by the two of you sharing resources. The Admiral has many houses and gentlemen at his disposal, and he could help you obtain those that are rightfully yours."

"What did he mean by all this, think you?" The question seemed ingenuous, but Elizabeth's tone was calculating.

Master Parry glanced behind him before he spoke. The ladies at the window were quiet, pretending to look out at the winter landscape, and I sewed busily on my stool. "That perhaps he wants you near him, as well? You know he has not broken up the household of Queen Catherine—he has her ladies and gentlemen together still."

"To wait upon Cousin Jane," Elizabeth said quickly. "He did it so that Jane Grey might have a household of her own."

Because, I knew, Seymour wanted Jane to marry King Edward. I had heard Aunt Kat and Parry, and even Uncle John, discussed that fact often enough.

"Perhaps." Parry sent her a furtive smile. "And what would you say, my lady, if Seymour offered for you? Would you have him? If the council approved, of course."

He added the last hastily. King Edward's council had frowned on Seymour's original attempt to ensnare Elizabeth, and well we knew it. Marrying without their consent would not only displease Edward but might bar Elizabeth from the succession and result in her forfeiting those lands and money the council was taking its time about handing over in the first place.

I watched Elizabeth sift through these thoughts, a lady weighing the consequences of being able to love a fascinating gentleman against forfeiting all possibility of inheriting the crown.

I could have lent an argument if I'd dared, that Seymour had blatantly chased Elizabeth while he was married to Catherine. If his stalking of me in the corridor that night was any indication, he'd pursued other dalliances as well. Not a man who would consider it necessary to be true to his wife. Many gentlemen were not so nice when it came to fidelity, and quick to break their wives' hearts.

I had no way of knowing whether Elizabeth would count this as a point against Seymour. I'd met more than one woman in love with a philanderer, who held absolute conviction that if said man were with *her*, he'd philander no more.

Whatever debates hummed through Elizabeth's head, when she opened her mouth to speak, it was in the tone of a man of law who'd calculated every word.

"If what you imagine comes to pass," she said to Parry. "Then I will do as God shall put into my mind at the time."

A lovely answer, saying neither yay nor nay. Parry bowed his head. "Of course, Your Grace."

After Master Parry had scuttled off to his coffers, I fitted Elizabeth into the dress I was creating. Her hands were ice cold, and she scarce seemed to notice me and my maidservant pinning the brocade to her frame—that is, until I accidentally poked her.

Elizabeth jumped and slapped my hand. "Do take care, Mistress Seamstress."

I humbly begged her pardon, words of apology now rote upon my lips. So often did I have to say them to Elizabeth.

Elizabeth's mouth trembled, but I saw a gleam of excitement in her eyes. "Master Parry is a prodigious gossip," she said abruptly. "Are you fond of gossip, Eloise?"

"Me? No, never, Your Grace." I spoke with all sincerity.

"Liar." Elizabeth laughed, the note shrill. "What a liar you are, my seamstress. I am surrounded by liars."

I had no idea what she meant by this and did not reply. Elizabeth then growled with impatience at the fitting, so the maid and I unpinned the gown and laid it aside for another time.

Later that evening I came upon Master Parry closeted with my aunt in her chamber. Chatter, chatter, chatter—they nattered away about my Lady Elizabeth and Seymour, gossiping and speculating as though they had every right to arrange the lives of two important people of the realm.

I liked Aunt Kat's chamber, small and cozy, lit with fragrant candles and warmed by a fire. Because Aunt Kat was a favorite of Elizabeth, she had candles made of true wax, a fire built high, cushions for her benches and stools, and a bed as plump as she was around the middle.

I remembered how, when I'd first joined Aunt Kat, the ladies and gentlemen of this household had ordered sumptuous meals to be served to the little princess in order that they could feast themselves. A small child could eat only a little of the spread, and the ladies and gentlemen had enjoyed themselves heartily on the remains.

Aunt Kat put a halt to that, much to the annoyance of the spoiled courtiers. Once Elizabeth had been restored into the succession, we all dined well and slept in comfort, lucky in our positions. A far better life, I always reminded myself, than I would have living with my mother and Sir Philip Baldwin, her priggish husband, who pretended I did not exist.

As a child, I'd amused myself drawing pictures on scraps of discarded paper of my stepfather and then sticking him with my scissors. Then I would hastily burn the papers, afraid anyone finding them would think me practicing witchcraft.

As far as I knew, however, my Sir Philip never took harm from it. Now, I simply pretended he did not exist in return.

Neither my aunt nor Parry ceased their blathering as I seated myself at Aunt Kat's table and helped myself to a thick slice of bread. Using this as a truncheon, I heaped warm meat and sauce across it. A watchful servant brought me a goblet and poured out a large measure of hock.

All the while Parry and Aunt Kat moved their mouths in

talk. So intent on each other they were that they never noticed me eating my meal at the other end of the table. Which was to my advantage, I decided, as I snatched the last sweetmeat from a tray and quickly stuffed it in my mouth before either of them saw me.

"What think you of all that, Mistress Ashley?" Parry was saying in satisfaction.

They'd kept their voices muted, but now I pricked my ears, though I kept my head down over my food.

"I've known of his wishes all along." Aunt Kat sniffed. "No reason she should not have the Lord Admiral to husband."

I remembered Uncle John's warning, the fear in his words. "Aunt Kat," I ventured.

Aunt Kat took as much heed of me as though I were a buzzing fly—less, because a fly she would swat.

"You've known no such thing." Parry laughed, confident that he possessed better gossip than Aunt Kat.

"Indeed, I do." My aunt leaned toward him. "The Lord Admiral was always taken with our lady, and why should he not be? A lovely girl is Elizabeth, so poised and regal. The perfect lady, not like *others* in her family I could mention, though they be *close* to her."

I stopped eating, overwhelmed by unease. Aunt Kat did not go so far as to name Princess Mary, who was small-statured and sullen, but I knew this was who she meant. This was exactly the sort of talk Uncle John did not wish his wife to indulge in.

Parry rolled his goblet between his palms. "We have ever been friends, have we not, Mistress Ashley?"

"Of course, Master Parry," Aunt Kat returned with warmth.

This surprised me a bit, because these two had quarreled plenty in the past, as Parry had dipped his fingers into Elizabeth's money from time to time. We all knew it—even Elizabeth did—but Aunt Kat and I had to look the other way about it.

Only Elizabeth could dismiss Master Parry, and so far, she'd shown no inclination to do so.

"Then you will tell me all, will you not?" Parry asked. "As we both have our lady's best interests at heart, and you know so much about it."

Aunt Kat loved to be praised. While an intelligent woman, she had a weakness for flattery.

She sent Parry a delighted smile, then to my horror proceeded to relate the entire story of Elizabeth's encounters with Seymour at Chelsea. Every morning romp, the cut-up dress, Seymour's visit to Elizabeth's chamber in his nightshirt, and Catherine's tacit condoning of his seduction until she could shut her eyes to it no more.

Thomas Parry lapped it up like a dog with a dish of scraps. He and Aunt Kat leaned closer and closer until their noses nearly touched, their sleeves in danger of ruin by cooling stew.

"I grant you," Aunt Kat went on. "Even if the Lord Protector does not like the match between our Lady Elizabeth and the Lord Admiral, when the king is of age, he will certainly smile upon it."

I could contain myself no more. "But surely the Lord Admiral is too old, Aunt Kat." I used the argument I'd tried with her before. By the time King Edward reached his majority, Seymour would be well along in his forties.

Aunt Kat sent me an irritated glare. "He is of an age with me, Miss Impertinence, and none too old for our lady. What young woman does not want to marry a man of wise years? And for all his *great age*, as you term it, Seymour is strong and finely shaped. I saw this when he went bare-legged into my lady's chamber." She tittered. "No quarrel there, I imagine."

"Aunt Kat!" I put as much shock into my words as I could. Aunt Kat had gone red with wine and excitement, the drink loosening her tongue a dangerous amount.

At last, Aunt Kat seemed to realize she and Master Parry

were speaking far too much about things that were dangerous to discuss. Aunt Kat shot a guilty glance at Parry, who closed his mouth at the same time.

"You'll not breathe a word of this, of course," Aunt Kat quickly admonished Parry.

Parry adamantly shook his head. "Never, Mistress Ashley. I'd never tell a soul what we discuss about our Lady Elizabeth. I have assured you of this time and again."

He looked quite sincere, and after a moment, Aunt Kat gave him a decided nod. The two exchanged a secret smile, lifted pewter goblets of wine from the Rhine valley, and drank to it.

I LEFT AUNT KAT THAT NIGHT, TORN ABOUT WHETHER TO REPORT the conversation to Uncle John. After much inner debate, I went to bed without disturbing him, reasoning to myself that Aunt Kat's and Master Parry's wild speculation in the privacy of my aunt's chamber would come to nothing.

No matter how high the two of them might believe their positions to be, they had no true power to affect Elizabeth's choice of bridegrooms. That was up to the king's council, Lord Protector Somerset, and Edward himself. Idle chatter about a man's legs would not bring down King Edward's reign.

I also had a nasty headache and did not fancy running to Uncle John to tattle on his wife. I kept my thoughts to myself and slept fitfully.

How Uncle John got wind of the conversation, I do not know—though I suspected the attentive servants. When I rose in the morning, I heard his voice booming from Aunt Kat's chamber.

I dressed quickly and scurried through the darkened gallery to her door.

"Gossip and meddling," Uncle John roared as I opened the

door a crack and peeped inside. "Have nothing to do with the Admiral, for the love of God, Kat. Nothing good can come of it, do you understand?"

Aunt Kat had never been a meek woman, nor readily obedient to her husband. She had a good opinion of herself, a strong will, and a voice as loud as his.

"I mean only well for Elizabeth," she shouted in return. "Only that. You, John, are the party who needs to understand my loyalty to her."

Uncle John banged out of the room, his eyes glittering with rage. He caught sight of me as I scuttled into the shadows, pointed a savage finger at me, and motioned me to follow him.

CHAPTER 6

My head gave an extra-hard throb as I hurried after Uncle John, who descended the stairs and made for the wide hall on the ground floor.

"Uncle do not look at me so," I pleaded when I caught up to him. "I cannot stop the Thames from flooding, and I cannot stop Aunt Kat when she wants to talk about something."

Uncle John swung to face me, his cheeks flushed, though modulated his voice when he spoke to me. "I do not blame you, Eloise, but you must understand. That man is dangerous, and all his smiles and beguiles do not make him less so."

"I know he is dangerous, Uncle. You do not need to convince *me.*"

Uncle John eyed me sharply. "And why are you so certain?"

I did not want to talk about the awful evening Seymour had forced his attentions upon me. I could still feel the imprint of his large hand, smell the sticky sweet scent that had clung to his clothes.

"I see through him," I said glibly. "Not all women are fools."

Uncle John let out an exasperated breath. "Your aunt is—at least in this instance—and I have told her so. I am bound for

London today. You will report to me any meddling Kat thinks to do as soon as I return. Do you understand?"

I clutched Uncle John's sleeve, the wool of it homey and comforting. "Why do you not stay and watch her yourself? Or take her with you?"

"I have business," he answered in clipped tones. "And no time for a wife who embroils in dangerous gossip."

Uncle John removed himself from my grip and strode through the hall, barking at a servant to help him prepare for his journey.

I remained forlornly at the foot of the staircase, thrust squarely into the middle of a husband-and-wife quarrel.

AUNT KAT SULKED ALL THAT DAY, ANGRY AT UNCLE JOHN AND AT me, calling me no better than a jailer.

The next morning she began to repent, admitting to me, shame-faced, that perhaps she had far too much interest in affairs not her own. She blamed Master Parry for dragging the story of Seymour's pursuit of Elizabeth out of her, though she conceded she should not have allowed him to goad her.

Several long, soggy days dragged by, while Aunt Kat became ever more unhappy and remorseful. She missed Uncle John and lamented that she'd so angered him. She wrote him a letter and waited eagerly for a reply, but had none.

When another week and more passed without word from Uncle John, Aunt Kat became resolute to go to London and make things up with him. Her excuse for leaving the princess's side was that her arm ached strangely, and she wished for a physician to examine it.

It was obvious that Elizabeth saw through the excuse for the journey, but she gave Aunt Kat a cool nod and permission for her to leave for a short while.

Wanting, I suppose, to reconcile with me as well, Aunt Kat bade me accompany her.

I went with her readily, because not only did I want Aunt Kat and Uncle John to patch up their quarrel, but the countryside had become gloomy in the dark of December. London, though it could be as muddy and cold as the country, would at least be interesting.

Vendors would sell hot nuts and cider, and there would be street entertainment aplenty. Though Aunt Kat admonished me that tumbling men and performing bears were low forms of amusement, I enjoyed them, and I noted that they could hold her attention as well. Elizabeth was also fond of bears, tumblers, and acting troupes of the sort my father had belonged to, whenever they passed through Hatfield in the warmer months.

I had also hoped, when we reached London, to shop a bit. I wanted a peek at whatever fabrics and trims were coming in on the great ships, as well as baubles and beads I could sew into patterns on the cloth.

When Aunt Kat descended the coach with haste at the dwelling of her friends, people called the Slaynings, she shut herself inside the house and refused to budge, admonishing me to remain with her.

The Slaynings' home was large but dark, and the fires did not draw well, making the rooms smoky and my throat sore. I tried to busy myself drawing designs for gowns and planning what I'd search for in the shops, but Aunt Kat made no sign that she wished to leave the house. She did not even emerge from the chamber her kind friends had prepared for her.

"Will you not seek the physician?" I asked her with impatience after a few days had passed. "I thought your arm pained you so."

"I cannot go out, Eloise," was Aunt Kat's listless response. "I have nothing to wear."

True, Aunt Kat had not packed very much above her travel

garments, but I knew this was only an excuse. She bore the demeanor of a woman who meant to stay the whole day indoors with her feet propped on a stool by the fire.

She'd come to London to find Uncle John, and no other reason. Her fabrication about seeking a leech had already been forgotten.

"Perhaps *I* should visit the physician on your behalf," I suggested. On the way, I could seek out the markets and immerse myself in my beloved fabric.

"Yes, do go, Eloise. You are restless as a sparrow." Aunt Kat returned her brooding attention to the fire, clearly uncaring of what I did.

I conscripted a maid and a lad of the house to accompany me, it being unfit for a young lady to wander the muddy streets alone. They resented being dragged out into the cold and muttered to themselves as we walked along.

The house in which we stayed was near the Strand. I turned onto this street and reveled in the carts selling everything from sweetmeats to trinkets from far-off places. I found ivory-colored beads that would look well against a white velvet bodice I was designing, and purchased a few with what pennies I had.

Durham Place—which should have been Elizabeth's, had not the Lord Protector confiscated it—was a fixture of elegance on the Strand, not far from the Lord Protector's own home of Somerset House.

The gates of Durham Place stood open this morning. As we strolled past in search of more shops, I craned my head to peer in beyond the gatehouse. A huge courtyard led to the manor itself, which was set far back from the street, its rear windows overlooking the Thames. I could well understand why Elizabeth was annoyed that the Lord Protector had pulled the lovely mansion into his clutches.

Farther along the Strand, near Temple Bar, we came upon a troupe of acrobats—three men and two women—in the middle of a lively performance. I and my servants joined the watchers in delight.

Wind scraped down the narrow lanes from the river, and a chill crept up my skirts and seeped into my gloves. The acrobats, climbing upon shoulders and tumbling to the ground, were smiling and rosy, but the audience stamped feet and blew on fingers.

The troupe finished their last move, landing solidly and raising their arms to our wild applause. They unfroze from their pose, the men bowing, women curtsying, then moved through the crowd, hats out for coins. I dropped tuppence in one, to the sweating tumbler's delight, and the maid and lad I'd purloined happily gave them a farthing each.

The heavy tramping of feet interrupted the proceedings. I spied liveried and armed gentlemen pushing down the Strand toward us, their presence indicating that an important personage was traveling this way.

The acrobats abruptly swung from the crowd, and all five nimbly disappeared down the nearest passageways. The audience dispersed, hurrying aside for whatever noble gentleman or lady came their way, and I did the same.

I hadn't gone more than three steps before a chillingly familiar voice called out to me.

"It is too cold to be abroad, kitten. Is your mistress so cruel that she does not allow you to laze by the fire?"

I stilled for a long a moment before I turned slowly. Thomas Seymour, Lord High Admiral of England, had halted with his guards and eyed me from among his entourage.

Why he, an exalted nobleman, should be tramping about on foot, I could scarcely say. It was easier to move through London using boats and barges on the river than through the filthy streets, but then, the athletic Seymour had always done as he pleased.

I curtsied as well as my stiff legs would allow and murmured, "Your lordship."

Seymour flashed his arrogant smile. "I asked you a question, seamstress. Does your mistress not keep you busy sewing?"

He took in my two servants, who'd faded behind me, and noted the absence of any other person or retinue. Clearly, he wanted to know whether Elizabeth was nearby or in London at all. I had no intention of telling him the answer to either question.

"You are too cold," Seymour announced. "You must come with me and warm yourself."

I did not answer, my heart pounding as I pretended that etiquette prevented me from conversing with my betters.

My thoughts, in contrast, were roiling, my previous fear of Seymour mixing with rage. This man had intruded on my person—I had no doubt he'd thought himself doing me a favor —and I trusted him not one whit. He was busy manipulating Master Parry and Aunt Kat, and by extension, Elizabeth, to obtain all that he wanted.

He was a lofty man not caring who he stepped on to make himself still more lofty.

Seymour's teeth worked his lower lip, making his beard move. He seemed in no hurry, and his men assumed the stoic expressions of soldiers awaiting orders.

"You must have passed the gates of Durham Place to reach here," Seymour said. "A magnificent house, is it not? Even if the stink of the river mars it."

He obviously wanted some response, so I murmured, "Yes, my lord."

"Our lady would rejoice to see it once more for her use, I believe." Seymour didn't bother to modulate his voice, no matter how many stood in the street around us. "As I have discussed with her clever Master Parry. It shall be, and so much more, very soon."

He gave me a nod, perhaps expecting me to utter words of delight. Or maybe he wished me to rush straight back to Elizabeth and share with her the intriguing hints the Lord High Admiral had dropped to me in the middle of the Strand.

I contrived a blank expression, pretending not to understand him. Seymour's eyes narrowed, and his ingratiating smile faded.

"You will come with me, little seamstress. I have need of you."

Seymour did not reach for me but instead jerked his head at his attendants. The men wheeled about with precision and proceeded to herd me back past Temple Bar and along the Strand the way they had come.

I intended to slip away the first moment I was able, but for now I was hemmed in by guardsmen with swords and pikes. My maid and footman had vanished, and I hoped they'd fled back to Aunt Kat for help.

I wondered what Seymour meant to do—confine me in one of his houses until he pried out of me what he could about Elizabeth? Or were his designs darker than simply wanting information?

I believed Seymour was not above holding me captive until Elizabeth agreed to aid him. Speculating what he would do to me while I was in his power reawakened my direst fears. Seymour was a ruthless man, and I was no one very important.

"Eloise Rousell, where do you go?"

Never had my uncle's deep voice sounded so beloved. The tall figure of Uncle John broke through Seymour's retinue, he the most welcome sight in the world.

"Why are you in London, niece?" Uncle John went on, as though Seymour and his men were not there at all.

Seymour scowled at the interruption, but I watched him check whatever sharp words had sprung to his tongue. He knew

Uncle John for a trusted gentleman of Elizabeth's household, one he could not manipulate.

"Ashley," Seymour said in a neutral tone.

Uncle John bowed diffidently. "Your lordship."

I wondered what excuse Seymour would offer for attempting to kidnap me, but he did not bother to explain. His flattering, beguiling manner returned, though I could have told him it would not work with Uncle John.

"The seamstress is a credit to you and your good wife," Seymour said.

"Your lordship is kind," Uncle John replied stiffly.

"I will make you a gift. Some trifle, to express my appreciation for looking after Her Grace so well."

Alarm flickered through me, which I saw reflected in Uncle John's eyes. Accepting a gift, even a small token, could be interpreted as conferring loyalty to Seymour, and pledging loyalties was a dangerous pastime these days.

"You are kind, my lord," Uncle John repeated. "But serving the princess is reward enough for us."

Seymour made a negligent flick of his fingers. "A bauble, perhaps, that your niece might present to the princess. I will send a messenger to her at Whitehall."

A man of single-mindedness was Seymour. He sought even now to learn whether we had traveled to London in Elizabeth's company.

"Her Grace is not at court," Uncle John said without changing expression. "I left her in Hatfield."

Seymour sent me a sharp look, and I did my best to appear ingenuous. I nodded to affirm my uncle's words, my eyes wide, as though I was a bit simple.

Having ascertained that his quarry was nowhere near, Seymour took his farewells with Uncle John. Seymour was scrupulously polite, so that Uncle John could repeat to Elizabeth what a pleasant and courteous fellow the Admiral was.

After that, Seymour signaled to his retinue and walked off once more toward Temple Bar, utterly ignoring us.

As soon as Seymour was out of sight, my two borrowed servants emerged from around a corner, both stuffing sweetmeats into their mouths.

I glared at them, but they showed no contrition. If I'd dragged them out into dirty London in the cold, their expressions said, then it was only their due to run off and gobble treats when my attention was engaged elsewhere. I doubted they'd even noticed that Seymour had tried to make off with me.

"What are you doing in London, Eloise?" Uncle John demanded as he towed me into a narrow lane, out of the crowds. "Where is Her Grace?"

"At Hatfield, as you told the Lord Admiral," I replied, the air fogging with my words. "Aunt Kat and I came to London on our own."

"Why?" Uncle John peered at me in anxiety. "Never tell me it was to speak with Seymour. What is she—"

"No, no, not the Lord Admiral," I said quickly. "To speak with *you*." My voice gentled. "Aunt Kat is quite sorry she quarreled with you, and she misses you so. She made the excuse that she needed to seek a physician, but in truth, she is waiting for you to send word that she is forgiven."

Uncle John's grip on me relaxed, and tenderness entered his expression. "She is foolish sometimes, is your aunt."

"Perhaps, but she is willing to be guided by you."

Uncle John frowned. "Cease when you have won, Eloise. Your aunt is not the most obedient of wives, though, to be honest, I prefer her that way." His mouth softened. "I miss her, too."

"Return to the house with me now, then. She is staying with the Slaynings, and will be glad to see you."

To my relief, Uncle John nodded, and we fell into step

together, making our way toward the house where Aunt Kat waited.

My assurances did not curb Uncle John's questions. "If your aunt came to London to make it up with me, why were you out here conferring with his lordship?"

"Hardly conferring," I said indignantly. "I was being abducted." I told him what had occurred, and Uncle John looked troubled.

"He is scheming something, as ever." Uncle John shuddered. "I hope whatever it is never touches us."

I fervently shared the wish. The conspiracies of the highborn could be perilous, and I knew Seymour for a dangerous man.

AUNT KAT WAS SO PLEASED TO SEE UNCLE JOHN WHEN WE reached the house that she welcomed him with open arms, all quarrels forgotten. Uncle John stayed to supper at the Slaynings' request, which was a happy reunion with his wife and friends.

By tacit agreement, neither I nor Uncle John spoke of my encounter with Seymour.

That evening, Aunt Kat retired with Uncle John to her chamber, and they did not emerge again until much later. I admit that before I went to sleep, I pressed my ear to their chamber door and was happy to hear their contented murmurs.

In the morning, Aunt Kat and I broke our fast with Uncle John, and Master Parry, who'd likewise come to London on business. We made no mention of Seymour, and Aunt Kat seemed to understand that the topic of the Admiral—and marriage at all—was forbidden.

Once we'd finished the meal, Aunt Kat told me that Uncle John had persuaded her to return to Hatfield with him. We packed our meager belongings, thanked our hosts, and departed on horseback, me clinging to Aunt Kat as I rode behind her on a calm palfrey.

We wended our way north through London to Smithfield and then took the long road to Hatfield.

By the time we returned home, news reached us that Thomas Seymour had begun a dangerous new mission.

He'd decided to use his position as Lord High Admiral to try to overthrow his brother and the stranglehold he and the privy council had on King Edward, and to grip Edward in his own fist instead.

"I am all amazed," Aunt Kat told Uncle Denny. "It must be a mistake."

Uncle Denny was taking supper with us and Master Parry and his wife in Aunt Kat's chambers at Hatfield on a cold January night. Uncle John had made another journey to London a few days ago, but this time, Aunt Kat and I had been content to remain home and cozy, with the world in winter's grip.

Also dining with us was William Paulet, who'd arrived at Hatfield this afternoon with Uncle Denny. Paulet had once been comptroller of the household for King Henry and now was young Edward's chief steward.

I stood in a little awe of Paulet, a graying man with a shrewd eye, who'd been among those who'd carried out the arrest of Anne Boleyn. He'd acted only out of duty at that time, he'd always claimed, and he now served Edward well, but that made him no less formidable.

Uncle Denny, who'd been one of King Henry's closest companions, peered down his long nose at Aunt Kat. His full beard was shot with gray, though the close-cropped hair on his head was still quite dark.

"The Lord High Admiral was found to not only be in collusion with pirates but to have obtained money by outright fraud," Uncle Denny explained. "He planned to use these funds to raise a force to take control of the king's person. The Admiral has been arrested and confined to the Tower," he finished with satisfaction.

Aunt Kat exchanged a bewildered look with Master Parry, who shifted in his seat.

I recalled that when Seymour had assailed me on the Strand, he'd been marching purposefully to do who knew what. His adamance when he'd tried to discover from me Elizabeth's whereabouts now took on an even more sinister cast. Seymour had nearly kidnapped me—would he have done the same to her?

Uncle Denny's revelation brought me great relief, truth to tell. Elizabeth was well quit of Seymour, safe now from him riding up to Hatfield, his charming smile in place, to coerce her into marrying him, the treacherous rat.

"It's scarce to be believed," Aunt Kat repeated. Master Parry had relapsed into silence, turning his wine cup nervously on the table.

"Unfortunately, 'tis all true," Uncle Denny said. "Seymour tried to woo the king to his side with gifts and the promise of riches, but I am afraid his overly obvious bribery simply annoyed the boy. And now with the evidence that Seymour was funding a private army coming to light ..." Uncle Denny shrugged. "Lord Protector Somerset is furious. King Edward is also furious, the more so because Seymour was his favorite uncle. It is quite embarrassing to discover one has been the victim of both charm and cunning."

"Indeed," Paulet added.

Uncle Denny set down his wine and swiped a droplet from his lips with his tongue. "You can imagine I did not like this errand, today."

Aunt Kat looked surprised. "We are always pleased to see you, Sir Anthony, whatever news you bring. I am sorry you have missed John. He is detained in London."

"That does not matter," Uncle Denny said slowly, as though choosing his words with care. "I am afraid that you and I, my dear sister-in-law, and Master Parry, must travel to London together. The Lord Admiral's plan to marry Her Grace Elizabeth has come to light. Coupled with consorting with pirates and arming himself against his brother, it does not bode well for him." He gentled his tone but spoke firmly. "You, Mistress Ashley, along with Master Parry, have been named accomplices in this matter."

"What?" I cried in indignation. All heads turned to me, the forgotten mouse at the table. "How could anyone believe such a thing of Aunt Kat?"

I knew full well how they could, of course. Master Parry must *not* have kept quiet about his talks with Seymour concerning Elizabeth, no matter how much he'd promised he would. Likely he'd been proud that Seymour had deigned to discuss Elizabeth's situation and her finances with him.

Aunt Kat had even tried to coax Elizabeth to write to Seymour and encourage his advances. Thank heaven Elizabeth's caution had nipped that avenue in the bud.

Parry's wife did not help matters by bursting into tears. "I knew no good would come of it," she sobbed. "Will I ever see my husband again?"

As she was next to me, I pinched her. Mistress Parry yelped, but at least she ceased babbling. I knew little about the law, but I had learned from observation that in these sorts of matters, keeping quiet was always best.

Aunt Kat sat in troubled silence. I doubted she'd fully under-stood Seymour's true corruption—she'd only seen a handsome, powerful man interested in her beloved Elizabeth.

I did follow Aunt Kat's reasoning. If Elizabeth married

Seymour, she would become Lady Sudeley, honored and titled. More importantly, at least to Aunt Kat, Elizabeth would remain in England.

Far better, in my aunt's view, than Edward marrying Elizabeth off to foreign royalty and sending her away. The husband might not want Aunt Kat and me to accompany her, and it was likely we'd never see Elizabeth again.

"You both must journey with us to London this night," Uncle Denny said to Aunt Kat and Master Parry. "I will give you a little time to prepare yourselves, but we must leave soon."

At this, Mistress Parry cried the louder.

Aunt Kat rose in agitation. "I cannot simply leave," she said breathlessly. "My Lady Elizabeth. I must see to her, I must speak to her—"

"No, madam," Paulet interrupted, rising. "You must not. I will ensure that word is taken to Her Grace of your departure, after you have readied yourself. Perhaps you would like to go and prepare now."

It was a command, not a question.

I noted a glint in Paulet's eyes that the flustered Master Parry and Aunt Kat failed to grasp. Paulet would never say so, of course, but I surmised he was giving the two of them a chance, out of sight of himself and Uncle Denny, to collude on their stories about anything Seymour had said to them.

From what I'd heard of Paulet, he was canny, always understanding which way the wind blew. If he was doing what he could now to keep Elizabeth from being implicated in Seymour's schemes, she might have a chance to stay free of this mess.

"May I accompany my aunt to London, sir?" I asked Uncle Denny in a small voice. "Aunt Kat will be distressed to be alone."

"No, niece." Uncle Denny's eyes were kind but unrelenting. "Your Lady Elizabeth will need you here all the more. There is nothing you can do in London."

Aunt Kat nodded her agreement, though her eyes were moist. "Stay with her, Eloise. She will need the comfort of her favorite ladies."

Take care of her for me, Aunt Kat was silently begging me. *Promise me that Elizabeth will be protected.*

It was now clear that marriage to Elizabeth had been only one part of Seymour's plot to seize control of the king and the country. Viewed in that light, Aunt Kat trying to convince Elizabeth to marry Seymour against the king's wishes could be considered treason.

Traitors died terrible deaths. I had witnessed the torn bodies of the condemned after such an execution, their decaying heads then displayed on pikes. I wondered if the Lord Protector would also accuse poor Uncle John of colluding, or would Uncle John simply have to live through the tragedy of his wife's execution?

As I assisted the trembling Aunt Kat from the room and to her chamber, my stomach churned with fear. I needed to put this right, but my thoughts were frozen, and I did not know what to do. I was a seamstress, not a courtier or a wise counselor.

Words could condemn Aunt Kat, or words could save her. The right words said at the right time, or omitted at the right time, would make all the difference.

The king's council, guided by the Lord Protector Somerset, had so much power—the power of words, the power of life.

In Aunt Kat's chamber I helped her don her cloak. An idea hummed through my brain, though I was uncertain if it would work.

"Aunt Kat," I said in a low voice, making sure the bustling but weeping maidservants did not hear me. "You had no intention of going against the king's wishes, did you? You thought only to marry Elizabeth to someone she would admire, though not if it meant displeasing the king and his council."

"No, of course not," Aunt Kat snapped, impatient in her fear. "John was right when he told me not to meddle."

"That is all that you must say," I said, stressing each word. "It is true that you thought Seymour would be a good husband for Elizabeth, but you never dreamed of her marrying anyone against the council's wishes. She would abide by the law always."

"Yes, but—"

"Aunt Kat." I put my hands on her shoulders and spoke carefully. "You never, ever once thought to see Elizabeth marry against the wishes of the council."

Aunt Kat gaped at me, and then I saw understanding dawn. She closed her mouth and drew a long breath. "Quickly, Eloise. I must speak to Parry ere I go down."

I nodded, my heart thumping, and ran off to find him.

WHEN I PARTED FROM AUNT KAT IN THE MUDDY YARD NOT LONG later, I could not stop my tears. Aunt Kat gathered me into a hard hug, her face wet, and told me to mind myself and Elizabeth.

Aunt Kat, Master Parry, Uncle Denny, and William Paulet rode away from Hatfield in the cold darkness, the four of them surrounded by armed outriders. The entourage disappeared too soon as Mistress Parry and I watched, holding on to each other to keep from collapsing in despair.

Though Mistress Parry slowly turned back to the house, I remained outside until I could see no more, my heart heavy but my thoughts spinning.

I had been advised by Uncle Denny not to inform Elizabeth what had transpired. She, by the council's orders, had been purposely kept in the dark about the reason for his and Paulet's visit.

However, after the riders were truly gone, hoofbeats dying

into silence, I sped into the house, hurried up to her chamber, and told her anyway.

WHAT DOES A WOMAN DO WHEN SHE DISCOVERS THE MAN SHE'S fallen in love with has only been using her to obtain something he wants? Especially when it is her first love?

Will she bow her head and meekly accept that her suitor was more interested in money, power, and connections than in tenderer emotions?

Or will she become toughened and angry, vowing never to experience such disappointment again?

When I told Elizabeth everything the night they took Aunt Kat away, including my admonition that all involved must state they would never dream of thwarting the privy council, she listened in stony silence. She sank to her chair as I spoke, and I knelt at her feet.

As I gazed up at her, I saw a new hardness enter Elizabeth's eyes. Tears beaded on her lashes, but she held those tears in check with an anger brighter than any I'd ever beheld in her.

The temper tantrums of Elizabeth's childhood abruptly made way for a fierce, adult anger that she honed into a weapon as I watched.

"Keep silent that I've told you, my lady, I beg you," I whispered. "Aunt Kat is innocent, and they surely will send her home on the morrow. This will pass us by."

"Perhaps," Elizabeth responded, but absently.

"Would you like me to stay with you tonight, Your Grace?"

Elizabeth blinked and brought her attention to me once more. "No." Her anger was grim, and I wasn't certain at whom she directed it—me, Aunt Kat and Master Parry, Thomas Seymour, Uncle Denny, Protector Somerset? Perhaps all of us.

"Stay away from me, Eloise," she said, suddenly harsh. "I do not want to succumb to the temptation to speak of this with you. Silence is best."

I nodded, wiping my eyes. "Others will wonder if we do not speak at all. It is known you confide in me."

"Then I shall pretend to be enraged with you, and not wish you by my side." The words were sharp and quick, like sleeting rain, then she dropped her voice to a whisper. "Tell me of all you hear."

"I understand." My heart beat faster. For some reason I was animated by this duplicity, by a secret Elizabeth shared with me and no other. I was ashamed of myself for my gratification, but it remained.

Elizabeth slapped me then, and not a contrived slap. Her fingers stung my face, her nail catching my lip.

The ladies on the other side of the chamber looked up in interest at this new bit of excitement, whatever the cause. I had little trouble bursting into tears as I fled the room.

I SPENT THE NEXT SEVERAL DAYS TELLING MYSELF THAT AUNT KAT would return right away, that Protector Somerset would admit his mistake about her complicity and send her and Master Parry home. Seymour might have leaned toward treason, but my aunt would never even consider it. Somerset and the king must understand this.

Uncle John remained in London. I feared to write him, in case my letter was intercepted, but he sent me one instead. He'd learned of Aunt Kat's arrest and was distraught but ordered me to stay at Hatfield.

I knew Uncle John was right—there was little I could do in London—but I chafed and worried about my beloved aunt.

Elizabeth walked with her ladies, took her meals, and studied as usual. She played music, read, prayed, and did not allow any speculation in her hearing about Aunt Kat's situation.

Ostensibly, she knew nothing about it. Somerset's instructions, according to Uncle Denny, had been to tell Elizabeth nothing of the matter. I assumed this was so Somerset could discover from Aunt Kat and Master Parry whether or not Elizabeth had been in on the plot before he made a move against her.

Somerset was a fool, though, if he thought servants would not gossip about events at Hatfield, especially something so extraordinary as Aunt Kat's arrest. The maids and their ladies might not disobey and speak to Elizabeth directly about it, but they certainly discussed it amongst themselves. I sewed in a corner, allowed into Elizabeth's presence only because my services were necessary, and hid my misery.

On a blustery, dark afternoon, not long after Aunt Kat's detainment, a contingency of people rode into the courtyard. The guardsmen wore the emblem of the Duke of Somerset, and they escorted several gentlemen and a lady, who were admitted to the house at once.

Upstairs in her chamber, Elizabeth read out a passage in Greek, in attempt to drown out the commotion downstairs. Her face was wan, but her voice remained strong.

I stitched in a window embrasure, pretending all my attention was on the fabric. True to our agreement, Elizabeth all but ignored me, deliberately turning a cool eye to me if she needed to give me an order.

One of Elizabeth's gentlemen ushers entered the room, bowed apologetically, and explained that Sir Robert Tyrwhitt had arrived and requested to speak to her.

"I will receive him when I am finished with my studies," Elizabeth said coldly. Lines pinched about her eyes, but she resolutely returned to her book. The gentleman withdrew, troubled.

"Tyrwhitt, Tyrwhitt," Elizabeth said when he'd gone. "I've

always thought his name sounded like a cheeping bird. Tyrwhitt, Tyrwhitt, ter-woo."

Her attending ladies laughed, though my throat was too tight join in. So was Elizabeth's—she put her hand to it and swallowed.

Her haughtiness did not stem entirely from fear. The idea that her governess and financier could be arrested under her nose, with no one informing her about it, had infuriated her. So did the fact that Seymour's duplicity had been brought to her door.

Elizabeth was well aware that not only had Seymour used her, but that Somerset was now likewise using her to build a case against his brother.

I saw frustration in the set of Elizabeth's lips, a burning in her eyes as she longed for a day when she was not the pawn on the chessboard.

Elizabeth kept Tyrwhitt kicking his heels for a good long while before she condescended to send for him. When he arrived in her outer chamber, where she waited, she was every inch a regal princess in crimson damask, while Tyrwhitt, disheveled from his journey, appeared very much an impatient suitor.

Robert Tyrwhitt had been Master of Horse to Catherine Parr when she'd been queen, and he'd obviously used the wealth of that lofty position to grow comfortable and stout. He had graying hair and a short beard, his eyes small and quick. His wife, who was the lady I'd seen arrive with him, had also waited upon Catherine.

Lady Tyrwhitt, who had a long and distinguished career of serving Henry's queens, was nowhere in evidence at the moment. Likely she'd been left downstairs so that she could not soften Elizabeth's interview with her husband.

Elizabeth, on the other hand, insisted that her ladies stay— including me—at which Tyrwhitt looked pained.

Tyrwhitt continued to stand, as we ladies did, while Elizabeth, who'd risen at Tyrwhitt's entrance, resumed the chair at her writing table. One of her ladies had turned it to face the room as she stood, so now she seemed to repose on a small throne.

Tyrwhitt cleared his throat. "It ill pleases me to announce such a thing, Your Grace," he began, a bit pompously. "But I must tell you that your governess, Mistress Ashley, and the treasurer of your household, Master Thomas Parry, have been detained at his majesty's pleasure in the Tower of London. They are being investigated for their part in the improper pursuit of a marriage between yourself and the Lord Admiral."

I wanted to crumple to the floor. Aunt Kat in the Tower? I felt sick, but I could do nothing, say nothing, to betray my distress. I was a nobody in the presence of greatness, and I must suppress my anguish.

Elizabeth watched Tyrwhitt coolly, as though trying to decide her answer.

Then she abruptly lifted her hands to her face and started to weep.

Tyrwhitt stared at her in astonishment, as though this had been the last reaction he'd expected. Had he thought to find her lofty and brittle, or perhaps sly and guilty?

He hadn't had much contact with Elizabeth, despite his role in Catherine's household, and probably had no idea of her true nature. Perhaps he'd expected a seductress, one who beguiled with coy smiles, like her mother purportedly had done.

Instead, he'd found a straight-backed, no-nonsense young woman, who cried when she learned that her beloved governess was in danger.

"Now then," Tyrwhitt said, clearly uncomfortable with the tears of a fifteen-year-old girl. Nervously he laid a few sheets of paper on the table next to Elizabeth. I glimpsed a signature at the bottom of one, in Aunt Kat's handwriting, and went cold.

"Katherine Ashley and Thomas Parry have made their first confessions," Tyrwhitt said. "They signed their names to the statements. It would be best, Your Grace, to confess all to me straight away, and let this be done with."

Elizabeth sniffled and dabbed her eyes with a handkerchief, but the hand that reached for the papers did not tremble. "May I have time to read them?"

Tyrwhitt gave her a thin smile. "Perhaps you will tell me what you know, and then we may read them together."

Elizabeth withdrew her hand and laid it in her lap, her fingers curling into her palm. "Mistress Ashley is a good woman and would do nothing to deceive my brother the king, or His Grace of Somerset. Or myself."

Tyrwhitt's smile became tight as Elizabeth reminded him just who she was—sister of a king and no commoner. He cleared his throat again. "Thomas Parry hints that the Lord Admiral was familiar with you, and Mistress Ashley says nothing to deny it."

"The Lord Admiral never offered marriage to me, if that is what you mean," Elizabeth returned. "I never made any sort of pledge to him. I would never agree to marry without the king my brother's consent, and I trust the Protector believes so."

The second reminder of her position irritated Tyrwhitt. He huffed. "Do remember, Your Grace, that though your brother is ruler of this realm, you are but a subject."

"Of course." Elizabeth's chilly manner returned. "Which is precisely why I know I may not choose my own husband. The council, the Lord Protector, and my brother must approve. Mistress Ashley knew that very well, and would never advise me otherwise."

As Tyrwhitt grew even more irate, I again wondered what he'd expected. That Elizabeth would throw herself at his feet and beg for mercy? That she'd confess that she'd conspired against the king? She'd never have admitted such a thing, even if it were true.

I learned much in that room as I watched Elizabeth match wits with Tyrwhitt, a man more than twice her age. He tried to cajole, to be stern, to threaten, and to cajole again, but Elizabeth never wavered.

She repeated multiple times that she had no intention of marrying outside the wishes of the council, and declared that the romps Aunt Kat and Master Parry might have described were nothing more than childish games, which Queen Catherine herself had joined.

As Tyrwhitt lost patience, his words became cruel. "My wife was in service with your stepmother, as you know. She waited on the Queen Catherine in her last days, was in the bedchamber when she died. The queen, in her delirium, declared that her husband had betrayed her. And Master Parry says you were sent away from the queen's household."

Tyrwhitt snatched one of the papers from the table and read from it. *"One time the Queen, suspecting the often access of the Admiral to the Lady Elizabeth's grace, came suddenly upon them when they were all alone, he having her in his arms. Wherefore the Queen fell out, both with the Admiral and with Her Grace also."*

Elizabeth sat as though carved of marble. Any reminder of how she'd hurt Catherine distressed her, and the statement coming from the self-satisfied Tyrwhitt made it doubly upsetting.

"I admit a misunderstanding with the queen," Elizabeth said in a brittle voice. "But it was cleared up soon after. There was ever great affection between us, as our letters to each other while I stayed at Cheshunt will show."

Tyrwhitt scowled. "You realize that your governess and treasurer will remain in the Tower until this matter is finished? My wife will now take the place of Mistress Ashley as your governess."

"I see no reason why she should," Elizabeth snapped. "Mistress Ashley is innocent, and quite dear to me."

"Mistress Ashley has revealed your secrets," Tyrwhitt said with his complacent air. "I wonder that you'd want her near you again. She has betrayed you."

Elizabeth's lips tightened. "She has done no such thing."

Tyrwhitt more or less shoved the papers at Elizabeth. "Right there, in her own words."

Triumph flared in Elizabeth's eyes. I realized she'd made Tyrwhitt do as she wished—to let her read the confessions before speaking further.

She skimmed through Master Parry's statement with a frown and tossed it aside. Her expression softened, however, as she gazed upon Aunt Kat's words.

Elizabeth read the pages in all seriousness then laid them neatly on the table. "Mistress Ashley has written here that the Lord Admiral paid me no more attention than he did my cousin Jane, and that my brother's wishes are what we will follow in matters of marriage. She is innocent of duplicity, do you see?"

Tyrwhitt snatched up the confessions, parchment rustling like dry leaves. "Nevertheless, Lady Tyrwhitt and I will remain here," he said sternly. "I suggest that you think everything over, Your Grace, and speak with me again on the morrow."

Elizabeth sent him a frosty nod and a little gesture of dismissal. I suppressed my glee when Tyrwhitt bowed and departed the chamber as though he were the accused and *she* the interrogator.

As soon as his footsteps faded, however, Elizabeth put her hand to her forehead and moaned that her head was splitting in two.

I and her maids put her to bed where Elizabeth remained, ill and unable to rise, for the next several days.

Tyrwhitt tried, every day that Elizabeth was well enough to leave her bed and meet with him, to make her say what he wanted her to.

He never succeeded. With the precision of an expert swordsman, Elizabeth evaded his every question about Seymour and his plots. She constantly brought Tyrwhitt back to the fact that she firmly intended to obey her father's last wishes, which had been that she'd never marry without the advice and permission of Edward's council.

Whatever Seymour's plans had been, Elizabeth implied without blatantly stating it, she'd had no intention of participating in them herself. She held herself apart, aloof.

I understood as I watched these interviews that Elizabeth had fallen out of love with Seymour as thoroughly as I had. When once her eyes would brighten at the mention of his name, she now spoke no word in his defense nor made any sign of protest about his arrest.

She had finished with him. Elizabeth could not stop what happened to him now, and so she strove to remove herself from the incident.

Tyrwhitt, faced with Elizabeth's coolness and her iron will, seemed amazed by her. The only human feeling she had, I heard him mutter to his wife, was for her governess, Mistress Ashley.

"They *must* have collaborated on a story," I also heard him say to Lady Tyrwhitt. "They sing the same tune, the three of them."

"She will have counseled them," his wife answered darkly. "The princess, I mean."

"She is a child, for heaven's sake," Tyrwhitt retorted. "God's grace, she is but a girl, for all her haughty ways. I will wager it was Parry who advised her." He sighed. "Though Denny and Paulet swore that they never allowed Mistress Ashley or Master Parry speak to Elizabeth after their arrest. I do not know how they managed it, but they must have."

I turned away from them, a smile on my lips.

A PIECE OF GOSSIP CAME TO US SOON AFTER THAT, WHICH brought Elizabeth out of her cold aloofness and sent her into a towering fury.

"It is untrue," Elizabeth exclaimed hotly to Tyrwhitt when he, torn between embarrassment and smugness, shared this news in her chamber. "As you can see."

She spread her arms, showing her slender figure hugged by a close-fitting blue satin bodice coming to a point over a skirt of the same color.

I'd heard the whispers myself before Tyrwhitt brought them to light and had made certain that the gown denounced the slander.

Tyrwhitt flinched at Elizabeth's outburst. "It is rumor only, Your Grace," he said hastily. "No one will believe it."

"Of course they will believe it," Elizabeth shouted. "Here I am, shut away from the world, unable to refute the tales. Take me to court and let me show myself. 'Twill be easy to make a mockery of the story that I am heavy with the Admiral's child and locked in the Tower if I am seen in my brother's company."

"I cannot allow you to leave Hatfield," Tyrwhitt said miserably.

Elizabeth whirled and abruptly swept all books and papers on her table to the floor.

Tyrwhitt jumped, but secretly I was pleased to see Elizabeth in a fine rage. The coldness into which she'd retreated in the last several days had unnerved me. I was used to her hot tempers—her icy control was new.

"Then I will write to *His Grace* Somerset." It was all Elizabeth could do to give the Lord Protector the honorific. "And ask him myself."

"My lady … "

Elizabeth sent Tyrwhitt a freezing glare. "My reputation is at stake, Sir Robert. The people of England shall not be laughing at me, or pitying the princess who has fallen so low. I have *not* fallen, and these slanders are insulting. How dare the Lord Protector allow them to persist?"

I could guess how he dared—it would be in Somerset's interest to paint Elizabeth as a whore and Seymour as a whoremonger. He'd state that the two had readied themselves to take over the kingdom, easily stopped by Somerset, of course.

Elizabeth won this round and wrote her letter: *Master Tyrwhitt and others have told me that there goeth rumors abroad which be greatly both against mine honor and honesty … which be these: that I am in the Tower and with child by my Lord Admiral. My lord, these are shameful slanders … I shall most heartily desire your lordship that I may come to the court after your first determination, that I may show myself there as I am.*

I heard reports that when Somerset received this letter, dutifully delivered by Tyrwhitt, he turned nearly green with fury.

Somerset's wife had snarled at the impudence of Elizabeth,

she who'd behaved so wantonly, nearly committing adultery with her own stepfather. What right had Elizabeth to write so peremptorily to Somerset, the first lord of the land, while Elizabeth was one step from being condemned as a traitor?

Somerset, it was said, ground his teeth before writing a curt and severe reply.

Thus began the battle of wits between Elizabeth and the Lord Protector of England.

WHILE ELIZABETH EXERCISED HER RAGE AT SOMERSET, I WORRIED about Aunt Kat. She remained in the Tower, how sequestered I did not know. Lady Tyrwhitt assured me she was well, but one of Tyrwhitt's manservants whispered to me that Aunt Kat had been put into a dungeon and made to sit in chains.

I recalled my vision not long ago of this very thing happening and could not ease the chill that took me. I did not believe I had second sight—I could hear my grandmother scoffing at such a notion even now. I must have simply realized what dire troubles Aunt Kat's meddling could bring.

I fretted about her and also about Uncle John, who was still in London. Finally, I begged Elizabeth for leave to journey to visit him.

Elizabeth at first was not inclined to let me go.

"I need you, Eloise," she said when we met for a fitting one afternoon. She still pretended to be put out with me, so that I could watch, listen, and report to her without anyone believing I was her confidant. "You are the one point of comfort in the madness."

I warmed to hear her say this, but even her praise could not banish my fears.

"I have to know what is happening," I said as I straightened a hem I was pinning. "I can find out things so much easier in London."

Elizabeth went silent as she weighed my argument until she at last gave me a nod. "Go then. But keep your eyes open and tell me what truly goes on. Master Ashley will know some of it, and you are clever enough to invent a way to learn more."

I had intended to question Uncle John thoroughly and try to gain admission to the Tower to visit Aunt Kat. Thus, I had no trouble agreeing to Elizabeth's stipulation. I doubted I'd succeed in speaking to Aunt Kat myself, but I meant to discover everything I could, regardless.

When I rose to my feet and helped Elizabeth step out of the unfinished skirt, she caught me briefly in her arms, crushing me in a spontaneous embrace.

"Do not let any harm come to her." Her whisper was hot in my ear. "She has always loved me, even when no others would."

It was true that when Elizabeth's mother had been condemned, many deserted her or were taken from her. Elizabeth was now proving fiercely loyal to the ladies who'd remained. The gentlewoman who'd been her protective nurse was one, and Aunt Kat another.

I did not know what I could do to prevent Somerset from condemning whomever he pleased, but I nodded and dared to kiss the pale cheek so close to my lips.

"I will keep her safe," I promised.

Elizabeth lifted her chin, her dignity returning. "See that you do," she commanded, then turned from me for her other ladies to re-dress her.

I RODE TO LONDON ON HORSEBACK WITH A CONTINGENT OF Tyrwhitt's and Uncle Denny's gentlemen, who'd been dispatched there to deliver messages to Somerset. We traveled at a swift pace—very unlike the stately journeys I took with the princess—and reached Moorgate in the north of London late that night.

Because the riders bore messages for Somerset, we were speedily admitted into the city. Two of Uncle Denny's guards were ordered to escort me to the house where Uncle John lodged, which they did, if grudgingly. I was glad of their company, truth to tell, because London could be a frightening place after dark.

"Eloise," Uncle John exclaimed when his manservant ushered me, travel-worn and dusty, into the sitting room of his lodgings. "What do you here?"

"I feared for you, Uncle." My voice cracked with fatigue and anxiousness, and I longed for a sip of hock to wet my throat.

Uncle John was gray-faced and weary, his hands shaking as he reached for me. "Worry not for me, but for poor, silly Kat."

He pulled me into an embrace, and for a moment, we both shed tears for her.

I drew away and wiped my cheeks. "Surely the king will not condemn his sister's beloved governess. He could not be so cruel."

"Young Edward, perhaps not." Uncle John led me to a seat, and the hovering manservant who'd admitted me brought us warm, spiced wine. "But the Lord Protector might. He has fixed all his jealousy and suspicion on Seymour, and he will pull in any he believes will help condemn him. Somerset has always been the bland, do-good Seymour while Thomas had the charm and received all the attention. Naturally that rankles."

"Hardly fair to punish Aunt Kat because Thomas Seymour is more dashing than his older brother," I said heatedly. "That is not her fault."

"But Seymour is a traitor, or as good as one." Uncle John sighed heavily, while I took an indignant slurp of wine. "Seymour's apparent plot, as far as I can learn, was to marry either

Mary or Elizabeth, overthrow Somerset, and rule behind Edward's throne, with Seymour's princess wife aiding and abetting him."

"Mary *or* Elizabeth?" I repeated with incredulity. "It made no difference to him which he wed?"

"I imagine he preferred the pretty and young Elizabeth," Uncle John said dryly. "But yes, either would do."

I studied my boots, muddy from the journey and flecked with dead blades of grass. "Elizabeth fell in love with him."

I did not mention the brief, foolish time I'd been infatuated with Seymour as well. But it gave me an understanding of his charm.

"I know she did," Uncle John said, voice gentling. "That is neither here nor there. A princess may fall in love and break her heart with no one to condemn her—so long as she keeps it to herself. But any action on that love determines her fate. The question is not whether Elizabeth fell in love, but whether she promised to marry Seymour and thus aid his schemes."

"She did not," I said with confidence.

"And that is why they are evil to our Kat. They wish to make her admit that Elizabeth *did* agree to marry him, with Kat as a go-between."

We sat in silence, hearts heavy, thinking of the woman we loved, wretched in the Tower.

Uncle John and Aunt Kat did not see eye to eye at times, which was obvious from their occasional quarrels. Uncle John believed her too ready to pry into things she should leave alone, but it was clear that he cherished her.

Theirs had been a match of love and friendship—I regarded it as an example of what a good marriage could be. I was broken-hearted, but Uncle John was doubly so.

"Will they let us visit Aunt Kat?" I asked after a time.

Uncle John shrugged tiredly. "I have tried, but without

success. They fear I will pass messages to her or advise her what to say."

"Perhaps I can be admitted. I am a seamstress—I can invent some excuse to enter—"

I broke off when Uncle John glared at me. "I'll not let my niece traipse into the Tower like a heroine and be arrested as a conspirator. 'Tis a foolish idea, Eloise. Let me hear no more about it."

His fear for me was genuine, so I subsided.

"How can we sit here, not knowing what is happening?" I asked as we drifted into moroseness once more.

"I do have *some* information. Not everyone belongs to Somerset. There are those who tell me things, ones who do not like Somerset's complete control over the king."

Some of my fears gave way before curiosity. "Who are these people?"

"No one you should trouble yourself about. Never repeat that I said this, but I believe Somerset's days are numbered." Uncle John lowered his voice and glanced around uneasily, as though he feared spies lurked behind the walls. Well, they might. "We will dine, niece, and you will rest. You must be worn out from your journey."

I obeyed him, seeing he would say nothing more.

I remained in London with Uncle John for a time, trying to live as routine a life as possible. We took meals in his lodgings, aided by Uncle John's servants, who were kind to us, and also concerned for Aunt Kat's welfare.

I'd brought along the bodice for the new gown that I'd been doing fittings on with Elizabeth before I'd departed. I tried to focus on sewing tucks that would make the bodice lie flat and embellishing it with seed pearls, but Aunt Kat's imprisonment remained a shadow over me.

I usually enjoyed excursions to London, taking the opportunity to visit shops that carried fabrics and trim brought from the Continent, Africa, and as far away as the Asiatic countries. I loved to browse the silks and velvets, damask and satin, laces and ribbons. Even the more common fabrics of lawn and linsey-woolsey could usually gain my attention.

This journey, I lacked interest. I kept myself in Uncle John's lodgings and wrote to various people of my acquaintance in London, trying to find out what information I could regarding Aunt Kat.

On the fourth day my stay, our fears for Aunt Kat were confirmed. One of Uncle John's cronies from court discovered that she had indeed been confined of nights to a dank cell. She was usually released in daylight hours, but only to speak to a secretary of Edward's council. Apparently, she was telling him all sorts of tales, including everything that had happened between Seymour and Elizabeth in Chelsea.

Somerset ordered guards to Uncle John's house and bade us not to leave. As frightening as this was, however, these guards proved to be a great source of information. Stultified by their assignment, the men at arms gossiped readily with us to relieve their tedium.

The guards had heard about Elizabeth's letter to Somerset denying she was pregnant by Seymour. Somerset had apparently written back to her, declaring that Elizabeth should name those who'd slandered her, so he could make an example of them.

Somerset had flown into another rage at Elizabeth's reply—that she would not be considered the sort of person who pointed fingers and punished rumormongers.

This news had filtered through nobles to their servants, and in turn to our guards, so I could not say how embellished all had become before it met our ears.

But I detected in the stories a grain of truth: Elizabeth had stood up for herself and her damaged reputation, laying it fully in the Protector's lap to prove she'd done anything wrong.

Somerset at last issued a statement saying that such stories about the princess were untrue and those who spread the lie would be imprisoned. I sensed an acid tone in the proclamation, but it was done.

Though Uncle John and I were more or less confined, I managed to gain permission to run the occasional errand, claiming to need thread or other notions that I trusted only myself to choose. I obeyed Uncle John and never went near the Tower, which was made easier by the guard who was always dispatched to follow me.

I met acquaintances at the markets and spoke to those I regularly bought fabric and other sundries from while in London. I learned through these sources that while Somerset was busily confiscating Seymour's lands and houses, there were other nobles, like the Dudley family, who believed Somerset was going too far. The Seymours' power was waning.

Again, I realized this information might only be hearsay, but I tucked it away in my head to relate to Elizabeth when I returned to her.

The Dudley family was run by the Earl of Warwick, whose son, Robert, had sometimes been Elizabeth's playmate or studied with her when they were children. I hadn't thought much about him at the time, as I'd had no interest in boys in my youth. My Lady Elizabeth and her beautiful clothes had been far more interesting to me.

Robert now served in Edward's court, as did his father, who'd become the Lord Great Chamberlain. I wasn't certain what a Lord Great Chamberlain did exactly, but I knew it was a very lofty position.

Robert's father and Somerset had always been good friends, from what I understood, and so this friction, if true, was intriguing.

I kept my findings to myself, as the cold February days wound on, as neither Uncle John nor I were allowed to communicate with Elizabeth. I'd hoped to send her a covert letter, but Uncle John convinced me it was foolish to try.

I obeyed him, to his relief, though I continued to pry as much as I could out of anyone I could speak to.

In my frustration, I began to ponder ways I could communicate with Elizabeth without writing, since letters were forbidden. The scheme that dawned on me would not help me at the moment, but I amused myself expanding on the idea and trying various methods. I'd have to explain it all to Elizabeth, if I was ever allowed to be near her again.

March began with the same cold dreariness of February. Then, as suddenly as they'd arrived, our guards were dismissed, and we were allowed to leave again for Hatfield. We had no explanation—the sergeant who headed the troop simply told us he'd been recalled, and the armed men marched away.

Uncle John elected to stay in London, to be near Aunt Kat, but he sent me home.

I retreated with a heavy heart. I'd miss him—I clung to Uncle John for a long while before I could make myself let go. I was still frantically worried about Aunt Kat and none the wiser about her fate.

I reached Elizabeth's house on a drizzly morning, having spent a night with the gentlewomen and guards Uncle Denny had sent to escort me at a wayside inn.

I found Elizabeth in another great fury.

"The Protector could get nothing from my fine Kat," she snarled as she stalked back and forth in her chamber. "She is innocent of anything but having a foolish tongue. Still, he dares to replace her with Lady Tyrwhitt, a woman of no great mind. I have done nothing to demean myself, and the council has no need to put any more mistresses upon me."

I crept out as she called for paper, prepared to write her anger to the Protector once again.

I imagined the tall, thin-faced Somerset, his white lips folding in on themselves as he read yet another tirade from Elizabeth.

"What of our dear Kat?" Elizabeth asked me later that night when her outrage had brought on one of her headaches. "What did you learn? Tell me at once, Eloise."

She lay in bed with a chamomile-scented cloth on her forehead, while I sat by her side. Fear made Elizabeth angry, and her rage could wind her into illness.

I told her all I'd learned—that Aunt Kat remained confined and that she'd confessed all of Elizabeth's escapades with Seymour at Chelsea. Master Parry had shared similar tales, including that Seymour had offered Elizabeth, via Parry, lands and money. I also related the rumors that Somerset was in danger of being toppled himself if he did not take care.

Elizabeth listened to all without interruption. When she did speak, her voice had quieted, as if worn out with bitterness.

"Why, then, should they keep our Mistress Ashley? She has told them all she knows, and Seymour has been condemned, his lands seized. Why is that not the end of it?"

"I do not know," was all I could say.

Elizabeth directed me to her writing table and told me to read the papers Tyrwhitt had brought that Aunt Kat had written herself. She'd continued denying that Elizabeth had any intention of marrying Seymour, but her final paragraph kindled my tears:

Good Master Secretary, speak that I may change my prison. For by my troth, it is so cold I cannot sleep in it and so dark that I cannot in the day see, for I stop the window with straw; there is no glass . . .

When I finally retired to bed, I wept, brokenheartedly.

This was the most terrible thing that had happened in my young life, and at fifteen, I could not imagine worse. The woman who had taken me from a home where I was unwanted and welcomed me with cheerfulness to hers, now suffered in the cold and dark, with no surety that she'd ever see daylight again.

Elizabeth cried for her as well, and the next day she wrote the Protector a strongly worded letter, explaining that Kat was more important to her than a mother. *Please relieve Kat's suffering—send her home, and be good to her.*

Tyrwhitt accosted me that afternoon when I was sewing in the light of the great hall, he having read Elizabeth's letter thoroughly before he dispatched it to London.

"You are close to Her Grace," Tyrwhitt said, his small eyes narrowing. "How is it she loves Mistress Ashley so well? Here is a woman who confessed all manner of lewd behavior on Her Grace Elizabeth's part, embarrassing her, even if trying to clear her from the Lord Admiral's plots. I would think Her Grace would like never to see the woman again."

I faced Tyrwhitt patiently, this moon-faced, elderly man who'd been given far too much power over us.

"The princess loves few people," I explained. "But those she loves, she loves very deeply, and she will never abandon them. My Aunt Kat took care of Her Grace Elizabeth when she had nothing—no status as princess, no household of her own, and had been declared illegitimate. Aunt Kat loved her anyway. Her Grace will never forget it, I think."

Tyrwhitt's frown grew as I spoke, his brows pinching in perplexity. When I finished, he cleared his throat, betraying his discomfort.

"I see," was all he could come up with to say. "Well, tell her she is a fool."

I made no such promise, and Tyrwhitt stalked away toward his chamber, clearly not understanding what I'd told him.

CHAPTER 9

On March 20, 1549, Thomas Seymour was led from the Tower to his execution.

Elizabeth and I dwelled at Hatfield still, both of us awaiting news of Aunt Kat's fate.

It was Tyrwhitt who brought word to Elizabeth of Seymour's death. He entered the upstairs chamber where she studied and cleared his throat.

Elizabeth let him linger a few moments before she condescended to raise her head from her reading. "Yes? What is it?"

Tyrwhitt coughed once more. "His lordship, the Admiral, has been executed on Tower Green, Your Grace," he said in a cracked voice. "This very morning. So said the messengers."

Elizabeth stilled, her pale lids lowering once over her dark eyes. She sat quietly, her hand on the page of her book. "I see."

I bit off a thread while I watched the drama, my lap piled with sumptuous brocade shot through with threads of silver.

I felt a twinge of guilt that Seymour's death did not upset me. I was a bit shocked that the Lord Protector would execute his own brother, but Seymour had been a hard man beneath his charm, skilled at beguiling others into serving his every need.

I was not certain if my mild satisfaction at his death made me an evil person, but that was the only emotion I could conjure.

Elizabeth dipped her head, as though thanking Tyrwhitt for delivering such difficult news. He waited for her reaction, clearly assuming she'd burst into tears and fling herself to the floor, weeping for her dead lover.

She disappointed him. Elizabeth gazed at Tyrwhitt calmly and stated, "This day died a man of much wit and very little judgment."

One corner of Tyrwhitt's mouth drooped. "Indeed, Your Grace."

He met her steady stare a moment longer but had to turn from her in defeat. At the door, he swung back.

"Another bit of news, Your Grace. Your governess, Mistress Ashley, and the cofferer, Thomas Parry, will be released forthwith and allowed to rejoin you here."

Again, Elizabeth made no reaction but to nod to Tyrwhitt in dismissal.

I dropped my needle and carved silver scissors as relief flowed through me. Aunt Kat was all right. She'd come home.

Only when Tyrwhitt's footsteps had faded into the distance did Elizabeth rise from her chair and beckon to me.

"Attend me, Eloise," she commanded.

I threw down my sewing and rushed to her. Elizabeth gave me a quick embrace and a kiss on each cheek.

"We shall be happy that Mistress Ashley is coming back to us," she said, eyes shining with unshed tears. "Shall we greet her with splendid gifts?"

I fervently agreed, and spent the rest of the day helping her plan the celebration for Aunt Kat's return.

But that night when I sewed alone in Elizabeth's outer chamber, I heard the princess in her bed, weeping for a long, long time. Her sobs of despair nearly broke my heart.

As April came with softer weather, I sketched my ideas for Elizabeth's summer wardrobe, toning down the exuberance of her earlier gowns into something simpler, more quiet.

I stared at what I'd done, realizing that I was seeing my lady as woman, her childish frivolousness behind her. And oak, not a fragile flower.

I felt Elizabeth's presence in my corner of her chamber, and I looked up to see her gazing at the drawings in curiosity.

"What are those?" she demanded.

"Summer gowns for you, and for your return to court." I tapped a gown I'd make in ivory with a dark gray overdress.

"A bit drab, aren't they?" Elizabeth lifted my book in her slim fingers, turning the sketches around to the light.

I relaxed. She was interested. If she'd hated the ideas, she might have ripped the pages from my hands and flung them onto the fire.

"They indicate that you are interested in matters of the intellect," I said. "You study, you read, you have discourse on history, philosophy, and the reformed religion. You converse with some of the best and shrewdest minds of the age."

"All of that is true." Elizabeth's eyes glinted. "What a fine idea, Eloise."

While I knew Elizabeth loved beautiful clothes and the luxurious fabrics they were made from, I saw her calculating exactly what message she'd send if she adopted the designs I'd just drawn.

"We can still use the velvets we've recently acquired," I said. "But make them into ensembles of sober elegance." I smiled, pleased with myself. "I vow every lady in court will try to emulate them."

"Perhaps." Elizabeth shoved the drawings back at me. "I will sew them with you. We will work side by side."

I warmed, happy that I no longer had to pretend to be at odds with her. Elizabeth was an accomplished needlewoman, so her assistance would be no hindrance.

"You honor me, Your Grace."

Elizabeth's glance resumed its teasing sparkle. "You are bad at dissembling, Eloise, my shrewd and wise seamstress. You are proud of your ideas, and rightly so. These gowns will show my brother's court that, far from being a wanton, I am a sober and quiet creature."

She sent me a triumphant smile, and I could not help returning it.

We began work at once. I sorted through my patterns and perused new books that arrived from London that spring, making more sketches and designs.

I decided to emulate the French and Spanish styles of a surcoat—a sleeved over-garment that closed at the throat and flowed open over the bodice and skirt in an upside-down V. The skirt and bodice would be of plain white taffeta, the stomacher ending in a soft point over the gathered skirt. A high collar would enclose Elizabeth's neck, with a banded hood to hold back her sleek hair.

I designed her entire wardrobe for that summer and into fall, enjoying the challenge of the new styles and making the light colors sing. I created another gown whose surcoat was decorated with lines of fur on high-capped sleeves, a little more ornate for the occasion that called for it.

Elizabeth joined me in sewing most evenings as she chatted with her women and Aunt Kat, who was now happily restored to our circle. Elizabeth and I exchanged instructions on stitching techniques, exclaiming at or laughing over the results, as though we were dear friends.

Elizabeth wore the ensembles we'd made to London when Edward at last sent for her to attend his court. In the chambers of Whitehall and St. James's, her clothes drew amazed attention but gained approval.

Princess Mary and her attendants continued to dress in low-cut gowns, with sleeves sliding seductively from shoulders. The ladies glittered in jewels that covered throats, fingers, and wrists, and ornamented the bands of their hoods.

Courtiers compared the two young women and favored Elizabeth. Elizabeth carried herself with decorum, they decided, as a princess should, while Mary, with her leanings to the old religion, indulged in glitter and extravagance. Elizabeth displayed a composure well-liked in a young lady, these courtiers stated, especially appropriate in a sister to the king.

Elizabeth and Edward resumed terms of affection, although it was a rather stately affection. Elizabeth gave him a recently painted portrait of herself, and, in return, Edward invited her to spend Christmas with him.

Life in Elizabeth's household settled down nicely. Uncle John and Aunt Kat purred together again, and I rejoiced.

Lord Protector Somerset, the boor, had lost much popularity by beheading his own brother. No matter how much perfidy Thomas Seymour had been plotting, he'd made himself many friends, and these friends now muttered that seeing Somerset be overthrown by Seymour would have been no bad thing.

I recalled the rumors that had flown about London earlier that year, and Uncle John's quiet prediction that Somerset's days were numbered. This became more evident as the golden summer wound to autumn.

Elizabeth, ironically, was now more admired than Somerset ever had been. When she rode into London with her retinue, people cheered for her. Elizabeth of England was all a princess should be.

Somerset was finally ousted from his office that October.

Robert Dudley's father, the Earl of Warwick, convinced King Edward that he, Dudley, would make a much better Lord Protector than Somerset. Twelve-year-old Edward, tired of Somerset's high-handed stinginess, agreed.

The Earl of Warwick was a popular general, much praised for his part in defeating a Scottish army a few years before and suppressing a recent uprising in Norfolk. Trusted by Edward, his rise was rapid.

And so, not long after Lord Protector Somerset had sent Seymour to the block, Somerset was banished from court, and Warwick filled his place. Elizabeth, when she heard the news, barely glanced up from her books.

The other change that year was that, though Thomas Parry resumed his post as Elizabeth's treasurer, she never again trusted him as she had in the past. She went over his account books herself, signing her name in the margins that she'd approved them, a practice she maintained for the rest of her life.

She also requested that William Cecil, who became Edward's secretary of state once Warwick took over, manage her vast properties, most of which the king's council finally relinquished to her after Somerset's fall.

I sewed her new gowns, Elizabeth grew in prosperity, and Aunt Kat, Uncle John, and Master Parry and his wife resumed their comfortable conversations—though they were careful not to mention marriage or Elizabeth's future ever again.

As the months passed, I grew a bit taller, my hair became less unruly, my figure lost its youthful roundness, and I took on the curves of womanhood. I let my gaze linger on handsome young gentlemen, though I kept my thoughts firmly to myself. I had no wish to repeat my foolish mistake about Seymour.

Aunt Kat was responsible for my virtue, I told myself, and I should not make things difficult for her. So, I eyed a fine body from afar and pretended I felt as Elizabeth did—that for now the unmarried life was preferable.

Elizabeth's friends, on the other hand, began to enter the married state with alacrity. In the spring of 1550 Elizabeth learned that Robert Dudley was to wed a young lady of Norfolk, one Amy Robsart. Elizabeth would attend the ceremony, as would Edward, her brother.

She and I traveled together in early June to the wedding, which was to be held at the palace at Richmond—the benefit of having the new Lord Protector as one's father. The weather had turned warm, and soft air brought the scent of new growth from the fields beyond the roads.

"Sweet Robin needs cash, and he must needs marry it," Elizabeth informed me as we supped in a wayside inn's private chamber. "A fifth son can expect little from his father, for all that man's lofty position." She sniffed. "*Lord Protector* might mean he has a larger purse, but he holds the purse strings all the more tightly."

It was clear Elizabeth did not approve of this marriage. She'd known Robert—or Robin as she liked to call him—for most of their life. Whenever Elizabeth had visited her father and Queen Catherine as a child, she and Robert had studied together. Robert had loved mathematics and astronomy, Elizabeth Latin and Greek. Though I'd paid little attention to Robert at the time, I recognized that he'd been charming even then, with his lopsided smile, dark good looks, and his devotion to Elizabeth.

The two were close in age—they liked to pretend they'd been born on the exact same day in 1533, but in truth Robert was about a year older, now eighteen to Elizabeth's seventeen. They liked one another well, and after Elizabeth had made her quiet return to court, they'd renewed their friendship.

It had pleased me to see her with Robert at Edward's gatherings, sharing dances and sometimes riding out together on the many hunts the royal family seemed to indulge in.

Elizabeth showed none of the strange infatuation with Robert that she'd given Seymour, although both men had a similar studied charm. Robert seemed a bit more practical than Seymour had been, more resigned to his place as younger son of a powerful father.

I was surprised—as many were—at Robert's choice in Amy Robsart. I'd glimpsed her various times throughout my life, and while she was pretty enough, she had none of the intellectual robustness of Elizabeth. She barely glanced at Robert as we gathered the day before the ceremony at Richmond. But of course, as Elizabeth had told me, her father was wealthy, and Robert would gain control of that wealth once they were wed.

Elizabeth did not deign to speak to Amy, that young lady being nothing more than the daughter of a country squire, albeit a well-off one. Elizabeth had bestowed a few small gifts on her via her ladies, and would congratulate her at the ceremony, but their worlds certainly did not mix.

The ball the night before the wedding was sumptuous. Warwick spared no expense to marry off his son, pleased Robert had found a young woman of child-bearing age who stood to inherit a fortune. Amy's dowry must certainly be large, I speculated, as I gazed about the ballroom that had been decorated with live trees that held masses of blooms entwined around them.

The musicians hired for the night had been, for the novelty of it, suspended on ropes from the high ceiling. The musicians gazed nervously at the hard floor beneath them and clutched their instruments as they floated about. The music was a bit strained, but the revelers did not seem to mind.

I danced with several gentlemen in the pavanes and galliards, including Robert Dudley himself and Robert's brother Guildford. I also danced with a young man called James Colby, tall and red-haired, who'd been introduced as one of Robert's friends.

Colby danced well, though he seemed to have little interest in me. I preferred Guildford, who'd inherited some of the Dudley charm.

Very late that night—indeed, in the early hours of the next morning—I pattered along an upstairs gallery, searching tiredly for the chamber I shared with Aunt Kat. Richmond Palace was vast, and I lost my way.

I rounded a corner and spied, in a dark window embrasure, my Lady Elizabeth snug in Robert Dudley's embrace.

I staggered to an abrupt halt. My heart beat hard three times before I realized that they were not kissing, but conversing. However, Robert's arms were firmly around Elizabeth's waist, and she smiled up at him, making no move to push him away.

If either saw or heard me, neither made a sign.

I decided, after a few sickening moments, that I had better stand at the end of the passage to make certain no one else came this way. I could not imagine what scandal would befall Elizabeth if she were to be discovered in the arms of a man who planned to marry another woman on the morrow. I turned my back on them, but I could hear their conversation clearly.

"An interesting choice of brides, sweet Robin," Elizabeth was saying. "As I told you before."

"She will do," Robert answered.

"Aye, she is rich and from good stock."

Robert tittered. "You make her sound like a soup."

"May you have many, many offspring from your soup," Elizabeth returned. "That is why gentlemen marry, is it not?"

"Gentlemen with ambitious fathers do," Robert said darkly, his amusement fading.

"Now, now, this occasion is happy," Elizabeth chided him. "In the hall you danced on light feet."

Robert laughed once more, his dourness vanishing. "Do not

tease me. Ever you tease me, dear Lizzie, as though you live to torment your Cock Robin."

Elizabeth's voice softened. "'Tis a pleasant thing to live for, teasing one's friends."

"But you tease me especially," Robert said. "Come, admit it. I am your favorite tease."

I tried not to roll my eyes at his obvious flirtation, and I debated making some noise so they would cease.

If I interrupted, however, Elizabeth would be embarrassed and possibly furious. She might send me from her side for days or even weeks before she decided to forgive me.

I also did not sense the danger in their silliness that had existed in Seymour's attempts at a dalliance. Elizabeth and Robert were old friends—it was natural that some flirtation had grown between them.

"Your ladies will be searching for you," Robert said, as though he sensed me hovering at the end of the gallery.

"They do fuss," Elizabeth agreed. "They forget that they work to *my* demand."

"Ever the imperious princess, are you not? I am certain they quake in their shoes."

"Your tongue speaks nothing but nonsense, dear Robin," Elizabeth said in mock severity. "It is silver coated."

"Then stop my tongue. Kiss me, to wish me good luck on the morrow."

"I wish you all the good fortune in the world," Elizabeth replied, and then she went quiet.

I turned in worry to peer at them through the gloom. Robert had bent to Elizabeth, his tall frame curving over her smaller one. Their faces hovered an inch apart, and then Robert closed the space and let his lips touch hers.

Elizabeth flowed into him as the kiss deepened.

This was not a friendly buss for luck, but a kiss filled with a passion that had grown between them. I suspected this was not the first time they'd kissed—they seemed familiar with each other, even comfortable in the embrace.

When they at last broke apart, I stepped back into the shadows to hide myself.

Elizabeth must have heard some rustle, for her crisp voice rang down the hall. "You may attend me now, Eloise."

She commanded in a tone I dared not disobey. I moved on numb feet along the passage to the window, holding my skirts still.

The pair stood apart now, Robert lounging against the embrasure's carved stone arch, his smile firmly in place.

"'Tis only Eloise," Elizabeth said as I halted and curtsied deferentially. "She knows how to keep her thoughts to herself."

"The pretty seamstress." Robert reached out and gently tugged a lock of my hair. "Would you like a gift, pretty seamstress?"

"No," I said abruptly, then at his surprised expression I softened the word with another curtsy. "No thank you, my lord. You are most kind." One was not rude to the Lord Protector's son, even if he'd just been wantonly kissing an heir to the throne.

"She does not need you to shower her with gifts, Robin," Elizabeth said, annoyed. "She is a dear friend who can keep her own counsel." She held out her hand. "Walk with me to my chamber, Eloise. The halls might be filled with lecherous gentlemen."

Robert laughed out loud. He gave my hair another tug before he waved me away.

"Take care of my lady," he said, and winked. "Stay ever vigilant by her side."

Elizabeth seemed to tire of the game. She frowned at Robert and pulled me to her side. "Good night, Lord Robert. My felicitations on your nuptials."

She started swiftly down the gallery, and I had to stride

quickly to keep from being dragged along with her. Behind us, we heard Robert's laughter lingering in the darkness.

"Not one word," Elizabeth said to me. "No tales to Kat or your uncle, do you understand? And never speak of it to me."

"Of course, I will say nothing." I was offended that she'd even think so. "But tell me, Your Grace—are you in love with him?"

Elizabeth bathed me in a glare that seared. "Do not be ridiculous," she said with her usual ice.

Then she towed me at a near run all the way to her chamber, and I could ask no more questions.

ROBERT AND AMY MARRIED THE NEXT DAY. ROBERT WAS RED-eyed, an indication he'd not retired after I'd last seen him but likely had remained awake to drink more. Elizabeth sat serenely in the seat set aside for her comfort, her expression never changing as Amy Robsart became Amy Dudley.

After the ceremony Elizabeth coolly kissed Amy, now risen in rank, and wished her good fortune. She bestowed an equally cool kiss on Robert. Throughout the banquet and the ball that followed, Elizabeth kept her gaze on Robert, but the pair never made any sign that they were more than childhood friends.

Once, when I'd paused to refill her cup of wine, and we were relatively alone, Elizabeth snapped at me, "Close your mouth, Eloise. You gape like a fish. When I asked for your discretion, I did not mean for you to frown upon us like a disparaging nursemaid."

My temper splintered, and I leaned to whisper into her ear. "You put yourself in danger, Your Grace. Have you forgotten how close you came to arrest and ruin?"

Elizabeth jerked to face me, her eyes narrow slits. "I am not a complete fool. Nothing has gone further than what you saw.

Robin is a dear friend, a trusted friend, and now he is married. That is that."

She turned away, finished with me.

I straightened, clutching the jug of wine so tightly that the silver's pattern indented my palm. Aunt Kat was watching me from across the room, so I contrived a neutral expression.

To my intense relief, Robert and Amy left the next day for Norfolk, and Elizabeth returned home and to her usual routine.

We did not see much of Amy Dudley after that, but whenever Robert came to court at the same time Elizabeth visited, I slept very little.

SEASONS PASSED, AS DID YEARS. EDWARD GREW CLOSER TO Elizabeth as his rule went on, but the court became a dour place. Edward left off his boyhood interests to endlessly discuss the reformed religion with men as dour and staid as he was.

Robert's father, Warwick, made himself Duke of Northumberland in 1551, not long after he finally managed to have Somerset executed for supposedly plotting against him and Edward.

Robert resided quietly in Norfolk with his new wife and was elected to the House of Commons by his Norfolk constituents. The rebellion that had been fomented there before his marriage —ruthlessly squashed by his father—showed no signs of returning. Robert, if not beloved, was at least respected.

Archbishop Cranmer presented Edward with a revised edition of the *Book of Common Prayer,* as Edward took his religion very seriously. Edward approved of Elizabeth's somber attire, which I continued to create for her, moving to new styles as the years slid one into the other.

Sweet Sister Temperance, Edward called her, and Elizabeth did nothing to disabuse his perception of her.

I could not help but remember Sweet Sister Temperance with her fingers entwined in Robert Dudley's dark hair, but outwardly, as far as I could discern, Elizabeth behaved herself.

Young Edward, on the other hand, ground his teeth over his sister Mary, who refused to give up her Catholic masses. When Edward blatantly forbade it, Mary attended mass in secret.

Elizabeth, by contrast, read the Bible in English and discussed scripture intelligently with Edward, earning her younger brother's praise.

Despite my worries about Elizabeth and Robert Dudley, life moved along calmly enough for the next few years. Then Edward, who as a boy had been hearty and athletic, suddenly grew sick, and then sicker.

It became known that his life was in grave danger. Elizabeth, riding to St. James's in early 1553 to visit him, was turned away at the gates and had to retreat to Hatfield. Catholics dusted off their icons and prepared for the country to return to the old religion under Mary.

But Edward, as ill as he was, had another card to play. When he laid down his last hand, he shocked us all, and plunged Elizabeth—and by extension Aunt Kat and me—into dire peril for years to come.

PART II
CAPTIVE

1553 -1558

CHAPTER 10

July 1553

In the middle of a sticky midsummer night, as I neared my twentieth year, I sat in Aunt Kat's chamber working on a velvet brocade, blue as the sky. The fabric's embossed pattern depicted flowers exploding from a vine that grew from golden vases.

I saw in the cloth great beauty and regality, but behind my usual obsession, I was uneasy. I sewed the gown for Elizabeth's next journey to court, but whether that would be to visit her sickly brother or to attend her sister Mary's coronation, I could not say. Either event troubled me.

When a manservant banged into the chamber, I jumped, the fabric sliding to the floor. I quickly caught up handfuls of it, praying it hadn't been soiled.

This particular young man, whose name was Tom, was in the employ of Master Parry, who tarried in London. Tom should have gone straight to Elizabeth's chamber if he came with news of importance, but perhaps he'd felt safer confronting Aunt Kat and me rather than facing the uncertain temperament of Elizabeth.

"Disaster, Mistress Ashley," Tom said breathlessly, his eyes alight, his pockmarked face holding too much excitement for his ominous words. "The king is dead."

Aunt Kat scrambled to her feet so abruptly that she upset a small table with a candle burning upon it. I rescued the candle before it could set her skirt alight and placed it and its holder on a shelf. I sat down again, righting the table.

Aunt Kat hurried to the door and slipped the bolt across it, then she closed the shutter against the night, though the July weather was close, the room, stifling.

She resumed her place on her bench and bade Tom stand before her. "Now, tell me," Aunt Kat commanded. "No embellishments, mind. I want the entire truth of what happened."

I leaned in to listen. Young Tom, flattered at our attention, burst into his tale.

"I heard from a servant outside the king's bedchamber that his majesty vomited black bile and coughed horrible spittle from his lungs before he died in grave weakness."

I felt a pang of pity for poor Edward, only sixteen. He'd been led first by Somerset, then the Duke of Northumberland, and hadn't had much chance to be a king in truth. Somerset and Northumberland had given away his lands, spent his money, and let him die.

Tom hadn't finished. "The high lords of the king's chamber do not want news of his death to come out yet. They are seeking the king's sisters—Mary-Mary of the Popery and ..." He broke off, feeling Aunt Kat's eyes hard upon him. "His other sister."

"But if His Grace the king is dead, then Mary is queen," I said, too agitated to keep my silence. "Mary must know by now. If not, she must be told."

"Nay, for neither sister will be queen now." Tom bounced on

his toes, reveling in his role as the bearer of bad tidings. "Bastards they be, by royal decree."

Aunt Kat surged from her seat again and caught Tom's ear in a tight pinch. He yelped, but he was no match for Aunt Kat.

"You're wrong, boy," she declared. "Mary is queen, and after her will be Elizabeth. That was Henry's desire, by his legal will. If Edward decided to change the succession, Parliament would have been called—and we'd have heard the uproar all the way to Hatfield."

Tom winced until Aunt Kat released him. "No Parliament but the king's bedchamber," he said gleefully, rubbing his ear. "We have a new queen. All hail Queen Jane, long may she reign."

My mouth went dry. "You must have heard a falsehood. A rumor started by idle servants with nothing better to do."

Tom grinned, enjoying us hanging on his every word. "'Tis no lie, Mistress Rousell. The grand Northumberland has married his own son to Lady Jane, the king's cousin, and made her queen of all England. The king himself struck his sisters from the list and commanded that the words *Jane Grey and her heirs male* be written instead. Then he died."

Aunt Kat and I gazed at each other, dumbfounded.

"He cannot have," Aunt Kat said when she found her voice again. "'Tis unthinkable."

I did not understand much about politics, but I recognized hole-in-corner dealings when I heard them. The king could not change the succession without approval from Parliament, but the Duke of Northumberland, sweet Robin's father, was a cagey gentleman who could twist events, and even a person's mind, to suit his own needs. He'd let Somerset be condemned on false charges and made himself duke without pausing to draw a breath.

"What will happen?" I asked, half to myself. "Will Mary stand for being ousted by Northumberland? Her will is as strong as Henry's ever was, for all I've seen."

Aunt Kat and I leaned to our informant once more, but alas, he'd run dry of information.

The gist of the matter was that Edward was dead, and he'd named Jane Grey as queen at Northumberland's instigation. Northumberland had married one of his sons—Guilford, it must be, as Robert was still married to Amy—to Jane.

Now Northumberland wanted to put his hands on Mary, before she could rightly protest her abrupt removal from the succession.

Aunt Kat and I exchanged another glance, understanding the lay of the land. If Northumberland sought to secure Mary before news of the king's death leaked out, he'd want to secure Elizabeth as well.

Aunt Kat's eyes met mine, and together we looked at Tom Messenger.

He never knew his danger. Aunt Kat grabbed one arm and I the other. Tom was too surprised to object, and I swear the ridiculous youth thought we meant to thank him for our news by smothering him with embraces.

Tom laughed in modest protest as we pulled him to the storage cupboard behind the fireplace. His laughter cut off when we tossed him in then slammed the door shut. Aunt Kat locked the door, and I helped her drag a large chest in front of it.

Tom yelled when he discovered the trick and pounded on the door in outrage.

I plopped down on the chest. "Shush yourself," I called through the wood. "'Tis only for a day or so. You'll be fed."

I understood, as Aunt Kat did, that no one in the world could know the truth just yet. Unless Tom had invented the story to make himself important—which I doubted he'd have the wits to—danger now cloaked the house.

Jane, innocent little Jane, Elizabeth's schoolroom companion who'd stitched with us when we were tiny girls, and whom

Catherine Parr had nurtured in her own home, was suddenly queen. Grandniece to Henry and granddaughter of his sister Mary, Jane had a claim to the throne, but not as direct a one as Mary and Elizabeth.

Northumberland, being no fool, would realize he had to control Mary and Elizabeth before he could proclaim Jane as monarch. The daughters of Great Harry would not meekly step aside and let Northumberland's new daughter-in-law assume the throne.

And so, Northumberland would hunt Mary and Elizabeth and bring them to heel, and possibly to the block.

My blood chilled, and Aunt Kat's face was ashen. "It must not happen," she said in a hushed voice. "It will not happen. We will not let it happen."

I agreed most heartily. We put our heads together and began to scheme.

ELIZABETH'S REACTION TO THE NEWS WHEN AUNT KAT BROKE IT was predictable. She waited, tense, while Aunt Kat explained what the servant had said, turning to me to confirm it.

Once Kat finished speaking, Elizabeth lifted a pretty glass ball from a table and hurled it hard through the window. Sunlight glittered on the sphere as it arced out to the gardens followed by splinters of the windowpane.

"He cannot," Elizabeth snarled. "He can*not*. Where is Mary? Does he already have my sister?"

"We do not know," I answered, my voice shaky. "We do not know if Her Grace Mary has even heard the news."

"Discover whether she has," Elizabeth commanded. "I want to know everything. I cannot simply sit here and wait for bloody Northumberland to decide what he will do with me—"

She broke off in a scream of rage, and a rain of books,

papers, pens, and pots of ink crashed to the floor. Aunt Kat and I, the only ladies in the chamber with her, scuttled away from Elizabeth until her tantrum wound to its close.

Elizabeth abruptly put her hand to her head and cried out in frustrated pain. One of the headaches that she'd fallen prey to more and more had come upon her.

"I HATE THE SILENCE." ELIZABETH LAY IN BED THE NEXT afternoon, her face pasty, the continuing headache so severe that she could eat nothing and drink little. Her fury had worn into cold anger, and her eyes held the calculation of a cornered fox. "I can send no messages and receive none. I must pretend ignorance. I can only wait and wonder."

"And plan." I had my feet on a hassock as I stitched again on the blue velvet. "We must decide what to do should the worst come."

The manservant, Tom, was still locked in Aunt Kat's chamber. We'd brought him breakfast this morning, and he'd tried to overpower us when we opened the door. Aunt Kat, who was quite strong, managed with my assistance to shove him back into the cupboard. Tom had kept hold of the bread and cheese we'd given him, but we feared opening the door again. So, he remained inside, fed but complaining.

"The worst," Elizabeth repeated bitterly, raising her head the slightest bit. "You mean my death. I will face *the worst* with dignity, but I will do everything in my power to keep it from happening. Damn Northumberland." She winced and eased herself back to the pillows. "Thank heavens Robin married himself off to that stick, Amy."

"You believe he'd have been the one chosen to marry Jane?" I asked in curiosity.

"Very likely. Robert stood to inherit nothing and was utterly dependent on his father. I would like to think my Robin would have had the courage to defy his father's wishes, had he been free, but who knows? Guildford is far more compliant. I imagine he didn't dare disagree when ordered to marry Jane. The Duke of Northumberland and the Duke of Suffolk have married their children to each other's to gain England." She sighed.

The marriage of Guildford and Jane this spring at Durham Place—a property Elizabeth was still being denied—had surprised us, but neither Elizabeth nor I had foreseen that Northumberland would use Jane to push Mary from the throne.

I wondered whether Guildford and Jane were yet husband and wife in truth, with Jane ready to produce the necessary heir. When the two had married, vicious gossip had put about that Jane had quietly rebelled and not let Guildford into her bed.

"Poor Jane." I stroked the cloth, trying to take comfort in its softness. "What must she think of all this?"

"Think?" Elizabeth scoffed. "She thinks nothing but what her father and mother tell her to think. If Suffolk says, *Be the queen of England, Jane*, she will curtsy and reply, *Yes, Father*. If he says, *Be a washerwoman, Jane*, she will curtsy and reply, *Yes, Father*."

I could not disagree. Jane had always been quiet and obedient, loving her books above all else. Granddaughter of King Henry's sister Mary, Jane was close in age to Edward, and she and Edward had liked each other well. I believed Northumberland and Suffolk would have succeeded in marrying Jane to Edward, if Edward had lived.

"When I am queen, I shall have wise men for my advisors, not landed men seeking the crown for their own heads," Elizabeth declared.

I noted that she stated the occurrence as a certainty.

"I scarce see how landed men can be avoided, my lady," I pointed out. "Gentlemen always want more, more, and more.

The Duke of Northumberland is powerful, I am sorry to say, and many now owe their positions to him."

"But he and Suffolk have put aside the true succession, the one decreed in my father's will," Elizabeth argued. "They have overturned the right way of things—God's way of things. They have dared to interfere with the body politic and the great chain of being."

Elizabeth was always interested in the great chain of being because she, if she became queen, would dwell somewhere near the top.

"God, angels, kings, then lesser men," I said. "Essentially. Is there room for displaced princesses and seamstresses?"

Elizabeth raised her head again. "You forget yourself, daughter of a strolling player."

"I do not, my lady." I busied myself making tiny stitches in a seam. "I never forget who I am."

Elizabeth, ever changeable, burst out laughing. "That is why I like you, Mistress Eloise. You and your Aunt Kat speak your mind, but you have shown great loyalty to me, and I will to you. Never forget *that.*"

"I will endeavor, my lady."

"Impertinent jade. Read to me Eloise. The light blinds me today."

Obediently I put aside the velvet. As I reached for the book she'd discarded on her bedcovers, she opened one eye and peered interestedly at the gown. "What is that you sew? The blue velvet for me?"

"Yes, Your Grace."

"Will it be a shroud, do you think?"

"No, of course not," I responded quickly. "It will be a grand ensemble, and all who see you will remark how splendid you are."

Elizabeth knew I flattered her on purpose, but she seemed

pleased by my assessment. "And they will see the skill of my beloved seamstress. Now, read to me."

I opened the book I'd lifted with some dismay, the strange letters dancing before my eyes.

"I do not read Greek well, Your Grace." I had told her this many times. "I can pronounce the words only with your guidance."

Elizabeth's mood shifted like lightning. "Then send me someone who can. I tire of this."

She moved to throw back the bedcovers, and I lifted my hand. "But you are ill, my lady. Wretchedly, miserably ill and can bear to see no one but myself and Aunt Kat."

I thought that Elizabeth would come at me with her fists. It would be my duty to bear her blows, to let her play out her fit of pique, but at the last minute, her eyes pinched in true pain.

"Yes, I am quite unwell. Most wretchedly and miserably, as you say." Elizabeth put her hand to her forehead and sank back to the pillows with a dramatic moan.

I was nineteen years old, a woman in truth, yet still young enough to giggle. Elizabeth laughed softly with me, but our forced levity did not chase away the darkness.

I struggled through the Greek without the least idea of what I read, while we waited for news of Mary and to discover what the Duke of Northumberland would do next.

MOST INTERESTINGLY, THE FIRST PERSON THE NEW QUEEN JANE summoned to court was me.

Riders came in the night, a hundred or so with lances and horses, making a great clatter around Hatfield. I was terrified they meant to cart the entire household off to the Tower, but Northumberland's man seemed quite courteous when he asked to speak to the Lady Elizabeth.

Aunt Kat and I told him he could not—it was impossible, as she was at death's door. We'd sent for a physician, and we had no way of knowing if she might live. Elizabeth would certainly not survive a journey, if she was being summoned to court. I, Aunt Kat, and her ladies of the bedchamber attested to this.

Why did the king want her? Aunt Kat asked the man ingenuously.

The gentleman smiled with false courtesy and said he came only with a message from Lady Elizabeth's friend and former playmate, Lady Jane Grey, asking to borrow the little seamstress of whom they were both so fond.

No mention of the king's death, no mention of Edward proclaiming Jane queen.

Aunt Kat and I retreated to Elizabeth's chamber and held our council of three. Elizabeth was at first furious and refused to let me go to Jane, but her mercurial character changed before long.

"Yes, you shall go, my dear Eloise." Elizabeth had risen, against our advice, and now she paced the room, her headache gone. "You shall sew and you shall listen and tell me every single thing Jane says and does. She and that blasted Northumberland and his cohort, the Duke of Suffolk, must be watched. Be my eyes and ears, Eloise."

Eyes and ears are dangerous things, I thought to myself. But I could keep my eyes on my needlework and my ears wide open. Servants gossiped and few paid attention to a seamstress.

"And discover what you are able of my dear Robin," Elizabeth went on. "Does he follow his father or counsel the man to prudence? The Robert Dudley I know is not much for prudence, but even so, tell me of him."

"Shall I write to you?" I asked hesitantly. I had other ideas on how to send a message, ones I'd pondered when I'd been in London with Uncle John, awaiting news of Aunt Kat. I'd toyed with the theory since but hadn't had reason to put it to the test until now.

"No." Elizabeth did another turn about the chamber. "Keep your knowledge in your head, as I know you can, and tell me all when you return. I will find a way to send a messenger you will recognize. Do this for me, Eloise. Or do you love Jane better, whom you think so kind?"

Her eyes held fire, and I answered sincerely. "You are foremost in my heart, Your Grace. And ever will be."

Elizabeth sent me a skeptical look but ceased pressing. She came to me, grasped my shoulders, and kissed my cheek. Her eyes softened, and she touched the place she'd kissed.

"God speed, my lamb," she whispered.

THE TOWER OF LONDON WAS A PARADOX.

The original keep and its surrounding walls housed royal families in great state. Those who inherited the kingdom spent the night here before they progressed through London to be crowned at Westminster. Knights were dubbed in the great hall, and storage houses held gold and silver plate, and jewels worth the entire kingdom's treasury.

On the other hand, the Tower was a royal jail from which there was little chance of escape.

A few prisoners did leave the Tower with their heads intact. The old Duke of Norfolk, uncle to Elizabeth's mother, had been reprieved by the good luck of King Henry dropping dead the day Henry was to have signed the writ of execution. Aunt Kat and Thomas Parry had been released after being questioned about the Seymour affair, and various others had gone in and out as their fortunes changed.

But those in the Tower lived in shadow of the scaffold, where black birds strutted about the green, their hoarse cries proclaiming the deaths they'd witnessed. The confined could only wait for word whether or not they'd join the toll of those before them—queens, dukes, lords, cardinals, bishops, and great men of state.

Jane had been brought to the Tower by her father, the Duke of Suffolk, and her father-in-law, the Duke of Northumberland, to be proclaimed queen.

I, arriving at a side gate in the hot night amid the rain, escorted by a contingent of Northumberland's men, was not supposed to know that.

Ostensibly, I'd heard only that Jane needed a needlewoman to help her with the new wardrobe she'd have now that she'd married. Why Northumberland believed he could keep his plot so secret I scarce knew, but those in great power sometimes thought all those around them blind fools.

The small courtyard we entered teemed with activity. Men in armor, guards in livery, pages and servants, and soldiers with swords or pikes—weapons of war—scurried here, there, and everywhere, despite the late hour. My mouth went dry as I hurried through the melee, following the gentlewoman who'd come to fetch me.

As it was long past midnight, I assumed I'd be shoved into a chamber to sleep, with Lady Jane sending for me in the morning. To my surprise, the woman chivied me toward a back staircase, hissing that *she* needed me.

I was tired, dirty, smelly, and irritated, but I could only obey. The lady took me by the elbow and propelled me up staircases and through passages until we emerged into the suite in which King Henry's queens had lived before being given their crowns.

Young Jane had changed little from the days when she, I, and Elizabeth had sewed together at Hatfield or Enfield, or when she'd shared lessons with Elizabeth in Catherine Parr's house.

Jane had large eyes in a slim face and was slight for her

sixteen years. She appeared even smaller under the vast beamed ceiling of the chamber in which she awaited me.

The enormous, embroidered robe she wore dwarfed her, its sleeves belling over her too-thin wrists. Her hair had been dragged back and pinned under a hood, from which her pale, rather rabbity face jutted.

Her figure was as slender as I remembered—it was obvious that, even had she shared a bed with Guildford Dudley in these last months, she had not yet conceived.

Jane was not alone in the large chamber. Her mother, Frances Grey, née Brandon, the haughty Duchess of Suffolk, paced the long room with impatience. The duchess did not even glance at me as I hurried in but lifted a long finger and pointed to a corner filled with bolts of cloth. "Over there."

I'd grown up sitting in corners while I sewed for royal women, and had learned early in life how to discover the most comfortable, out-of-the-way spaces in a room and make them my own. Sometimes I, sewing with all my might in a nook by the fireplace, was far warmer and more content than the great people who shivered across the chamber in cushion-strewn chairs.

The niche to which the duchess directed me was dark, shadowy, and not to my taste, but the July night was stuffy, and the corner was the coolest in the room. I took up my place without a murmur.

The duchess paced and fanned herself vigorously. Jane stood out of her mother's path, beads of sweat on her face, her gaze following the duchess's stride back and forth.

"It must be done by morning," the duchess said abruptly, as though I knew exactly what she was talking about. Her glare fixed on me, and I dropped my gaze in deference. "You will finish, won't you, girl?"

My temper splintered. I was the daughter of a gentlewoman, a Champernowne. Though my mother had made an unfortunate marriage, I was not, and never had been, of the serving class. I did not mind waiting on great ladies I respected, like Elizabeth, or even Jane, but I was here at the insistence of Northumberland, who had risen to a dukedom from nothing, *on* nothing but ambition.

But the daughter of old King Henry's sister Mary, and now Duchess of Suffolk, had royal blood in her veins and never let anyone forget it. Thus, she glared at me and called me *girl*.

I did not speak directly to Jane, but I made it plain my words were for her. "This cloth is quite fine. 'Twill make up in no time, as long as I know what it is I am to create."

The duchess's lip curled. "Everything is there for a gown. You will sew."

"I will need light." I could hardly cut a pattern and seam a skirt without being able to see. "And perhaps assistance. There is enough cloth here for two or three garments. How many did you wish?"

As I hoped, I goaded Jane into speech. "Bring her light." Jane waved to the servants who occupied the shadows. "Bring them now, and I will assist her."

"You will *not*." The duchess rounded on her daughter. "Remember who you are."

I thought Jane would crumple to the floor. She had never been one to defy her elders, and her duchess mother had a personality that flattened all before her.

However, Jane, like most timid people, retained a stubborn streak, which, when invoked, hung on like grim death. Jane didn't quite meet the duchess's eye, but the corners of her mouth firmed.

"I will sew with Eloise," she announced. "It is something I *can* do."

The duchess flushed. I could point out that sewing was a most royal pastime—Henry's wives sewed his shirts and helped in the making of linens. Mary sewed and embroidered quite well and so did Elizabeth, although Elizabeth did not always have the patience.

I had chosen a bench so I would not have to perch on a precarious stool or sit on the hard floor. I busied myself sorting the cloth while Jane had her quiet confrontation with her mother in the middle of the room.

They had certainly supplied her with sumptuous fabric— cloth of gold, green brocade, thin silk taffetas, sumptuous velvets, damask lined with silk and fur. *Fur,* I thought in incredulity, *for hideous July weather. But they want to present her as a great queen.*

I pictured the gown I'd make—a velvet overskirt revealing a sheath of the brocade, with the same green brocade trimming the sleeves. The costume would be beautiful on Jane, wearable art, and I would create it for her.

Jane must have won her small rebellion, for she plunked herself onto the bench beside me and snatched up a skein of silk. "All this is because I am married now," she said to me. "A matron must have a larger wardrobe than a maid."

A ridiculous explanation for cloth fit for a sovereign. I smoothed the silk in her agitated fingers before she could tear it, and found her skin ice cold.

A halo of light touched the window above Jane's head, the rising sun, but the brightness immediately dimmed as a cloud passed over it. Inky darkness seemed to surround Jane, eating the golden light like a hungry malaise.

I shivered suddenly, sucking in a breath.

The duchess, who'd hovered to keep watch on Jane, forced my head up with a hard hand under my chin.

"What is the matter with Mistress Rousell?" the duchess demanded of Jane. "Is she ill? If she is ill, she must go at once. You cannot take sick."

I was exhausted and longed for bed, but I held my tongue. If the duchess sent me scuttling back to Hatfield, there would be nothing to report to Elizabeth except that Jane was having new clothes made, and that her mother loved to harangue her.

The duchess mercifully released me, and I shook my head. "I am not ill, Your Grace, I promise you. I had a long journey and not much to eat, and this room is close."

"She ought to sleep," Jane tried. She put a chilled hand on my forehead, and it was all I could do not to shrink away from her.

"No," I said quickly. "I will carry on."

The duchess regarded me, stone-faced, but ceased her questions.

I sewed. Jane helped, or pretended to, but she was fairly useless this night. Pins slipped from her nerveless fingers, and I could not trust her at all with the scissors.

The duchess did little but storm up and down the room and demand servants fetch wine and cakes, which she devoured without offering any to Jane or me. Jane flinched at the mere sight of the food, but I, healthy and in no danger of becoming queen of England, was quite hungry.

Though the duchess and Jane believed themselves to be secretive, I knew quite well that I sewed Jane's coronation wardrobe. Though I saw no evidence of stately robes and ermine, the gowns that would come from these cloths would be worn at banquets, balls, and ambassadorial visits Jane would attend after her crowning.

The weight of the dresses would crush her. I predicted Jane would collapse when she had to face the mass of people in Westminster Abbey, no matter that the Duke of Northumberland and her mother stood behind her to prop her up.

I could better see Elizabeth in these gowns, her slim, upright form regal and strong. She'd watch with steely eyes as her ministers as well as ambassadors from foreign lands bent knees to her.

Edward's dying deed, however, might ensure that Elizabeth never wore the robes of a queen.

The dawn light that had brushed the window grew brighter as the duchess swallowed her cakes and Jane and I quietly worked. By the time the chamber was fully lit, we heard horses and the heavy tramping of boots in the courtyard below.

I had not thought it possible for Jane to become any more pale, but her face went as white as linen. She began to sway on her stool, a small noise of terror in her throat.

The duchess marched to Jane and jerked her to her feet.

"Get *up*. Stand. Meet them. And you." She kicked my bench over as I scrambled up beside Jane. "Do not sit in her presence. Ever. Do you understand?"

I held my breath, understanding very well. They were going to do it.

The ambitious, turbulent, handsome Dudleys, aided and abetted by Jane's parents, were going to turn England upside-down.

I thought of Robert Dudley and the wicked kiss he'd shared with Elizabeth just before his wedding. I wondered, as Elizabeth had, if he were party to this conspiracy to keep Mary and Elizabeth from the throne. Robert stayed mostly in Norfolk these days, when he didn't attend Parliament, but his father could have compelled him to obey.

The duchess nearly dragged Jane from the chamber. With no one watching me, I followed, keeping well behind the crowd of servants who scrambled after Jane and her mother.

The Tower's large hall was now filled with men—the Duke of Northumberland himself, the Duke of Suffolk eyeing his approaching wife in trepidation, and Northumberland's sons, Guildford Dudley and Robert, in Norfolk no longer.

Gentlemen of the king's council tarried in the hall as well, along with William Cecil, his nervous gaze darting about, and the aged William Paulet, who held himself steadily in the tumult.

A canopy had been set up at one end of the great hall, which

I recognized as King Edward's cloth of gold. My heart thumped as I squeezed among the crowd, unnoticed.

Northumberland held a paper that dripped with seals, including the large red one of the dead young king. He waited for silence, though I had the feeling every single person in that room already knew exactly what he would say.

"This *Devise*," Northumberland began in a loud, clear voice, "was drawn up by Edward the King of England and signed by his council not many days before he died. For yes, as I stand before you, I bring you grievous news. King Edward is dead. Long live Queen Jane!"

"Queen Jane!" Suffolk bellowed, his face already red with whatever wine he'd drunk in celebration.

He pulled his daughter forward and thrust her under the canopy, forcing her to turn and face the room.

The crowd took up the cheer, the Dudleys in enthusiasm, the men of the council less so. Paulet and Cecil stood in silence, unsmiling.

Jane, the new and regal queen, gazed upon the faces of her subjects and dropped to the floor in a dead faint.

CHAPTER 11

I was at last able to sleep, because with everyone hovering around the wretched Jane, I could slip away and find a bed. I crept into one that a maid had just abandoned to serve the invading Northumberlands, the straw mattress warm from her round body. I slept hard for a short time then awoke, restless and worried.

What young Tom—whom Aunt Kat had released when Northumberland's men arrived at Hatfield—had reported to us was true. The darling Dudleys had somehow persuaded the council to let them steal the throne from under Mary's nose.

I did not doubt that though the crown would be on Jane's head, it was Northumberland and the Duchess of Suffolk who'd truly have the power. They would rule England, and Jane would let them.

Guildford Dudley might try to put his hand in. Jane's father, Suffolk, obviously thought he'd have much say himself. Northumberland would be the true monarch, though, with Jane's mother to make Jane's decisions for her.

I studied the ceiling above my borrowed bed, watching a spider crawl across a crack that must seem a chasm to it. So must the abrupt accession to the crown seem to Jane, with her parents standing behind her to push her into it.

I knew Jane would never have chosen this for herself. She loved reading and scholarly pursuits, not the trappings of power. Her tutors had praised Elizabeth's quickness but loved Jane for her devotion to her studies.

What would Princess Mary do? And where was she? Someone surely had given her the news by now. Strong-willed Mary would never simply bow her head and step aside. She'd even now be planning a way to keep her crown.

Mary had made her resentment clear when her father had stripped her of her titles during her girlhood, and she'd make it clear now. With her fixed stare and deep convictions, Mary would never allow an upstart like Northumberland and a mouse like Jane keep her from her rightful place.

I threw back the thin covers and climbed from the bed. I had to shout into the hall for a maid to come and help me dress, then I followed her down to the kitchen and demanded breakfast.

The cooks wanted nothing to do with me. I told them I'd come at Lady Jane's special request and advised them not to anger the new queen on her first day. The kitchen staff threw me evil looks but also handed me a good helping of stew.

After I filled my stomach, I returned to the chamber where I'd worked in the night before and found it empty. The beautiful fabrics had spilled from the bench the duchess had knocked over, and my needle box lay in a jumble where it had fallen.

I quietly tidied my things and brushed dust from the cloths, folding them neatly. I resumed working on the patterns, my head bent, so that if anyone peeked in, it would appear as though I'd remained virtuously at my post all morning.

The first person to find me was Sweet Robin himself, dressed in finery fit for a queen's brother-in-law.

"Is it Eloise Rousell?" Robert asked as he peered into the cool shadows. "But it is. Dear Mistress Rousell. Dear, dear, Mistress Rousell."

"Leave off your dears, my lord," I said, raising my head. "Or have they made you a duke as well, and I must call you Your Grace?"

Robert sent me his quick smile, his pleasant face lightening. "Always impertinent, is our little Eloise."

We were near the same age, so he had no business calling me *little*. "You have not answered my question, my lord."

"My father and brother have all the duking," Robert said jovially. "I am simple Robert still. Tell me why you are here."

"My lady Jane asked me to help her with her wardrobe." I explained this calmly, but my heartbeat sped.

Robert was no fool, and he knew Elizabeth well. He'd reason she'd not lend her favorite servants willingly, which either meant I'd abandoned Elizabeth, or she'd sent me here for her own purpose.

I did not know where Robert's loyalties lay—with his father and the Suffolks? Or with Elizabeth, for whom he felt friendship and more?

Robert could easily tell his father that Elizabeth had sent me to spy on them. He could also use me for his own purposes, perhaps to feed me information for Elizabeth, true or false.

I saw in his eyes, which danced with possibilities, that he hadn't yet decided what to do with me.

Our conversation might have turned in a hazardous direction if we'd not been interrupted. I recognized the man who entered as Robert's friend, with whom I'd danced at Robert and Amy's wedding—James Colby.

Colby had fiery red hair and a look of the Welsh about him, though I'd heard he was English, from Shropshire. He was tall and rawboned, his face not particularly handsome, though it was strong, and he possessed eyes of keen blue.

Those eyes swept over me without much interest and fixed on Robert. "Dudley, they're looking for you."

No *my lords,* no obeisance. Merely a blunt *Dudley.*

Robert bowed to me as fairly as he would a lady at court. "Au revoir, my little seamstress. Colby," he nodded to the man at his side.

Colby sent another gaze over me, an assessing one this time. Likely he tried to decide why Robert favored me with his courtly bow.

Was I a mistress, friend, Northumberland's servant? Colby's reddish brows drew together as he tried to reason it out.

Robert, already finished with me, swept from the room. Colby, with a final baleful glance at me, which I met with my head high, followed in his wake.

LATER THAT DAY JANE, LIKELY FOR THE FIRST TIME IN HER LIFE, stood up to her mother and father.

William Paulet, who had arrested Aunt Kat and Master Parry that fateful night four years ago and who'd had a hand in the trials of both Anne Boleyn and Lord Protector Somerset, arrived in the hall, where I continued to sew, with a casket in his hands. He moved to Jane, where she stood near her father and Northumberland, and bowed to her.

"What is that, my lord?" Jane asked, her tone barely curious, though she was, as ever, deferential.

For answer, Paulet opened the box. Jane flinched as she gazed down into it, her hand stealing to her throat.

Not until Paulet lifted the heavy pointed circlet studded with jewels did I understand—he held the crown of the monarchs of England.

"I did not ask to see that," Jane said rapidly. "Why have you brought it?"

Paulet regarded her without expression. "To see how it fitted, Your Grace."

Jane backed a step. "I will not put it on. It is not time. I did not ask for it. Please, do not make me." Tears clogged her voice, but her spine remained straight, no more fainting fits.

"You must take it boldly," Paulet answered, some kindness in his tone. "Soon I will have another made to crown your husband."

Jane stilled. Her tears ceased to flow, drying on her face in the July heat. "My husband?" she asked in bewilderment.

"Aye, Your Grace," Paulet said. "Your husband, who will be king beside you."

Jane flicked her gaze from the world-weary Paulet, who waited calmly for her response, to the dukes of Suffolk and Northumberland, who stood side-by-side like the conspirators they were.

"There is no need to make a crown for my husband," Jane said clearly. "Guildford Dudley will never be king."

Father and father-in-law went slack-jawed, as though they'd heard a dog suddenly speak English.

Northumberland was the first to recover. He moved quickly to Jane, reaching a long hand to rest on her shoulder.

"Guildford is your husband," he said, as though explaining to a child. "Of course he will be king. He is married to the queen."

Jane faltered beneath her father-in-law's stern gaze, but her neck remained unbent.

"I am queen because my mother is the daughter of King Henry's sister," she declared. "I am Henry's grandniece—his sister's blood is in my veins. Guildford is a Dudley. He is not royal-born, and God has not decreed him king."

Northumberland glared at her a moment then turned away with a snarl. "Suffolk, tame your daughter."

It was not the Duke of Suffolk but his wife who sailed from the doorway to Jane and slapped her across the face.

"You will obey your father," the duchess commanded. "He has made you queen, Jane, so that the reformed religion may continue, unencumbered. You do not want Mary and her popery to rule us all, do you?"

Tears trickled down Jane's cheeks, but she stood resolute. "I will never deliver England back to the Pope." She wiped the tears from her face, the pearls in her hair shining in the summer sunlight. "I will be queen, yes, but only if Guildford is never king."

Northumberland regarded Jane incredulously. He had underestimated her, I saw from my vantage point, a grave mistake.

However quiet she was, however beaten into obedience she was, Jane was a Tudor. She shared with Elizabeth, Mary, Henry, and Edward the conviction that God's will alone had brought them to the throne.

Northumberland swerved his gaze to Jane's father. "Suffolk," he growled.

Suffolk lifted his shoulders in a shrug. "If she will not, then she will not. We will make Guildford a duke in his own right."

"Duke of Clarence," Jane said quietly. "A lofty title."

My estimation of Jane rose. Clearly, she had thought long about this, as though she'd known it would be no use to fight her parents. Therefore, she would impose her conditions. I suspected she'd exerted the same stubbornness to keep herself out of Guildford's bed for as long as possible.

Paulet viewed the scene with a canny eye. I wondered if he'd brought in the crown to provoke Jane's declaration, and to make certain Northumberland knew where things stood.

Paulet's face held no expression, but this gentleman, having survived the long reign of Henry and the short one of Edward, was a wise old bird. I had no way of knowing whether he supported Northumberland's scheme, but I had the feeling he'd be among those standing at the end of the day.

Northumberland surrendered, though he stormed from the room in fury. The Duchess of Suffolk vented her feelings on Jane, while her husband stood by in resignation. Paulet returned the crown to the casket and glided, unnoticed, from the room.

Jane would be queen, but Guildford Dudley would never be called king.

THE NEXT AFTERNOON, NORTHUMBERLAND MADE ANOTHER announcement, this one more somber. Mary had staked out a territory in East Anglia and had declared herself Queen of England. She had plenty of men at arms who'd sworn loyalty to her, and she was raising an army.

Jane paced and wrung her hands, eyes wide like a frightened child's.

The Duchess of Suffolk swept an icy glare over her husband. "You did not secure Mary?"

I sat once more in my nook, forgotten in the dark, cutting the velvets meant for Jane. Robert Dudley lounged by the fireplace, one booted foot propped behind him on the grate. His friend Colby stood in the shadows near him.

"My men tried," Suffolk answered his wife wearily. "She eluded us."

"You let her," the duchess boomed. "Go and retrieve her. You have London, you have an army, and your daughter is the queen, not Mary."

Northumberland looked upon the duchess as though she were a roach he barely kept himself from stepping on.

"Lady Mary is a cunning woman, who uses the most of the devil's wits," Northumberland told her, tight-lipped. "An army shall be dispatched, and a ship is standing by to take her. 'Twill be over by the week's end."

"And what of the Lady Elizabeth?" the Duchess of Suffolk demanded.

My heart hammered, but I continued carefully snipping, keeping my focus on my scissors.

"My reports tell me that the Lady Elizabeth is very ill and cannot travel," Northumberland said. "That is no matter. She can be held at Hatfield as well as anywhere, and moved when she is better. The Tower is reinforced. It was meant to be a stronghold, and a stronghold it will be. Suffolk will lead the army against Mary and bring her to heel."

At this, Jane shrieked. "No, Father. Do not leave me!"

Northumberland's face clouded. Perhaps Jane had the correct blood to be queen, but she did not have a queen's mind.

Were it Elizabeth they'd elevated to the throne, she'd face down Northumberland and the Duchess of Suffolk, her eyes glittering as she decided who had the best chance to capture Mary. Her own feelings in the matter would be held in rigid control. She'd not beg any man or woman to stay with her, nor would tears wet her face. Elizabeth might rage, but only against fools.

Jane's mother scowled at her. "Your father will not be long. He'll command the army and bring Mary to London in a trice. You will be so busy preparing for your coronation that you will scarce know he has gone."

But Jane was as stubborn in her own way as any of them in this room, as she'd shown yesterday. Like many gentle souls, she could dig her heels in so hard that a regiment could not move her.

"You cannot leave me, Father," she proclaimed. "No one will listen to me if you go. They listen to *you*. You must stay."

Suffolk's hard face softened as he went to Jane and took her hands. Jane sank to her knees, gazing up at him piteously, while her mother rolled her eyes in disgust.

"Please, Father," Jane whispered.

At the fireplace, Colby murmured something to Robert, and then the pair of them turned their gazes to me. I met their stares briefly before bowing again over my work. Colby's eyes, I'd noted, burned with a strange light.

Meanwhile, Jane was busily getting her way.

"I will stay," Suffolk conceded. "Never you worry." He held Jane, letting her weep against him, while her mother and Northumberland regarded them with annoyance.

Jane's tears were effective. Northumberland, along with his sons, agreed to go snatch Mary from the east of England and deliver her to the Tower, while the Duke of Suffolk remained behind with his daughter and wife.

THAT NIGHT I WAS AWAKENED BY A HARD HAND ACROSS MY mouth.

I jerked upward, striking out at my assailant, struggling for breath to scream. I heard a satisfactory grunt as my fist connected with flesh, then a strong grip forced me back to the pillows.

"Do not rouse the house, you idiot woman," a male voice came at me. "I am here to help you."

My thoughts immediately flashed to Thomas Seymour, his fingers tight on my breast as he admonished me not to call out.

Fear lashed through me before I forced myself to banish my panic. Seymour was dead, and this voice was nothing like his. The man's grasp held urgency, not seduction, his words tinged with alarm.

I strained to see who he was, but the darkness was complete. Nor could I place his voice. Not Suffolk or any of the Dudleys, and not a servant. The ungloved hand over my mouth was broad and callused.

"You must return to Hatfield at once," the man commanded.

"Without anyone seeing you. Get up and dress yourself. Dudley is departing with his father, but he said you were sensible. Do not give his words the lie."

I finally realized who he must be. Colby, Robert's friend, who'd shown him no deference and me little enjoyment when we'd danced. As my eyes adjusted to the dark, I made out his tall body, long face, and glint of red hair.

I lay still to convey that I would not scream if he released me, but I do not think Colby quite believed me. He lifted his hand very slowly, ready to clap it to my mouth again if I cried out.

"*Why* must I return home at once?" I asked in a whisper. "What has happened?"

Colby made a noise of annoyance. Had he expected I'd instantly obey any gentleman who entered my room in the night, pinned me to the bed, and hissed orders at me?

From the growl he emitted, he had. Colby had underestimated me as much as Northumberland underestimated Jane.

"There is danger here," Colby said. "Mary will win. Her sister must be protected."

"By me?" I sat up, hugging the bedcovers to my body. "You are optimistic. Shall I fight with my scissors and needle?"

He ignored my ridiculousness. "You must go to the Lady Elizabeth and tell her all. There will be much confusion here, and you might not have another chance to slip away."

Colby must know me for the spy I was and realized that Elizabeth had sent me to report what happened. Robert must as well. Why the pair had not simply dragged me to Northumberland, I could not say.

Colby backed from the cot and stood waiting. The July night was hot, but a cooler breeze wafted through the high, open windows. With it came the sounds of horses snorting, chains rattling, and men shouting to one another in the courtyard below.

They were leaving to fight Mary's troops. Whoever won this battle—Mary or Jane—Elizabeth would be the loser for it. Northumberland had said he wanted Elizabeth secure, and I shuddered to think what that might mean.

I did not really trust Robert or Colby, but nor did I want to stay any longer in the Tower.

I slid from the bed and padded to the hooks that held my clothes. It became apparent that Colby had no intention of leaving the room or even turning his back while I dressed, so little did he trust *me.*

Nothing for it. I faced the wall and threw off my night rail. Cool air touched my naked skin, raising goosebumps on my flesh. It was so dark, Colby could not possibly see me, or so I assured myself as I dropped my chemise over my head.

I slid on stockings and tied my skirt around me, then I held my bodice against my chest and glanced over my shoulder at Colby.

"Lace me, please."

Colby hesitated, a typical man who did not realize how much assistance a woman needed when dressing.

"If you want us to be so secret that I cannot call a maid, you will have to do it," I informed him.

Colby's breath was loud in the dark as he came to me. His fingers fumbled against my back until he found the laces, then he began the tricky business of threading them through the grommets.

Once he got them started, however, he seemed somewhat competent at the task. He tied off the laces more quickly than I'd assumed he would.

"Do you have sisters?" I asked as I hooked the bodice to my skirt and then scanned the floor for my sturdy shoes.

"I had a wife."

Colby spoke in neutral voice, and I could not see his face, but the words were tense.

"Has she died?" I asked softly.

"Two years ago, in childbed."

Colby was perhaps only a few years older than I, but that age was enough for him to have married and sired children. A woman dying bearing a babe was not unusual, but still sad.

"I am sorry." I touched his arm. "That is a tragedy."

He did not answer, and I had to leave it at that.

Colby twitched in impatience to get away, scarcely giving me time to gather up my needle case and tuck it into a bag. I suppose he'd have liked me to simply throw a cloak over my nightgown and flee with him, but sewing accessories were expensive. Mine were precious to me, a gift from Aunt Kat long ago.

Once I was ready, we descended through back stairs that were deserted, the old Tower cold and musty, even in the heart of July. We wound through a narrow, bricked yard in the pitch dark, the torches in the main courtyard and the sounds of men and horses not a breath away.

Colby led me to a water gate, our feet slipping and sliding on the damp stone stairs to the river. The tide was out, but a tiny boat rocked on the Thames not far from the sludge of shore.

Colby propelled me onward, his fingers biting my arm. Mud sucked at my feet as I splashed toward the boat. The two of us climbed aboard the tiny vessel, and Colby took up the oars. I sat in the bow, watching him row us downstream, my bag of accoutrements at my feet.

I was trusting him, which could be a mistake. He could be taking me straight into the arms of Mary, who might not be happy that I'd been helping Jane the so-called queen. In addition, I was deserting Jane—poor Jane, who had no one on her side.

But for some reason I believed that Colby wished to aid me in returning to Elizabeth. Robert cared for Elizabeth's person, but Colby seemed a man who might be more loyal to her as princess.

Also, I could not object to leaving the Tower. A palace it might be, a fortress to protect kings and queens, but I could never forget its bleaker function.

I huddled in my cloak against the wind that skimmed up the river from the sea. Colby strained at the oars, moonlight brushing his dark tunic and trousers tucked into riding boots. No flashy court colors, no hat with plumes, just plain garments for escaping.

We moved as silently as smoke, my cloak and Colby's subdued clothes blending into the shadows.

Colby rowed for an hour or more at an even tempo, taking only brief rests. After this, he angled the boat for a dark bank until we bumped against a deserted dock jutting into an inlet. Colby leapt out, then reached down and hauled me up beside him.

Beyond the jetty lay a village, typical of mid-England, with thatched-roofed houses surrounding a green. I had no earthly idea where I was. The houses were small and silent, and no lights shone as we hurried through the high street.

Where the high street became a road leading from the village, a lanky young man waited with two horses, one a well-bred animal, the other more ample and placid. The young man sagged in vast relief when we appeared out of the darkness.

He—Colby's servant or squire, I could not tell which—helped boost me into the saddle of the fine horse, and Colby swung up behind me. He apparently did not trust me to ride alone.

The servant mounted the staid beast, and we rode off into the night.

The sun tinged the horizon with gray not long later. We headed north and west, I saw by where the sunrise lay. Colby's charger moved swiftly, though I sensed Colby holding the horse back to prevent winding him.

I felt it safe to speak now, so I pried a fold of cloak from my mouth and turned my head to look up at him. "You never told me why you and Lord Robert decided I should return to my lady."

Colby took his time answering, as though deliberating what to say. When he spoke, it was through tight lips, his face stained pink from the wind.

"Mary will return the old religion to England."

I waited, but Colby pressed his mouth closed, no more forthcoming.

"Every simpleton will conclude *that*," I said in exasperation. "Let me see if I understand you aright. You supported Jane at first, because she and Northumberland would retain the reformed faith. You now believe Northumberland cannot stand against Mary, and so you want Elizabeth safe. Her claim on the throne is likely to be restored when Northumberland is overthrown."

Colby said nothing for three or four of his horse's strides. "Women gossip overmuch," was his enlightened comment.

"It is not gossip but simple reasoning. You want to save the reformed faith, not the throne. At least *you* do. What Lord Robert wants I can only guess."

"He wishes you to keep watch," Colby said. "And to report any difficulties to him."

"I will not spy on my lady," I began.

"You will do as you are told."

His high-handedness grated on me. I did not have much experience with gentlemen, but most in Elizabeth's household were deferential to me, because it was well known that I was one of Elizabeth's favorites. Colby didn't give a toss about my favored status, except that it would allow me to be close to her.

"I will do what is best for my Lady Elizabeth," I informed

him. "I will watch over her, as I always have, and keep her from the grip of conspirators like you. If you drag her into your secret dealings, you will lose the very cause for which you strive. She must be free of your schemes and plans, and be able to prove it."

"That is why we will speak to *you* and never to *her*," Colby said tersely.

"I see. Because if I am caught and executed for treason, 'twill be no great loss for you. You can easily find another informant, but not another princess."

Colby actually smiled, a brief flash of teeth that disappeared as soon as it came. "You learn quickly."

I suppressed a shiver. "I am not a silly prattler you can pay to repeat everything that occurs in my lady's household. I serve Elizabeth, not Lord Robert. If our interests coincide, then of course, I will help you. But at *her* command, not yours."

Colby did not answer. We rode, as the sun rose, in complete silence until we turned onto a road that I recognized ran to Hatfield.

At that point, Colby muttered something under his breath that sounded like *bloody women*, but the wind was in my ears, and I could not be certain.

CHAPTER 12

For the next tense few days at Hatfield, Elizabeth and I anticipated news of Mary's defeat or of Northumberland's, but unnervingly, no news came at all. Elizabeth quietly mourned her brother's passing, and we waited.

I thought through Colby's bidding that I look after Elizabeth and be his go-between, and I did not like any of my conclusions. I didn't trust Colby, but well I knew that times were dangerous and Elizabeth needed her friends close about her. I determined to be a good one.

When I could finagle a private moment with her, I told Elizabeth all that had transpired with Jane and her family. Elizabeth turned her face away when I relayed that Robert had ridden off with the soldiers, though I did not know if he'd act for or against Mary.

He'd likely do what his father ordered, I mused. How could he do otherwise?

Whether Robert fought for Jane or Mary, I believed his first loyalty would be to Elizabeth. What I'd seen in his eyes, combined with Colby's words and actions, told me that.

At last, nine days almost to the hour that Jane had been proclaimed queen, messages at last flowed to Hatfield.

The gentlemen of Edward's council, who'd been kept more or less prisoner with Jane in the Tower, had slipped away one by one, once Northumberland had gone off to subdue Mary. This included old Paulet, who'd escaped to his country home. Once free, these gentlemen, surmising that Northumberland's plans would come to naught, had declared for Mary.

In East Anglia, Mary won the day. Many of Northumberland's own soldiers and officers had turned on him to join Mary.

Northumberland finally conceded he'd lost and had reportedly proclaimed loudly, "All hail Mary, the queen!"

At the Tower, the Duke of Suffolk tore down the gold canopy they'd erected for Jane. "These things are not for you," he told his daughter in sorrow.

I imagined that Jane, despite her fright, could only bleat relief that she did not have to be queen. I heard that she sat down immediately to write to Mary to beg forgiveness for what her father and mother had made her do.

The people of England cheered Mary. Catholic or no, she was the rightful heir, and Northumberland had no business meddling with the succession. They had tolerated Jane as queen for a week or so but now danced in the streets to rejoice that Mary had prevailed.

"What of Jane?" I asked Uncle John when he returned from London. I thought of the anxious girl I'd deserted and the flash of stubbornness she'd revealed when she'd refused to let Guildford be named king. "Surely Mary will never believe that the plots were Jane's. She knows Jane better than that."

"Jane remains in the Tower," Uncle John informed me wearily as we gathered in Aunt Kat's chamber where Uncle John refreshed himself with wine. "But Mary has said she will be merciful to Jane and Guildford. She has already released the

Duke and Duchess of Suffolk—as arrogant as they are, they would have been harmless without Northumberland. Northumberland will pay, of course, and he knows it."

"It wasn't Jane's fault," I repeated.

Aunt Kat sniffed. "Well, why do you not run to Whitehall and tell Mary so? I am certain she will listen to you and release her right away."

Her sardonic tone made me flush. "I feel sorry for Jane, is all."

"As do I." Aunt Kat softened. "Pray for her, Eloise. Her innocence is sure to touch Mary, and all will be well."

"It will be," Uncle John reassured me. "Mary will release her, in time, you will see."

I thought of Jane weeping pathetically at her father's feet, and I realized that her very innocence could be her downfall. Both Northumberland and Suffolk had believed she'd be the perfect pawn-queen.

Had Northumberland chosen Elizabeth as his pawn, things would have been much different.

Elizabeth, in the first place, would never have been coerced into marrying Guildford. She'd learned a hard lesson with Seymour about how gentlemen used women to put forward their own ambitions. She'd not have meekly gone to the altar.

I wondered if Elizabeth might have been tempted had the suitor in question been *Robert* Dudley, but with Robert safely married to Amy, that was not to be.

Now, Sweet Robin was in the Tower with his father, having raised men against Mary in Norfolk. He waited, with Jane, Northumberland, and Guildford to discover what Mary would do.

In the meantime, I hastily designed clothes for Elizabeth, who would ride in Mary's coronation procession.

I had progressed in the world enough by now to have two seamstresses working under me. I drew designs for gowns and chose the fabric for each from the vast quantities provided for Elizabeth's use, and they cut and stitched to my direction.

I sewed beside them when we were in a great hurry. I could put together a bodice quickly to near perfection, and other ladies of the court envied Elizabeth having me all to herself.

Elizabeth once speculated, in those days before Mary's coronation, that Mary might steal me away to make her clothes fit for a queen.

"Never," I vowed. "She'd never request it anyway. Everyone knows I am of the reformed religion. She would have much difficulty converting me to popery."

"Guard your tongue," Elizabeth admonished me in a low voice. "My sister will bring back the mass, and you will be required to say it."

"You as well?" I challenged.

Elizabeth went quiet, her expression guarded. "That remains to be seen."

I had learned that with Elizabeth it was often a battle of wills, even if she fought silently. She was a good fighter, and I wondered who would win in any wars between herself and her much older sister.

The wardrobe I assembled for Elizabeth remained in keeping with her role as the virtuous Protestant princess. However plain the garments were, though, I made them of lush satins, velvets, and tissues, including the velvet with the burst of flowers I'd been working on when we'd heard the news of Jane.

I designed the bodices to be unadorned and narrow, with overskirts that draped modestly over rather plain underskirts. I kept the sleeves close-fitting and uncomplicated without the voluminous oversleeves Mary's ladies continued to wear. The colors I used for Elizabeth were pale, including much white and silver, thinking it could not hurt to draw attention to her virginal state.

At the end of July, we made ready for Elizabeth to ride to

London, accompanied by two thousand riders and most of her household of ladies and gentlemen. Aunt Kat had stayed behind, claiming she needed to rest before the strenuous undertaking of the coronation, and she tasked me to look after Elizabeth in her place.

Our journey would be not only to greet Mary as queen, but to remind all we passed that Elizabeth was her sister and heir to the throne.

To that end, the company was splendid. We had outriders with swords, the gentlemen of Elizabeth's household in armor, the ladies in their finest. I was on horseback among the gentlewomen, dressed like a lady myself in dark greens, the style of my garments of similar plainness to Elizabeth's.

Elizabeth rode bareheaded, surrounded by men with banners to both protect and proclaim her.

Crowds turned out to watch as we left Hatfield and moved along the roads to London. Villagers cheered as we rode through their hamlets, and children ran forward to hand Elizabeth gifts of garlands and fruit. She took the adulation as her due and smiled beneficently at all she passed.

"They like a princess to look like a princess," she told me when we stopped to rest along the way. "They shall always have that, I assure you."

As we rode on, I lagged a little behind the other ladies, and an outrider came close to me. A fold of his streaming cloak flowed back to bare a sword and the raw-boned body of James Colby.

"Greetings, Mistress Rousell," he said formally.

I did my best to nod at him equally as formally. Colby steered me apart from the others, so that we could speak in relative privacy.

"I do not remember you joining Her Grace's household," I remarked to him.

"But I have joined it, at the request of John Ashley." Colby gave me a slight bow from his saddle. "Ashley is a friend of my father's, and he obtained me the position."

I had not heard this. I would have to question Uncle John about Colby when we I had a chance.

"Why are you not in the Tower with the Dudleys?" I asked him. "Keeping Jane and Guildford company?"

"I managed to be on Mary's side when it mattered." Colby shrugged as he gave the evasive answer. "I am pleased Northumberland did not prevail, no matter what I think of Mary's religion. Most of the council and Parliament agree with me, as you've no doubt heard."

"Did you betray Robert and his family?" I glowered at him. "Did you desert them to ride to Mary's side?" While I was happy Mary had prevailed over Northumberland's and the Duchess of Suffolk's schemes, I disapproved of Colby so callously abandoning his friends.

"There was no betrayal." Any lightness left him. "What I did was meant to happen, though I can say no more of it here."

"You seem determined to draw me into dangerous intrigue. Why do you trust me?"

Colby sent me another glance, this one assessing. "You have proved yourself. Elizabeth told me of the ladies in her household she put her faith in, and you were the first she mentioned."

"She spoke to you?" I asked in surprise. I was equally surprised that my name had been at the top of her list.

"The princess granted me a short audience with herself and her estate manager, Cecil. She knows where my loyalty stands."

Elizabeth had not mentioned this to me, nor had Uncle John. Who Elizabeth had in her household was her business, I told myself, but for some reason, this omission of information about Colby rankled.

"But do *I* know where you stand?" I asked in a hard voice.

"I serve the princess," Colby answered without heat. "I have been told you do as well. Mary is very much of the old religion, and Elizabeth sees that danger. Mary can be fair-minded, but when her religion is challenged, she is blind. I have seen this."

I had seen it as well, in a distant sort of way, throughout my life, though I'd never paid much attention. I'd expected Edward and his sons to rule for many years, and Mary's beliefs not to matter. Now everything about Mary was of severe and sharp importance.

Colby sent me another of his assessing stares before he nodded at me and rode on, as though finished with my company. The man made me impatient, though I was not certain why.

Rude, I told myself. I was simply bothered by his abrupt comings and goings and his high-handed demands.

I caught up with the other ladies and tried to push Colby from my thoughts.

Not long later, we arrived in London.

Our large retinue had to slow as we entered via Aldgate and paraded through the cheering City to Fleet Street. We passed Temple Bar and flowed into the Strand, following it a short way to Somerset House, the huge estate that had been granted to Elizabeth after Somerset's downfall.

This manor was enormous, with large grounds and a pile of buildings backing onto the Thames.

My lodgings were high in the rear of the house, the damp and stink of the river wafting into my chamber. It could not be healthy, I thought, but we'd not linger here long.

Indeed, we rode out of London again the next morning to meet Mary north and east of the city at Wanstead.

I stayed near Elizabeth for this leg of the journey, keeping my eye on Colby. Elizabeth had not brought her entire entourage today, but I spied him with us, dressed in her colors as one of her gentlemen.

I did not know what to make of Colby, nor could I decide whether he truly had Elizabeth's best interests at heart. I could not help but wonder whether he and Robert Dudley worked schemes of their own, using her for their gain. Sweet Robin, in his own way, could be as canny and manipulative as his father.

I drew a breath of relief once we were free of London again. While life in Town could be entertaining after long stretches of rustication, I preferred the air of the country. Too many bodies pressed together in the city, and the air was thick with the stench of privies plus animals living without the sun or the grass beneath their feet.

I thought the country air more salubrious, my belief justified by the fact that plague gathered mostly in cities.

Mary waited for us at a great house near Wanstead. Once she'd won the battle against Northumberland, she'd traveled to London to be proclaimed queen before retreating here to meet her sister.

I did not know what to expect of Mary now that she'd come into power. She'd been a bitter and angry young woman when I'd first arrived in Elizabeth's household, commanded to wait upon her small half-sister, and I hadn't really blamed her.

She'd been much criticized at both Henry's and Edward's courts for her religious leanings and her Spanish heritage, and she'd turned a frosty demeanor to the world that disapproved of her.

Edward's rather stiff-necked ladies and gentlemen had found fault with Mary's expensive costumes and jewels as well as her stubbornness. They'd also disparaged her short stature, deep voice, and dark brows drawn too often over her piercing eyes.

Mary had felt their disapprobation keenly and had responded by becoming more pious and disagreeable than ever.

All that seemed a long time ago as Mary greeted Elizabeth in the middle of a great hall festooned with garlands that must have been hastily hung. Mary was very royal in an ensemble of golden velvet with large pearls decorating her bodice and seed pearls lining her French hood. Rubies and sapphires glinted on Mary's plump fingers, and a diamond crucifix hung from her neck.

She waited for Elizabeth to glide to her and curtsy, then Mary caught Elizabeth's hands and pulled her to her feet, beaming her a wide smile.

Elizabeth, at least a foot taller than her older sister, stooped so that Mary could kiss her on both cheeks. When they straightened and stood toe to toe, hands clasping, the contrast between the two women was remarkable.

Elizabeth was twenty, Mary thirty-seven. Mary had an almost rectangular body, her shoulders, waist, and hips nearly the same width. I noted that her seamstress had padded her bodice to emphasize her chest and likewise her hips to make her waist seem smaller in proportion. Mary's face was rectangular also, barely curving at her chin, her eyes wide-spaced, her mouth small.

Elizabeth stood tall, her posture naturally upright, with shoulders thrown back to show off her slender figure. Her hair was red gold, like King Henry's had been, her brows and lashes fair, her dark gray eyes glittering.

The gown I and my assistants had created spoke of simple elegance—bodice closed at the throat, gray velvet surcoat drawn back to reveal a dress of white and silver brocade. The costume was a work of art and far more subdued than Mary's showy finery.

I watched Mary busily compare Elizabeth to herself and draw a different conclusion than I had. Mary's eyes gleamed with satisfactory pride as she perceived that *her* jewels were more numerous, more costly, and larger than Elizabeth's. Mary's gown rippled with velvet, her sleeves trimmed lavishly with furs, while Elizabeth's ensemble was deceptively simple.

More importantly, Elizabeth was only a princess—an illegitimate one in Mary's eyes—while Mary, daughter of Catherine of Aragon and granddaughter of Isabella of Spain, was now queen.

After years of being shunted aside, ignored, and disdained, Mary reigned at last.

The Catholic queen and the Protestant princess, I whispered to myself. Foreboding filled me, even as Mary turned to Elizabeth's ladies, her smile welcoming.

Each lady was presented to Mary in turn, by rank, including myself, as a gentlewoman.

A heavy wave of perfume engulfed me as Mary raised me from my curtsy and kissed my cheek. The perfume could not quite hide the musty smell of a warm body sweltering under too many layers of clothing.

Mary pressed a gift into my hand, as she had the other ladies, a small brooch of gold with a crucifix emblazoned on it.

"Your Grace does me honor," I murmured, hoping my voice was not too hoarse.

Mary's indulgent smile faded as she looked me up and down. "You are the seamstress?"

I curtsied again. "I have that privilege, Your Grace."

Mary took in my gown, which was, as usual, a humbler version of Elizabeth's—I could copy the style, but I would never presume to wear the fabrics of a royal princess. Mary's gaze then flicked to Elizabeth, and her mouth turned down in one corner.

She disapproved of the plainness of the gown, I realized. Simplicity was the Reformed way. Elizabeth's religion did not favor ornamentation—not on the body and certainly not in the church. Mary's garments spoke of her convictions that God was to be worshipped with the most glorious jewels and precious metals money could buy.

Mary likely never contemplated it in these words, but she saw the contrast, and it annoyed her.

She turned to the next lady in line with her smile fixed in place and gave her the kiss, the greeting, and the gift.

Elizabeth dined with Mary that evening, and we ladies were given the privilege of waiting on them. The topics Mary chose were safe ones—the weather, the ease of the journey, Elizabeth's health and hers, the coming coronation.

Not one word of Northumberland, or Jane trembling in the Tower, or Edward's duplicity in changing the succession at the last moment. Nothing that would bring anger or recriminations to this festive occasion.

Next to Mary stood a woman I'd met often when Elizabeth and I had sojourned at Edward's court—Jane Dormer. Jane was a few years older than Elizabeth and unmarried. With delicate movements, Jane carved a slice of meat out of the haunch presented for Mary and laid it on a plate, then cut it into smaller pieces for her. Jane lifted her sleeve out of the way as she poured wine, glanced my way, gave me a nod of greeting.

I nodded back. Jane and I had become friends, of a sort. Jane's family was very Catholic, and what's more, her family in Buckinghamshire was close with that of Sir Philip Baldwin, my stepfather.

Mary's gaining the throne, I had well to worry, might not simply restore the nation to the old religion, but it might make my stepfather and mother insist that I be restored to it as well.

"... for the coronation," Mary was saying to Elizabeth. "What say you, sister, that you'll wear as fine a cloth of gold as any ever saw? I will send you the material myself."

"You are kind." Elizabeth took a delicate sip of wine. "My seamstress will be pleased. She is quite the artist. Perhaps the sleeves puffed over the shoulders in the new way?"

"Have you kept up with fashion then, in the country?" Mary asked, with a hint of derision.

Elizabeth's eyes glinted like a snake's. "As well as can be expected, Your Grace. I have been fortunate to be instructed on the subject by the ladies of the court. They have given me much advice."

Which she obviously had not followed. Some among the courtiers whispered that Mary depended far too much on the counsel of her ladies. Elizabeth was declaring that she, for her part, did not.

"You are a Tudor, and a princess," Mary said, missing the reference. "You must now wear clothes as befits your station. Perhaps another seamstress can be found?"

Cold washed through me. If Mary had me dismissed, I might have to return home to that awful man for whom my mother had gladly deserted me.

"Mistress Rousell sews to *my* dictation," Elizabeth said. "If I am to be more at court, then of course, my wardrobe will reflect this. She shall prepare gowns worthy of my position. I wish to do honor to the queen."

Mary only smiled and inclined her head, while I let out a quiet sigh of relief.

I DID NOT SEEK MY BED UNTIL LATE, AS I SPENT THE TIME AFTER supper in Elizabeth's chamber, helping her ladies undress her for the night. Elizabeth bade me to stay after that and listen to another lady read from the Bible—in English—as she lay abed. By the time I sought my own pallet, I was exhausted and dropped off to sleep quickly.

I dreamed of Mary, her musty odor hidden by perfume when she embraced me, and behind that came a cloying odor of smoke. Incense, I first thought, but the scent grew stronger and the emotions that came with it flooded me—despair, anger, fear, and determination. All very odd and somewhat frightening.

The dream changed, and I saw Mary and Elizabeth standing together, facing each other, as they had this afternoon in the hall. Elizabeth grew in stature while Mary shrank, until finally Mary put her hand over her face and screamed in despair.

I woke abruptly in the quiet of the night. Royal houses were never completely silent—somewhere servants tramped through passageways to wait on the ladies and gentlemen who in turn waited upon the royals. Guards outside patrolled the grounds and stablemen looked after horses, but this night not much sound reached my bed in the attics.

The smoke of the kitchen fires wafted up the chimney in my chamber, the cooks already roasting the meat for the next day. I reasoned that the smoke must have tickled my nose and entered my dreams, nothing more, but still it troubled me.

WE REMAINED ONLY A SHORT TIME AT WANSTEAD BEFORE THE two sisters rode back to London together. I bedecked Elizabeth in a gown with enough gold brocade to please Mary, but I was careful to not let her outshine the queen.

The people of London lined the streets as Elizabeth and Mary rode into the city side by side. It was early August, the weather warm and clear, which seemed a good omen. Men cheered as we passed, children tossed flowers in our path, and women bounded out to hand up gifts to both queen and princess.

These gifts touched my heart—knitted gloves or handmade tokens like pressed flowers or drawings, things a family had spent much time and what little money they had on. Both ladies, I was pleased to see, accepted them graciously.

Bells rang from every church tower we passed, and the City guard turned out in their livery to salute us and escort us through the streets.

Mary radiated pure happiness. Elizabeth seemed content to

ride a few paces behind her once we were in the City's narrow roads, nodding regally at the crowds.

The people of England have much power, Elizabeth had always told me. *Their happiness or unhappiness can make all the difference to a prince's reign. Contented and serene, or angry and rebellious.*

Under the summer sun with the crowds celebrating, it was difficult to believe that Mary's reign would be anything but joyful.

"No," Elizabeth said in a hard voice. "I cannot possibly do as she wishes. Let me speak to her, and explain why I cannot."

We were at Richmond, several weeks after Elizabeth and Mary's triumphal entry into London.

Elizabeth sat upright on a cushioned chair in her chamber, facing Bishop Gardiner, who was now the Lord Chancellor, and other gentlemen of Mary's council. Their task: to make Elizabeth explain why neither she nor any of her ladies had attended mass since their arrival at court.

We lodged in Richmond Palace at Mary's invitation, where she prepared for her coronation with the enthusiasm of a bride for a wedding to a beloved.

Mary lavished much attention on the upcoming pageantry and fretted over who would have what position in the procession. She'd pore for hours over the written details of what she was to wear, what responses she'd give in the ceremony, and who would stand next to whom.

Thus far, Mary had shown every sign of becoming a tolerant ruler. She made no secret that she wanted the old religion restored but had proclaimed, not many days ago, that she'd be merciful to those who'd grown used to the reformed services. There need be no forced conversions, she said. Those who'd strayed would soon understand their error and turn quietly back to the true church of their own accord.

Generous Mary had caused a murmur when she'd released Edward Courtenay from the Tower, where he'd spent many years in a kind of limbo since Henry's reign. His father had been accused of trying to overthrow Henry and was executed, and Edward had grown up in the Tower alone, more or less forgotten. Bishop Gardiner had looked after him, as he himself had been a prisoner there, and I imagined that his influence had assisted with Courtenay's release.

Mary had gifted Courtenay with a ring when he was presented to her, which he'd romantically proclaimed made him *her* prisoner.

Courtenay's mother, the Marchioness of Exeter, a close friend to Catherine of Aragon, had been freed and pardoned years earlier. Now Mary requested that the marchioness become a lady of the privy chamber.

As Uncle John had told me, Mary had released the Duke of Suffolk and others who'd conspired with Northumberland against her, though Northumberland and his sons remained under arrest, and Jane was still a prisoner.

But Mary's tolerance began to wane as Elizabeth evaded attending mass or even having it read to her in private by one of Mary's clergymen.

Elizabeth had not out-and-out refused, of course, but her excuses for not attending chapel became many and varied. We ladies of her household had done nothing overt against Mary's wishes, but we continued to read our daily devotions in English rather than Latin, and like Elizabeth, contrived to be elsewhere when it came time for mass.

Now Elizabeth faced the Bishop Gardiner—whom Mary had also freed—as he stood before her and interrogated her about this lack.

Bishop Gardiner was a rather handsome man, clean-shaven

with an almost triangular face and thick-lashed eyes. Those eyes had seen much and had grown hard and arrogant.

"The opportunity to attend mass is given to you six times a day," Bishop Gardiner said, his voice a dry crack. "Perhaps your duties have been too strenuous to allow you to attend chapel, Your Grace?"

"Indeed," Elizabeth responded coolly. "I have much to do."

"Then your tasks will be lightened," Gardiner answered without hesitation. "The attempt at the reformed religion is over, Your Grace. It failed. Her majesty the queen will restore the nation to the faith."

And restore you to power, you old goat, I thought from my place among Elizabeth's ladies.

Gardiner, once he'd knelt at Mary's feet and accepted his new position of Lord Chancellor, had plunged himself into restoring the church to its old glory. As far as I could tell, this meant rich robes on his back, money in his coffers, and the permission to cuff those against whom he held a personal grudge.

Today he'd decided to cuff Elizabeth. Elizabeth represented all Gardiner disliked, and he'd apparently decided to relieve his pique by lecturing her.

"It distresses the queen," Gardiner went on, "to have a sister who leans dangerously toward heresy. Her Majesty is in fear for your soul."

"I have no doubt." Elizabeth swept him and the nobles who'd accompanied him an imperious gaze. "I have been ill. My headaches are frequent, and my ladies remain to attend me."

"I am unhappy to hear of your poor health," Gardiner returned, though he looked not the least bit concerned. "The queen will send a priest to your chamber in the event you are too ill to attend chapel."

Elizabeth sat up straighter, her pale face more icy than usual.

She was not going to win, and the flash in her eyes told me she knew this.

However, she would not give Gardiner the satisfaction of witnessing her hanging her head, mumbling an apology, or begging him to intercede with Mary for her.

Elizabeth rose from her chair, indicating the audience over as far as she was concerned.

"I will give some thought to what you say." She nodded to the gentlemen of the council, who bowed as she swept from the chamber.

Gardiner's eyes sparkled in fury as he watched her go, which worried me not a little.

MARY HAD NOT SPOKEN MUCH TO ELIZABETH IN PRIVATE SINCE we'd arrived at Richmond, which I took to be an ominous sign. We did attend the queen's entertainments—which involved dancing, card games, or little theatricals put together for her.

Elizabeth loved to dance and would rise from her ostensible sickbed for that. I also knew she left it for the opportunity to chat and flirt with Edward Courtenay, who had swiftly become a popular gentleman.

Courtenay had spent most of his youth in the Tower, and now, at age twenty-seven, he found himself a member of Parliament, restored to his estates as Earl of Devon, and having a favored position in the queen's court.

I considered him rather pallid and foppish, but rumor had it that the queen's council hoped Mary would wed him. Courtenay was of the correct blood, being descended from Edward IV through his father, making him a second cousin to Mary and Elizabeth. He was of a good age to sire a son, and most importantly, native to this land.

I could not decide what Mary thought of him. She treated

him with courtesy but one that came more from pity than fascination.

Courtenay made it a point to smile at Mary and flatter her, but I heard scurrilous gossip that he enjoyed walking about London of nights and seeking the company of street courtesans. I supposed being locked away for so long had deprived him of the ordinary pleasures of gentlemen, but from what others whispered, he was now rather overdoing it.

He and Elizabeth made a good pair, I thought as I watched them dance, despite the vagaries in Courtenay's character. Both were young, energetic, and graceful. Courtenay knew he had the attention of both Mary and Elizabeth and preened under their interest.

"The queen considers him a match for Elizabeth," a voice said in my ear. I did not jump, because Colby had the habit of popping out of nowhere and beginning conversations in the middle of them.

"I would hope for someone rather better for her," I answered without turning to him.

"Are you a snob, Mistress Rousell?"

I heard amusement in Colby's voice. I glanced at him, taking in his slight smile as he fixed his gaze on the dancers in the middle of the warm room.

"Not usually," I said. "'Tis just that I do not think much of Courtenay. I've also heard rumors of a Continental marriage for Elizabeth, and that sending her from the country entirely would be best for Mary."

Colby's nod told me I'd heard aright. "They debate it in Parliament. But after Elizabeth, the heir is Mary Stuart of Scotland, with her very French ties. Mary prefers Elizabeth to a French-Scottish queen, no matter that Mary Stuart is so very Catholic."

"Then Elizabeth had better stay," I said decidedly. "But I still don't like Courtenay as a suitor for her." I studied Courtenay and his too-ready smile as he turned Elizabeth in the dance. "'Tis a pity Lord Robert is already married and that he so obediently raised an army in favor of poor Jane."

"Dudley is too ambitious and flies too high," Colby replied. "He will bring himself to grief."

I turned to him in surprise. "I thought Lord Robert your great friend."

"He is." Colby flashed me one of his rare grins. "Which is why I know he overreaches himself. He and the princess are matched in spirit, but that may not be a good thing."

I had to agree. "It is a bit worrying. What will become of Elizabeth, I mean."

"More than a bit."

The music had ended, the musicians stretching their fingers in fatigue, but Mary clapped her hands. "Another. A pavane. It is most diverting."

Ladies and gentlemen returned to the floor. Colby offered his hand to me and led me out.

Colby danced well, as trained as any courtier. As we moved in the steps of the pavane, I realized I still knew very little about him. He came from Shropshire, had been married young and was now a widower, as he'd told me, and Robert Dudley counted him a friend. Nothing more.

"At Lord Robert's wedding, you danced with me," I reminded him.

"Yes," Colby said as we turned toward the couple opposite us. "I recall."

"You seemed to find it tedious." I put annoyance into my tone.

Colby did not apologize or even appear contrite. "My mind was on other things that evening."

"Some scheme you were concocting with Lord Robert, no doubt."

"No doubt," he said, his amusement returning.

"I saw little of you at court before this," I remarked once we were relatively alone in the dance again.

A shrug. "I spend much time in the country."

"In Shropshire?"

"There, and other places," Colby answered without changing expression.

"You have many lands then?"

Colby bent an exasperated glare on me. "Not really. Why do you wish to know?"

I wanted to know because I was curious about this man no one ever talked of, and of whom I knew almost nothing.

Growing up in Elizabeth's household, and under the tutelage of Aunt Kat, I could recite the family trees of almost everyone Elizabeth came into contact with. I knew where they lived, what estates they owned, and could pinpoint them almost as well as Elizabeth herself.

Against this knowledge, James Colby was an enigma. It was clear he resented my prying, so I gave him a banal smile and went silent.

Colby continued the pavane with a frown. After the dance finished, he led me back to Elizabeth's ladies, bowed courteously, and departed without further word.

I watched him stride away, more curious about him than ever.

No one mentioned me speaking with Colby in a corner or even dancing with him, but when I returned with Elizabeth to her chamber later that night, she pinned me with a cold stare.

"I hope I shall not have to search for another seamstress once you marry yourself to a nobody, Eloise."

Marriage being the furthest thought from my mind, I gaped at her in amazement.

"Do close your mouth," Elizabeth said in irritation. "It will rust open if you do not."

I popped my lips together, but I could not let the matter

pass. "I have seen too few good examples of marriage that would make me want to pursue that state," I said vehemently. "Aunt Kat and Uncle John perhaps, but none other."

"Good." The word held finality. "I dislike it when my ladies marry and leave me, as though they no longer care for me. Would they all be like my mistress Blanche, who has been with me since my cradle." Her waspishness faded, and Elizabeth sent me a placating smile. "I have too much affection for you to let you go, Eloise."

I assured her again she would never lose me to marriage, and the matter was dropped.

CHAPTER 13

Autumn 1553

S everal days later, the agate-hard light reentered Elizabeth's eyes as she marched through Richmond Palace to have another audience with Mary. As I scuttled along behind her, I wondered if she would express her hot rage to Mary or be coldly offensive with her sister as she had been with Bishop Gardiner.

Mary likewise was in a temper by the time we reached her chamber. She thrust out her hand for Elizabeth to kneel to and kiss then snatched it away, leaving Elizabeth on her knees with no permission to rise.

"My council is displeased with you," Mary snapped. "And this displeases *me.*"

Whatever sisterly affection Mary had expressed in the euphoria of her rise to the throne was nowhere in evidence. She glared at Elizabeth with an outrage that reflected Henry Tudor.

Elizabeth stared back at Mary, their father reflected in her as well. Just when I thought Elizabeth might respond in kind, she burst into sobs and pressed her hands tightly to her face.

Elizabeth's body shook, but she never removed her fingers from her eyes. Perhaps she waited to manufacture tears before she raised her head to Mary again.

"You must forgive my backwardness, sister," Elizabeth said, her voice muffled. "I was raised in a household that taught nothing but the reformed faith. How can I transform myself in the space of weeks to something I have never known? I am all ignorance. Tell me, dear sister, what I can do to overcome this?"

While Mary's expression did not soften, I saw her unbend slightly at Elizabeth's contrite plea. She'd steeled herself for a long argument with heated, perhaps hateful words, and here was Elizabeth at her feet, weeping and begging for forgiveness.

"I am pleased to hear you acknowledge your error," Mary said stiffly. "I know so many who refuse to even admit they've been led astray. You will come to chapel with me, sister. You will show the world what it is to repent your sins and beg God and the Virgin for forgiveness."

I held my breath, waiting to see what Elizabeth would do.

I knew, through my whispered meetings with Colby whenever he sought me, that many in England were pleased that Elizabeth remained of the reformed religion. They hoped it meant that the reformed church could continue intact, in spite of Mary's wishes. If Mary would not force her own sister's conversion, they could believe the queen sincere in her wish for tolerance.

Mary appeared anything but tolerant as she stood over Elizabeth, her small hands clenched, her agitated breath pressing her bosom against her too-tight stomacher.

"Will you be willing to do as I ask?" Mary demanded.

Elizabeth gazed up at her sister, true tears on her face. "I beg you to give me books to read and a priest to instruct me. Help me to learn."

Mary bent to Elizabeth, the sapphire crucifix at her neck nearly swinging into Elizabeth's nose. "You will attend the

Chapel Royal with me next week at the Feast of the Nativity of the Virgin. May I send a litter to you for your convenience?"

"I will come." Elizabeth's voice held a quaver. "You are a kind, dear sister."

Mary at last relented. She lifted Elizabeth to her feet and then embraced and kissed her. Elizabeth daintily wiped her eyes and returned the kisses.

Mary dismissed her, watching her go with some suspicion, despite the hope Elizabeth had given her.

Mary's suspicions would have been justified if she'd witnessed Elizabeth storming into her chambers when we returned to them, overturning tables and flinging aside anything she could lay her hands on.

"The fool," Elizabeth snarled as I quickly closed the outer door. "She's buried herself in her piety all her life, and now she wants to drag me down with her. Can she not see that people do not want her church, can she not hear their muttering?"

One of her ladies, Elizabeth Sandes, a staunch believer in the reformed faith, snorted. "Not over the droning of Latin and the ringing of chancel bells," she said.

Elizabeth whirled on Mistress Sandes, her face red with rage. She glared at her lady for a few seconds, then abruptly burst into uproarious laughter.

Elizabeth began the morning of the Feast of the Nativity of the Blessed Virgin by being sick in a bowl, the stink of it tainting her bedchamber.

She'd not been fabricating when she'd informed Mary and her chancellor that she was a victim of severe headaches. They could confine Elizabeth to bed for days, with her ladies in constant attendance to place cool cloths on her brow and dose her with herbs.

"I am wretched," Elizabeth whispered. She clenched her teeth, her skin as colorless as the linens on her bed. "The pain tears at me like claws."

Mistress Sandes suggested we send word to Mary and beg her to let Elizabeth rest, but Elizabeth instructed Mistress Sandes to help her stand, determination in every move. "Lace me into my gown, Eloise. My sister shall see what I am made of."

We got her bathed and dressed, though it consumed most of the morning. The escorts who'd arrived to accompany us to the Chapel Royal grew impatient and irritated as Elizabeth kept them waiting.

It took a long while for us to traverse the grounds of the palace in the litter Mary had sent, as we had to move very slowly to not upset Elizabeth's head. Elizabeth lay against the cushions, a cloth on her forehead. We hovered beside the litter with herbal balls and worried expressions.

Inside the chapel, Elizabeth descended the litter, her cheeks almost gray. As she entered the royal box, high in the chapel, she pressed her hand to her stomach and sat down next to Mary, breathing heavily. Jane Dormer, sitting behind Mary, scowled her disapproval.

Mary slid out a hand to clasp her sister's. "I am pleased you have come. I shall not forget this."

"My head pains me something terrible," Elizabeth whispered back to her. "Let me sit quietly, or I am undone."

Mary nodded in understanding. Jane Dormer continued to frown, her skepticism evident.

Below us Bishop Gardiner began his chanting, the syllables filling the chapel. A huge Bible was open on a lectern before him —I could see its colorfully decorated pages from my place behind Elizabeth.

As Bishop Gardiner read the Magnificat—the Song of Mary

—his assistant priests waved smoking censers, coating the air with the thick scent of sandalwood and patchouli.

I found it oddly soothing, but Elizabeth groaned audibly, her voice mixing with the bishop's intonations. "My head. Mistress Sandes, quickly."

Mistress Sandes, who'd grimaced as soon as Gardiner had begun chanting, handed Elizabeth a silk ball filled with chamomile and lavender. Elizabeth pressed the pomander gratefully to her nose, closing her eyes and shutting out the heavy smell of incense.

Below us, the Holy Roman Emperor's ambassador, Simon Renard, scowled up at the box, his smooth face set in annoyance. Mary, though, showed only concern for Elizabeth as she held her sister's hand and chafed her wrist.

"*Gloria patri, et filio, et spiritui sancto,*" Gardiner sang.

The words were echoed by a soft retching sound from Elizabeth.

The service finally ended. Elizabeth, with Mary's blessing, climbed painfully into the litter, and we retreated to her chambers. Elizabeth complained loudly not only about her head but her stomach all the way back.

But her theatrics were successful. Not a few days later, Jane Dormer led several of Mary's ladies to Elizabeth's rooms and presented Elizabeth with jewels from the queen, a ruby-studded crucifix among them.

Elizabeth expressed her gratitude through them to Mary and accepted the jewels as though they were her due.

The crucifix she pushed to the back of a drawer and never took out again.

AUNT KAT, UNCLE JOHN, AND I WERE PRIVILEGED SPECTATORS OF Mary's coronation that October, allowed to watch the new queen enter the Tower and then leave it the next morning to process to Westminster.

Elizabeth, dressed in white and silver, rode in a carriage behind Mary with Anne of Cleves, Henry's fourth wife. I witnessed firsthand the cheers that arose when Elizabeth appeared, the Tudor princess, shining in the sunlight.

Luckily, Mary believed the adulation all for her. Wine ran freely in the streets, pipes flowing from wine shop to wine shop to dispense the drink to all. At Westminster Abbey, Mary stood proudly after the crown was lowered onto her head. Tears flooded her eyes as every man and woman bent knee to her.

During the coronation banquet, Elizabeth sat with Anne of Cleves, and both ladies were made much of.

"They say Elizabeth looks far more like a queen than her sister," Aunt Kat remarked to me as we celebrated that night in Elizabeth's chambers at Whitehall. "In many's opinion, the crown is on the wrong head."

"Kat," Uncle John admonished. We stood in a quiet corner, but Mary's spies could be anywhere.

"Not to worry, husband," Aunt Kat said quickly. "I've learned my lesson. No more dabbling in affairs of the crown. But I cannot help what others say."

"Mary is queen now, whatever that may bring." Uncle John released a resigned sigh. "Though I admit it did not bode well, Mary having to request one of her noble gentlemen to dub knights at her coronation instead of doing it herself. That only emphasized that she cannot do what a man can do. A woman cannot don armor and lead an army, and she cannot dub the naked knights of the bath."

"Will she marry Courtenay, then?" My mouth was full of sweetmeats, which I had overindulged in today. A serving man had let me take a tray of them into my hands, more fool he. "I cannot imagine Edward Courtenay as king. He would cause more trouble than Mary could soothe, I should think, from all I have heard about him."

"Mary is old," Aunt Kat said, forgetting that she herself was at least ten years Mary's senior. "Courtenay is the sort who will always want a young and pretty woman. Like our own princess."

Uncle John rumbled in his throat, and Aunt Kat flushed. "Never mind, John. I shall not give it another thought. She looked fine today, did our Elizabeth. She would make a regal queen."

I squeezed my eyes shut. "Please tell me you have not turned conspirator, Aunt."

"Of course not," Aunt Kat said in surprise. "But Mary isn't yet married, is she? She might be too old to bear children, in any case—she is thirty-seven after all. Elizabeth is her heir. Elizabeth may be queen before our time on earth is out. No need for conspiracies at all."

Colby, I mused as I nibbled another sweetmeat, thought differently. He did not seem to be a man willing to sit back and wait to see whether Mary bore children or not.

I'd decided that Colby wanted me to remain close to Elizabeth for two reasons—first to keep her safe, and second to ferret out whether she would support any schemes dreamt up by him and Lord Robert.

I understood why Colby might plot to put Elizabeth on the throne. Elizabeth was English, born of Tudor Henry and an English gentlewoman. Mary was half Spanish and sympathetic to the Holy Roman Empire.

Mary wanted to pull England back under the harness of the pope, while Elizabeth wished England to remain free and unencumbered. The Holy Roman Empire was strong and vast, its Hapsburg princes more than ready to snare England in its net.

Colby and Dudley were clever, popular, and rash. Colby had dragged me right into the heart of things by confiding too much in me. If I were sensible, I would flee at the very sight of the man and refuse to speak to him again.

But secretly I agreed with Colby. If a plot came to oust Mary, I would be in the thick of it, risking my neck to help my princess. I knew this as well as I knew my own name.

"SHE IS SLY," SIMON RENARD, THE IMPERIAL AMBASSADOR, SAID. "Not to be trusted."

Mary nodded reluctantly, her misgivings visible in the stiffness of her response.

I had no business eavesdropping on the queen and the Empire's ambassador, but I took the opportunity that had dropped into my lap. I'd entered an antechamber of the queen's rooms to visit Jane Dormer, who'd sent word that she had messages and gifts for me from my mother. Jane visited her far more frequently than did I—I'd had little to do with my mother since entering Aunt Kat's guardianship.

When Jane had departed to fetch the items, I'd remained seated on a stool behind a screen in the little room, out of the drafts. Before Jane could return, Mary and Ambassador Renard had strolled inside for a private chat.

I stilled, peering through slits in the ornate wooden screen, but it was clear they did not see me. Renard, the imprudent man, began speaking before he ascertained whether the room was clear.

"I do *not* trust her," Mary said with hesitation.

I could hear in her voice that this declaration made her unhappy. Lonely Mary, who wanted a happy family, was having to acknowledge that becoming queen had not ended all hardship in her life.

"She has wriggled out of mass for nearly a month," Renard went on. "And she has not made use of the books you sent her. I hear she laughs with her ladies about them and openly defies you."

My skin prickled with anger. It was not true that Elizabeth openly defied Mary, but ignoring the books could be taken as such. Damn Renard for interpreting her actions so.

"I open Parliament tomorrow." Mary put her stubby fingers to her lips, her many rings flashing. "Where the old religion will be restored, and my mother's marriage to my father reinstated as lawful."

"A perfect time to remind others that your father's marriage to the Boleyn woman was never valid." Renard almost purred with his satisfaction. He had a large nose below wide, rather intense dark eyes, ones that might have made him attractive if they weren't so cooly calculating.

"It was not, was it?" Mary's voice took on a note of eagerness. "My mother was England's true queen, as am I. My father's second wife was … inappropriate." Pious Mary could not bring herself to say the word *whore*, which was what Anne Boleyn's detractors had always called her. "I have ever wondered, you know, whether my sister was born my father's daughter at all. She bears resemblance to that musician from her mother's court, Mark Smeaton, who was condemned to death for having improper relations with the Boleyn woman." Mary rocked on her feet as she warmed to the subject. "I imagine that it is true, that Smeaton is Elizabeth's father. Why should such a person be heir apparent to my throne?"

The words shocked me all the way through, and I knew them for a lie.

I had never known Mark Smeaton, being a tiny girl when he'd died, days before Anne herself was executed. But I remembered Henry, and I had seen Henry and Elizabeth together.

Elizabeth had Henry's red hair, his flashing eyes, his mercurial moods, his temper. When Elizabeth worked herself into a rage, her expressions and her movements were all Henry's.

But I knew enough of court machinations by now to realize that the truth did not always matter. If Mary convinced enough people to speculate on Elizabeth's legitimacy, to cast doubt on her possessing any Tudor blood at all, she could effectively bar Elizabeth from the throne forever.

"I will speak to my council about it," Mary continued, her conviction growing. "You are correct that my supposed sister is crafty. Her blatant disregard of my wishes over her conversion sets a dangerous precedent. I am willing to forgive those who have strayed from the church, but not Elizabeth, if she is so obstinate." Mary's voice rose as she began to pace, the light from a brazier catching on the pearls of her hood. "She will not have the throne. She will remain in the country or be married off abroad, but she will not rule. Never. That is my wish."

Renard sent her an assessing glance. "As we talk of marriage, dear lady, the earl—Courtenay—he is too frivolous for you. A wiser, steadier gentleman is what you deserve, one who will love you and help you rule in your best interest."

Mary plopped down on the room's one armchair in a rush, color flooding her face. "Courtenay is too fond of worldly pleasures, I agree. I had already decided that."

From the rise and fall of her bosom and her easy dismissal of Courtenay, I guessed that she'd already entertained the notion of another. Courtenay was to be disappointed, if he thought he'd be king.

"I believe we are of one mind, Your Grace," Renard said, approval in his voice.

"Indeed."

The pair fell silent, and for a moment I thought they would depart without revealing the name of this sainted man Mary would woo, but then Renard chuckled.

"We speak of Philip, the son of Charles, our Emperor, do we not?" he asked. "A perfect match. I believe your affection lies in that direction?"

Mary smiled, her blush almost girlish. "I *am* a woman."

A silly one, I thought vehemently. I knew nothing about this Philip, but I gleaned that a marriage to anyone connected to the Empire would be a mistake. Courtenay, for his faults, was at least from these isles.

Mary sprang up on light feet. "I believe Philip and I will deal well together. I now have another proposition to put before Parliament."

She shared a smile with Renard, then Renard bowed as she turned and walked from the room, leaving the ambassador behind.

I tried very hard not to move or make a sound, but perhaps a breath escaped my lips. Renard turned sharply as he prepared to follow his queen out and surveyed the room.

At that moment, the shutter of an open window high above creaked in a sharp breeze. Renard glanced at the window, relaxed, and padded out of the chamber.

When I reported this conversation to Colby, he regarded me with pure alarm.

We stood in a little-used corridor, I with my arms full of fabric, he having entered from outside. We'd arranged the meeting, but to anyone passing it would look as though we'd come upon each other by chance in the middle of errands, perhaps even halting a moment to flirt.

"She cannot possibly cut Elizabeth from the succession," Colby said in a low, fierce voice. "Nor can we tolerate a marriage to Philip of Spain. We shall be in the hands of the Empire, and England will be swallowed whole. If Mary pushes this marriage through, we will have to act."

"Act?" I repeated, my breath deserting me.

"Yes, act, Mistress Rousell. Did you believe us only full of pretty words?"

I was uncertain what to think. Conspiracies were fashionable during any reign—young, wealthy, and well-born gentlemen grew restless and decided that they'd change the world to suit them.

Their need for change often dwindled into nothing more than bold words sworn over ale in taverns, but Colby's angry gaze told me he had moved from words to careful planning.

Planning meant raising money and gathering men at arms, leaving hearth and home to march against the monarch.

I realized as we stood in that chilly passageway that Colby had told me far too much. He could not risk that I would not run straight to Mary.

Colby must have read the worry in my eyes, because he placed strong hands on my shoulders. "I trust you, Eloise. It is not blind trust, either. I know you love Elizabeth and would do anything to keep her from harm. I would do the same. You may put your trust in *me.*"

"I am not reassured," I said, lifting my chin.

"There is danger coming. Much danger—to you, to me, to *her.* If you cannot bear that, then leave her household immediately and return to your mother. Stay quietly in her popish home and forget about our Lady Elizabeth."

I swallowed as Colby gave me details about my life I had not told him. "You know much about my family."

"I know everything about you, Eloise Rousell." Colby's grin flashed. "I would not have approached you had I not found out all about you. I believed I had measure of you."

I hid my flinch. "How comforting."

"Dudley trusts you, though he can be more of a fool about people than I. But in this instance, he was correct."

"More comfort." My heart thumped. "You know much about

me, but I know nothing about you. How can I be certain I can trust *you*?"

Colby lost his smile, and his cheekbones stained red. "You know all you need to know."

"Which is next to nothing," I continued stubbornly. "Not even the name of the wife you married."

"She came from no important family. You would not recognize her."

Colby's mouth had tightened, not with anger, but with trepidation, I realized in surprise.

I wondered what he was hiding, and I resolved to find out. If my fate was in his hands, I needed all the information about him I could gather.

"There is someone approaching, Master Colby," I said as footsteps sounded in the passageway beyond us. "Perhaps you ought to release me."

Instead of complying, Colby pulled me all the way against him and pressed a kiss to my mouth.

The kiss was brief and unexpected, but my lips went hot beneath his, and my breath came close to choking me. Colby held me firmly but not harshly, his touch almost tender.

He stepped back as one of Mary's ladies came around the corner. A mercy he did, because I thought I'd never breathe again.

Colby was not quick enough to prevent Mary's lady from spying us. Her brows went up and her mouth down, but she passed by with the barest of nods.

I understood what he'd been doing. Better that Mary's lady spread the news that I was kissing James Colby in back corridors, than that we'd been speaking about preventing the queen's marriage scheme, by force if necessary.

Colby gave me a somber nod before he turned and strode away from me, his dark tunic and riding breeches soon lost in the shadows.

I spent a long time trying to catch my breath, my heart burning.

Colby had kissed me, but it had been a ruse. On the other hand, the soft imprint of his lips refused to fade and stayed with me the rest of that afternoon and long into the night.

I DETERMINED, AFTER THAT ENCOUNTER WITH COLBY IN THE passageway, to discover everything I could about him.

But strangely, though I asked as many questions as I dared over the next several days, I found no one who truly knew anything about the man or what his life had been before he'd joined Elizabeth's household. Even Uncle John, who'd obtained the position in the guards for him, confirmed he'd come from a quiet, genteel family in Shropshire, but little else. The one gentleman who might know—Robert Dudley—remained locked in the Tower.

I informed Elizabeth of the conversation I'd overheard between Mary and Ambassador Renard about cutting Elizabeth out of the succession.

Not surprisingly, Elizabeth flew into one of her rages. Not only was Mary trying to bar her from the throne, but she'd speculated that Elizabeth was not even Henry's child. The entire business made her ill again with fury.

Elizabeth stewed in a foul temper the day Mary opened her first Parliament, but Elizabeth's anger and my fears turned out to be premature.

Mary managed to restore the legitimacy of Catherine of Aragon's marriage to Henry—implying that his marriage to Anne Boleyn therefore was not—but Mary's wish to disinherit Elizabeth was never entertained.

I learned later from Uncle John that the wiser gentlemen in Mary's council had persuaded her that cutting Elizabeth out of the succession posed far more risk than retaining her as the legitimate heir. All Mary had to do, the council said, was to find a husband and provide an heir—naturally, Elizabeth would then be moved down the line of succession.

Mary capitulated, though I heard that her words to her advisors on the matter were harsh.

After that, she seemed to decide that if she could not stymie Elizabeth by law, she would severely cut at her in personal ways.

In the cold days of early winter, Mary invited Margaret Douglas—King Henry's niece by his sister Margaret, and a firebrand in her own right—to live with her and be her closest companion. The pair of them cut out Elizabeth at every turn, who by rights should be next to her sister in importance at court gatherings.

Margaret now rode with the queen when they went out for exercise, leaving Elizabeth behind. Margaret followed just behind Mary when she moved through the palace, forcing Elizabeth to trail after them. Margaret did this gleefully, making certain everyone knew she'd been honored above Elizabeth.

Elizabeth's temper soured, and her headaches grew worse.

When one day Mary chastised Elizabeth for having a private chat with the French ambassador—implying that Elizabeth leaned toward treachery—Elizabeth came to the end of her patience.

She asked stiffly to be allowed to retreat to her estate at Ashridge in west Hertfordshire for Christmas. Mary's crowded and hectic court hurt her health, Elizabeth claimed, and she needed to heal in the country air.

Mary smiled and acquiesced. She bade Elizabeth a pretty farewell and bestowed on her lovely furs to keep her warm during the journey.

CHAPTER 14

The problem with returning to Ashridge was that, no matter how beautiful I found this corner of Hertford-shire, we were isolated from the court and its gossip. While the privy council believed that anything decided within its body was secret and private, rumor of every discussion and decision ran through the halls of the palaces almost the moment they happened.

In the country, on the other hand, the news we received was days stale. Elizabeth, however, made it clear she was determined to rusticate as long as Mary held sway with her foolishness.

We would rusticate with her, as Elizabeth liked her ladies close to her at all times. I asked Colby, somewhat waspishly, what on earth I could do to help while stuck in drafty cham-bers at Ashridge Priory. He told me that watching over Eliza-beth and reporting to her what intelligence he brought me was enough. He'd said it serenely, but I chafed at the inactivity.

Elizabeth allowed Colby, as a gentleman of her household, to come and go as he pleased. Because he was not an important nobleman, he was often able to discover information others could not. Most of what we learned about Mary's plans and desires in the next months came from him and Uncle John.

Thus, we were aware when Mary succeeded in ramming her proposed marriage to Philip of Spain down the collective throats of Parliament.

The gentlemen in the House of Lords had at least persuaded her to agree that Philip would not rule as king over Mary's English subjects. Mary conceded, though reluctantly, but all believed Philip would have more sway once he fathered the heir to the English throne.

I did not need to be at court to learn that the proposed marriage was opposed by all. Even those in the village at Ashridge shared the sentiment.

"They'll sing Spanish songs in the streets and outlaw the good English tongue," one woman said darkly to me when I'd gone to the high street to purchase extra pins. "No good will come of it."

I heard that phrase repeatedly: *No good will come of it.*

No more, *Blessed Mary, Queen of England.* It was grumbling that a woman could not possibly rule well—she needed a husband, but an *English* one.

Philip was heir to the kingdom of Spain and son of the Holy Roman Emperor. His father, lofty Charles the Fifth, was encouraging the marriage so he could use England as a contingency against the uncertainty of France and the Netherlands.

If Philip and Charles had their way, England would become an adjunct of Spain and the Empire, and even the lowest, most illiterate farmer in the fields around Ashridge knew it.

Worries were echoed all over England.

If the marriage to a Spaniard takes place, a man in Norfolk was reported to have said, *the Spaniards should have our houses, and we should live like slaves.*

Edward Courtenay, who'd fancied himself husband to Mary, was openly disgruntled and styled himself ill-treated.

"No good will come of it," Aunt Kat repeated to me one afternoon as I supped with her and Uncle John. "Mary has stated that her private wishes are more important than her privy council's or even Parliament's advice. Can you credit it? Says *she* knows the hearts of the people." Aunt Kat harumphed and shook her head. "She cannot be listening with her ears if she believes that. If she marries this *Felipe,* she will be hated as the queen who let another realm rule us. Church bells will ring dirges instead of joyous peals."

Her words dredged up the dream I'd had when we'd met Mary at Wanstead in the summer—the pall of smoke and the feeling of despair.

"Philip is Catholic," I pointed out. "And Mary loves the church more than anything."

"Courtenay is Catholic," Aunt Kat said vehemently. "Even if he is ridiculous."

"Too fond of bodily pleasures," Uncle said. "Gluttony, avarice, and lechery will be Courtenay's downfall."

"And pride," I added.

"How short-sighted you both are," Aunt Kat snapped. "Courtenay could be brought to heel by Mary's council. He'd prance around with his crown and enjoy himself, without threatening the queen's rule. This foreign prince will be the death of us."

Neither Uncle John nor I had any argument to that.

COLBY WAS OFTEN GONE FROM ASHRIDGE FOR LONG STRETCHES of time. Elizabeth never discussed these absences, and when I once mentioned, casually, that I hadn't seen much of Master Colby lately, she quieted me with a sharp word.

I longed to speak to Colby, because he was the only one who

confided in me. Uncle John kept Elizabeth informed as he could, but Colby usually knew details Uncle John did not. Colby seemed to have ways to dig deeper and discover truths.

Ashridge was cold and dismal that winter. Its buildings were old and oddly laid out, with huge, drafty halls downstairs and tiny, uncomfortable rooms above them. The house and grounds had once been a monastery, and little had changed since the days of the monks twenty years before.

I began to lie in wait for Colby in the chamber he'd been given—he shared with no one, which was most unusual. The first night that I waited until dawn, he did not appear, nor did he on the second.

On the third night, my effort was rewarded. At the hour after midnight, his door scraped quietly open.

Colby beheld me dozing on his bed by the small hearth, and quickly shut the door.

"Mistress Rousell, what do you here?" he asked softly and angrily.

I slid off the bed as he lit tapers with a spill from the fireplace's flames. Cold radiated from the cloak he tossed to a bench, and his clothes were scented with smoke and the outdoors.

"Please tell me what is happening," I begged him in a low voice. "I can hardly be your go-between if I know nothing."

Colby's expression was hard and stern, more so than I'd ever seen it. "Seeking me is dangerous, Eloise."

"That is most obvious. But I am already in danger—you placed me squarely in it. I'll not be like dear Jane, shutting my eyes to the plots around me even when I am in the thick of them."

Colby regarded my resolute face before he let out his breath. "Very well." He swept his cloak from the bench and indicated I should sit there with him while we warmed our feet at the fire.

"We have been meeting," he began, keeping his voice hushed. His shoulder brushed mine, his body warm despite the fact that he'd come in from the freezing rain. "I and others, and Courtenay."

"Courtenay?" I whispered, surprised. "What on earth for?"

"Courtenay has money, and he is not happy with Mary for deciding against marrying him. Courtenay is descended from the Yorkists and considers himself an heir to the throne—which he more or less is, by blood. He opposes the marriage to Philip as much as the rest of us do. Perhaps not for the same reasons, but it hardly matters."

"He was released from the Tower not a six-month ago," I pointed out. "Is he so anxious to return to it?"

"He is not worried. There is enough resentment against the queen that we have a chance at prevailing. We'll put Elizabeth on the throne, and Courtenay will not return to prison. I, like you, do not much fancy the man as king, but one thing at a time."

A shiver ran through me. "So, you mean to actually dethrone her?" I murmured. "Not simply petition her to change her mind?"

Colby huffed a mirthless laugh. "Mary does not listen to her Parliament or her counselors, not even to her beloved Bishop Gardiner. Gardiner wishes her to marry Courtenay, but Mary has done the equivalent of stamping her feet and declaring she will act as she pleases. She'd never bend to a petition by her nobles."

"Next you will tell me that gentlemen in Parliament will not meekly bow their heads and go about their business," I said darkly.

Colby gazed at me for a long time, his eyes almost azure in the firelight. "You have guessed correctly. I can give you no details, but things are in motion. There will be a French fleet.

Elizabeth was able to speak to the French ambassador before she left court. We will succeed."

I digested all this in silence. I remembered Mary's anger when she'd discovered Elizabeth's meetings with the French ambassador. Had she an inkling of what was going on, or had she simply been annoyed at Elizabeth for charming the gentleman behind her back?

"You are putting our lady in grave danger," I said. "Any move against the queen will draw Mary's attention to Elizabeth like a hound on the scent of the largest hart."

"There will be no communication with Elizabeth directly," Colby said. "That is why we need you. You will tell her all, but she must do nothing. Like you, she need not have all the details. If it comes to pass that the plot is revealed, she will know no more about it than do her questioners."

I recalled Aunt Kat's lurid descriptions of the dark Tower room in which she'd been confined, with no fire to warm her and no certainty she'd live to return home.

Aunt Kat had been ashamed that the threat of torture had loosened her tongue, but I could wholly understand why it had. The same fate might come to me, or Aunt Kat again, or to Elizabeth herself.

"I am not afraid," I said, my voice steady. "I can keep my silence."

Colby's glance was approving. "You are a good and loyal friend to her."

"It is more than loyalty. Elizabeth has a nasty temper, and she can be haughty and selfish, but that does not matter. She is who she was born to be, and I will protect her from Mary as long and hard as I can."

"You are an unusual woman, Mistress Rousell," Colby said in a tone of respect.

I shrugged. "Perhaps because I was rejected by my own family. Her family cast her off when she was a child, so we have that in common. Elizabeth has rewarded me well for my service, even befriended me, and now she trusts me. Perhaps I took to her as an orphaned lamb might take to a shepherd boy."

One corner of Colby's mouth turned up. "Either that, or you lie very skillfully, and tomorrow my head will be on the block."

His humor was grim, and I studied him quietly. "Let it rest easy on your pillow tonight." I lightly patted the head in question, finding springy russet hair. "Although I must say, having slept here the past two nights, that while Elizabeth has awarded you privacy, she must have given you the most uncomfortable bed in the place."

Colby's brows went up. "You slept here?"

"I had no way of knowing when you would return, and I was too weary to make my way to my own chamber. No matter, I aired the bedding each morning, so you have no cause to worry."

"I'd not worry over that." Colby's blue eyes fixed on me. "We must invent a better way of keeping you informed that will not endanger your reputation."

I rose, my cold limbs stiff. "There is no danger in that regard. No one notices what seamstress Eloise does. That is why you chose me to help you, is it not?"

"One of the reasons," Colby said quietly.

We shared a long look that I could not interpret. He did not rise, as a gentleman should when a lady got to her feet, but his tallness meant I easily met his gaze.

I flashed him a sunny smile as he stared at me, and then left the room for the overly cold passages of Ashridge in December.

COLBY DISAPPEARED AGAIN A FEW DAYS AFTER THAT, AND I SAW nothing more of him for a long while. I reported our conversation to Elizabeth, who listened without a flicker of emotion.

She ordered me, once I finished, to never say anything aloud about it again. Also, I was to keep everything I knew from Aunt Kat. I agreed. After the debacle with Seymour, we could not rely on Aunt Kat not to chatter in the excited way she had, wishing to prove to others she knew something they did not.

We spent a quiet Christmas season at Ashridge which led into a dark and cold January. Mary sent Elizabeth religious books, chasubles for her priests, and ornaments for her altar. Elizabeth packed them away and never looked at them.

Mary held lavish entertainments to celebrate Christmas and Epiphany while Elizabeth seethed, knowing Margaret Douglas would be at Mary's side.

"All will be pitying me," she said with irritation one evening as we faced each other over a chessboard. "Or they are gloating. The shunned bastard sister festers in the country, while Margaret plays the virginals and smiles at the queen. Margaret, Countess of Lennox, once sent to the Tower for behaving like a wanton. A plotter and a schemer is Margaret. Now she is the favorite of the queen." Elizabeth abruptly seized the white marble queen from the board and hurled it into the flickering hearth fire. "Fine company my sister keeps."

I forbore to remind Elizabeth that she'd loathed being at Mary's court so much that she'd begged for permission to leave. I feared one of the heavy chessmen would be fired at me if I mentioned it. "Things might be different, come spring," I said.

Elizabeth's temper did not ease, though she pitched her voice so only I could hear. "God save me from plotting men. Plans can go wrong, and here I sit, unable to direct them, a help-less pawn." The chess piece in question flew across the room to splinter against a wall.

Her ladies looked up from their embroidery, but wisely said nothing and resumed stitching.

Earlier that day, a message had come to Elizabeth from one of her gentlemen, Thomas Wyatt, who'd encouraged her to move to Donnington, an estate she owned, carefully not saying why.

"Ridiculous," Elizabeth had said to me. "How would it look if I fled Ashridge now? Guilty. I must sit here as though I know nothing, as though I am utterly astonished that anyone in the realm could move against the queen. I will wait and do as I see cause."

She had begun to write as much in a letter to Wyatt, but before she'd penned more than two words, I stopped her with the extreme caution I'd developed since the Seymour affair.

"Easy to deny a spoken word, Your Grace," I'd said. "But if anything goes wrong, and a letter by you to Wyatt is found ..."

"You have become devious, Eloise." Elizabeth had immediately risen from her writing desk and burned the sheet. "And cleverer than you ought to be. But I believe you advise well. Say no more of this."

I assured her of my silence, and she sent one of her ushers to Wyatt with a message so banal that no one but the conspirators would be able to make anything of it.

Now, Elizabeth leaned over the chessboard to me, bitterness in her voice. "The trouble with being the second person in the realm is that there are those constantly plotting to make you the first. So that you will reward them well, of course."

"Not Colby," I said quickly. "He understands the damage Mary's marriage will do to the kingdom. He knows that the best person for England is you."

"Guard your tongue," Elizabeth said curtly, but she did not look angry. She serenely set up the chess pieces again, though how we were to play without her pawn or my queen I did not know. "These are things *women* would not think to discuss."

"Of course, you are correct, Your Grace," I responded with a nod. "Forgive me."

"I would, though, devise a way in which I might speak to these men. Writing, as you say, is too perilous."

"Colby is trustworthy," I said with great assurance. I'd come to believe in him.

"Indeed, I believe he is, but he can be in only so many places at once."

She frowned at the chessboard, and I leaned to her, excited I could at last contribute something practical.

"I have had ideas about that," I said. "I would be honored to use them to assist you, Your Grace."

"What ideas?" Elizabeth's eyes glittered as they did when she was adamant about something.

In a low voice I described what I'd pondered when Aunt Kat had been in the Tower, and I'd longed to communicate with Elizabeth.

No one thought anything of me stitching in corners and showing Elizabeth my work. Sewing messages blatantly into fabric could be found and interpreted, but I'd devised a sort of code using short and long stitches, or knots or edging, each of which could represent certain letters or phrases. In the few years between the first concept and now, I'd developed the code into what I thought would be most useful.

Elizabeth grew as eager as she listened and agreed my scheme would work, though she wanted a hand in perfecting it.

We drew back from the discussion and composed ourselves, resuming the game of chess, but her confidence had returned.

"You speak of Master Colby much," Elizabeth said as she moved a knight to intercept one of my bishops. "Are you in love with him?"

I started, dragging my mind from the intriguing business of ciphers. "In love? Goodness no, Your Grace. I do like Colby, though. He is sensible."

Elizabeth very carefully removed her fingers from the knight. "Because I could not do without you, Eloise."

So she'd said to me at Richmond after she'd seen me dance

with Colby. "I have no intention of leaving, Your Grace," I answered with all sincerity.

"My affection for you is too strong," Elizabeth continued in a hard monotone. "And I would be broken-hearted to lose you to marriage."

"No fear of that," I assured her.

The wrong husband, I had learned from watching Jane Grey and now Mary, could land a woman in a world of trouble.

CHAPTER 15

Toward the end of January, the worst happened.

Mary's spies discovered that a French fleet waited across the Channel to sail to England at a moment's notice. Next, Mary decided to recall to court one Sir Peter Carew, but he, being too busy raising and training troops for the rebellion Thomas Wyatt planned, ignored the summons. Thereupon, Mary dispatched trusted gentlemen to find out what he was up to.

Once all this was known, Edward Courtenay, the weak link in the chain, lost his nerve. Taxed to tell what he knew, he broke down and confessed the entire plot to his mentor, Bishop Gardiner.

Gardiner was horrified. Courtenay was one of his favorites, a young man he'd nurtured when they'd both been sequestered in the Tower. Likely fearing he'd be implicated by association, Gardiner immediately reported the entire tale to the queen.

The conspirators panicked when Courtenay babbled all and began their armed rebellion months before they'd planned to.

The gentlemen leading it—the Duke of Suffolk, Sir Peter

Carew, Sir James Crofts, and Thomas Wyatt—had rather counted on their countrymen rising with them. However, the farmers and yeomen they tried to recruit didn't wish to risk their lives against their queen's soldiers and stayed home. Only Wyatt was able to raise any sort of force at all.

The other conspirators gave up quickly, but Wyatt resolutely marched to London with his army. Wyatt must have been gifted with a silver tongue, because Mary's troops sent out to stop him turned around and joined him. This large force then made its way toward Mary, who waited at Whitehall Palace for news.

I heard the details of the entire affair from Colby later. At the time, Elizabeth and I shivered in the cold, dark manor at Ashridge, knowing little.

Apparently, Mary, in desperation, made her way to the City of London—whose people at first were fervently on the side of Wyatt's rebels—and asked for a personal audience with the Lord Mayor and the guilds.

The City had always intrigued me, one square mile surrounded by high walls, within which the people had their own laws, their own guards, their own lives, so different and removed from any other place in London, or indeed, England. Even the monarch lived outside it, apart.

If the men of the City opened the gates and admitted Wyatt's soldiers, Mary would be finished, and she knew it.

Wyatt would take Mary captive—and then what? Would he dare execute the true monarch? Or would he imprison her in the country, as her mother had been imprisoned, stripped of her rank and wealth, a condition in which Mary had spent much of her young life?

Mary must have known all this, because her speech, as I heard of it later, was impassioned.

I am your queen, she began to the gentlemen of the Guildhall. *At my coronation, I was wedded to the realm and the laws of the same.*

The spousal ring I have on my finger, which never hitherto was, nor hereafter shall be, left off.

I imagined her standing in the lofty hall, perhaps on a bench or platform so she might be seen over all heads, lifting her hand so that her coronation ring flashed in the light.

You promised your allegiance and obedience to me. And I say to you, on the word of a prince, I cannot tell how naturally the mother loveth the child, for I was never the mother of any. There would be pain in this statement, unfeigned. *But certainly, if a prince and governor may as naturally and earnestly love her subjects, as the mother doth love the child, then assure yourselves, that I being your lady and mistress, do as earnestly and tenderly love and favor you. I doubt not but we shall give these rebels a short and speedy overthrow.*

She'd paused for a moment, then added, for the few unmoved: *I never intended to marry outside the realm, but by my council's consent and advice. I assure you now, I shall never marry anyone but he with whom all my subjects shall be content.*

They cheered her, those men of the City, bolstered by her words and her fervent speech.

Mary had swept from the hall, surrounded by her gentlemen and ladies, to return to Whitehall and wait to discover whether her plea had any effect.

ON ASH WEDNESDAY, AT THE END OF FEBRUARY, WYATT LED HIS forces into Southwark, where he meant to cross northward over the Thames. The City, its people won by Mary's eloquence and her bravery at facing down the Guildhall, closed off London Bridge to him.

Wyatt was forced to march his troops far to the west to cross the river, and so from there made his way to Whitehall.

Mary had been sitting in the gallery above the Holbein gate

when Wyatt's men stormed it. I heard that Mary's yeomen guards had fled their posts before the enemy, allowing Wyatt and his soldiers to batter the gates unopposed.

Only Mary herself stood fast, sharply telling those in the room to stay and defend her person.

As it happened, Mary's guards did not have to fight to the last man. The gates below remained closed, strong enough to hold against the onslaught.

Wyatt continued past Whitehall toward the City, with Mary's soldiers, more heartened now, chasing after them.

Thus, Wyatt found himself squeezed between Ludgate, which had been closed and barred by the Lord Mayor's command, and Mary's soldiers behind him. He had no choice but to surrender.

The rebels were led to the Tower to await Mary's judgment.

ELIZABETH PACED HER CHAMBER IN AGITATION, SUNLIGHT flashing on the gold flowers embroidered on her gown.

"She tells me it is for my safety," Elizabeth snarled to Aunt Kat, who had just read aloud the letter Mary had sent Elizabeth.

The rebellion was over. Wyatt reposed in the Tower along with the Duke of Suffolk and other noblemen who'd wanted Elizabeth on the throne and Mary off it.

Just before the fighting had begun, Mary had sent a pleasantly worded letter to Ashridge, inviting Elizabeth to join her at court, where she would be safe.

She'd sent a second letter, now that the uprising had been quelled, repeating the request. Elizabeth might be in more danger, Mary claimed, if any who had escaped arrest decided to retaliate against both queen and princess.

"It is nonsense," Elizabeth scoffed. *"Run to me, sweet sister, and I will keep you safe.* In a nice, locked room in the Tower, no doubt. I hear that Jane Grey's father has returned there to his beloved daughter and son-in-law Guildford. Mary was a bloody idiot to let Suffolk out, and he was a greater idiot to get himself tossed back in. She cannot let them live now, you know."

I thought of Jane sitting innocently in her prison, by all reports happy that people had left her alone with her reading. She was guilty of nothing but obeying difficult parents.

"You're not going to answer this summons are you?" I asked worriedly.

"I have no intention of it." Elizabeth ceased pacing and glared at Aunt Kat and me both. "I am ill, and it is far too cold to travel. Mary must make do with keeping me penned here. What can I, stifled in the country, do? I had no knowledge of these deeds, and I will hide here from the bad men. Bring me paper, Mistress Kat, and I will write it to her."

The letter was penned and dispatched, and not long later came Mary's curt reply that Elizabeth must attend her, *immediately*. Mary would send an armed escort, she said, to see that Elizabeth was protected on her way to London.

Elizabeth's claims of illness were unfeigned—she'd been quite unwell all winter. Her head had ached worse than ever, and her limbs had bloated until she could wear none but the loosest garments.

Mary, of course, did not believe her. Hard on the heels of Mary's summons came a physician, who closeted himself a few hours with Elizabeth. When he finally emerged, he declared she was indeed fit to travel, at least as far as London.

"The man is a damned charlatan," Elizabeth raged once he'd gone. "If I drop over dead en route, blame will be laid at his door, but small comfort that will be to me."

Her fury made her even more wretched, but there was nothing for it. If she did not go, Mary might simply arrest her and drag her to prison with the rest of the rebels.

We began our journey to London on a chill day not long

after Wyatt's surrender, Elizabeth in a litter. I rode with the rest of her gentlewomen behind the main entourage, trying to ignore Mary's armed riders who accompanied us.

It was fine weather for a journey, crisp and cold but fair. Elizabeth's banners snapped in the wind, and her gentlemen ushers wore her colors. As we passed through villages, people ran out to wave and cheer.

Our progress was slow. After only six miles, the cold and Elizabeth's pain forced us to put up for the night. The outriders took us to a large house well off the road, the gentleman who owned it scrambling to accommodate us.

The house that emptied for us was cold. Aunt Kat ordered fires built in every room, chivying the house's servants, much to the country gentleman's dismay. Aunt Kat bustled about shouting orders to Elizabeth's ladies, many of whom were exhausted and almost ill themselves.

"Lord, help me." Elizabeth spoke the words in fury once she reached her chamber, as though to hide her pathetic weariness. She hated to face Mary and whatever waited in London from a state of weakness, although I suspected she'd find a way to use the weakness to her advantage.

Being of a robust nature, I found myself recruited to make Elizabeth comfortable in her small chamber, to lay rugs and hang curtains, to fetch warm drinks and wine. I supported Elizabeth's head while she sipped from a cup, and I massaged her wrists. Her hands and face had again swollen, and she groaned in earnest when she sank back on the bed.

"Now will they believe me ill?" she demanded. "I hardly could have invented this. Oh, take the wine away, Eloise, and cease your fussing."

I backed from her, secretly pleased that she barked at me, because her temper indicated she was not in grave danger. Mistress Sandes, Elizabeth's favorite, took my place, and Elizabeth turned her groans and growls to her.

I did more running about for Aunt Kat and for the other ladies who were unwell, working far into the night. When the chaos in the house wound to a dull clamor—Elizabeth at last slept, and the ladies and gentlemen of her household had settled themselves—I wrapped myself in a cloak and slipped out into the darkness.

My goal was the stable yard and the outbuildings that enclosed it. Here Elizabeth's and Mary's soldiers and several of the lesser-born gentlemen had put up for the night. I had seen one among their number I was anxious to speak to.

The stable yard had calmed by this time, the horses fed and bedded down, stable lads cleaning saddles and harness. The soldiers were eating, drinking, and nattering, and I withdrew into the shadows, not wishing to be noticed.

As though he'd been waiting for me, Colby walked out of a well-lit brick building and casually strolled in my direction. A cluster of trees stood not far from the outbuildings, and we met beneath their deep gloom.

"We cannot race to London," I said as soon as he stopped next to me. "She is truly ill. You may tell that to Her Majesty's soldiers."

"Aye, I hope she *will* tarry as long as she can," Colby answered in grim tones.

He was so tall that his voice came from a long way up. I shivered for no reason—the night had not grown colder. In fact, the absence of wind made the chill fairly tolerable.

"Why?" I asked sharply. "What has happened?"

"Guildford Dudley and Lady Jane Grey were executed today on Tower Green."

"No." I pressed my hands to my mouth, nausea stirring. "Oh, no, no. What has happened to the world?" Tears slid silently down my cheeks. "Jane was innocent. She had nothing to do with plots—how could she? Without a word to say for herself, how could *Jane* threaten anyone?"

My voice rose in my distress, and I found myself pressed against Colby, his arms coming around me. I leaned against him in gratitude and cried my fill.

My imagination filled in the details, which were confirmed when I heard the entire story later—Jane dressed all in black, led across the Tower green by her ladies, her lips moving as she read from a book of prayers she carried.

Her taut face as she turned to the people who'd come to watch her die, her stammered words that she was guilty of loving the world and worldly things too much. Jane, saying these things.

Then her ladies helping undress her to her chemise, and Jane stepping onto the straw.

I shoved myself away from Colby, trying to blot out the vision, but it insisted on playing itself out to the end. Jane kneeling at the block, tears running down her face, and the final, sharp blow. The vision did not spare me the blood, the wails of Jane's ladies, the *thump* of the executioner's ax. Then Jane's blood, innocent blood, on the straw.

I learned later that, more horrible still, Jane had not been able to find the block once she'd been blindfolded, and a man had darted out of the crowd to help her to it.

I fell to my knees in the mud, trying to banish the image from my head.

It vanished as suddenly as it had come, and I saw only the frozen ground under the trees, and a thick root that had poked itself above the earth. The folds of Colby's leather boots and glint of spurs came into view as he crouched beside me.

I gasped for breath, drawing the sweet scent of the night into me, welcoming the cold.

"Eloise?"

I could not say if Colby was upset at my distress or annoyed that I'd broken down.

"I am unhurt," I said, the only words that came to my lips. "I simply …"

Colby's hands were large and warm, lifting me to my feet. "I told you too abruptly. My apologies."

I wiped my eyes with cold fingers. "I grew up with Lady Jane, you see, and designed gowns for her. I started to sew her a queen's wardrobe." I shuddered. "I dared hope that Mary would spare her. Jane did nothing."

"She was a banner to flock to, just as Elizabeth is," Colby rumbled in the darkness. "Whether Jane had any desire to become queen was not the point. So long as any man could use her, she was a danger to Mary. Elizabeth is an even greater danger, which is why we must take our time riding to London. If Elizabeth arrives too soon on the heels of Jane's execution, Mary might simply follow with another. A lightning trial, a night in the Tower …"

"Enough," I said sharply. "I do understand, though I am but a foolish woman, weeping on your cloak."

"Not so foolish." Colby's voice became surprisingly gentle. "Dudley is sometimes led astray by a pretty face, but not in matters of importance."

I gazed at him, barely able to make out his features in the gloom. "If I were to think that through long enough, I might twist it into a compliment. Thank heavens you stayed away from Wyatt and his followers in the end."

"But I was in the thick of it." Colby touched my face with rough-gloved fingers. "I fought with the soldiers in London against Mary. When Wyatt saw that his quest was futile, he sent me back to Ashridge to protect Elizabeth. They battled at the very gates of Whitehall, and the queen's personal guard were nearly too cowardly to protect her. Had not the City stood by her, we would have gained a foothold in London. It might have ended in victory. But it did not, and I slipped away and rode to rejoin Elizabeth's household."

I absorbed the story, cold fear twisting my heart. Elizabeth could well share Jane's fate if Mary saw fit. If Mary was angry enough, if she could be convinced that Elizabeth had set Wyatt and his soldiers on her, she might be merciless.

"Damn them all," I said between clenched teeth.

"We will protect her," Colby promised. "You and I."

"We are doing naught but gossiping in the mud in the dark. How can this protect her?"

Colby firmly clasped my shoulders. Even through the thick fabric of my cloak and his gloves, his hands were warm.

"You will. You must. There may soon come a time when all our princess has is you, when Mary will take away everything *but* you. Then you must stand by her. You must insist on it."

I knew there was much Colby was not saying, but I was not certain I wanted to learn more tonight. "I will always stand by her," I said indignantly.

"It will be difficult. Very much so. But I believe if anyone can keep her from falling, it will be you."

His confidence surprised me. "You have much faith in my abilities, James Colby."

"I have come to know you." His words were rapid and soft. "You are clever, though you try to hide it behind that guileless face. I realized at once that the method Elizabeth used to communicate with the rebels was invented by you."

I tried not to warm to his praise. "I simply made it practical."

"No one else could have." Colby gazed down at me a moment longer then finally released me. "Go to her now and convince her to tarry here as much as she can. And prepare for the worst. Do not let my faith in you be misplaced."

"It shall not be," I replied with irritation. "You give and take back compliments quite easily, Master Colby."

"If we survive this," Colby said in light tones, "I will toast your many accomplishments."

"Elizabeth would not approve." I drew my cloak more tightly about me. "Good night, sir."

Colby stepped from me and let me go, his eyes glistening in the darkness. I walked away from him, uncertain of my heart as I always was after speaking to him.

But he was not wrong about Elizabeth's danger. Jane was murdered, Elizabeth could be next, and we were heading directly into Mary's waiting arms.

CHAPTER 16

O ur journey slowed to a crawl, much to my relief. We managed at best five or six miles a day, and even that, though she reclined in a litter, taxed most of Elizabeth's strength.

She complained of aches throughout her body, and her arms and legs swelled as before. Her physician bled her, Aunt Kat and Mistress Sandes fed her herbs mixed in wine, and I tried to take down the swelling with warm cloths.

I'd had an intense conversation with Elizabeth the morning after I'd spoken to Colby. She'd lain in bed, pale and sweating, as I told her of Jane's execution and Colby's suggestion that we take as much time as possible arriving in London.

We should give Mary's temper time to cool, I emphasized, and keep out of sight while Mary was signing execution orders.

"I did not need you to meet your dashing adventurer in the dark to tell me that," Elizabeth snapped at me. "I could not manage a faster pace even were I in a tearing hurry to reach Whitehall." Her brows drew downward. "Can you credit what Anthony Denny has told me, Eloise? That there is a rumor that I hide myself and will not come to court because I am great with child, probably made that way by one of the rebels."

The usual accusation against a woman, I thought in irritation. If she walks openly with head high, she is a wanton, but if she remains discreetly at home, it is because she is shamefully belly-full.

"A servant of this house must have mistaken your illness," I said. "And gossiped to Mary's soldiers of it."

"And if I discover who, they will be sorry they have a tongue."

I placed a soothing hand on her arm, I being one of the few allowed to touch her person. "The day we ride into London, we ought to go in full daylight. I advise you to wear your white and silver gown and travel with the curtains of your litter open."

"To show them how *not* pregnant I am?" Elizabeth flashed a sudden smile at me from her pillows. "It will not stop Mary doing as she pleases, but I'll not let her tarnish my reputation. The people of England want the pure princess, and that is what I shall be."

Her determination made me proud to be her lady, but still, I feared.

THE SLOW JOURNEY AT LEAST GAVE ELIZABETH TIME TO HEAL AND compose herself. By the time we reached London, she was much better and the strange swelling in her body had dissipated.

I carefully sewed a plain bodice to one of her white and silver brocade gowns and laced her into it.

As planned, Elizabeth rode through Smithfield toward the City, surrounded by her guardsmen. She wore shining white, her body slender and erect, every inch a Tudor princess.

London turned out to welcome her home. The road was lined with well-wishers who not only waved and shouted but thrust gifts at her, as they had when she'd ridden with Mary at her accession.

Elizabeth acknowledged her admirers with the stateliness of a monarch, smiling her thanks. They adored her, and she absorbed that fact as though she'd known and expected it.

We rode across Fleet Bridge and through Fleet Street to the Strand and so on to Whitehall. At the opposite end of London, in the Tower, the Duke of Suffolk, Jane's father, went to his execution.

When we reached Whitehall, Elizabeth's personal guards dispersed, not allowed into the palace itself. I accompanied Elizabeth and her ladies to chambers set aside for her, where she awaited Mary's summons.

The summons never came. Elizabeth paced for several days, her health regained, her anger evident.

She demanded constantly to know what went on outside the walls. What of Wyatt—what had he said to his questioners? Had he named Elizabeth as a conspirator? What had happened to the others, and what were Mary's plans for all of them?

Colby kept an eye on comings and goings and reported to me, and I in turn reported to Elizabeth.

"Wyatt has said nothing against her," Colby told me when we met one morning in a cold passageway high in the palace. "The men of the rebellion name each other, but not our lady. One of her gentlemen has been accused of delivering a message from Elizabeth to Wyatt, thanking him for his suggestion she remove to Donnington, but that has not been proved, as it was not a written message."

"I remember when he sent her the letter," I said, recalling the day I'd prevented Elizabeth from penning a reply. Verbal only, I'd warned.

"Please forget it, Eloise," Colby said swiftly. "You do not want to be put to the question."

"Why haven't *you* been?" I asked curiously. Colby, who knew what was happening better than most, who'd been among the fighters in London, should have been arrested with the others. I thanked God he had not been, but I had to wonder why not.

A look of self-loathing crossed his face. "I am too careful. I abandon honor to keep myself alive."

I had no idea what he meant by this. "I, for one, am happy you do. Elizabeth needs friends, needs information. She needs *you*." I decided not to share with him that I did as well.

"For the greater good," Colby finished bitterly.

"Indeed. Do not flog yourself for not being tortured in the Tower with the others."

Colby's eyes flashed with recrimination at himself. "They have not named me. They truly believe they die for the betterment of England, but they wish to leave enough of us alive to try again."

"Try again?" I echoed in renewed excitement.

"Good Lord, Eloise, you sound eager. Women should cringe in their chambers, not dash to be in the middle of things."

"You do not know women well then," I said. "We are far more ruthless than the gentlemen, when we see a need. I am willing to fight for Elizabeth. She is my lady. Why should this puzzle you?"

A smile crossed his lips. "Thinking of my mother, I well believe in the ruthlessness of women."

Learning that Colby had something so human as a mother made my interest quicken. "Your mother? Have I seen her at court?"

"No, no. She died years ago. My father as well, the better for this business." Colby shook his head. "If something happens to me, I cannot harm others connected to me, because I have no more connections."

Colby had lost his wife, and he'd never spoken of brothers or sisters. A man alone in the world. Sorrow should hang heavy on him, but he was resilient.

"Is that why you are willing to risk your life for all?" I asked. "Because you have nothing to lose?"

He shrugged. "Not the only reason, but the fact that no one else will be punished for my crimes allows me to act more resolutely."

"Well, I should be sorry if you were put to the block." I strove to keep my tone light. "Even though you have dragged me into your plot—quite literally at times. But I should not like to see you suffer, so I am happy they have not named you."

Colby studied me, his unruly hair framing a strong face, his chin dusted with golden-red stubble.

"I am sorry now that I did drag you into it." Colby brushed my cheek with the backs of his fingers, his hand warm despite the coolness of the passageway. "You ought to be creating famous costumes for queens, not mucking about in conspiracies."

"Elizabeth's downfall would likely be mine," I said without hesitation. "I may as well help keep her safe."

Colby let out a breath and removed his touch, my face growing colder without it. "Take care, Eloise."

"I always take great care, Master Colby," I returned with sincerity. I walked away from him then, feeling him watching me all the way.

WE REMAINED AT WHITEHALL FOR THREE WEEKS WITHOUT WORD from Mary, to Elizabeth's growing frustration.

Thomas Wyatt went to his trial, was pronounced guilty, and condemned to die. Wyatt admitted to sending messages to Elizabeth but constantly declared she'd provided him with no answer or made no sign of condoning, or even knowing about, the rebellion.

Elizabeth's gentleman who'd gave Wyatt her response

admitted to it, but the council had nothing in writing and nothing could be proved. It began to seem as though Elizabeth might be spared.

I dared hope Mary would simply send Elizabeth back to Ashridge and ignore her again. As the days dragged by and nothing happened, my hopes increased.

But I had not calculated the influence that the Spanish ambassador Renard and Bishop Gardiner had on Mary.

"She brings evil to this realm," they whispered into Mary's ears. "Courtenay and Elizabeth should lose their heads," Renard stressed. "It is the only way to keep peace."

Bishop Gardiner had always been fond of Edward Courtenay, and it was likely that only his affection saved the young man. Gardiner had no affection for Elizabeth, however, and fed Mary malevolent thoughts.

A few days after Wyatt's trial, I heard hurrying footsteps in the passageway outside the room where I sewed with Aunt Kat. A maid I'd asked to report to me what went on in the castle outside our chambers burst in upon us.

Out of breath, her hair straggling from its pins, she panted, "They are coming. They are coming for Her Grace. We are undone."

She began to weep loudly until Aunt Kat shook her to be quiet.

I hurried to the inner chamber and found Elizabeth rising from her chair, the books she'd been reading falling to the floor in a flutter of pages.

"Quickly, Eloise, my gown."

I knew what she wanted. I hurried to the wardrobe and gathered up a velvet and gold ensemble I'd finished after our arrival and hastily laced it on her. I positioned her near the window, angling her body to catch the light on the fabric, her overskirts coyly revealing the glittering brocade of the underskirt.

Her ladies grouped themselves around her, not protectively, but in a little tableau that put Elizabeth in the middle as the sun and they the stars around her.

When the first man, the Earl of Sussex—who was a cousin to both Mary and Elizabeth—marched through the door, ramrod straight, no bowing, he found Elizabeth regal and haughty, as though awaiting an inferior.

Mary's entire council piled in behind Sussex, from Bishop Gardiner, eyes alight in triumph, to William Paulet, who remained carefully neutral, as usual.

"We have come to arrest you." Sussex put a slightly apologetic note in his voice.

While Henry Radclyffe, the second Earl of Sussex, was one of Mary's staunchest supporters, he was very aware that Elizabeth was of royal blood. Sussex had a wife called Anne Calthorpe, who drove him a bit mad. She not only opposed the old religion but had once been arrested and confined in the Tower for sorcery. This accounted, I thought, for the worried lines about his eyes.

The rest of the council, save Paulet, turned hard faces to Elizabeth. Paulet managed to reflect some reluctance—after all, Elizabeth might be queen someday herself. Paulet had survived three Tudor reigns thus far. Why not four?

Sussex cleared his throat. "Sir Thomas Wyatt has been convicted of treason," he said to Elizabeth. "You have been accused of knowing of the plot as well as aiding and abetting it, with evidence brought forth. You are to be taken to the Tower of London, there lodged at Her Majesty's pleasure until such time as you will be tried for your crimes."

The council remained a stern wall of men turned against a woman. They waited for her to fall to her knees, or perhaps weep, plead, or even collapse in a dead faint.

Instead, Elizabeth raised her head, her eyes glittering.

"What evidence?" she inquired icily. "There is no evidence

that has not been manufactured, for I am innocent of this charge."

"Nonetheless." Sussex's voice firmed. "Tomorrow you will be escorted to the Tower. Tonight, you will remain here to prepare yourself."

"Let me speak to my sister," Elizabeth demanded as though she hadn't heard him. "She promised me before I left court that she would hear me if I were accused of any conspiracy, as I have been accused today."

"Her Grace, the queen, does as she pleases," Sussex tried.

"Tell her, my lord, that I beg humbly to see her."

Sussex regarded her steadily, finding no humility in Elizabeth. "I will deliver your message," he said. "Though I cannot speak for the queen."

"But you *do* speak for her, my lord Sussex." Elizabeth's words were razor sharp. "You tell me from her that I am accused."

Sussex flushed. "Even so. We will return for you in the morning."

The gentlemen of Mary's council turned their backs on Elizabeth. They walked out, neither shuffling nor ashamed, hats firmly on their heads, their backs straight. The insult was complete.

"This is Gardiner's influence, I will wager," Elizabeth seethed when the doors had shut again. "Gardiner keeps her from seeing me. He fears that she will soften with sisterly affection. I doubt she will—she has none—but I wish to plead my case. If Mary hears me, she will change her mind. She is not stupid."

No, but Mary was careful, I reflected. This was made evident when, not much later, the Earl of Sussex returned without the council but with a contingent of armed guards.

"You are to remain in this room," he informed Elizabeth. "Your gentlewomen must go, save only two needed to wait upon you. You will not leave here, nor will they, nor will they pass on any communication from you to any other person."

Elizabeth's face was stark, her red-gold hair standing out like fire against her skin. "Mistress Ashley and Mistress Rousell shall stay with me."

"Not Katherine Ashley," Sussex said, eyes narrowing. "But as Mistress Rousell comes from a pious family, she may remain."

I did my best to appear pious, or at least to keep the satisfaction from my face. I knew quite well how to get word to and from Elizabeth under Mary's guards' noses, but I could not do so if Sussex banished me.

"Mistress Norwich, then," Elizabeth said without argument.

Sussex nodded as though he did not much care who she chose, as long as the dangerous Mistress Ashley was far from Elizabeth's side.

I tried not to smile at the irony that I, a staunch supporter of Elizabeth, should be allowed to stay with her simply because my mother had married a Catholic.

Elizabeth regarded Sussex coldly, pretending she was not gleeful for having her own way. I knew she'd named Aunt Kat first because Aunt Kat would obviously be rejected—then by contrast Elizabeth could ask for who she truly wanted.

His mission complete, Sussex departed, again without bowing—but his expression before he left the room conveyed that he was sorry he'd been chosen for the task.

"Not all are in agreement, it is evident," Elizabeth muttered to me after the earl departed. "Some of these gentlemen are reluctant to choose which royal they will offend. They wish me to remember, if I become queen, which of them disliked to see me so harshly treated."

I agreed, but worried that Mary's council's divisiveness would encourage Mary to bring about Elizabeth's end that much faster.

Mistress Norwich and I saw to Elizabeth's needs at supper that evening, then undressed her, put her to bed, and read to her. Elizabeth's Bible and Prayer Book had been confiscated, but she had books of devotion and poetry, and Mistress Norwich could read Greek and discuss what she read with her.

At last, we snuffed out the candles, but the night dragged on. When I peered out of the window in my corner chamber, I spied men in armor pacing in the courtyards below. Mary was ensuring that no rescue attempt would whisk Elizabeth out of her reach.

In the morning, Mistress Norwich and I dressed the princess again, and we were ready and waiting when Sussex and Paulet came for her.

If any ever did try this old saying, ELIZABETH WROTE, ANGER evident in every curl of ink, *that a king's word was more than another man's oath—I most humbly beseech your majesty to verify it in me, and to remember your last promise and my last demand: that I be not condemned without answer and due proof.*

Elizabeth had gotten her way with Sussex, who'd at last allowed her to write a letter to Mary. Elizabeth had taken her time, penning it carefully in her own hand, with me nearby, so that I could read every word.

And to this present hour I protest afore God (who shall judge my truth, whatsoever malice shall devise) that I never practiced, counseled, nor consented to anything that might be prejudicial to your person . . . therefore I humbly beseech your majesty to let me answer afore your-self and not suffer me to trust your Councilors—yea, and that afore I go to the Tower.

In the next paragraphs Elizabeth reminded Mary of the words of the Duke of Somerset, who'd claimed that if he had spoken to Thomas Seymour before condemning him, letting his brother explain himself, Seymour might not have been put to death.

I pray God as evil persuasions persuade not one sister against the other . . .

She finished in a bolder tone. *And as for the traitor, Wyatt, he might peradventure write me a letter, but on my faith, I never received any from him. And as for the copy of my letter sent to the French king, I pray God confound me eternally if ever I sent him word, message, token, or letter by any means, and to this my truth I will stand in to my death.*

Elizabeth's letter ended near the top of a second page. She drew heavy diagonal lines across the remaining empty space so that Mary's councilors might not fill in something unwanted, then signed it.

She handed the finished letter to Sussex, not bothering to fold it or hide the words from him.

"I thank you, my lord, for delivering this to my sister, before setting me in the boat for the Tower."

Sussex took the paper, frowning his annoyance. "We cannot leave for the Tower now, Your Grace. The tide has turned, and we must wait for tomorrow."

Elizabeth shrugged her slim shoulders, the set of her lips telling me she'd known full well that she'd taken too long over the letter. If I calculated aright, the tide would turn again near midnight, but Sussex would never chance taking her on the river so late—one of Elizabeth's loyal men might arrange for her to be plucked from Sussex's care and rescued.

Sussex left the chamber to deliver the missive, his back quivering. He returned later to say that he'd given the letter to Mary, and that she'd read it, but she'd made no reply.

Hope faded from Elizabeth's eyes, but she did not wilt. She merely thanked Sussex loftily and called for her supper.

Sussex gave her a shallow bow and ordered the servants to fetch her a meal.

Elizabeth, for her part, utterly ignored him. She turned from him, calling for Mistress Norwich to bring her wine.

CHAPTER 17

The journey down the Thames the next morning was one I would remember for the rest of my days. The weather had turned for the worse with the tide, and a cold rain beat on us as I and one of Mary's armed gentlemen assisted Elizabeth into the barge that would carry us downstream. Sussex and Paulet accompanied us, though neither man looked happy about it.

Water ran from Elizabeth's cloak and pooled in the bottom of the barge, its flimsy canopy little protection against the cold and wind. Mistress Norwich huddled against Elizabeth on one side, I on the other, as we tried to shield her from the worst of it.

I had been able to get word to Colby about our predicament, though there was little he could do. The lead guard had gazed at me most suspiciously when I'd darted out of Elizabeth's chamber this morning with a pile of handkerchiefs and commanded that someone bring us clean ones.

The guard had inspected the cloths to see whether I'd buried a letter between the folds, but of course, I had not. I'd spoken a truth when I'd told Elizabeth that day at Ashridge that a thing written was tediously difficult to deny.

But stitches were not writing, at least not to those who couldn't read the messages. The code Elizabeth and I had perfected could be used in handkerchiefs, cloaks, gloves, sleeves, and even stockings, which were given to a launderer and intercepted by someone Colby trusted.

In this way, I'd communicated during the rebellion where Elizabeth was and that she was safe. Anyone caught with the garments I'd smuggled from Elizabeth's home, or her chambers in Whitehall, would never realize what information they contained.

The guard at last summoned a serving maid to take the handkerchiefs away and bring me more.

Now, Elizabeth's barge made its way slowly downriver, past the pile of Somerset House, then the Temple on the north bank and the fields of Southwark on the south. The shore was empty, but bells pealed from the churches and cathedrals—it was Palm Sunday, a feast day, and ordinary citizens rejoiced at the coming end of Lent.

The City's wall flowed past, then the shadow of London Bridge, the houses built upon it appearing as though they'd tumble into the water at any moment. The boat rocked and tossed as we floated under the bridge, the strong current threatening to carry it into pilings on either side of us.

The boatmen strained against their oars, sweat mingling with the rain, while I clung to the gunwale with both hands. I imagined Aunt Kat having to explain to my mother how I'd gone to a watery grave with the princess she despised. Somehow, I suspected neither my mother nor stepfather would be very sorry.

The barge at last shot from under the bridge, the speed sending us toward calmer waters. We passed Billingsgate, and all too soon the crenellations of the Tower drew close.

The boatmen guided the craft out of the current to the landings, they being the only ones happy to reach our journey's end. The barge bumped stone, the relieved boatmen throwing ropes to those waiting above to tie us fast.

Sussex immediately sprang ashore, as did Paulet, the elderly man hunched against the rain.

Elizabeth's face was carved in icy anger. When one of her gentleman ushers climbed out and reached a hand down to help her to shore, Elizabeth remained under the canopy, folded her arms, and sat still.

The man gazed down at her, troubled, the rain streaking his beard and matting his hair to his head. "Your Grace, we must go in," he said tremulously.

Elizabeth set her jaw and remained under the canvas. Paulet scowled and slid a fold of his cloak over his nose, as though irritated that his appointed task might result in a bad cold. He was nearly seventy, far too elderly for capers in the rain.

Sussex regarded her impatiently. "Your Grace, if you do not leave the boat, I must give the guards instruction to lift you out. I do not wish to do so, as I do not wish anyone to lay hands on your person."

Elizabeth did not answer. She glared at Sussex with all the fury she could muster, letting it spill beyond him onto Paulet. Then, without a word to either of us ladies, she scrambled to her feet and launched herself up onto the stone wharf.

"Here landeth as true a subject, being prisoner, as ever landed here," Elizabeth stated. She then sat herself down on the stone steps, full in the rain, and folded her arms again.

I climbed out of the boat, my body cold and stiff. It was a black day, quite literally. The rain pelted from dark clouds, and the afternoon didn't seem likely to be any brighter than the morning.

I expected Sussex to growl at Elizabeth to move, but he stood very quietly, waiting for her to choose what to do.

Hedging his bets, I thought once more. The other councilors, including Paulet, copied his stance. Only the gentleman usher, who was one of Elizabeth's own men, seemed distressed.

"Your Grace, you must not sit here in the rain," he said, anguished. He was nearly as elderly as Paulet, with a wife, children, and six granddaughters. I knew him as a gentle person, and now his kind eyes leaked tears. "Please, Your Grace, this is a bad place."

"Better here than a worse place," Elizabeth countered.

Her gentleman continued to quietly weep. Elizabeth gazed at him in exasperation, then she sighed and nodded.

Perhaps she took pity on the poor man—I could not tell. Elizabeth could be impatient with even the kindest people, and then she could turn around, soften her heart, and do everything in the world for them.

Elizabeth held out her hand for me, and I and the gentleman usher helped her to her feet. She swirled her cloak about herself in a dramatic fashion and ordered Sussex to proceed. Behind us, Paulet sneezed.

We walked along cold, flooded paths that skirted the ancient stone walls, our way lined with yeomen of the guard. A few pulled off their hats as she passed.

"God save Your Grace," one said to her.

Elizabeth acknowledged him with a gracious nod.

The accommodations we were escorted to were bleak, though not the rat-infested dungeons I'd feared. It was bad enough—plain rooms that held small hearth fires, but nonetheless dreary.

The two ladies Elizabeth had been allowed to retain would be prisoners with her. We'd not be permitted to leave the Tower, in the event that we'd conspire with outsiders to rescue her. Mary had sent several of her own gentlewomen to watch over Elizabeth and keep an eye on me and Mistress Norwich.

Mary's ladies waited in the long chamber that was to be Elizabeth's, standing like jailers near a bed hung with heavy curtains.

Elizabeth glanced around the spartan room, not in despair but with haughty annoyance.

"Did Jane Grey stay here?" she demanded of Sussex.

"No, Your Grace. She did not."

Colby had told me that at first, Jane had been allowed to live in the comfortable accommodations where she'd been originally housed with her mother, before she'd been moved to the half-timbered Lieutenant's lodging. From the windows of Elizabeth's chamber, I glimpsed a corner of Tower Green, where Jane had met her death.

Elizabeth refused to look out of the windows. "You may leave us," she said to Sussex, a royal personage dismissing him.

She turned from that retreating gentleman so she would not have to watch him refuse to bow to her.

Elizabeth flinched slightly when the heavy door of the outer chamber closed, and the key turned in the lock, but I was the only one who noticed.

WE WERE KEPT INSIDE THE TOWER FOR NEARLY TWO MONTHS TO the day. During that time, I saw few people, save the ladies waiting on Elizabeth and the elderly gentleman usher with whom I was allowed to run the occasional errand inside the Tower. Anything that was needed from outside the walls—food, linens, and the like—was brought by men loyal to Mary and passed to the ladies Mary had sent.

I did my best to be guileless to find out what was happening in the outside world. I managed to pry *some* information from the ladies and gentlemen who were allowed to go back and forth from our prison, who were unwary enough of me to gossip.

First, they told me that Wyatt had steadfastly refused to say anything against Elizabeth, even when he was promised pardon for admitting that the entire plot had been instigated by her. Wyatt stubbornly would not speak, and neither would any of the others so questioned.

Second, the most damning evidence the council had against Elizabeth was the belief that she'd been preparing to move to her house at Donnington and fortify it. Elizabeth denied this at her preliminary questioning, feigning to forget she even had a residence at Donnington.

Of course she had not forgotten. William Cecil oversaw all her properties, and she consulted with him often, questioning him pointedly about each of her estates. She was careful of her money and properties, and we all knew it.

However, none of her accusers could come up with a scrap of evidence to prove she'd even contemplated moving to Donnington. So what if Sir James Croft and Wyatt had advised her to go? Elizabeth had stayed at Ashridge, hadn't she?

Elizabeth stuck with that story, and the council could get no more out of her.

I began to have hope. If the interrogators could not come up with solid proof against Elizabeth, then they couldn't risk bringing her to trial. If they stood her before a jury, as was her right, that jury might acquit her. If that happened, then by law she'd be free of all the charges.

As it turned out, the juries were plenty lenient with the conspirators. Thomas Wyatt and the Earl of Suffolk had been the obvious ringleaders, and they were condemned—Suffolk already dead. Courtenay, who'd never hidden the fact that he'd hoped to be king one way or another, remained imprisoned, but Bishop Gardiner's friendship with him kept him from trial.

After all, Gardiner argued, Courtenay had not actually *done* anything.

Other conspirators—such as Nicholas Throckmorton, who'd been in it up to his neck—were pardoned. James Colby had eluded capture, and no one named him, for which I was fervently thankful.

I held onto my hope through the long weeks we waited. On the dreadful April morning when Wyatt was executed, he declared on the scaffold that neither Elizabeth nor Courtenay had anything to do with the plots.

I knew this to be a lie, but Mary could do nothing about it. The condemned man's last words did much to keep the council's actions toward Elizabeth cautious ones.

It became clear that Elizabeth's fortune had changed when Mary sent word that Elizabeth was to be moved to more agreeable accommodations, although the chambers were still within the Tower.

The change scarcely put Elizabeth in a better mood. She expected every day to be dragged to trial, for Mary to manufacture evidence, for a scaffold to be built for her. Elizabeth wavered between fear and anger, choosing the latter to relieve her feelings.

As we waited, the spring days lengthened and warmed, the chill dank of winter waning. Elizabeth was eventually allowed to walk in the privy garden, supervised by Mary's ladies, of course. We strolled slowly, soaking up as much of the outdoor air as possible before we had to return to the rooms inside.

As the conspirators, one by one, were released or ignored, Elizabeth walked among the pruned hedges with a lighter step. Daffodils and crocuses burst through the soil, perhaps a promise of coming freedom?

One morning a small girl came to Elizabeth and handed her flowers. Elizabeth bent down to her and smiled sweetly, calling her a dear child. Mary's ladies hovered behind Elizabeth in disapproval, and a guard strode over to monitor Elizabeth's conversation with the mite.

This was an answer to a message I'd covertly sent elsewhere in the Tower. While the ladies and guards were thus distracted by the child, I strolled to the far end of the garden and out through a gate to a little walk between two walls.

On another side of this narrow passage lay a second gate, locked, behind which a dark-haired man waited.

"God grant you good health, Mistress Rousell," Robert Dudley said to me. "And how is our princess this fine morning?"

"She is very well," I answered. "How is your good wife?"

Robert laughed, sounding merry, as though he'd not been held prisoner here for many months. "I have not seen her, but she is often sickly, poor thing," he answered. "Whereas our princess is robust."

"She is, indeed."

Robert beamed his smile at me. I recalled the passionate kiss he and Elizabeth had exchanged the night before his wedding, and wondered if he were thinking of it as well.

"The weather warms," Robert remarked.

"Indeed." I shifted from foot to foot, in a hurry to speak of something more interesting.

"A mutual friend praises you," Robert said, a sly note to his voice.

Assuming he meant Colby, I kept silent. What was between Colby and me was none of his business.

Robert was far more informed than I at this time. I had directed a few messages out, but none had come *in.* Would there be a rescue, or another rebellion? Had Elizabeth's followers abandoned her?

Robert read my expression. "A little knowledge is a dangerous thing, Mistress Rousell."

"I dislike speaking in riddles, my lord," I answered stiffly.

Robert laughed again. His dark hair was trimmed and neat,

his small beard framing a good-humored mouth, his body lithe and well-built. I could not blame females for being captivated by his handsomeness, although his nose, in my opinion, was rather on the bulbous side.

I personally found his charm overblown. I preferred plain speaking and sense to extravagant compliments and clever witticisms.

Elizabeth, however, was no giddy girl. She would not like Robert so much if he hadn't possessed an intelligence to match her own.

Still, I could not help being happy that Robert could have no husbandly domination over Elizabeth. A man in a flirtation might profess to be a woman's humble servant, but in marriage, he was master.

The ironic glint in Robert's eyes made me wonder if he knew in which direction my thoughts went. I realized I'd been assessing him most carefully, and I blinked to ease my scrutiny.

"I have nothing to speak of apart from the weather," Robert said in an amused tone.

"No message for the princess?" I asked, voice low.

"None at all. Save to greet her, poor fellow prisoner, and to ponder what joyous days we will have when we are past this place." Robert winked. "That is if we walk out *our* way, not Mary's."

I frowned in impatience. "That is nothing more than you have told me before." We'd met in a similar way several times over the past weeks.

"What do you expect of me, Mistress Rousell? Would you have me deliver ten written messages that rescue is at hand, naming all those who will be involved? Perhaps a map our lady may follow as she flees before Mary's army? Nay, my dear Mistress, look not to me for those."

A lady of my station—a mere gentlewoman—could hardly

admonish a duke's son, but I wanted to scold Robert for his flippancy and perhaps tweak his nose to relieve my pique.

"I am a plain woman," I said. "With plain understanding."

"You are hardly that." Robert dragged an impertinent gaze down my person. "But if you insist, I will speak plainly. She is to do nothing. Sentiment changes, and she is liked. Our mutual friend has more ideas. You are to stay close to her." Robert grinned once more, his haughty face lightening into the charm other ladies loved so well. "Is that plain enough? Or shall I write it in my blood?"

"Plain enough, my lord. I thank you."

Robert's smile faded abruptly, and he glanced behind him as though he'd heard a step. "Excellent. Now go back, Mistress Rousell, before you are missed."

He turned and walked away, not bothering to say farewell.

Another reason I did not like Lord Robert—he expressed courtesy as it pleased him, only to those he wished to please. He made it clear that as much as he had looked me over with a gaze bordering on lascivious, it was not *me* he wanted, but her.

IT WAS NOT UNTIL MAY THAT FORTUNE STEPPED IN TO AID US, and then in an odd way. One morning a man called Henry Bedingfield came to the Tower to take charge of Elizabeth.

Sir Henry Bedingfield had a large face, a long, wide nose that he tended to peer down, and close-set eyes. His long moustache drooped into his beard, giving him a perpetually woeful look.

Not that Bedingfield smiled much. He regarded Elizabeth in sorrow as he knelt before her, clearly wondering how a young woman could turn against her sister and her queen, and told her she would be his prisoner.

Elizabeth had measure of him before their first interview was finished.

"I noted that the Tower is being fortified," Elizabeth declared, staring Bedingfield down. We had seen new soldiers marching in this morning. "Am I so dangerous a prisoner? All this for one weak woman?"

Bedingfield took her statement at face value. I had watched Elizabeth fence and win with Tyrwhitt over the Seymour affair, and Tyrwhitt had been a much worthier opponent than Bedingfield. This match would be ugly.

"You are too humble, Your Grace," Bedingfield answered. "But no, the guards have nothing to do with you."

His eyes flickered, and I knew he lied. Elizabeth, of course, discerned this as well. From what I'd understood from the cryptic hints Robert gave me whenever I met him at the garden gate, Elizabeth's prisoner's status had changed. I could not tell— and Robert seemed not to know—whether that change was for good or ill.

"I have asked Her Majesty my sister whether I might walk in the great hall," Elizabeth said to Bedingfield. "Have you brought her answer?"

"I have not had word on this." Bedingfield's brows came down as though he were reading from a long list in his mind. "But she forbids you to speak with anyone in the gardens who are not your attendants."

"That is no worry. I do not."

Again, the eye flicker, as if reading from instructions inside his head. "You speak on occasion to a little girl named Alison, who is the porter's daughter," Bedingfield said.

Elizabeth's brows climbed. "The child? Who kindly brings me wildflowers, because she thinks me beautiful?"

"Such an easy messenger to bring you news from the outside world." Bedingfield nodded, certain he'd said something clever.

Elizabeth sent him a look of lively contempt. "A little girl, a messenger? From whom? Thomas Wyatt? He is dead and can dream up no more plots. Edward Courtenay? He is watched most closely, I believe, by his beloved Bishop Gardiner, and even the queen herself. There is no one to send me messages, Sir Henry. I am alone."

At the dramatic statement, Bedingfield cleared his throat. "Nevertheless, you must not speak to anyone again. The child's mother has been warned to keep her close."

"Dear God in heaven." Elizabeth sent the pretty vase of crocuses on a table next to her crashing to the floor. Bedingfield, stuck on his knees, could not scramble out of the way of the water and flying porcelain that rained across his person.

"An innocent child of seven years as a conspirator," Elizabeth raged. "It is scarce to be believed. Let me write a letter to my sister, I beg of you."

Bedingfield wiped his beard, and shards of porcelain tinkled to the floor. "Out of the question, Your Grace."

"Out of whose question? Mine? Or yours? Or hers?"

"It cannot be done, Your Grace. I have not leave to give you permission."

Elizabeth glared at him. "You must ask her leave, then. And her permission to give you leave to give me permission."

Bedingfield glanced heavenward as he tried to unravel this. Elizabeth sent him a smile that held no humor.

"I will inform Her Grace," Bedingfield answered after a time, sounding relieved he could at least say that.

"See that you do."

Bedingfield climbed painfully to his feet, made certain to give Elizabeth another low bow, and backed from the room. I fancied I heard him hurry frantically off after I closed the door.

Once he was gone, Elizabeth snatched up more breakable objects and flung them from her, we ladies dutifully cleaning up the mess.

Elizabeth's anger pleased me, however, because it meant she hadn't given way to despair. Mary's preoccupation with and suspicion of the innocent little girl pleased me as well, not because I had any desire for the child to be harmed, but because it meant nobody had noticed Eloise Rousell dashing away to whisper to Robert Dudley through a grill between the gardens.

Elizabeth's walks continued. Mary's guards watched Elizabeth closely, the little girl was kept away, and everyone ignored me. I continued to pass Dudley's messages—helpful and otherwise—to Elizabeth, with none the wiser.

CHAPTER 18

On the nineteenth of May, the exact day Anne Boleyn had been executed eighteen years before, a great number of armed guards filled the halls and courtyards of the Tower, alarming us not a little.

Bedingfield appeared and gave a peremptory command for Elizabeth to accompany him, her ladies to pack her things and follow.

Elizabeth paled until her brows stood out in fiery red lines. "Am I to have no trial, then? Is Jane's scaffold waiting for me?"

"You are to be moved from the Tower," Bedingfield said in his careful way. "I am to accompany you far from London, there to live in a house at her majesty's pleasure."

"It is a trick," Elizabeth insisted. "You will take me out into the country, and your men will assassinate me there."

"I assure you, Your Grace," Bedingfield began.

His tone and manner were anything but reassuring, and Elizabeth turned her back on him and stalked away across her chamber.

I wondered if Mary *would* have the audacity to murder Elizabeth outright. She would not dare, I didn't think. If assassins knifed Elizabeth in the night, all the world would know in the morning that Mary had ordered her death.

Elizabeth's popularity had not waned during her sojourn in the Tower. If Dudley's information was to be believed, it had even increased. Dudley regaled me with tales of men sentenced to the pillory for loudly declaring that Elizabeth was innocent, and of women and men alike voicing concerns about Elizabeth's health.

A quiet assassination would only lead to more conspiracies to topple Mary. Dudley had also told me that Mary had again attempted to disinherit Elizabeth, but Mary's council had strongly advised her against it. Unlike with her stubbornness over her upcoming marriage, she had capitulated.

The council's hesitancy, I thought, was why we were now being hustled into a barge that moved upriver toward Richmond on this fine day in May.

For my part, I was relieved to have sunshine on my face and wind in my hair, no matter where we were going. Even the presence of Bedingfield's men when we disembarked—a hundred of them, all armed—could not erase the feeling of freedom. I never wanted to see the Tower of London again.

That I was allowed to accompany Elizabeth at all had been difficult to finagle. Mary had wanted every one of Elizabeth's ladies dismissed and replaced with Mary's own, but she'd relented at the last minute and allowed Elizabeth to retain three women as well as three gentlemen.

Elizabeth had begged for me to accompany her on the journey itself, saying she had need of a seamstress who knew her well. Again, because of my mother's marriage to a staunch Catholic, Mary agreed.

So, the rest of Elizabeth's household was sent away with many tears, and she and I, with Bedingfield and his outriders, began the journey from Richmond, heading north and west.

THE ROYAL ESTATE WE REACHED AFTER FIVE DAYS OF TRAVELING reeked of isolation and mildew. Woodstock Manor in Oxfordshire was a huge place, rebuilt by Elizabeth's grandfather, but now rundown, as neither Mary nor Edward had been inclined to reside there. To reach it, we had to travel over a muddy causeway, which increased our feeling of seclusion.

Elizabeth surveyed the mess of the house in some dismay, then briskly inquired of Bedingfield if it were to be their last stopping place.

"Indeed, Your Grace," Bedingfield told her in his mournful tones.

In the outside world of Oxfordshire, through which we had just traveled, spring had arrived, with lambs trotting after their mothers, flowers budding, fields greening. Here at Woodstock, the dark and forbidding air of winter still clung to the wood and stone buildings.

Elizabeth gave the house and outbuildings a grim glare and then demanded to be taken to her quarters.

"I LOVE TO DANCE." ELIZABETH THREW HER ARMS OUT AND whirled in circles about the stone room.

I chuckled because I knew she did not mean in the literal sense.

We had settled into life at Woodstock. May had blended into a warm June then moved into hot July. Elizabeth walked the unkempt gardens, read and studied, played tunes on a virginals brought into her chamber at her request, and held her daily verbal fencing match with her jailor, Bedingfield.

I enjoyed watching her feint with him this way and that, and knew she quite despised him.

Bedingfield knew it, too. His hesitancy annoyed her, as did his mule-like stubbornness in writing almost daily to Mary for instruction and to note to her every word that left Elizabeth's mouth.

Elizabeth was aware he'd never be swayed to her side, but at the same time, his obvious reluctance to upset her because she might become queen someday was irksome.

"He, like others, tries to play both sides," she snarled to me in derision. "I would respect him much more if he were stern with me and meant it."

"Would you listen to him?" I asked with curiosity.

"Of course not," Elizabeth answered, and we broke into peals of laughter.

Our laughter was always strained, however. Elizabeth worried constantly that she'd been brought to Woodstock to be murdered, far from prying eyes. We learned from messages Colby was able to smuggle to us that Mary's advisors had strongly warned her against such an act. However, such advisors could die or be dismissed and replaced with those who told Mary what she wanted to hear, so we did not rest easy.

I and the two other ladies of Elizabeth's household allowed to attend her had been deemed "safe" by Mary. Aunt Kat was under house arrest far from us. Mistress Sandes had been summarily packed off, and she'd fled to the Continent, along with others who were considered to have too much influence on Elizabeth.

But while Elizabeth's former ladies and gentlemen might decry the country's return to the old religion, they could do nothing to prevent it. Mary had already made Parliament obedient on the subject, although the wealthy men in that body who'd eagerly scooped up the monastic lands doled out by King Henry balked at returning them.

Accept the Catholic faith?—*Yes, if we must.* Return our lands and wealth to monasteries?—A fervent *no.*

Mary did not always get her way.

In mid-July, one of Elizabeth's loyal gentlemen took me aside in the privy garden and told me that Colby would wait for me at a woodcutter's hut not far from the grounds.

"How am I to get away?" I whispered, mindful of one of Mary's ladies approaching.

"You will know when to go," the gentleman answered. "Linger in this garden tomorrow when Her Grace finishes her afternoon walk."

Mary's lady, a tall woman with a beaked nose, swooped down on us and informed me that there was mending to do. She gave Elizabeth's gentleman a severe look, which he returned blandly.

All the next day Elizabeth was in foul temper. A few days before, she'd at last gained permission to write directly to Mary and had received a reply that morning. In summary, Mary's letter stated that Elizabeth was ungrateful for the bounty her queen had bestowed upon her, and that she should be more humble. Furthermore, Elizabeth was not to write again.

Elizabeth fumed, and our garden walk was swift as she strode out her anger.

I continued to ponder how I'd escape the grounds to meet Colby. Elizabeth's few gentlemen were allowed to come and go to the nearby village, but we ladies were prisoners with her.

I loitered, as instructed, in the garden after Elizabeth and her ladies had stormed back into the house, with the excuse that I wanted to study the flowers, with an eye to designing a gown in a fabric that would reflect them.

Also, I claimed to need more air—not entirely feigned. I found the house stagnant. Though young Edward had caused some repairs and reinforcements to be made during his reign, it still needed much work. This palace, of all the monarchs' homes, was the farthest from London and therefore easy to neglect.

Stories had it that Henry the Second had built a bower on the palace grounds for his mistress, the Faire Rosamund, a legendary beauty. Their love had blossomed here, Henry besotted. I had to imagine that the house had been much more sumptuous then than it was now. I also wondered what Henry's wife, the formidable Queen Eleanor, had thought of the arrangement.

As I studied flowers that covered a hedge in a riot of color, I heard a commotion at the gate of the outer courtyard. I skirted the house toward the disturbance, taking care not to be noticed by Bedingfield's guards.

A young man who looked familiar stood in the courtyard, surrounded by armed men. A red-faced Bedingfield interrogated him at the top of his voice.

"Books," he shouted. "What business have you to bring Her Grace books? There will be messages in them I'll wager."

"Indeed, no," the young man replied haughtily. I recognized him then as the son of Thomas Parry's wife by her first husband. Young John Fortescue was presently reading at one of the colleges at nearby Oxford and must have been sent here by Master Parry. "They are tomes my stepfather thought Her Grace would want. Her Grace is a learned woman."

Bedingfield stared at Fortescue in grave suspicion, then turned to his guards. "Search the books, and search *him*, for any messages."

The guards did not look happy to dip their thick fingers into the books, grumbling as they did as they were bid. Mr. Fortescue complained about having to turn his clothes inside out like a common thief, but he had to obey.

While Bedingfield's attention was thus occupied, I slipped back to the garden and out a small gate that had been left unbolted for me.

I found the cottage not far up a woodcutter's track, deep under a canopy of forest. The tiny house boasted one window, whose shutter, worn and cracked, appeared as though it should have hung askew, but someone had fastened it quite firmly over the window. Likewise, the door had obviously been broken once, but its hinges were newly mended.

The rest of the house was ramshackle—thatch sliding from the roof to leave patches like a balding man's head, its whitewash gray, the chimney's bricks crumbling. Seedlings surrounded the house, as did undergrowth, nature reclaiming what human beings had abandoned.

I stepped into the dim interior, which was a single room, and waited for my eyes to adjust to the gloom. I appeared to be the only one present.

"Close the door."

I stifled a shriek as Colby's voice came out of the darkness. Admonishing myself to breathe normally, I obeyed and pushed the door shut.

"If I am caught, Bedingfield will write of it in great detail to Mary," I warned him in some irritation.

Colby sent me a hint of his smile. "A young woman slipping into the woods might only be keeping a tryst."

"You do not know Bedingfield. Should Elizabeth sneeze, he writes to Mary's council to inquire whether they believe it a code. All her friends are suspect, and even some of her enemies."

"I tease you, Mistress Rousell," Colby said. "It is put about that Elizabeth's enemies might think to infiltrate her ladies by flirting with them, but none would dare try it with you."

I considered his words as I laid my summer cloak over a stool that was whole and somewhat new. "I believe that is vaguely insulting."

"It should not be." Colby's tone lost its amusement. "I mean that you are shrewder than most and see through guile disguised as flattery. Your head is not easily turned."

"I see." I eyed him narrowly. "I had no idea I was such a paragon."

"The primary source of this idea is Dudley." Colby studied

me, his arms folded across his chest. "He finds it difficult to take your measure."

"Perhaps because I've taken *his* measure," I answered with heat. "He knows his own charm and uses it to his advantage."

Colby shrugged. "When his advantage runs parallel to my needs, I concede him his charm and let him use it."

"I grant that," I answered. "Is it law that conspirators have to love one another?"

"Decidedly not." Colby softened enough to grin at me, appearing almost like an ordinary person.

"Well, I am here. What are we conspiring today?" I asked.

"Nothing." Colby came out of his closed stance and spread his hands, his light cloak moving loosely on his back. "We only wish to know how Elizabeth fares. Bedingfield, we hear, is a strict master."

I huffed a laugh. "He attempts to be. Elizabeth is far more intelligent than he, and she plays upon it. I've seen Bedingfield clutch his head trying to decipher what she has said to him. Her Grace speaks in roundabout ways, wheedling him into permitting her to do more than Mary would like. It is a good source of amusement, where we have so few," I finished morosely.

"I heard that on her journey here, she was hailed by the farmers and their families she passed," Colby said. "They rejoice that the princess is free."

"Yes, and I wish they would cease," I said in exasperation. "The people so clearly favoring Elizabeth must fuel Mary's fears."

"It does." Colby nodded.

I began to restlessly pace the small room. "'Tis a strange imprisonment. Elizabeth's every move and every word is reported, but her gentlemen freely visit Master Parry in the village, where he oversees Elizabeth's coffers."

"Bedingfield's own fault," Colby said, uncaring. "I'm told

Mary gnashes her teeth every time she receives a letter from him, and she receives one nearly every day."

"Good." Mary, on her righteous high horse, deserved to be annoyed.

"Every plotter in the land goes to The Bull to see Parry," Colby said. "So much so that they will ruin all if they are not careful. Every day a new idea is dreamt up for rescuing Elizabeth, but none so far have proved plausible. The gathered gentlemen enjoy a good talk of treason."

I regarded him with alarm, but Colby stood calmly, the dim light darkening his fiery hair. "Do they endanger her?"

He waved a dismissive hand. "They are hotheads. We wish to triumph in the end, not simply stir up trouble. Parry brings a surprising measure of reason to the discussions, as he understands that anything planned must be paid for in real coin. He has kept Elizabeth's estates running smoothly and her tenants paying—though I imagine she'd faint away at the state of the books."

I didn't smile. "More likely she would fly into a tantrum. She is frustrated at not being able to attend to her own business. Bedingfield spends most of the time with his brow permanently puckered." I let out a breath in some sympathy. "Poor man. Mary could have chosen a shrewder jailer."

"Not really. Bedingfield will do exactly as he is told, no more, no less. He will not be won over by Elizabeth and betray Mary, and Mary knows it."

"That is obvious. Turning against a monarch takes imagination."

Colby chuckled at that, then went silent a moment. "Philip arrives in a few days' time," he announced, serious once more.

I stilled, cold running through me. "So, the marriage will take place."

I had not really doubted it would. The ladies-in-waiting Mary had appointed to Woodstock spoke of it often, wishing they could attend the wedding. I'd nursed hope that Mary would finally realize that the only person in her country who desired the marriage was herself, but I'd recently let that hope go.

"She purports to love him," Colby said.

"Love?" I stared at him incredulously. "She's never met the man."

"Philip has written and sent her his portrait. Mary is convinced that Philip has esteem for her, which will develop into love." Colby shrugged. "The rest of us know that his father, Emperor Charles, wishes to secure England to aid his ongoing fight with France. That, and to use our country as a wall against the German heretics filling his realm. Charles believes an alliance with England is worth sacrificing his best-beloved son."

I sat down hard on the stool, my legs giving way.

The thought that England, having struggled to stand on its own, putting its tongue out at the world, would abruptly be reduced to a satellite kingdom of the Holy Roman Empire, threatened to overcome me with despair.

The world's affairs did not always benefit the ordinary person, but I had believed my country to be different. Here, if the people did not like their monarch, they could and did say so —forcefully. They'd rejected Jane and rallied around Mary, never mind that Edward himself had assigned Jane to the throne.

Sixty-odd years ago, they'd declared themselves tired of the Yorkist and Lancastrian battles by letting the grandson of an upstart Welshman take over the throne and end the bloody struggle.

Now the Holy Roman Empire would create an heir through Mary and Philip, and England would forever be ruled by Continental powers.

I clenched my fists. "I will not have it."

"You are a spirited fighter, Eloise," Colby said in admiration. "A seamstress against the mightiness of the Empire."

"Do not tease me. You would not have asked me to meet you here if you didn't need my help to stop the marriage."

"We cannot stop the marriage, short of assassinating Philip," Colby said decidedly. "That would be a foolish deed, because it would bring the wrath of the Emperor down upon us. We couldn't survive a direct fight at the moment, even if France came to our aid. The only thing we can do is keep Mary and Philip apart as much as possible and pray that Mary does not conceive an heir."

"That is all?" I leapt to my feet. "Sit by the fire and hope she does not become pregnant?"

"The Spanish prince already knows he is not welcome here. He and his followers will want to stay as far away from England as possible. Mary will die childless, and Elizabeth with inherit." Colby's voice softened. "Elizabeth prizes loyalty, Eloise. She will reward well those who stand by her."

I regarded him with the shrewdness I'd developed since I'd met him. "Is that why you do this?" I asked. "For the hope of reward?"

"Not the only reason," Colby answered, voice light. "I do it for the good of England."

"Oh, yes? Many who claim they work for the common good often mean they work for the good of themselves. Why do you so much wish for Elizabeth to succeed?"

Colby's expression revealed nothing. "I have told you. So, England will remain free from the Empire and from domination by Rome."

"But why?" I persisted. "Why are you so opposed to Mary's religion and her dedication to Philip? Or do you simply not like Spanish food?"

Colby didn't smile at my witticism. His gloved hands curled

at his sides, his blue eyes tight. "If the heresy laws are reinstated, and the Inquisition takes root here, things will be very bad."

"That fact is evident. I do not wish to be dragged off and tortured because I recite the paternoster in English." I let out a dry laugh. "Which Bedingfield would immediately report to Mary, of course."

"Aye, Mary chose Elizabeth's jailer well. Stubborn and blind at the same time."

"You are wandering from the subject," I said.

A chance beam from the shuttered window touched his red hair. By his stance, the shape of his face, and his coloring, he was very Tudor-like—Elizabeth's hair was red and gold, Mary's dark but tinged with red as well.

"Why do you wish to know all my reasons?" Colby asked softly. "Suffice it to say they are good ones. I want foreign rulers to stay far from England."

I pressed my hands to my stomacher, chilled. "I haven't quite decided I trust you, James. I know nothing about you—not who your people were nor why you do not remain in Shropshire puttering about your estate. I do not see in you the feverish obsession of a fanatic, and so I must wonder what you gain by helping Elizabeth."

We squared off, Colby's face taut with the effort of holding in his temper.

"What must I do to gain your trust?" he asked in wariness.

"Tell me the truth. You are not an idealist, like Thomas Wyatt. You are not a cocksure courtier, like Robert Dudley. You do not have ruthless aspirations to rule through a puppet-queen, like Northumberland."

Colby's gaze flicked from mine to the wall behind me. "You ask too many questions."

"Because you refuse to answer them. I will therefore have to give you my conclusions, and you will not like them."

Colby's brows drew down as he focused on me again. "I have no interest in your conclusions."

I stepped to him and wound a lock of his hair around my first two fingers. "Tudor red."

Colby moved impatiently, disentangling himself from me. "Many a man in England has red hair. It is not unusual."

I touched his chin. "You remain clean-shaven, and you do not put yourself forward. You are taller than he was and quite slim, but when you are out of temper ..." I drew back. "I should take care with that, were I you."

Colby's voice went hard. "You know nothing, Eloise."

"You cannot trust me with this secret?" I demanded. "You trust me with so much, and not, I believe, because Lord Robert assured you I had integrity."

"My secrets are dangerous." Colby glared at me, his expression so like Elizabeth's when she was in a temper. "Everyone who knew this secret is dead, save me."

I remained close to him, with no desire to run. Colby's body was warm, his strength apparent. I placed my hand on his chest to feel his heart beating beneath my palm.

"I must know one thing," I said calmly. "Do you plan to overthrow her, or rule through her? Or blackmail her to keep it secret that Henry has a living, male son?"

Colby grew very still. When he spoke, his voice was deadly quiet. "If any of that were my intention, I would kill you before I left this house."

I drew a sharp breath. "Then the fact that I remain alive means you have no designs on the throne?"

"None whatsoever." Colby's lip curled. "Why should I?"

"For one thing, Mary would not be queen and planning to marry a Spanish prince."

Colby shook his head, and the tension in him eased slightly. "I would have to fight hard for the crown, and even if I won, I could not prove my claim. I was never acknowledged. My true mother was a milkmaid of Gloucestershire. I was taken off her hands and given to the Colbys of Shropshire to raise, and I never saw my mother again. She is dead. The Colbys are dead as well, and so is Henry."

"Such difficulties never stopped men with lesser claims," I pointed out.

"Aye, that is so," Colby acknowledged. "But I have observed the men and women who surround these pretenders to the throne. I have no wish to be jerked about and manipulated by ruthless people for their own gain and then executed when their plans go awry."

Something tight in me began to unwind. "You have some inkling how Elizabeth feels, then."

Colby rested gentle hands on my shoulders, his gaze holding mine. "Why do you believe I've appointed you as her guardian? To keep our lady safe and distant from the plotters, to have her head remain intact. You are an excellent watchdog, Eloise."

"A fine compliment," I said in my ironic tones. "I thank you. Does Elizabeth know any of this?"

"I have told *you*. As I say, everyone else who knows is dead. Except you."

I understood that Colby was capable of strangling me and leaving me here on the stone floor—silly Eloise, who ran off into the woods alone to meet a stranger.

It would be my own fault. I'd allowed myself to be caught up in the rivalry between Elizabeth and Mary, proud that I'd been chosen to watch over Elizabeth. I'd lauded myself for perfecting the scheme of using stitching to convey messages into and out of Elizabeth's house.

Not only that, but I'd found it exciting to meet a handsome man like James Colby in out-of-the-way corners. I knew he had no lover, because I'd have heard the gossip, nor any woman with whom he liked to dally. The only lady he spoke to intimately was me, and I'd pretended to myself that his interest in me went beyond taking care of Elizabeth.

I'd been a fool. I made myself let my ridiculous fantasies about him go, and met Colby's gaze squarely.

"No one listens to the prattling of Eloise," I said. "Even if I blabbed far and wide that you were Henry's bastard, no one would believe me."

Colby's grip tightened. "Perhaps not at first, but they'd begin to look twice at me and to wonder. I am in your power now, Mistress Rousell," he finished softly. "What must I do to ensure you will keep my secret?"

"Nothing." I put truth in every word. "I would never, ever betray you to a soul."

Colby's dangerous expression relaxed into perplexity. "Why not? Knowledge like this could give you much power."

I smoothed his cloak where it lay against his chest and then turned from him and caught up my own. "I will not tell you why not. That will be *my* secret."

I believe he guessed because he tugged me back to him and pressed a brief, warm kiss to my lips. It was a sincere kiss, a kiss of gratitude, not an offering for my silence.

"Be well, Eloise," he whispered.

I told him I would and departed.

CHAPTER 19

July 1554

"I am very ill, Master Bedingfield," Elizabeth said in a hard voice. "This is why I am silent at mass."

"But you are not silent," Bedingfield countered, his drooping moustache quivering with his words. "Only when prayers are said for the queen."

"Perhaps that is when my headaches flare," Elizabeth returned. "I do have them, sir. In fact, I have one now and must lie down. Mass must be sung without me, today."

Bedingfield gazed at her more mournfully than ever and scuttled away to write of the conversation to Mary.

Love was a strange thing, I mused as I went about my duties. When one is very selfish, love is about how the object of desire makes one feel. A cruel woman could make a courtier her abject servant and be kind to him only when he pleased her.

A less selfish love not only wishes for the pleasure the other person can bestow on one but also wants to make the desired person happy. A mutual pleasing, as between a fond husband and wife.

More selfless still is love that expects no return, a need to keep the beloved safe and ensure their happiness. This love can be beautiful, as a mother with her children or a daughter to an elderly father ... or it might turn dangerous and slide into obsession.

I did wonder as much as Colby had why I wanted to keep his secret, why I did not want to see him used by ambitious men or beheaded for the blood in his veins.

I knew only that I wished Colby to be safe, and that I admired him for his sensible acceptance of his position. If he'd been greedy and zealous, he'd have used the opportunity of Edward's—or even Henry's—death to sail in and claim he was Henry's son, despite the difficulties in proving such a claim.

Colby hadn't done this, because he did not covet the throne. He wanted nothing to do with it, but fervently wished Elizabeth to have it.

I thought of love for another reason the day that Bedingfield admonished Elizabeth about omitting prayers for her sister during mass. In Winchester that morning, Mary had married herself to Philip of Spain.

I learned the details of the wedding and its splendor a few days later from a reliable source, Uncle John. He wrote to Parry, who in turn gave the letter to Colby, who let me read it at the empty cottage in the woods. Because I was searched whenever I came back from my walks, I memorized relevant passages before I returned the missive to Colby.

Philip had arrived in Southampton with great pomp and pageantry and then progressed to meet Mary in Winchester. The Spaniards who'd accompanied him were described as haughty and sneering, though Uncle John, a more charitable man, declared they were no more so than any other aristocrats.

Twenty-six-year-old Philip, their prince, was apparently handsome, blue-eyed, and athletic, and had drawn much praise for his appearance. Rumor had it that he put his attractive body to use in the bed of any lady who would have him, but that same physique also made him regal and every inch a king consort.

He'd made it quickly clear that although he was glad to pull heretic England back into the fold of the mother church, he would not oppose the fact that Mary was England's sole ruler. This pleased the bishops and lords in Parliament and on the council, who had only at the last moment given in about the marriage—with that stipulation.

Philip also had begun organizing tournaments, with all their grandeur, so that the lords of the land could compete as they had done in Henry's time.

Clever, I thought as I read Uncle John's letter. *Philip knows he's not wanted and works to soften the blow.*

Mary had emerged from their chamber the morning after their wedding a very blushing bride. Uncharitable onlookers claimed Philip was pale and red-eyed from having to fortify himself against the onerous task.

I read of the couple's consummation with a qualm. A pregnancy would weaken Elizabeth's position and at the same time strengthen Philip's.

The royal couple was, at the time of Uncle John's letter, traveling to London where they would continue their quest to pull England firmly under the dominance of the Catholic church. Charles, Philip's father, had given him kingship over Naples and also styled him as King of Jerusalem, and so Mary perforce was now queen of those as well.

"And so it begins," I sighed as I handed the letter back to Colby. "Are you still willing to wait and see whether Mary conceives?"

"It is the best thing we can do," he answered. "For now."

I disliked having to be idle, but Colby was correct. I could think of no other solution that would not involve bloodshed.

Colby kissed me again before I left that day, but I was too distracted to take much pleasure in kisses. Or so I told myself.

When I returned to the palace, my basket, cloak, and pockets were searched, and as usual, they found nothing. I sought Elizabeth to tell her what Uncle John had written and found her in another towering rage. Bedingfield, rigid on his knees, regarded her timorously.

"He refuses to give my Bible to me," Elizabeth shouted when I entered her chamber. "Can you credit such a thing, Eloise? Shall I not read and study God's word?"

"I assure you, Your Grace, you may have a Bible," Bedingfield said in desperation. "Your Grace reads the Latin so well, I am certain it will be a joy for you to read God's word in that tongue."

Elizabeth screamed, fists at her sides. Bedingfield fled, and Elizabeth shouted obscenities at his retreating bulk.

THE CHILL OF AUTUMN GAVE WAY TO WINTER. IN NOVEMBER WE heard—openly through Bedingfield, and covertly though Parry —that Mary was with child. Elizabeth became quiet as Bedingfield read the official dispatch, her hands clenched fiercely in her lap.

One Cardinal Pole, who'd been exiled by Henry for opposing his marriage to Elizabeth's mother, returned from the Continent bearing an edict by the Pope forgiving the nation of England for its heresy. The English people, apparently, were not to blame for their error in leaving the Church of Rome, despite two kings that had led them astray.

So, at one stroke, we were Catholic again. Mary had her handsome husband, her Church restored, and an heir inside her body. Her joy was complete.

"Meanwhile," Colby said when we next met, "the rest of us wait and watch."

"She will have her child," I said unhappily. "What will become of Elizabeth, then? And me?"

"There is rumor of a plot to make certain Mary miscarries the child," Colby said slowly. "A poison that will cause her to lose the babe."

I flinched at the cruelty of this. "How awful. Is it true?"

"I do not know." Colby sat beside me on the bench he'd brought in to furnish the little cottage. It had a table now too, and stools for that. "It is rumor only at this point. It would be most difficult to get near enough to her, in any case."

"I must draw the line at that," I said resolutely. "Even if such a child might be the death of us all."

"It might not be."

Colby's tone went thoughtful, and I glanced at him, my interest caught. "Why do you say so?"

"Philip is trying to persuade Mary to be more lenient to Elizabeth. He's told her that there is no need to disinherit Elizabeth entirely. Whether or not Mary manages to produce an heir, it is best to keep Elizabeth as a possible holder of the crown—reformed church or no."

"Philip, pawn of the Holy Roman Emperor, prudent?" I asked with a smile. "Who would have thought it?"

"Philip is shrewd, rather. Better Elizabeth than Mary of Scotland, Philip and his father believe. Scotland is in the firm grip of France, and young Mary seems to be an easily manipulated person. She would make England become French too, and the Holy Roman Emperor does not want that."

"They'd be besieged on all sides," I said. "Better to gamble on Elizabeth, they suppose." I sighed. "So, we still do nothing?"

"For now. Philip's presence keeps conspiracies at bay, because he has the might of Emperor Charles behind him. But we shall see what Fortune brings."

I rose and shook out my skirts. "I perceive nothing but bleakness ahead. Please send my love to Aunt Kat."

"I will." Colby pressed my hand and kissed my cheek. "God speed, Eloise."

By tacit agreement we had not spoken again of his parentage, but it was there between us, an unacknowledged spectre. I sensed that Colby did not trust me completely, but as with Mary's pregnancy, he would wait and see what happened.

My knowledge was dangerous to him, but then, he'd passed himself off as the Colbys' son all these years. Why would anyone disbelieve him now?

I had no idea what he meant to do. These games of intrigue were growing too deep for me.

ALL THAT DARK WINTER AT WOODSTOCK, WE WAITED AND watched, uncertain of our future. The house was cold and the roof leaked. Fuel, for some reason, was difficult to obtain, and I had no fire in the room where I slept. I admit I often purposely ingratiated myself with Elizabeth so she'd invite me to spend nights in her bedchamber with its warm fire.

In comfortable London, Mary made happy plans for her babe to come. That she was quick with child, she had no doubt, and the news was broadcast to all corners of England.

Advent arrived and then Christmas. The priests at the chapel in Woodstock sung many long masses, which were supposed to be festive celebrations, but which I found tedious in the extreme.

Elizabeth sat in sullen silence as incense wafted through the cold chapel to choke our throats and burn our eyes.

Though Elizabeth was not allowed the luxurious garments she'd worn before her arrest, I continued to sew gowns with fabric Bedingfield was persuaded to ask Mary for. I kept the cut plain and the frocks somber, but I made certain Elizabeth always looked regal.

Spring came none too soon for me, with Candlemas in February and then the quiet season of Lent. We waited for news of Mary's lying in, and while those around us prayed out loud for her safe delivery, Elizabeth remained silent.

Colby and I met regularly at the little house, but we were not the only spies whispering clandestinely. Elizabeth's gentlemen attendants spent much time at The Bull in the village, where Master Parry lodged, and Elizabeth, through me, was seldom short of information.

Bedingfield *must* have known of these meetings, but he either was stupidly oblivious or simply did not want to deal with the complexities of the situation.

Colby and I became closer. Whether he was relieved to have someone with whom he'd shared his secret or whether he simply wanted to keep an eye on me, I could not tell.

I realized he might be using my growing attraction to him to manipulate me, but I was so confused about what I truly felt, I did not mind. All I knew was that I looked forward to my encounters with Colby and missed him grievously when he roved about England keeping watch for Elizabeth.

Whenever Colby and I met in private we kissed, though with little of the passion I'd witnessed in Elizabeth and Robert on the eve of his wedding.

I never spoke about what was blossoming between us, deciding to enjoy the friendship as I had it. Woodstock was a lonely place, and I was lucky to be able to occasionally stroll to the village and back, speak to Colby in the woods, and communicate—even underhandedly—with Aunt Kat, who was still under house arrest in Highgate, north of London.

It was the strangest winter of my young life. That year, 1555, I would be twenty-two.

The loneliness at Woodstock came to an abrupt end in April.

At Easter, Mary had gone into seclusion at Hampton Court for her lying in, and she sent for Elizabeth to attend her.

The summons both stunned and relieved Bedingfield, but not me or Elizabeth. We knew that Philip had been gradually persuading Mary to release Elizabeth and embrace her as sister once more. This apparent reconciliation was his idea, not Mary's.

As we prepared to depart, Elizabeth paced through the rooms that had confined her, glaring at them in distaste. "A horrible place," she declared. "Whenever I am queen, I shall burn it to the ground."

One of Mary's ladies sent her a disparaging glance, but I believed it was more for Elizabeth's assumption that she'd become queen than for her vow of destruction.

My gaze fell on the window frame, glass, and shutters where Elizabeth had inscribed verses, much to Bedingfield's irritation, though he hadn't stopped her. One in particular now caught my eye.

Much suspected by me, nothing proved can be.
Elizabeth, A Prisoner.

It was the last thing I saw of her jail at Woodstock.

WE LODGED AT HAMPTON COURT FOR SEVERAL WEEKS IN quarters that had been built for Edward when he'd been a boy prince, without word from Mary. One morning we were startled by bells pealing all over the palace and throughout the town.

"The queen must have had her child," one of Mary's women exclaimed. "God be praised."

Elizabeth quietly put aside her breakfast and returned to her bed. The bells continued to ring but then quite suddenly faded away.

"It was a mistake," I passed the news to Elizabeth later that day. It had not been difficult to discover the information—the palace halls were full of the tale. "Some poor soul thought the queen had borne her child, a boy. They were so ready to believe it that the churches were ordered to ring their bells."

"Oh, poor sister," Elizabeth exclaimed, with a hint of genuine pity. "A cruel humiliation."

The pity was only a hint, however. Bishop Gardiner had visited Elizabeth during these first weeks and attempted to badger her into admitting her guilt in Wyatt's conspiracy. Elizabeth stubbornly insisted on speaking only to her sister and would admit nothing.

Gardiner, aged, stubborn, and fire-eyed, and Elizabeth, young and just as stubborn, had faced each other, neither of them with any remorse. Watching them, I worried we'd spend another year at cold, dreary Woodstock.

A few nights after we'd heard the bells, I was aroused from bed by a frightened maidservant. Wide eyes regarded me in terror over a single candle flame.

"Her Grace sends for you, miss. She is to go to the queen— now, in secret. I fear this is the last we'll ever see of Her Grace, miss."

I struggled to climb out of bed and dress myself, my fears mounting alongside the maid's. Would Mary have Elizabeth murdered, here in the queen's own house?

She might, I thought darkly. Elizabeth had arrived at Hampton Court with no announcement or pageantry, brought inside through the back gates at night. I doubted the populace at large even knew she was here.

I reached Elizabeth's chamber and found her waiting impatiently, already dressed, with a heavy velvet cloak over her gown. A gentleman of Mary's household stood with her, his lantern throwing a circle of warm light through the gloom.

"This is your waiting woman?" the gentleman asked abruptly.

Elizabeth sent him an irritated look, both for his impertinence and his ignorance. "She is. My sister knows of her. Shall we go, and not tease the queen's patience?"

Elizabeth was as poised as ever, but when I went to her, she gripped my arm with panicked fingers. "Do not leave my side," she whispered as we followed our guide out of the chamber. "I fear what this night may bring."

The gentleman with the lantern hustled us down a staircase, out through a dark garden scented with flowers that had closed their petals for the night, and back into the palace via a door on the garden's far side.

I had always disliked Hampton Court, which had been seized by Elizabeth's father from the unfortunate Cardinal Wolsey. Wolsey had recklessly flaunted his beautiful manor, more sumptuous than anything Henry owned. His punishment had been the forfeiture of his house, and his life.

Henry had remodeled Hampton Court to woo Anne Boleyn. He'd ordered the intertwined initials *HA* to be carved on the dark wooden moldings that decorated the halls, passageways, and royal chambers.

After Anne's downfall, workmen had hastily chiseled away the initials so that Henry could bring Jane Seymour to live here, but the work had been done so quickly that several carvings had been missed. Here and there, a lone *HA* remained high in the wall, a reminder of royal fickleness.

People heard ghosts at Hampton Court—the echoed screams of Catherine Howard in one gallery, a strange cold figure glimpsed stalking through another.

I had no idea if this gloomy atmosphere upset Elizabeth as we climbed the staircase to the queen's privy chamber. She darted nervous glances toward the shadowy corners, as though expecting assassins to spring from them, and kept tight hold of me. Whether my presence reassured her, or whether she planned to thrust my body between herself and an assassin's knife, I could not tell.

We reached the queen's chambers without mishap and were admitted at the knock of the gentleman who'd brought us here.

Mary's chamber was deserted except for one lady attending her—Susan Clarencieux, I recognized her as. Mary reposed in a chair near a dark window, a tapestry-draped screen behind her chair to cut the draft. Her stomach was somewhat distended under her loose gown, though not as much as I would have thought for a woman eight or nine months with child.

Mary had aged since I'd last seen her. Her cheeks were heavier, and the lines about her mouth had deepened. Her eyes showed satisfaction that she'd restored her religion to these shores at last, as well as frustration that all was still not as it should be.

With a swollen, beringed hand, Mary motioned Elizabeth to her. Susan, a stern-faced woman with iron-gray hair, detached herself from Mary to stand by me, the two of us giving the sisters a moment of privacy. Our escort disappeared from the room in evident relief, his task done.

Elizabeth knelt before Mary and bowed her head, kissing the coronation ring held out to her. Candlelight touched Elizabeth's unbound hair, deepening its red hue.

Mary regarded Elizabeth with a sour frown. "You believe then, do you, that I wrongfully punished you?" Her deep voice rolled through the room. "Your letter to me implied as much."

Elizabeth's head moved slightly, but she kept it piously bowed. "I may not say so, not to Your Grace."

"You say it, I believe, to others."

Elizabeth remained in her posture of supplication. "I have never been, with one word or deed, unfaithful to Your Grace. I promise you that I have always been—will always be—your truest subject."

Her beseeching words could have melted the iciest heart, but Mary's face remained like stone. "I have heard of your behavior from Master Bedingfield, in tedious detail. Your conduct is not that of a prisoner, he tells me. You did not accept your punishment as you ought."

"If so, 'twas only because I was maddened at being driven from your side." Elizabeth dared raise her head, and she sent Mary a look of appeal. "I waited for one word, for one sign from you of sisterly forgiveness." A sob choked her voice.

I hoped Elizabeth would not take the contrite pathos too far. I'd observed this sweet, penitent princess unmercifully abusing poor Bedingfield, even tricking him into writing to Mary's council whatever she dictated.

"Well, you are here now," Mary said with finality. "Here you will remain until the birth of my heir. Then we will speak of better days to come."

She spoke stiffly, as though she wished to say other words, but had forced herself to speak these. As though someone stood behind the screen at her back and murmured lines to her.

"There *is* someone there," I whispered to Susan, who'd remained beside me. "Behind the screen. I saw a movement through a crack in it."

"Hush," Susan advised me in a severe tone. "This is none of your affair."

Mary glanced at me as though she'd noted my observation, and I dropped my gaze as I should before the royal stare.

"You are good to me," Elizabeth was saying. "Though I do not deserve it."

Did I detect a softening in Mary's expression? I could not tell from this distance. Mary's pregnancy, I reasoned, had bolstered her confidence. She could afford to be generous to Elizabeth when the next heir to the land grew in her belly.

I started when I detected another furtive movement behind

the screen. "Someone *is* spying on them," I hissed to Susan. "Friend or foe? And whose foe?"

Elizabeth had excellent hearing and jerked her head up at my questions. She shot a searing gaze at the screen behind Mary, while Mary turned a bright, angry red.

The tapestry-hung screen was suddenly shoved aside and around it stepped the last person I expected to see: Philip, King of Naples and Jerusalem, Regent of Spain, consort to the Queen of England.

CHAPTER 20

"Well met, Your Grace," Philip said to the still-kneeling Elizabeth.

Elizabeth remained fixed in place and watched Philip with steel in her eyes.

I hadn't decided what to expect of the man, whom I'd never beheld either in person or in painted likeness. I could understand, though, why so many ladies found him pleasing.

Philip stood tall next to Mary, though in truth, he wasn't much taller than I was. His hair was so light brown it was nearly blond, and his neatly trimmed beard framed a strong face. He had an athletic body hardened by tournaments and sport on horseback, which gave him an upright grace.

On looks alone, I could understand why Mary had fallen for him, this dashing, handsome hero who'd ridden in to rescue her and her country.

Not being Mary, I studied Philip with rather more objectivity. He did not carry an aura of either evil or foolishness, as his detractors claimed. Instead, he exuded strength of character and the determination to succeed at whatever it was he set his mind to. He might practice much diplomacy to obtain what he desired, but he'd have it in the end by pure force of will.

He did not love Mary. I saw that at once when he turned to her. Mary was another piece of diplomacy he'd use as means to the greater glory of the Hapsburgs. He'd put up with her deteriorating looks, her temper, and her stubborn piety so that he could hold England in his hand.

"Dear sister," Philip said to Elizabeth. "We are pleased at this reconciliation."

By Mary's pinched mouth, she had not seen the interview thus. A chance to vent her pique, perhaps, but never a reconciliation.

Philip took Elizabeth's hands and raised her to her feet, pressing a chaste kiss to her cheek. Elizabeth returned the kiss but warily.

"We should have wine," Philip declared. "To celebrate."

Mary remained seated, her sour look more evident, but she nodded at her husband.

"Have it brought," she barked to Susan, and Susan slipped out the door, pulling me along with her.

I'd wanted more than anything to remain in that room so I could report to Colby every word Philip uttered. But Susan curtly gave me orders that I in turn relayed to the servants.

Despite the late hour and exhausted staff, we soon collected wine and cakes from the kitchens and carried them back into Mary's chamber.

They awaited us, Mary rigidly in her chair, Elizabeth on a stool at her feet, Philip standing behind his wife. They made an elegant tableau, one begging to be immortalized by the court painter, Hans Eworth.

Philip crossed the room to us as Susan and I entered. I clutched my tray while I curtsied deeply to him.

With chivalric grace, Philip relieved me of the tray and then Susan of hers, placing each on a table before he poured wine for us all. I momentarily feared he meant to poison Elizabeth, and perhaps she did as well, because she glanced into the cup Philip handed her without enthusiasm.

Philip carried wine to Susan and me, the pair of us curtsying again to receive it. Philip touched two fingers under my chin, and I looked up a gold-embroidered silk sleeve studded with rubies to his face.

Over his crimson doublet he wore a waist-length black velvet cloak, also embroidered in gold. It was a beautiful costume, and the ease with which he wore it told me he was used to such sumptuousness.

Philip's brows rose slightly, as though he sensed my assessment, but he turned away, uncaring of my scrutiny.

Once I creaked to my feet, Susan and I remained in the corner while the three royal personages spoke together—or rather, Philip held forth, Mary murmured responses, and Elizabeth listened. They drank wine—Elizabeth barely wet her lips with hers.

It became clear, as Philip chided Mary, that no matter how much Mary feared Elizabeth's popularity, Philip had more or less demanded that Mary pardon her. I remembered what Colby and I had discussed at our meetings in the cottage near Woodstock—how Philip and his father worried far more about Mary of Scotland inheriting England than they did Elizabeth.

Philip's welcoming of Elizabeth had nothing to do with compassion, friendship, or sisterhood, no matter what his silver tongue said. He played politics in this room, and Mary had to have realized this.

Elizabeth understood it, and Philip knew the two Tudor women were aware of what he was doing. I seemed to be watching a staged drama in which only Philip had learned all the lines. He fed them to Mary, who obediently stated the correct responses, and Elizabeth, who maintained her silence.

By the time Elizabeth was allowed to leave the chamber,

Mary had tentatively agreed to bridge the chasm between them, repeating that she wanted Elizabeth near her during her lying in.

We returned to Elizabeth's chambers, my lady gleeful but cautious.

"Perhaps, just perhaps, we might return to better times," she said. She turned a thoughtful look to the dark window, above which a stray *HA* remained. "'Twas a curious night."

I could not disagree.

Our stay at Hampton Court stretched through May and June, and then into July, with no sign of Mary's child arriving. Mary's midwives and physicians began stammering that they must have been mistaken about how far along she'd been before she'd confined herself.

Elizabeth resided with Mary in the royal apartments, no longer a prisoner, but on the other hand, not encouraged to leave again for one of her own estates.

Philip's Spanish courtiers who filled the palace were aloof and strange to me. The noblewomen's gowns ranged in color from black and silver to deep blue and crimson, and were spangled with gold lace, pearls, and glittering jewels.

The ladies had dispensed with the fashion of low-cut bodices and shoulder-baring necklines for close-fitting sleeves with padded sleeve caps pushed well above the shoulder. The overdresses were sometimes fastened all the way down the front rather than split open over the underskirt, though many ladies did like to hook back their overskirts to display a sumptuous kirtle. I took note of these new styles, as I had not had my notebooks with me or news of the changes of fashion on the Continent during our long sojourn at Woodstock.

The Spanish gentlemen wore velvet, silk, and satins even

when they rode out in the mud and rain. When they ruined their garments, they tossed them away then complained when replacements were too slow to arrive from Spain. They behaved as though they belonged to a court in exile, and lamented its lack of the comforts of home.

Following Philip's commands, these courtiers stoically looked the other way when Englishmen jeered at them or threw mud and worse when they strayed from the palace.

One afternoon I entered Mary's bedchamber to deliver linens to her and found Mary on the floor, her knees drawn to her chest, her maids and midwives hovering anxiously around her. Mary's face was twisted in agony, her hair hanging down, and as I stopped, astonished, she emitted a low, guttural cry.

"Is it the baby?" I whispered to one of the midwives.

The woman shook her head. "She has had this illness since spring. Naught to do with the child."

Mary moaned, a piteous sound. She leaned her head back, her breath coming fast, her body tight. I thrust the linens to another attendant and slipped out of the room.

"Poor Mary." Elizabeth conveyed genuine sympathy when I relayed this event to her. "I know well how frustrating pain can be." Her headaches of late had gone, and the swelling that had plagued her last spring and again at Woodstock had not returned, disappearing as mysteriously as it had come. "All I can say is she had better have this child soon, because what they are saying … It is horrible." She broke off, shuddering.

"What things?" I asked with alarm.

"That she miscarried," Elizabeth said. "That the baby the bells rang for earlier was dead. That God is punishing her for marrying Philip. People wanted an heir, and now they are angry."

Through the open window, we heard Mary moan in her chamber across the courtyard, her cries echoing with hollow sorrow. I disliked Mary, but the sound broke my heart.

Now that Elizabeth was no longer officially a prisoner, her ladies and gentlemen could come and go as they pleased—although her favorites, such as Aunt Kat, had not been restored. Elizabeth gave me leave to make visits outside Hampton Court when she did not need me, and I happily departed, rejoicing in freedom and the warmth of summer.

I no longer had to meet Colby in the woods in secret. He lodged near the palace with a man called Sir Shelby Williams and his wife, who'd served Queen Catherine and had been pensioned off by her will. The Williamses were a kind family, not only friends of Colby, but also of William Cecil, Roger Ascham, Uncle John, and others who'd made up Elizabeth's household once upon a time.

In addition, the plotters who'd surrounded Master Parry in Woodstock often paid visits. We would sit at Sir Shelby's long table, our elbows on the board, partaking of fine joints of meat and warm wine, while we conversed freely.

We were prudent enough not to openly talk of Mary or Elizabeth, except in a general, gossipy way, but we discussed many other things long into the night. The time was made merry by song and good company.

Colby and I liked to speak together at length, alone in the hall after others had departed or retired, Sir Shelby and his wife making a tacit agreement not to disturb us.

"I heard that Mary miscarried," Colby said to me one night in July. We sat side-by-side on a bench facing a small hearth fire, the summer night having turned cool.

"Whoever says so is wrong," I answered. "Poor Mary is in much pain, and her entire body is swollen, but not from carrying a child. She never did carry one, she has now realized."

"She ought to show herself, then," Colby said grimly. "Stories are circulating in London that Mary is dead."

I huffed a laugh. "What nonsense. If Mary were dead, Philip would depart, taking his Spanish court with him." I went somber. "The villagers near Hampton Court despise the Spaniards. I cannot help feeling sorry for Philip's gentlemen and their ladies, though at the same time, I do wish they would go away."

"That time might come sooner than you think," Colby said, his blue gaze on the flames. "Philip has other kingdoms to worry about, and England is only a small corner of the Empire."

"England is an independent nation," I said indignantly. "And part of no empire."

Colby flashed his smile at me. "You echo the sentiment of the English people."

"And of Princess Elizabeth, I am afraid."

Colby nodded, returning his attention to the fire. "True."

I let out a sigh. "Even Philip knows he is not welcome, but Mary will not admit it. She is so certain God will not desert her, so certain she is right."

"God *has* deserted her." Colby's tone was so stern I blinked at him in surprise. "He must have, and for good reason. She has revived the heretic laws. We have not spoken of it in this house, because it is so terrible, but she has already had people tried and burnt alive in London." His large hands tightened on his knees. "Ordinary people, Eloise, who refuse to give up their beliefs and who cannot afford to flee to someplace like Geneva. The Archbishop of Canterbury and his cronies have been imprisoned at Oxford for creating the Book of Common Prayer at Edward's command. It is madness."

I'd heard about Archbishop Cranmer's arrest, because he'd been housed not far from us at Woodstock. I'd learned that he'd quickly recanted his reformed faith, but it is easy to recant anything when your fingers are being crushed.

"You are in no danger of being arrested yourself, are you?" I asked in concern.

I'd not put it past Mary to imprison Colby out of pique because he'd been in Elizabeth's company of gentlemen. Once interrogators began torturing him, what truths might be revealed?

I wondered if Colby's adoptive parents had recorded his birth and baptism, claiming him as their own son, or whether anyone traveling to Shropshire could discover that he'd been a by-blow.

I also wondered if the milkmaid who'd borne him had officially revealed the identity of Colby's true father, and whether anyone had written this into some record or other. No one had any reason to check Colby's antecedents, but if Bishop Gardiner and Mary's council decided to try him for heresy, who knew what might come to light?

"Do not fret, Eloise." Colby took my cold hand between his warm ones. "I mouth pious Catholic prayers and attend mass like a good lad. Martyring myself for the cause will help nothing. I do what I must to stay alive."

"Good," I said fervently.

"*Good* because I work for Elizabeth?" Colby's lips quirked, a sparkle entering his eyes. "Or *good* for my own sake?"

"On both counts." I regarded him without blushing. "On both counts, James."

I strangely did not mind whether Colby returned the affection I felt for him or not. I wanted his safety, and his happiness, more than I cared about anything for myself.

Colby kissed me with more warmth than usual when we parted. He studied me thoughtfully, but I refused to be embarrassed.

AT THE END OF JULY, MARY LEFT HAMPTON COURT, commanding Elizabeth to accompany her. No trumpeters or heralds raced before us, and no lavish pageantry proclaimed the queen's progress as we sailed downriver, back to London.

Mary's depression ran deep. She stoically faced the humiliation that she'd been wrong about her pregnancy, but another followed close behind it—Philip announced to Mary that he was leaving England.

It would not be for long, he adamantly promised, but everyone in the court except Mary herself understood he was deserting her. The marriage and the attempt at an heir had been a failure.

Nobody but Mary was sorry the Spaniards departed, sailing from Greenwich where we'd traveled to see them off. Mary mourned for days after they were gone, her dream of marriage, a child, and perfect happiness dashed from her.

"Such a thing shall never happen to me," Elizabeth vowed quietly as we watched Mary's gaze return again and again to the window of her chamber. Below her, the Thames on which Philip had taken ship ran wide and full. "I shall never ruin myself with a bad marriage. A woman must always be careful whom she marries, especially a queen."

I silently agreed. I'd received an alarming letter from my mother not many days ago positing that it was high time *I* married. I hoped it to be a passing whim on her part—or rather, her husband's. I knew quite well who had prompted the letter.

I determined that I, like Elizabeth, would refuse any suit I didn't wish, and asked Elizabeth to stand by me against my stepfather.

Not many weeks after Philip's departure, I was allowed to meet Aunt Kat in London and ride with her to Hatfield, where we would join Elizabeth. Mary had finally allowed Elizabeth to leave her side—as long as she stayed at Hatfield and behaved herself, she'd admonished.

Aunt Kat and I had a tearful reunion, with much embracing and many kisses. I quickly realized, however, as we rode north from London, that Aunt Kat's house arrest had not made her any more docile and compliant than had Elizabeth's.

"It does a body good to go about where one wishes." Aunt Kat sighed with contentment as we rode our palfreys at a slow pace, the outriders happily dawdling along with us. "Our time is coming, Eloise, you mark my words."

"What do you mean?" I asked absently, paying more attention to the soft green of the countryside than her nattering words.

"Mary is barren, her husband is gone, and old Bishop Gardiner is at death's door." Aunt Kat sounded meanly pleased about all this. "Our princess shall be queen, and sooner than you think."

I turned to her, my alarm rising. "How do you know this, Aunt Kat? You have been confined longer than I have."

Aunt Kat sent me a sage nod. "I have my ways. I know that Mary wishes to confiscate the lands of good people who fled to Geneva and other more tolerant places, but she has enough opposition not to act too hastily. Well, we'll see if she has her way, but I think not. A mistake, the burnings at Smithfield. London chokes on the smoke of her victims, and Mary will not last."

I could see that Aunt Kat had not lost her taste for meddling.

"James Colby has been often to visit me," Aunt Kat continued. "He was able to bring me messages. No, Elizabeth's cause has not died." She smiled, a woman content.

"Mary watches her," I cautioned. "Philip might have persuaded Mary to let Elizabeth out of prison, but Philip is gone, not to return, I think."

"Mary will obey Philip whether he be near or far," Aunt Kat said. "Mary lives to hear a word of praise from him. But there are plenty who want Mary gone, and they hardly keep a secret of it."

"You hardly keep a secret of it either," I pointed out.

Aunt Kat seemed perfectly willing to chat openly of treason, with riders around us, although they were out of earshot. Her boldness showed me more clearly than the crowds who'd come out to laud Elizabeth as we'd ridden to Greenwich how much love for Mary had waned.

Mary had snatched shopkeepers out of their homes and burned them for reading the Bible in English and refusing to recant. These people were not wealthy enough to flee England and live in comfort abroad, which meant they had to remain and face Mary's wrath.

Mary had bullied Parliament into allowing her marriage to Philip, who cared nothing for England but how it profited his father's empire. Now, that prince had run off to the Netherlands to make them behave, and Mary had not produced an English heir.

Therefore, Elizabeth had become the new hope. I felt a qualm of direst foreboding.

CHRISTMAS THAT YEAR WAS PARTICULARLY FESTIVE. ELIZABETH was home with her favorite ladies and gentlemen, including the Parrys, Roger Ascham, and the Countess of Sussex, Anne Calthorpe, who was estranged from the husband who'd led Elizabeth to the Tower. Aunt Kat and Uncle John were reunited, and Elizabeth even had visits from Dr. Dee, the famous astrologer.

As Advent wound on, people came and went from the surrounding countryside—including a Mr. Kingston, two young men called Verney, Sir Christopher Ashton, who was fervently devoted to Elizabeth, and James Colby. At Hatfield, excitement mounted, and because of Colby, I knew everything that was being planned from the start.

"The French ambassador is with us," Kingston said as we sat

at table in Aunt Kat's private chamber at Hatfield one night in December. Outside, the world was cloaked in darkness, and a cold rain had fallen, but it was still not icy enough for snow. "Sir Henry assures us that the money will come from France's coffers. He will lead a force from there."

The reason for this new eagerness to form an uprising was Mary's continued obstinacy. She'd raged at her Parliament this autumn when they'd fought her taking away lands belonging to the Protestant exiles, and again when she'd declared she wished to return her own lands to the monasteries that had been broken up by her father.

The men of Parliament had tried to point out that the Crown actually had very little money. Returning the monastic lands would be a financial disaster.

But Mary adamantly wished it—God had informed her that this was necessary to heal the rift between monarch and church that her father had created. Mary had gone so far as to lock the men of Parliament into the debating chamber until she had her way. They'd resisted, and now they wanted no more of her.

"Mistress Rousell is our go-between with the princess." Kingston gazed straight at me. "You know how to keep her informed, with no one the wiser?"

"Better than you can know, Mr. Kingston," I assured him.

"Eloise is trustworthy," Colby said, and my pride warmed at his words.

They had great courage, I thought, to sit here over ale in Elizabeth's own house and plot to overthrow the queen. Sir Christopher promised he would depart to France and meet with Henry Dudley, a cousin of Robert, and together they would raise an invasion force.

Kingston, with Colby's help, would put together an army in the west, and other loyal gentlemen would gather in the south and east. The French king would pay for much of this rebellion, in return for us driving Hapsburg Philip and Mary his wife out of England. The armies would take London and Mary's person this time, placing Elizabeth on the throne before Philip could act.

Kingston fished a coin from his pocket. It had been severed in two, the cut half ragged. "When I am sent the other half of this, they will be ready in France. And we will see an end to this hideous farce."

I believed them rash and foolish, but I knew better than to state that opinion among these half-drunk, conspiracy-mad gentlemen. They wanted Mary gone, dead if she had to be.

I thought again of Mary as we'd left her in Greenwich, ill and melancholy. Her only desire now was God's work, she'd made known. She vowed to return the lands and money the Crown received from the raided monasteries and to convert those stubbornly clinging to the reformed religion.

"They should be punished with fire," she'd said fiercely the day after Philip had gone. "It is God's will. The flames will free their souls."

The men in this room wanted her stopped, and they were willing to pay any price to do it.

CHAPTER 21

I did my duty throughout Christmas and Epiphany to keep Elizabeth informed of what went on in and outside of Hatfield.

We never wrote or spoke a word that could be misconstrued or used in evidence, as I was able to convey the information to her in our code. I sewed what she needed to learn, and she read it in silence.

When Thomas Wyatt's rebellion had come precariously close to costing Elizabeth her life, I'd been angry with the gentlemen who had put her into such a position.

This time, things were different. Two years ago, Mary had simply wanted to marry whom she pleased, even if her choice of bridegroom was not popular. Now, she burned people alive because they clung to their beliefs.

I did not truly understand the full horror of it all until early in 1556 when I had cause to travel to London. My route brought me near Smithfield on a day when several burnings took place.

Two women and a man, the women fairly young, the man

elderly, were being led to three pyres. The day was cold and misty, damp under leaden skies.

"Shopkeeper's daughters," a woman said near me as I strove to view the scene over heads around me. "And their old uncle." She lowered her voice. "A shame to see it."

The woman took in my fine clothes, fur-lined cloak, and the servants waiting for me, who gazed in as much shock as I did at what was transpiring. The woman I spoke to was middle class, and she was aware that most wealthy gentlewomen served Mary in some capacity or other.

"A shame, I agree," I said, then added, "I am with the princess."

The woman's grim countenance lightened. "Blessings be on her, I say. The blessings of God be upon her." The woman then abruptly closed her mouth and moved from me, as though she feared she'd said too much.

In the center of the cleared space, the two women were being bound to their biers, the man openly weeping. I tried to turn away, to flee the sight, but the dense crowd hemmed me in.

The number of people between me and the pyres prevented me, mercifully, from seeing everything, but I could still hear and smell. Torches were lit and thrust into the wood, but the damp had got into the pyres and the sticks scorched and smoldered. Before long, the girls began shouting and pleading.

"The wood's too wet," a man near me shouted. He swore. "It's too wet to burn 'em quick."

The cries of the girls turned to screams. I heard nothing from the elderly man, but I glimpsed him standing in the midst of smoke and smoldering wood, tears running down his black face, his hair singed and gone.

"Fan the flames," one of the young women cried. "Good people, I beg of you."

Several people pushed forward, trying to help them end their lives quickly, but the guards shoved them back. I desperately scrambled away, squeezing between people who openly wept or shouted for others to help the victims. The smell of slowly burning flesh pursued me as I fled, as did the girls' pathetic screams.

"Stopped. It must be stopped." Tears ran down my face, and I growled the words between clenched teeth. I'd become separated from my servants, and passers-by stared at me as though I were a madwoman, but I did not care.

I scuttled from one side of London to the other without realizing it, my skirts dragging in mud and filth, my shoes ruined.

Anguish and anger dogged me every step of the way. The thought of Mary sitting in her palace, watching the river for any sign of Philip's return and feeling sorry for herself, infuriated me beyond reason.

"Stopped. It must be stopped." I babbled the litany over and over, my tears unceasing.

I'd reached Somerset House, my feet somehow taking me where I needed to go. Aunt Kat came hurrying downstairs when I stumbled in through the front entrance and caught me in her arms.

"It must be stopped," I sobbed into her shoulder.

"'Twill be, love." Aunt Kat stroked my hair as she'd done when I'd been a young lass, and let me cry. "That is why we work so hard, my dear. To stop her and her foul bridegroom. We will win through."

I DID NOT VERY WELL SEE HOW WE COULD WIN ANYTHING. IT WAS fine and good for men to sit around tables and make vague plans, but I began to itch for something tangible to do, though I was not certain what.

Aunt Kat and the others had not been idle, however. Aunt Kat had collected pamphlets against Mary, which she distributed to all she could. Lord Robert Dudley, though living mostly at Norfolk now that he'd been released from the Tower, still attended Mary's court from time to time, and had many chats with his old friend Colby. Colby, in turn, passed on plenty of information to us about Mary.

Lord Robert even went so far as to sell land from one of his properties and smuggle the money to Elizabeth, for raising an army. Elizabeth accepted it and thanked him sweetly.

In March, the Archbishop of Canterbury, Thomas Cranmer, was condemned to burn. During his imprisonment, he'd signed six statements recanting his conversion to the reformed faith and affirming his loyalty to the Pope. But then Cranmer, who'd made it possible for Henry to divorce Mary's mother and wed Elizabeth's, did the remarkable.

At his condemnation, he gave an eloquent speech, much to the distress of his accusers.

I have written many things untrue, and for as much as my hand offended in writing contrary to my heart, therefore my hand shall first be punished. For if I may come to the fire, it shall first be burned.

And as for the Pope, I refuse him as Christ's enemy and antichrist with all his false doctrine.

I imagined the gaping mouths and angry starts of the host of Mary's bishops who'd put the old Archbishop on trial. They'd confidently believed they'd terrified Cranmer into siding with them and supporting Mary's stance on the heresy laws. But in the end, Cranmer died a martyr, another around whom Mary's opponents would rally.

I heard that when Cranmer stood on the pyre that was to burn him, he'd stated in a loud, clear voice, "This is the hand that wrote, and therefore shall it suffer the first punishment."

He'd thrust his hand into the flames and held it there until he died. Mary had been so angry, Colby reported, that she'd overturned the furniture and gone to bed ill.

Stopped. It must be stopped.

I would stop her. No matter if I died for it, as long as I ended Mary's cruelty, I would consider it a deed well done.

DURING MY STAY IN LONDON, I RECEIVED A MESSAGE FROM MY stepfather. He and my mother were lodging near Lincoln's Inn, and he demanded that I visit them. My mother had been writing to me all winter, continually hinting about my unmarried state, but this was the first summons I'd had.

I ground my teeth and ignored their first message, but the second one was borne by a large manservant who would not leave until I accompanied him.

"Why should they be in London at all?" I growled as the stoic man led me toward Fleet Street. "They have a snug house in Buckinghamshire in which to roost."

The manservant said nothing. I could not slip away from him, as he was watchful and strong, and presently we came to a modest house that I entered with trepidation.

My stepfather, Sir Philip Baldwin, was a wealthy man, and the house he'd hired reflected this. Tapestries hung on the walls to guard against drafts, and the floors bore clean rushes scattered with herbs. A gallery encircled the second floor of the house, its elegantly carved railings polished and smooth.

A maidservant met me at the door and led me up the staircase to this gallery, the wooden steps creaking under her tread. The maid was as tall and strong as the manservant—their resemblance in build and taciturnity made me guess they were brother and sister.

If my mother had awaited me alone in the cozy room that the maid ushered me into, I might have tolerated the visit well. As it was, my stepfather sat near the fireplace on a chair filled with cushions. It was the only chair in the room. My mother reposed on a bench, albeit softened with small tapestries, her head bent over some stitchery.

Neither my mother nor Sir Philip rose as I entered. They waited in silence, as though expecting me to pay them the deference I would a great lord and lady.

My mother, once Margaret Champernowne, then Mistress Roussel, and now Lady Baldwin, was complacent and plump like a partridge in a nest. She wore an elegant French hood that lined her rather round face, and had wide rings on every finger. My mother had been slim in my childhood, but good living and rich food had put much flesh on her bones.

My stepfather had dark hair going gray at the temples and a hint of ruthlessness that my mother lacked. Sir Philip was loud in his support of Mary and had benefited from it. Mary had given him a sinecure with an income, and I'd heard that Sir Philip was as proud of his small position as he would be a dukedom.

I curtsied with feigned respect, trying not to let my impatience show. As I straightened, my mother held out her hands without rising from her bench.

"It is grand to see you, daughter." Her gaze hungrily roved my bodice and velvet sleeves. "Are those facings silk? So pretty you look. A credit to us, I have always said."

Sir Philip was less impressed. "You will sup with us, Eloise," he said. A command, not a request.

I went to my mother, took her offered hands, which were warm and moist, and kissed her cheek.

"I cannot stay, sir," I said, turning to Sir Philip. "We ride to Hatfield soon, and there is much to be done."

Sir Philip sent me a chilly smile. "You will not be returning to Hatfield, daughter. It is arranged. Tomorrow you will be betrothed to Sir Henry Felsham, a friend who is in need of a wife. As you are in need of a husband, he has agreed to marry you."

The bottom could not have dropped out of my world more assuredly than if I'd fallen from atop a tower. I gaped at Sir Philip while time slid by, the fire crackled pleasantly, and a group of men passed, arguing, in the street below.

"I would have more words of gratitude." My stepfather's growl snapped me out of my daze.

I raised my head and gazed at him with imperiousness worthy of Elizabeth herself. "I will *not*," I said in a clear, ringing voice.

The ruthlessness in Sir Philip's eyes turned swiftly to savagery. I saw in him a man who would do anything to obtain what he wanted, and I understood that my mother had long since learned to be meek for him.

"You defy me?" he said in furious incredulity. "I am your guardian, Eloise Rousell. I would think you delighted to rid yourself of a low name and rise in the world. Felsham is a wealthy gentleman, with three estates. You will be Lady Felsham, and your son will inherit his baronetcy. What I have done for you is far, far more than one of your sort could hope."

"*One of my sort*," I repeated. "How dare you?"

"Eloise," my mother tried.

My stepfather launched himself from his cushions and slapped me across the face. "Ingrate." Spittle flecked his lips. "Blood tells, as I knew it would. You *will* marry him, and he will have the keeping of you. That is all."

I touched my fingers to my stinging cheek, barely feeling the pain. "I am twenty-two years old, nearly twenty-three. I do not need your permission to marry as I please."

Sir Philip raised his hand to slap me again, but my mother made a noise of distress. He glanced at her in derision but took a step back. "You are impudent and disrespectful," he informed me. "Felsham will cure you of that. He is not afraid to punish his wife."

My fury mounted. "I cannot leave the service of my princess.

She does not like her ladies to desert her. She will never allow me to go."

"Your monarch is not Elizabeth, but her majesty, Queen Mary," Sir Philip said with a sneer. "I am certain Mary will give me every power to take you from Her Grace's household and marry you where I see fit."

I had no doubt he could do just that. Mary was soppy about her true and loyal subjects, and she'd gleefully send away Elizabeth's favorite little seamstress if she had excuse to do so.

I forced my voice to cool. My gamble might not work, because Mary still might have the power to stop me, but I had to try.

"I cannot marry your friend," I said, returning my stepfather's irritated glare with an icy one of my own. "I am married already. Last week in a parish church in Bedfordshire. To a Mr. James Colby."

Silence descended upon the room for a few thick moments. Then my mother let out a little scream and pressed her hands to her face.

My stepfather gaped at me exactly as I had gaped at him, before he lifted his hand and expertly and thoroughly beat me.

CHAPTER 22

I must retrace my steps and explain how it happened that when my stepfather was ready to bind me into an unwelcome match, I was already legally sworn to a more welcome one.

After I'd begun receiving the letters from my mother this winter, I had sought out Colby at Hatfield, cornering him alone in the gardens one late January afternoon.

He'd been speaking of Sir Christopher's plans and our part in them when I'd grasped his sleeve and said, "James, you would do me a very great favor if you would marry me."

Colby had stilled, his red brows climbing slightly higher on his forehead, his only reaction. "Marry …"

"Yes, right away, please. I would be in your debt."

Colby regarded me for a few moments while chill winter wind whipped at my hood and threatened to dislodge it.

"May we wait?" he'd asked after a time. "Elizabeth will be on the throne sooner than we think, and I need you where you are now. After that …"

"No, James, it must be now." I told him in rapid words about my mother's letters and my fear she'd marry me off. "My stepfather will do it—I know he is making her write the letters. If I marry where they choose, I will have to leave Elizabeth, and you would certainly lose my help. I will have nothing to do but sit in a house saying rosaries all the long day. Please, James."

He watched me with his pale blue eyes, taking in every hurried word. "Are you certain?" he asked quietly. "Considering what you know about me? I can think of several gentlemen who are above suspicion I could convince to take you. You could continue your work that way, and Elizabeth would keep you at her side."

"No." My answer was adamant. "Of all the gentlemen of my acquaintance, I can only envision myself married to you. That is why I asked you."

Colby looked away from me, across the green to the woods beyond the village, where Elizabeth sometimes rode out to hunt.

"This is not what I wanted," he muttered.

I'd come to this interview prepared to make a businesslike arrangement with James—if he married me, I would somehow make it worth his while, perhaps use my influence with Elizabeth to bring him money and position. Also, I'd assure him I'd do everything in my power to make certain his secret stayed buried.

Nothing, however, prepared me for the stab of hurt at his words. Prickles of heat spread across my face, and my palms grew cold.

I should respond, to say that it did not matter, and ask him about these other gentlemen he had in mind. But I could not speak.

Colby turned back to me, a half-smile touching his mouth. "I wanted it to be so grand, Eloise. I planned to wait until Elizabeth gained her throne—she has promised me a position in her government as well as a baronetcy. I wished to offer you so much more than a hasty wedding to a nobody."

My hurt evaporated into confusion. "Why?" I asked, my mouth stiff.

Colby's smile remained in place. "Someday I will explain it to you, but the garden behind Hatfield is not the place." He let out a breath. "Never mind. I will fix it, we will marry, and I will hand you heaven and earth later."

I stared at him in shock, almost afraid to understand. "Are you in love with me?"

I truly wanted to know, as I had no experience with men in love, at least not men in love with *me*.

James turned his smile upon me full force, and I had to move back a step, so little could I take the promise of happiness he was sending me.

"That is another of those things we will discuss later," he said. "What is your full Christian name?"

At this moment, I barely recalled it. "Eloise Alice Rousell."

"Eloise Alice." Colby nodded. "I will find a priest we can trust."

My throat went suddenly dry. In the space of a few short sentences, I was betrothed.

"You will make certain it is a legal marriage?" I asked worriedly. "Something not even Mary could put asunder?"

James's grim, businesslike manner returned. "If I take a wife, it will be legal and binding. You leave it to me. Will you tell the princess?"

I hesitated, glancing at the windows of Hatfield from which no doubt someone watched us. "Not yet. I think the fewer who know of this right away, the better."

"I agree," Colby said. "Very well, I will find a priest who will keep it from both Mary and Elizabeth." He paused and sent me a long look I could not decipher. "When we are wed, even if none know it but us, I shall want to be your husband in all ways. Do you understand me?"

I flushed, my heart beating faster. "You mean, in the bedchamber?"

"Aye. Will this change your mind?"

My flush deepened, but not from embarrassment. "Decidedly not."

"Good." Colby touched my cheek, so briefly that anyone watching might miss it. "I am pleased to wed someone with whom I am in complete rapport. Thank you for asking me, Eloise."

He teased me. I smiled back at him to show I did not mind.

COLBY HAD ARRANGED FOR THE BANNS TO BE READ THREE Sundays running in a little church in Bedfordshire, just over the border from Hertfordshire. Four weeks after our agreement, I met him in that little church, where we were married. Colby had paid the priest there handsomely to register the marriage but stay quiet about it.

We'd ridden back to Hatfield separately. The household had assumed we'd been away on errands for Elizabeth, as she went about fortifying her estates while pretending not to. Aunt Kat and Uncle John were too busy to pay attention to my comings and goings, and so no one was the wiser at my change in state.

Colby and I had arranged to meet later in secret to begin our married life. We chose an inn along a road leading west toward Ashridge, one in which none of Elizabeth's people currently stayed. The wind chilled me as I rode to meet my new husband, my cloak hardly enough to keep out the late February cold.

Hatfield had been in an uproar when I'd departed, because Henri of France had written via his ambassador that Elizabeth should give up on her plans for now. The French king advised Elizabeth to remain quiet and take the long view—in other words, France was pulling back from paying for the uprising.

Messages flew to and from Hatfield, and in the midst of it I had left alone, wondering if Colby would be able to keep our appointment.

Elizabeth's ladies and servants had stayed often enough at this inn whenever we traveled from Hatfield to Ashridge that the landlord and his wife knew me. Assuming I was on business for Elizabeth, the landlord's wife let me hire a private parlor without fuss.

I discarded my cloak after I closed the door and warmed myself by the fire, worried that Colby would not come.

The day we'd married Colby had not said much to me, had barely even glanced at me. Since then, he'd been busy carrying messages or closeting himself with those who were secretly shoring up Elizabeth's manor houses.

Such things were far more important than meeting with a new wife, I surmised. Not an auspicious beginning to our marriage, but I supposed it was my own fault for rushing him into it.

I paced the floor as the sun dipped below the horizon. I'd have to stay the night here if it grew too dark, and I busily began inventing stories to explain my absence to Elizabeth and Aunt Kat.

I never heard his step, but suddenly Colby was there. The chamber door closed and he stepped behind me, warm hands on my waist.

"Did any follow you?" he asked.

"No. I did as you instructed."

Colby turned me to face him. I thought he would begin speaking, probably about what he'd been doing for Elizabeth, but instead he kissed me.

This kiss was different from the brief brushes of mouths we'd been enjoying whenever we met in private. He kissed me with a man's kiss, with the taste of passion I'd never been privy to before this.

Strange to feel the roughness of his unshaved whiskers against my lips, his strong mouth on mine. I wrapped my arms around him, and Colby held me tightly in return as the savoring kiss went on.

The ghost of Thomas Seymour and his rough games rose in the back of my mind, before fading into quiet oblivion. Seymour had been oppressive and demanding, but Colby wanted *me*, Eloise. He saw me as a woman for whom he had affection, not a female to conquer.

For a long time we held each other, enjoying each other's warmth.

"What do we do?" I asked him softly.

A hint of Colby's smile flashed across his face. "Whatever we can."

The little chamber was cold, but the bed had been piled high with comforters and warmed with a hot brick wrapped in cloths. James helped me undress then lifted the covers so I could burrow into the bed.

His doublet and shirt came off quickly, and soon the heat of his body warmed the little nest I'd begun. He pulled the covers over us and for a moment, the newlywed couple simply lay together under the weight of the blankets, shivering.

Colby's hands found my skin, which he touched with utmost gentleness, raising his body a little to support the tent of blankets over us. I relaxed beneath him in the dark while he caressed me.

The feelings he engendered in me were strange but not unwelcome. My body lifted of its own accord, liking his warmth.

Colby heated my mouth with a kiss as he slid himself over me, and then he changed me from girl to woman in truth.

"Are you well, love?" he murmured when it was over.

For the first time in my life, I had no words. I nodded

mutely, my wanton hands traveling his body. This was a beautiful man, my husband, and God had given him to me to enjoy.

Colby continued to kiss me, his warm weight covering me better than any quilt. We drowsed together, then he began the dance with me again.

The wooden bedstead creaked, the headboard bumping the wall. Patches of dislodged whitewash floated down to scatter like snow in Colby's hair. That made me laugh, and he opened his eyes, his smile like summer sunshine.

"Do I amuse you?" he demanded.

"Yes." I started to laugh.

His eyes widened in the faint firelight. "Dare you mock your husband?"

"Yes," I repeated and grinned broadly. "I dare."

Colby punished me by loving me so well I could laugh no longer. The little bed scraped across the floor, and at one time I heard an ominous snap, but nothing collapsed.

CHAPTER 23

My stepfather tried to petition Mary to have my marriage to Colby made illegal, but his plea never made it farther than Mary's secretaries. I doubt Mary ever learned of such a minor problem, and if she did, she saw no reason to intervene.

My grandmother, on the other hand, had plenty to say. My mother had immediately sent her word after my visit, and I received a summons, before I could flee London, to wait upon her.

The message came to Somerset House, where'd I'd retreated, bruised but not defeated. Aunt Kat had gone back to Hatfield before my stepfather's command to attend him, so she was not there to comfort me, but the house's staff had been tending to me.

My grandmother lived in Surrey, south and west of London in the gentle countryside. Her house was not as large as the rambling, grand manors I'd been living in with Elizabeth, but was a substantial brick home behind a gate with a square court-yard and a wide garden beyond it. I'd admired the house as a child, and I admired it now when I arrived on horseback, sore and tired, with one manservant and a maid to attend me.

My mother had thought to send me here when I'd been a toddler, but my grandmother had declared she didn't have the vigor to look after a child. Hence, she'd decided I'd live with Aunt Kat. She truly had known I'd have more advantage with Aunt Kat and Elizabeth, and I hadn't regretted her decision for one day.

Grandmother waited for me in her upstairs sitting room, one I fondly recalled from sporadic visits with Aunt Kat when we'd been given leave to travel here. I'd certainly not had the chance since Elizabeth's confinement at Ashridge, then the Tower, and Woodstock.

I curtsied to my grandmother, who remained seated, her hand on a walking stick. Unlike in my stepfather's house, there were several chairs in this wood-paneled chamber, all softened with coverings, along with stools for my grandmother's feet. The fire in the stone hearth was built high, Grandmother believing a person had every right to be comfortable in life.

"Let me look at you," Grandmother began in her usual stentorian tones. "Turn around, girl, do."

She'd called me *girl* since I could remember, and I supposed I still seemed so to her. She'd turned seventy in January.

Obediently, I spun slowly in place, my woolen skirts rustling softly in the silence.

"Humph," my grandmother said. "You'll do. You dress in fancy finery now, do you?"

My own clothes resembled the styles that I created for Elizabeth, though I continued to design them in a subdued fashion. I did not use the same silks and velvets that garbed her—I wore practical wool today because of the rain-drenched roads.

But I prided myself on looking well, so that any who knew I served the princess would see I was turned out smartly, a credit to her, without overshadowing her.

My grandmother scanned my gown and the little jacket that covered my bodice with undisguised interest. While she'd never say so, she too liked to dress well. She enjoyed little luxuries, as her very comfortable home attested.

The maidservant, Helene, who'd been with my grandmother for many years now, carried in a tray with steaming mulled wine and sweet pastries, which I knew would have come fresh from the bakery in the village.

"I am a seamstress," I answered Grandmother, hiding my amusement. "I can make even drab fabric seem fine."

"Have a care with vanity," Grandmother returned. "It might be the end of you."

She gave Helene a curt, dismissing nod. Helene sent me an encouraging smile and withdrew.

"I am careful," I promised her. "How are you, Grandmama?"

"As well as can be expected for someone of my age." Grandmother's dark eyes snapped. "My physician threatens to bleed me, despite my health. He's a quack but an interesting conversationalist, so I send for him when I am weary of everyone else's company. So." She sat up straighter in her chair and thumped her stick once to the floor. "You've got yourself married, have you?"

"Yes." My back stiffened but I did not feel the utter defensiveness I'd had with my stepfather. "James Colby is a good man."

"From Shropshire." My grandmother went thoughtful. "I've heard of the Shropshire Colbys. Decent people," she said grudgingly.

"They've passed away now," I replied, which saddened me. Not only for James's sake, but I would have liked to meet them. "James is alone in the world."

"Sometimes that is better," Grandmother said. "No awkward connections to make your life difficult. He is good to you?"

"So far," I acknowledged. "He is an honorable man. Kind. And he cares for me."

"That is all very well, but be certain he has a warm house where you can be lady of the manor, and an uncomplicated will so you won't have to go to court to claim your inheritance from him."

"I imagine he'll take care of such things," I said, my heart lightening. Grandmother approved of Colby. She'd have said otherwise, decidedly, if she hadn't, and possibly had Helene march me back out into the road.

"You are young and gullible. Ensure he does right by you and that you have entire control of his household. Then you can remain on your estate with people to look after you when he decides to turn his sights to a pretty young mistress. Let her have the bother of him while you live in great luxury."

I hadn't known my grandfather, but apparently, he'd been quite fond of Grandmother and never gave a thought to another woman. He'd provided for her well, as this house attested, and he'd been devoted, so she was not speaking from harsh experience.

However, I'd observed the gentlemen of the court I'd grown up around and knew that many of them lived two lives—one with a wife, the other with a mistress. Grandmother was not wrong to warn me.

At the moment, I was giddily in love and also knew James didn't have much time for a mistress, or a wife either, for that matter.

"Have you told her?" Grandmother asked.

I knew she did not mean Aunt Kat. "Not yet," I admitted, then rushed on. "It has only been a week or so, and Her Grace has been quite busy—"

"Tell her," Grandmother interrupted in hard tones. "'Twill be better for you in the end. I hear that young Elizabeth can be harsh with her ladies but also that she will do anything for the ones she loves. It is the only explanation for her putting up with your Aunt Kat all these years," she finished in a mutter.

I did want to tell Elizabeth—I prided myself in keeping nothing from her—but I feared the interview. Elizabeth had told me repeatedly she did not want to lose me to a husband, and I'd always promised to remain unmarried.

I'd wed Colby to prevent my stepfather from forcing me into a marriage I did not want. Sir Philip had threatened to go through the courts to bring me to heel, but the judges and lawyers might balk at trying to end a marriage that was very legal. They'd have to prove that Colby and I were too closely related, or were already married to others, and things of that nature, none of which was true.

The parish priest Colby had chosen was Catholic, but he'd once been of the reformed religion and performed Catholic masses now to keep himself alive. The bishops would be reluctant to end a Catholic marriage, and the correctly signed registers, with witnesses, showed the marriage was valid, no matter what religion the country embraced. Colby had been very thorough.

I sank to a chair my grandmother waved me to and took up a cup of the warm, spiced wine. "Elizabeth will dismiss me," I said glumly.

"That is possible." My grandmother's words were blunt, but I needed to hear them. "And possibly not. If you are indispensable to her, she'll keep you on, as she did Kat when she married John Ashley. She brought Ashley into the household, where he remains to this day."

Elizabeth also liked Uncle John. The fact that he'd been related to her mother clinched the matter, as Elizabeth had a soft spot for her Boleyn relatives.

Colby was a relation to her as well, but in a much different way. I could never tell her about *that*.

I gazed around the cozy chamber, the fire crackling in a cheerful way on the hearth. I knew Helene hovered outside the door, waiting to fulfill Grandmother's every wish, and likely listened to the conversation as well.

"If she dismisses me, may I come and live with you?" I asked wistfully. I had good memories of this place, and it was quiet and sheltered. "Helene can look after both of us."

Grandmother snorted. "No, you may not. You have a husband now. Let him tuck you into his manor house, which you have just assured me he has. Besides, you'll bear him children soon, and I told your mother long, long ago that I do not have the vigor to look after a houseful of toddlers."

"I may visit though, can't I?" I asked, unwilling to move from the comfortable chair. "I want to see you."

"Because I am old, and soon it might be too late?" Grandmother asked sagely. "Of course, my dear. You are welcome at any time. I want you to bring this Colby when you come again, so I can look him over. Any children can stay with your Aunt Kat."

"Of course." I hid my smile with another sip of wine.

"This house will be yours anyway," Grandmother surprised me by saying. "Oh, yes. It belongs to me outright, because your grandfather was very clear about who would inherit his properties. Which is why I advised you to have your husband do the same. Your Aunt Kat will be provided for by Elizabeth and her husband for a long time to come, and doesn't need it. Your Aunt Joan is married to a successful gentleman, and your mother …" Grandmother glanced heavenward. "Well, she has made her bed, and she must lie in it. That leaves you. This house and grounds will be yours. Helene will be pensioned off in her own home, in return for putting up with me, so you will have to find your own housekeeper."

I could only stare at Grandmother in amazement which

quickly softened into gratitude. She, like Elizabeth, loved well, but hated to be caught admitting it.

I plunked down my wine, launched myself from my chair, and bent to catch her in my arms.

"Thank you, Grandmother," I sobbed. "You have ever been so good to me."

I felt her start, then her warm, plump arms came around me, her embrace so like Aunt Kat's.

"None of this, now," she said softly in my ear. "Someone had to be good to you. Wasn't likely to be your mother, was it?"

I laughed through my tears as I released her. "Still," I said. "I am grateful."

"Sit down and eat them pastries," Grandmother said sternly. "Helene sent someone all the way to the village for them."

I wiped my eyes, still smiling, and docilely resumed the chair and my repast.

I RETURNED TO HATFIELD AFTER SPENDING A FEW DAYS WITH Grandmother, resolving myself to confess to Elizabeth.

It took some time, because she was often in consultation with her advisors like Cecil about her properties and money, Elizabeth ever diligent. Or she'd be speaking with Uncle John or Master Parry about what went on with Mary. She might be isolated, but never ignorant.

At last, I insisted she be fitted for a new gown, made in case Mary recalled Elizabeth to court.

I knelt on the floor at Elizabeth's feet but kept my pins and scissors inside their wooden box. "Your Grace, I have something to confess," I said.

My voice wasn't very strong, and Elizabeth had to lean to hear me.

"What is it?" she asked with sharp suspicion.

"I have married James Colby."

I spoke the words in a rush, fearing I'd never say them if I didn't simply blurt out the truth without preliminary.

Elizabeth's eyes flickered in relief. I wondered what she'd thought I meant to tell her—that my mother and stepfather had convinced me to convert? That I'd betrayed the conspirators who continued to come up with daring and overly rash plots?

"Married," she repeated, her voice hard. "When you knelt in this very room and promised me you would never leave my side."

"I haven't left you," I said with fervor. "I never will." Rapidly I told her the whole tale, of how I worried, with justification, that my stepfather would coerce me into marriage, and how I'd gone to Colby to prevent such a thing, without any plans to leave Elizabeth's side.

When I finished, out of breath, Elizabeth gazed down at me with a cool expression. I saw anger in her, but not the lashing rage I'd braced myself for.

"You could have come to *me*." The words were cold and clear, like the rain beating on the windowpanes. "You could have showed me your mother's letters and told me your fears. Did you think I could not prevent an unwanted marriage?"

I'd reasoned she could have done nothing at all, not when Mary watched her every move and gave her no concessions. I kept my head bowed, not answering.

Elizabeth's hands were near my face, and her slender fingers curled into her palms. I expected to be cuffed at any moment for my impertinence and my conviction that she could not have helped me.

Then her hands relaxed, and Elizabeth let out a long sigh. "If Mary had condoned your stepfather's choice, then no, I could not have prevented it." Another sigh, with a growl to it. "Cease staring at my feet, Eloise, and look at me."

I raised my head, my mouth trembling as I gazed past the

white velvet, gold embroidered bodice to her very pale face, framed with flame-red hair.

"Your marriage to Colby can be put aside if there were no witnesses, or a record, or a clergyman," she stated.

"We had all of that," I assured her. "Master Colby is no fool."

"Indeed, he is not. It can also be undone if the parties do not live as man and wife, if you understand what I mean."

"Like Jane and Guildford." I nodded. "The marriage has been … consummated."

I flushed. While my time snuggled with Colby represented some of the best moments of my life, thoughts of it embarrassed me. And yet, I had no regrets whatsoever.

Elizabeth's mouth hardened. I saw the envy in her eyes for what I'd experienced, but also conviction that the step I'd taken was irreversible.

"What of Colby?" she demanded. "Does he expect you to reside in his home and preside over his suppers? While he claims he is in council all day but really means the public house in the village?"

I shook my head fervently. "No, Your Grace. He knows I won't relinquish my place in your household. I will stay with you—if Your Grace will have me."

I bowed my head once more, my fear unfeigned. I loved Elizabeth as much as I loved Colby, if in a different manner, and it would break my heart if she sent me away. I wasn't certain the joys of marriage would compensate.

Another growl left her throat. "I will think on this, Eloise. Colby is a gentleman of my household, and he should have come to me first. You both should have." I dared raise my head again to find her brows pinched in one of her foul tempers. "It was inevitable, I suppose. I saw how you watched each other whenever you were together, but I hoped you wouldn't do anything quite so rash."

"I can pack my things and be gone in a trice," I said, my voice shaking. "If you desire it."

"Go where? Shropshire? There's a ruined castle of my ancestors at Shrewsbury, but I hear it does not amount to much." Elizabeth became firm once more. "No, Eloise, you will remain here until *I* see fit to dismiss you." She took a step back. "Now go from me. I do not much wish to be near you at the moment."

I unfolded myself from the floor, my heart thumping in relief. If she'd been outraged and furious, she'd have banished me at once, not debated the point. Elizabeth might *still* banish me, but she'd think it over coolly instead of impulsively ordering me from her house.

"I should unpin the gown first," I said.

"No." Elizabeth flicked the skirt from my reach. "Send Mistress Blanche to me, my most loyal lady. And tell your aunt I wish to speak to her."

"Aunt Kat did not know," I quickly assured her. "None knew but Colby and me, and now you."

"And your mother and stepfather, of course," Elizabeth snapped. "Go, before I change my mind and toss you out into the rain."

"At once, Your Grace." I bowed low and then fled, remembering at the last instant to snatch up my box of scissors and pins before I went.

I hugged the carved box to my chest as I slipped into the outer chamber and rested my back against the door to catch my breath. The interview had been terrifying, but I reflected that I preferred begging Elizabeth for mercy a hundred times more than facing my stepfather who openly despised me.

LIFE CONTINUED AT HATFIELD MUCH AS IT HAD BEFORE. I remained with Elizabeth, who at first eyed me with displeasure whenever I entered a room. Gradually, her disappointment in me gave way to acceptance. Colby continued to work for her, bringing her intelligence about all that went on in the realm. I resumed my needlework, sewing gowns, caps, and hoods. Mary never invited Elizabeth back to her, but Elizabeth continued to ask for new designs from me.

Once Elizabeth convinced herself that Colby and I were in no danger of rushing off in a fit of passion and deserting her altogether, she ceased her silent torture of me. Truth to tell, I looked forward to my infrequent encounters with Colby, when we could be private together, but I was careful never to let on to Elizabeth about my yearnings for him.

As spring wore on, Elizabeth grew more confident as public opinion turned firmly against Mary.

The many terrible burnings, especially those of Hugh Latimer, Bishop of Worcester; Nicholas Ridley, who'd been Bishop of London; and finally, Archbishop Cranmer that spring, resulted in Mary being openly hated. It did not help Mary that these men—supposedly evil heretics—all died heroically.

Bishop Latimer had said to his fellow condemned, "Be of good comfort … We shall this day light such a candle by God's grace in England as I trust shall never be put out."

Then, in late March, Mary began making arrests of our group of conspirators.

As with all would-be rebellions, the greatest problem stemmed from trying to raise money. When Thomas Seymour had planned to rise against his brother, Somerset, he'd not only recruited pirates, but he'd bribed a man at the Bristol mint, who'd betrayed him. This time, Christopher Ashton, our leader, had tried to corrupt those at the Exchequer. This part of the plan was found out, and arrests began.

At first, I was blissfully ignorant of the crumbling plot. I had concentrated on proving my devotion to Elizabeth, as well as enjoying my newfound haze of love.

Colby and I were able to meet on occasion and share a bed, and the stolen encounters were beautiful. I was new enough to bodily desire that it transported me to great joy, and I thought there was nothing more wonderful than a husband and wife in love.

Colby was always gentle, though he could be teasing and playful, and we laughed a great deal. Marriage so far had been a heavenly state. I was hard-pressed to keep a smile from my lips and a tune from my throat as I stitched jewels into fabrics and chivied my assistants.

Aunt Kat, Uncle John, and many of Elizabeth's ladies now knew Colby and I had wed. Both Aunt Kat and Uncle John heartily approved of him, to my relief. The ladies all teased me, but I did not mind.

The gentleman who brought the news of Mary's arrests shattered this fragile happiness.

"They've thrown them into the worst of cells," our messenger reported grimly to Elizabeth in her sunlit chamber. "The queen cares nothing for their rank or family—all have been shoved into a noisome pit that would turn your stomach, and one of them has already been racked."

Elizabeth listened, her face like cold marble. "What men has she arrested?" she asked, voice brittle.

"Edmund and Francis Verney," the gentleman replied, his words quiet and angry. "Henry Peckham. James Colby. It's Colby who'd been racked and then tossed into the foul hole."

I dropped the stomacher I'd been stitching, and the steel bands struck the floor with a clatter. I'd risen when Elizabeth had, but now my legs gave way, and I sat down hard on my bench.

Elizabeth glanced at me, eyes like night, then signaled to Aunt Kat. Aunt Kat quickly retrieved the fallen stomacher, but I sat frozen, the needle like ice in my fingers.

Colby, my wily, careful Colby, imprisoned and tortured.

He'd be tried, certainly condemned, and then executed. The husband I'd loved for a few short, sweet months, the friend I'd known for years, had been abruptly torn from me.

Sudden pain burst through my abdomen, bringing bile to my tongue. The bench seemed to slide out from beneath me, and I covered my mouth with my hand as I tumbled to the floor.

CHAPTER 24

Aunt Kat cried out in distress. Skirts swished as Elizabeth swung toward me.

"Eloise," Elizabeth said in alarm.

I heard Aunt Kat's small scream then the voice of the Countess of Sussex. "She is quite ill, Your Grace. The poor child is bleeding."

I felt it then, the trickle of blood on my legs, the hurt as though someone had gripped my insides and twisted them. I heard a cry, loud and wailing, and realized it had come from me. Hands reached out to me, some wrinkled and worn, others beringed and soft.

"Miscarried?" Elizabeth's voice rang among the chatter. "She was with child?"

The ladies broke apart, and Elizabeth stood above me, glaring down like an eagle from an aerie. Tears soaked my face, my entire body wrenched in misery.

"You were with child, Eloise?" Elizabeth demanded of me. "Why did you not tell me?"

"I didn't know," I gasped out. I hadn't understood what the

nausea meant, and I'd been too busy to notice I'd missed my courses. "I didn't know."

I wasn't certain whether Elizabeth believed me, but I saw her perceive that bullying me while I curled in pain at her feet would not look well.

She gestured sharply to her ladies. "Get her to bed and send for a surgeon. Hurry."

Aunt Kat was there, lifting me to her bosom, and then a gentleman usher—a tall, strong man with a kind face— scooped me up and carried me away. Aunt Kat trotted anxiously alongside us and put me to bed in her own chamber.

I lost the child who'd been less than a month along, and then I lay in bed, too melancholy to move. Not only was my babe gone, but my husband was in a foul prison, likely to leave it only to go to his death. I wept for hours, tears quietly leaking from my eyes, and I could eat nothing.

Aunt Kat hovered at my side, trying in vain to persuade me to take food. I wanted news of Colby, but we could discover nothing. Aunt Kat had no idea what was happening, and Uncle John learned little more than that Colby was being questioned repeatedly with the others.

Once when I awoke, it was Elizabeth's long-fingered hand holding a cloth to my forehead. She gave me a smile, her affection in place, which loosened a tightness in my heart.

"Poor, Eloise," she said softly. "We must get you well."

"Are there gowns to be made?" I whispered.

Elizabeth laughed her charming laugh and dabbed at my face with the cool cloth. "Always impertinent, is my Eloise. We must get you well for *your* sake, and to reunite you with your husband."

Hope flared in my heart. "He still lives? Will she release him?"

Elizabeth's smile faded. "In truth, I do not know. I will do my best to discover what happened to him." She leaned to me. "His loyalty will be rewarded, Eloise."

I could not stifle a groan, and I turned my head away.

I wondered very much if Elizabeth would be so generous if she realized that Colby was her own half-brother. Or perhaps she already knew—perhaps Mary had found out the secret as well, and James would die for it.

I began to cry again, and Elizabeth called for Aunt Kat, some exasperation in her voice.

As I convalesced, I began each morning fearing to hear news of James's death, and every night tried to sleep, no wiser than before.

Uncle John told us that the entire plot had been revealed. While Ashton, the leader, was safely in France, every other man had been rounded up and interrogated. Unlike two years ago, when Thomas Wyatt and others had been swiftly arrested and executed, time ticked on while Mary kept the men prisoners without release.

April dragged into May, which was tediously warm, and toward the end of May two men came to arrest Aunt Kat … and me.

"My niece is ill. She has lost a child and cannot travel," Aunt Kat babbled as the two courtiers Mary had sent waited impatiently for us.

"No, I will go," I said resolutely. I had recovered in body from my ordeal, although a grief lingered inside me that I knew would never vanish. "I want to go, Aunt Kat."

We were forbidden to say goodbye to Elizabeth—Aunt Kat was not even allowed to speak to Uncle John. The gentlemen made us ride side-by-side, while their soldiers surrounded us and set a hard pace to London.

The metropolis was warming, mud from spring rains drying. The streets teemed with ordinary people on ordinary business, ignorant of plots and plotters, rival queens and princesses, prisons and tortures. No smoke drifted from Smithfield today, thankfully, as we passed southward through the City.

Mary's guards took us not to the Tower, but to Fleet Prison.

Fleet Prison was dank and cold, despite the warm sun outside. It was also noisy and smelled of human waste and the Fleet River, which rushed below its grated windows.

Our jailer, a large, silent man, gave me a look up and down with his hard eyes, and Aunt Kat stepped protectively in front of me. He shrugged and took our money—we had to pay for our own keep—and gave us a cell to ourselves. The small chamber had a table, one stool, and a narrow bed we'd have to share, and that was all.

"I have failed her," Aunt Kat said as she sank to the stool once the jailer had gone. "I have been her teacher since she was a tiny child. She liked to slap me when she was displeased, and I let her, because I knew she loved me as I loved her. I have tried to help her, to guide her, to raise her to where she belongs." Aunt Kat's head drooped in despair. "I have done nothing but make a mess of it."

I laid a comforting hand on her shoulder, though the Lord knew I had little comfort to give. "You love her well, is all, Aunt Kat. Even if you are not always wise."

Aunt Kat brayed a laugh. "I read too much in my youth and was happiest with my books—those classic tomes of ancient Rome. Small good it has done me." She shook her head. "When I first joined Elizabeth's household, she was a nobody, a cast-off bastard none knew what to do with. Her father's council would not even send her clothing, and she went about in threadbare garments too small for her. I had to write and beg for decent gowns for her. At last, King Henry restored Elizabeth as she should be, but still she is deprived of her rightful place. I only want to see her achieve it—that is all I have ever wanted. But my husband is right. I am a fool."

"Love can make one foolish." I twined my arms around Aunt Kat and rested my cheek on her hair.

It had made a fool of me, I thought with heavy heart as I envisioned Colby in his cold cell. I had loved too hard, and now I paid a dire price.

THUS BEGAN SOME OF THE HARDEST DAYS OF MY LIFE. AUNT KAT and I were confined to Fleet Prison all through the summer of 1556, enduring the heat behind walls that sweated with damp.

Halfway through our incarceration, we were moved into slightly better accommodation, two rooms with a few more pieces of furniture. We were not allowed to write to Elizabeth or even Uncle John. I learned nothing of my husband, whether he was alive or dead, though no rumors ever came of executions.

Mary's men interrogated us repeatedly. A search of Aunt Kat's chambers at Somerset House had turned up her box of pamphlets—diatribes against Mary, Philip, and England's return to Catholicism.

Aunt Kat feigned ignorance. "I know nothing about such papers," she bleated, but it was clear our questioners did not believe her.

Even then our jailers did nothing but keep us confined, Aunt Kat and I waiting and wondering what would become of us.

It was easier to learn of Elizabeth's fate than my husband's, because Fleet Prison was a font of court gossip. Those coming in eagerly told stories to those who had been imprisoned for a time, and the jailers and guards readily talked together without worry about who might be listening.

Apparently, Elizabeth had been confined to Hatfield after

Aunt Kat and I were arrested. Though Mary was in a fury, she'd done nothing to punish her sister, allowing her to live at home instead of dragging her back to the Tower.

Mary had informed Elizabeth that her servants—including Aunt Kat and me—had confessed to a conspiracy to overthrow Mary, though they claimed to have acted without Elizabeth's knowledge or consent. Mary, incredibly, had told Elizabeth that she would not hold the actions of her ladies and gentlemen against her.

Aunt Kat and I had stared at one another in disbelief when we learned this.

"Has the queen run mad?" Aunt Kat wondered. "I cannot imagine her smiling sweetly and telling our Lady Elizabeth that she believes in her innocence."

I could not imagine it either. But I recalled the handsome Philip concealing himself behind a screen in Mary's chamber to make certain Mary reconciled with Elizabeth after Woodstock. I had little doubt that the same voice guided Mary this time, although most likely in letters penned from afar.

"If Philip told Mary to cover herself with feathers and cluck like a chicken, I believe she'd do it," I said darkly.

"Eloise," Aunt Kat admonished, but the sparkle in her eyes told me that she agreed.

IN AUGUST MARY'S GUARDS RELEASED US, BUT WE WERE NOT allowed to return to Elizabeth. Rather, we were instructed to remain far from her.

Aunt Kat cried bitterly about this stricture. We stayed with Uncle John in London, where I tried to resume my needlework that I'd been deprived of in the prison, and listened in vain for news of my husband.

All we knew was that Colby had not been publicly executed.

Whether he'd died in prison, either from illness or of his injuries from torture, I could not discover.

Elizabeth continued living at Hatfield under house arrest, but had been allowed to retain most of her household, except, of course, Aunt Kat and me. We had to be content with that.

I tried to contrive ways to find news of Colby. I thought of Robert Dudley, now one of Mary's courtiers, who could possibly discover his friend Colby's whereabouts.

But Robert—despite the fact that his Dudley cousin had been up to his neck in the recent plot against Mary—was sitting quietly at home in Norfolk with Amy. William Cecil was also carefully watched, and I had no chance to approach him.

Neither did I know whether Colby had been informed of my own arrest or of my release, or if he'd known I'd carried his child. That last thought always brought tears, which furthered my anguish.

"No more intrigue," I snapped at Uncle John on a day I was at my darkest. "I want my husband and my life. I never wish to hear a prison door shut on me again."

Aunt Kat and her husband exchanged glances. "She has been like this since she lost the babe," she murmured to him.

I fell silent, frustrated. Aunt Kat lived for Elizabeth, as she'd revealed while we stewed in the Fleet. Aunt Kat loved Elizabeth even before her own husband, I'd witnessed many a time.

I was not so certain of my loyalty these days, because my love had caused me to lose everything.

Aunt Kat and I moved to the country in September, though not to Hatfield, because Mary still considered Aunt Kat a dangerous person. We dwelled with Uncle John's friends in Woolwich, far from court and any intrigue.

Elizabeth continued doing as she pleased, Uncle John told us, ostensibly overseen by Mary's guards, but she had most of her usual entourage about her. The wishes of Philip protected Elizabeth, and Mary dared make no move against her.

Toward the end of the year, Mary must have relented still further, because I was allowed to return to Hatfield, even if Aunt Kat could not. Aunt Kat sent me off with many well wishes for the princess, and I arrived in time for Elizabeth to be summoned to court to spend Christmas with Mary.

Elizabeth's greeting to me after months of separation was to demand I help ready her wardrobe.

"Your Grace," I ventured, my heart beating thickly. "Have you any word of Colby?" I swallowed as Elizabeth turned her cool gray eyes to me. "I have heard nothing of him. No word whether he be dead or alive."

My downcast countenance softened her a little. "My poor, sweet Eloise. Rest easy, my friend. Your husband, I believe, has gone to France."

I gaped in sudden amazement. "France? You *believe* so? Do you know for certain? Why—?"

Elizabeth made a curt gesture, cutting off my tumbling questions. "He was turned out of the Tower once he'd recovered from his injuries, and put on a ship for France. He had no time to search for you, as he had to leave at once."

My limbs grew suddenly weak, and I had to sit down before I could ask permission. Elizabeth merely glanced heavenward and returned to where her maids waited to continue her fitting.

Sweet happiness flooded me. My husband was not dead, not prisoner. He was in France, safe.

Where exactly he was, how safe, and for how long, I did not know, and I doubted I could discover the answers. For now, it was enough to know that Colby lived, in a place out of Mary's reach.

I RODE WITH ELIZABETH TO LONDON AT THE END OF NOVEMBER. She surrounded herself with liveried outriders, traveling once more as a princess in fine style. I'd created a gown of white velvet, thick against the winter cold, for Elizbeth to wear on the journey. Chance sunlight caught on its gold embroidery as we went, as though the air itself promised her better tidings to come.

When we arrived at St. James's Palace, Mary invited Elizabeth almost immediately to her privy chamber. No more ignoring her sister and leaving her to pace and stew—Mary sent an entourage to escort Elizabeth to her the day after her arrival. I accompanied Elizabeth, at her request. She'd scarce wanted me to leave her side since my return.

In her chamber, Mary grasped Elizabeth's hands and kissed her cheek.

"You look well, sister," Mary said. "The time spent in contemplation and study has been good to you."

Mary's countenance was smiles, her square face lighting as though she had genuinely missed Elizabeth. But her eyes were as hard as ever, a darkness flickering behind her sunny gaze. Her friendliness rang false, and I could only wonder what she was up to.

"Indeed," Elizabeth answered. She imitated Mary's cheerfulness, not objecting when Mary threaded her hand through the crook of Elizabeth's arm.

"What a lovely gown," Mary said. She looked over my gold and white creation as she arranged Elizabeth on a stool at her feet. The jewels bedecking Mary's garment and fingers flashed in the candlelight, and a heavy sapphire crucifix hung from her neck. Elizabeth had regulated herself to subdued pearls on her pale gown and a few unadorned silver rings.

"My seamstress is quite clever." Elizabeth nodded to me.

"Ah, yes, I remember her. The niece of your gentlewoman, Katherine Ashley, is she not?"

"Indeed."

Mary glanced at me without much interest, although she

must be remembering how Aunt Kat had been hoarding malicious pamphlets against her. Because I had been at Somerset House shortly before the pamphlets were discovered there, I was guilty by association.

Mary had arrested and tortured my husband and consigned me to several months in Fleet Prison, but other than giving me a slight frown of disapproval, she ignored me.

The queen and Elizabeth shared a meal, and both Elizabeth's gentlewomen and Mary's waited on them. Jane Dormer greeted me pleasantly enough, even though she'd heard of my scandalous secret marriage, to a heretic no less. Jane did not have as much sourness in her as my own parents, though, and she seemed to forgive me.

Elizabeth and Mary supped as we carried dishes to and fro, poured wine, and performed various other chores to make the royal ladies comfortable. Elizabeth was as graceful as a swan, her white gown showing her red-gold hair and gray eyes to advantage.

Mary had covered her plump body with purple velvet, sleeves turned back to reveal bright gold silk, and a stomacher too tight for her broad waist. Vast quantities of sapphires studded her headdress, echoing those on her crucifix.

"His majesty the king sends you his fondest regards," Mary said as she munched a sweetmeat. Elizabeth had finished her meal and sat quietly.

I half-expected Elizabeth to retort, "He does, does he?" but she only inclined her head and murmured her thanks.

Mary continued. "You well have cause to thank my husband, for he has kept your welfare and your future in mind above all things."

"Indeed?" Elizabeth asked, a touch of acid in her voice.

Mary missed her sarcasm. "His last letter to me outlines a fine idea. His Grace has entered into discussions with the Duke of Savoy, and he wishes to offer the duke as a husband to you."

CHAPTER 25

Mary's words dropped into silence. Elizabeth's colorless lids slid over her eyes once, twice, while we all waited for her response.

"Savoy?" Elizabeth inquired in a voice like frost. "The dispossessed Prince of Piedmont, ruler of nothing?"

The temperature of Mary's reply dipped as well. "Emmanuel Philibert is courteous and a man of chivalry. He is neither a boy nor an old man but ripe for marriage. I would think any young woman would be grateful for his offer."

"*Not too old, not too young.* This is a recommendation?" Elizabeth scoffed. "The king your husband has him on a tight lead. Savoy is dependent on Philip for everything."

"Philip thinks much of you," Mary said in annoyance. She lifted her goblet, found it empty and snapped her fingers at Jane, who hurried forward with fervent apologies to refill it. "Marrying Savoy will strengthen your chances of remaining in the succession," she told Elizabeth. "After the fruit of my body with my husband, of course."

"It seems I would owe much to Spain and the Empire then," Elizabeth responded tartly.

Mary slammed down her cup, wine slopping over. "A woman needs a husband. You are young enough to find the married state pleasing, young enough to bear children." Her voice broke over the last word.

"The *un*married state is the one that pleases me," Elizabeth declared.

Mary drew a breath, as though forcing herself to cool her temper. "You have no idea what you mean. God has seen fit to bless you with this gift, as he blessed me with the king."

"And I see what such a blessing has done," Elizabeth returned. "You brought in a foreign prince to ruin the nation of England, and you wish me to follow in your footsteps? A fine example you have set—the people mock you and throw things at you in the streets, because your husband is a Hapsburg."

Mary shrieked. She half-rose and backhanded Elizabeth across the face, knocking over her own goblet at the same time. Elizabeth's head snapped back, and wine arced over her white dress to stain it like blood.

"How dare you," Mary shouted at her. "You impudent, ungrateful daughter of a … Jezebel. Blood will tell. Get out of my sight and out of London. Ride back to your house and do not put one foot out of it until I give you leave. Go!"

Eyes blazing, jewels flashing, Mary flung out one arm, an imperious finger pointing at the door. She was breathing hard, her flushed face streaked with perspiration.

Mary's ladies rushed to the queen at the same time Elizabeth's ladies hurried to open the doors, all of us regarding one another with frightened eyes.

Elizabeth rose and swept from the room with dignity despite her wine-splotched gown, but I saw her mouth trembling.

I reflected as we raced to her rooms to pack what we'd unpacked only a day ago, that Mary's words were nearly the same as the ones my stepfather had thrown at me.

Elizabeth retreated to Hatfield and remained there as ordered, but in a fury. She raged at Mary's high-handedness and vowed to anyone who would listen that she'd never marry, least of all a Hapsburg courtier.

Curiously, Mary said nothing more about the matter, either in letters or messages, at least not that winter.

March of 1557 brought rains, as well as Philip of Spain back to England.

Mary was in transports of joy to see her husband again, but it turned out that Philip had not come for love of Mary. His purpose was twofold—one, to force the Savoy marriage upon Elizabeth, and more importantly, to persuade Mary to give him an army for his war against France.

The Savoy issue foundered, to Philip's intense frustration. Philip greatly desired the match, but Mary, astonishingly, abruptly switched her stance to take Elizabeth's side.

I thought I understood why. Philip wanted to marry Elizabeth to his cousin Savoy in order to keep England under his thumb when Elizabeth inherited the throne. No matter what sins Elizabeth and her followers had committed, Philip assumed Elizabeth part of the succession and England's potential queen.

Mary did not want Elizabeth in the succession at all, and so for the first time, she disobeyed her husband. The two sisters stood against Philip, to his exasperation, and eventually the matter was dropped.

But to Philip's second request, aid for the war in France, Mary was compliance itself. Despite her privy council's fervent advice to the contrary, Mary gave Philip his army. Philip departed at the end of 1557 to fight, taking Lord Robert Dudley and many other prominent gentlemen, including the spurned Duke of Savory, with him.

Philip and the English, with, it must be said, the talents of the Duke of Savoy, won a glorious victory at Saint Quentin in northern France.

Soon after that, disaster struck. Calais, the symbol of English glory for nearly two hundred years, fell in the cold of January 1558.

"It is inconceivable that she has done such a thing," Elizabeth stormed when she heard this news. "A war led by her damned husband—a man who had the gall before he left to gaze at me with desire in his eyes. As though I were a prized hart to snare. Philip knows his wife is a loss, and I have refused his cousin, so why should he not have me?"

"He would have to get special dispensation," I pointed out as I sewed demurely. "As you are currently his sister."

Elizabeth ignored my impertinence. "Mary has driven the last nail into her coffin. She hopes herself with child again, but it is a farce. She is very ill and will not acknowledge it. Serves her right for handing Calais back to France on a platter."

With that unsympathetic remark, Elizabeth continued raging, vowing to restore Calais to England during her own reign.

The fall of Calais filled me with mixed feelings, because when Mary's army returned, beaten, bedraggled, and ashamed, Robert Dudley brought James Colby with him.

I did not realize this until I beheld a tall gentleman with dark red hair under a rain-soaked hat, a thin beard on his chin, riding through Hatfield's gates behind Lord Robert. The man's left arm hung slightly askew, as though it had been broken and hadn't healed correctly, and a long scar marred one side of his face.

He dismounted and strode toward me as I stood in the courtyard, trying to decide who the stranger was. Lord Robert bathed me in a sudden grin, and then I realized.

Letting out a shrill scream, I abandoned all decorum and ran straight at James. I'd not seen him in nearly two years, and anything could have happened in that time—my death or his, or he finding a lady in France he liked better than me—but I did not care.

Colby swept me up and held me hard, his arms shaking with the effort of it. He kissed me right there in front of everybody, and I heard Dudley laughing.

"Such a display," Elizabeth said later when the gentlemen were welcomed home with wine and entertainments. "I believe you were pleased to see your wife, Master Colby."

Colby did not look in the least embarrassed. He'd worn a warm smile since his arrival, and he'd not moved far from my side.

I could not hold onto him for hours as I longed to, because I had to serve the princess. But I pushed aside all others to fill his wine cup, and he turned that wonderful smile to me each time.

"Devotion is touching," Elizabeth said, and laughed. "Dear Robin, you must show such devotion to *me*, or I will think you have forgotten all about me."

Robert gave her a devastating grin and a mock bow. For the rest of the evening, he served Elizabeth with exaggerated courtesy, and she giggled at him like a girl.

I feared Elizabeth would not allow me to leave her tonight, but she dismissed me without much interest early in the evening. I quickly retired to my chamber to wait for James.

He was not long behind me, and we had a reunion in truth. He lay with me far into the night, the pair of us loving each other with increasing frenzy as we rejoiced in each other. In the small hours of the morning, I curled up next to him, not sleeping, but simply enjoying the warmth of my husband's body at my side.

Colby did not sleep either, contenting himself with touching and kissing me softly. I ran my hand along his twisted left arm, the skin on the inside of it mottled and smooth.

"It broke," he said. "In the Tower."

When he'd been racked. His arm had been gruesomely pulled apart and then clumsily healed.

"I was horribly afraid for you," I said, then my voice hardened. "I hate Mary for doing this to you."

Colby tapped the scar on his face, which curved from his cheekbone into his short, red beard. "This came from the fighting in France."

I traced the scar as well. It marred his handsome face but helped disguise any resemblance to his true Tudor father. "Why did you fight for Philip?" I asked him. "Our enemy?"

"For a full pardon and a chance to come home," Colby answered with ease. "Philip cares nothing for these petty uprisings to put Elizabeth on the throne. He *wants* Elizabeth to be queen and is taking a stern hand with his wife."

"She should not have lost Calais," I said with disapproval. Calais had been the last English stronghold on the Continent.

Colby rumbled a low laugh. "Mary did not lose it. The French took it with their canny attack, when those inside the fortresses least expected it. We marched to try to save it, but to no avail. Calais is French once more. But perhaps not for long. The agreement being floated is that France will return the city in five years or pay a large sum to England for it."

I had not heard these details, but they scarcely mattered to me. "Elizabeth is furious with her."

"Many are." Colby touched my cheek. "As for myself, I am only happy to be home."

I was happy as well, wanting to drown in the joy of his warmth. I did have to tell him about the child I'd lost, after which he held me tenderly, both of us sharing sorrow.

After a long time, I wiped my eyes and asked, "Did you know that Aunt Kat and I had gone to Fleet Prison?"

"Yes." Colby's voice darkened. "I found out after I'd been hustled off to France." He pressed a kiss to my hair. "I wanted to rush back and tear down the walls to get you out, believe me, but Dudley restrained me. He had a better way, he said. He has some influence with Philip."

I thought about the timing of all that had happened. "Was that why Aunt Kat and I were released without a trial?" I wondered. "Dudley spoke for us."

Colby nodded. "Very likely."

"And Philip pardoned you for joining his army. It seems we owe much to Philip of Spain."

"Yes." James pulled me close. "Ironic, that."

I had to agree. "I thought you would forget about all me," I said as I snuggled into him.

Colby chuckled, his laughter vibrating pleasantly. "Eloise, how could I ever forget *you*?"

He kissed me for a while after that, both of us contented.

MARY NEVER TRULY RECOVERED FROM THE DEVASTATING LOSS OF Calais. Later that spring she claimed she was again pregnant, although this time her midwives reserved judgment.

When I made a journey to London with Colby in the summer to purchase fabric for Elizabeth, Robert Dudley had us as his guests at St. James's Palace, and I saw Mary in passing there.

She did not look as though she was belly-full. Instead, Mary was bloated and ill, with a gray cast to her face. Her clothes hung on a body that was swollen at the midriff and bone-thin in shoulders and chest, her face nearly skeletal.

"She is dying," I whispered to Colby that night. He agreed with me, but we dared speculate this to no other, including Robert.

That visit was in August. By November, everyone admitted what I had seen on that sojourn.

Queen Mary, abandoned and forgotten by her husband, faced her last days.

THAT NOVEMBER IN 1558 IS A TIME I WILL NEVER FORGET. ON the sixth of the month, Jane Dormer approached Hatfield, surrounded by outriders who bore the queen's standard. She curtsied low before Elizabeth and offered her jewels Mary had sent as a peace offering.

Elizabeth received Jane in her presence chamber and took the casket without expression. "My sister still lives?"

"Yes, Your Grace," Jane answered with quiet deference. "She is sore ill, but still alive."

"And she has named me as her successor, at last?"

Jane nodded. "On two conditions, Your Grace."

"Conditions?" Elizabeth's voice sharpened, but only Jane Dormer, the dearest and closest of Mary's ladies, would be tolerated giving Elizabeth conditions. "How interesting. Name them, and I will give my answer."

Jane was not in the least intimidated. "First, that you pay the queen's debts. She fears too many will be ruined if you do not."

Elizabeth gave a nod. "That shall be done. And the other?"

Jane raised her head and dared meet Elizabeth's gaze. "That you uphold the religion of the one true church. That you continue the work Mary has done."

Elizabeth's red-gold brows rose. "This is her stipulation?"

"Indeed, Your Grace."

Elizabeth laughed once, a derisive sound. "She need not have bothered with conditions. I will pay her debts—she can be assured of that. And I pray to God that the earth might open up and swallow me alive if I am not a true Roman Catholic."

Jane peered at her in some amazement. I did as well,

although I strove to hide my expression from Jane and her servants.

"I may tell this to the queen?" Jane asked. I could forgive her for sounding skeptical.

"You may," Elizabeth answered. Her voice softened. "Also, that my prayers are with her, as well as my hope that she goes easily and quickly to God."

Jane curtsied. "As you wish, Your Grace."

Elizabeth smiled, and Jane departed for London.

Several days later, Jane Dormer's betrothed, Count Feria, who was a Spanish ambassador to England, rode to Hatfield to dine with Elizabeth.

Very few sat down with Elizabeth at table these days. She supped like the heir to the throne she was, eating alone at her board, with highborn ladies waiting on her. She liked court etiquette and was well aware of where everyone fit into the vast chart in her head.

After Jane Dormer's visit and revelations, Elizabeth carried herself even more like a queen. Her household rapidly expanded —prominent ladies and gentlemen deserted Mary in her last hours to seek a place with the new monarch.

I found it sad that more and more abandoned Mary each day but had to admit excitement about the coming change. No more leaky roofs and cold prisons.

Elizabeth had chosen gentlemen for prominent positions in the coming government, these men ready to slide into place as soon as word came of Mary's death. Elizabeth had also brought some of the highest-born ladies in the land into her service, and she awaited the imminent return of several favorites who had fled into exile.

Gomez Suarez de Feria, Jane Dormer's affianced, had become Philip's eyes and ears, and Elizabeth received him as she would an ambassador from a far land. She treated him with the courtesy due his rank, at the same time realizing he would report everything she did or said to Philip.

Even so, I do not believe Feria was prepared for her.

He approved of Elizabeth, it was clear in the way he looked her over, as though sizing up an unfamiliar horse to determine its soundness.

"I congratulate you, Your Grace," Feria said in pleasant tones. "You have survived dark times. And ever in these troubles was His Grace, Philip, reaching his hand out to steady you. Because of my master, you will be queen of England. A generous gift from Spain and the Empire."

His words fell into cold silence. Elizabeth glanced up from her venison—game caught in her own parks—her knife balanced expertly in her hand.

"A gift from Spain?" she repeated.

"It was His Grace Philip who released you from your prison." Feria, confident, trundled on. "He, who prevented your sister from doing you harm. And so, you come to your inheritance."

Elizabeth laid down her knife. Candlelight touched her hair and the pale gown studded with pearls I'd finished only this afternoon. She studied Feria, her gaze as piercing as Mary's ever had been.

"It is not Spain or the Empire who gives me my crown," she said in a voice like winter ice. "It is the grace of God and the people of England who grant it to me. The rule is mine, by right of my succession as laid down by my father, King Henry. Not a gift from *Spain*."

Feria flushed. I felt a bit sorry for him, but the absurd man had expected Elizabeth to clap her hands in glee and bestow hearty thanks upon him and Philip.

Elizabeth had more to say. "Your master, dear Philip, tried to induce me to marry the Duke of Savoy, as you doubtless will recall. My refusal stemmed from one thing only, and that is from witnessing how my sister the queen lost much affection from her people by marrying outside the realm. Therefore, I never will do as she has done."

Feria swallowed. "I see, Your Grace."

"It is clear that you do not," Elizabeth said. "You have affection for my sister—you are to marry one of her most trusted ladies after all—as well as affection for your ruler. I find that commendable, Lord Feria. But do not expect me to share it."

She lifted her goblet with a dismissing gesture, the subject closed.

THE ABASHED COUNT FERIA RETURNED TO LONDON TO CONFIDE to his beloved Jane his forebodings about Elizabeth's accession. The true faith, he predicted, was doomed in England.

He and Jane later retreated to Spain to live in exile with other English Catholics—Jane, from all I heard, was happy married to her Spanish count, who later became a duke. I wished her well.

Not long after Feria's visit, I was awakened very early in the morning by a commotion in Hatfield's courtyard. The house had filled with so many guests that they now overflowed to the outbuildings. The servants were already stirring at dawn, rushing to build fires and ready meals for the many who resided here.

The noise came from more than the usual bustle of servants. I scrambled from my bed and pattered to the window to peer out. James pulled on his nightshirt as he joined me.

A rider had charged through the gates and was pelting hard for the main doors. I felt a ripple move through the house, beginning with the rider and flowing all the way to the attics. I snatched up a wrap and ran downstairs, sliding into Elizabeth's chamber before anyone else could reach her door.

"Who is it?" Elizabeth asked me from her bed.

"A rider." My mouth was dry, my words a croak. "I could not see who."

But we guessed.

Elizabeth tore back her covers and wrenched herself out of bed. "Help me," she commanded.

I assisted her into a dressing gown to cover her night rail and smoothed her hair into some semblance of order. Only when she was satisfied that she appeared calm and tidy did she let me open the door.

Elizabeth glided regally into her outer chamber, nodding to the crowd of her gentlemen and ladies who'd hastened there as they bowed or curtsied.

The man they stood aside to admit was not the messenger we'd expected. Elizabeth had told Sir Nicholas Throckmorton to come to her when Mary had at last died, but the young man who entered was not Throckmorton.

The youth bowed low and thrust something at Elizabeth. Her face changed as she took it.

I saw what lay on her palm—a plain, unadorned ring, the betrothal ring Mary had worn on her finger since the day Philip had placed it there. She would have parted with it only at her death.

Elizabeth fell to her knees. I ran to assist her, but she waved me away, tears flowing down her cheeks, though she smiled as hard as she could.

"This is the doing of the Lord," she said, her voice clear. "And it is marvelous in our eyes."

PART III
QUEEN

THE FIRST YEARS: 1558 - 1560

The difference between being seamstress to a princess and seamstress to the queen was that, from the instant Elizabeth received the ring in her chamber, I had not a moment to call my own.

By the end of November in 1558, we'd already made a progress to London, Elizabeth in robes of purple velvet that I and my assistants had hastily sewn for her. We stayed for a week at the Tower, in far more sumptuous apartments than during our imprisonment, then moved to Somerset House.

All this while I was expected to pore over the fabrics, trims, and jewels to bedeck the queen during her everyday audiences and make a start on the coronation gowns.

Mary and her Spanish husband were gone, Elizabeth was queen, and England heaved a collective sigh of relief. A pretty, young, and very English queen was ascending to the throne, and the dark days were over. The people, tired of winter, longed for spring.

Elizabeth's councilors and courtiers moved into in place within days of the official news that Mary had died. William

Cecil was busily making myriad plans in his new position as secretary to the queen.

Aunt Kat joined us happily in London and received Elizabeth's fond embraces. Elizabeth instantly made Aunt Kat First Lady of the Bedchamber—an honor that surprised everyone but me.

Robert Dudley became her Master of Horse, Uncle John the Master of the Jewel House at the Tower. To James Colby Elizabeth gave a captaincy in her personal guard and promised a knighthood and a baronetcy at her coronation. I became First Seamstress to the queen.

Being First Seamstress meant that though I longed to be near my husband, we perforce saw very little of each other. We had but a few stolen moments whenever we met in a passageway, and a few words before we fell, exhausted, into our bed at night—and that only when Elizabeth allowed me to sleep elsewhere than her chamber.

The coronation was foremost in our minds, and I spent every minute of the day consulting about Elizabeth's clothes, picking through the sumptuous fabrics presented to her, drawing designs, bullying my assistants to sew faster, and taking up a needle myself when it became clear that we'd never finish in time.

The gown for the coronation itself we remade from the one Mary had worn. As Elizabeth had a completely different build from Mary, the entire garment would have to be reconstructed.

Elizabeth was not the easiest to fit these days. People surrounded her from morning to night, most of them men, most of them high-placed, most of them trying to talk to her about everything at once. A lesser woman would have fainted away under all their fussing, but Elizabeth simply told them what she wanted done, expected them to do it, and moved on to the next crisis.

The coronation would be held on January 15, the date

chosen by Dr. Dee, the court astronomer now welcomed by Elizabeth, as the most favorable. Dr. Dee might believe it an auspicious day, I grumbled darkly to myself, but *he* was not the one who had to finish the wardrobe in time.

The state robes of red and purple velvets had to be done, then the gown Elizabeth would wear under them, a gold silk patterned with silver thread and pearls. We trimmed the long, pointed bodice with precious jewels and sewed ermine to the close-fitting sleeves.

I attached a small ruff for Elizabeth's neck, which would make her rather long face seem rounder. The gold skirt had a train trimmed with ermine that required extra time to stitch, and we were sorely rushed. The dress would be covered by a mantle of cloth of gold, embroidered with red roses and lined with ermine and gold tassels.

The costume was complicated and ornate, and I was never entirely happy with it. I felt added tension, because I knew all of London would be watching. The entire world as well, as countless reports and drawings of the event would be circulated throughout the kingdom and abroad.

I was never certain how we managed to finish it all, but we thankfully did. We'd have to pin a few of the gowns on her and hope—but on the appointed day, Elizabeth was ready to travel through the streets on her progress to Westminster.

Elizabeth rode in a large litter borne by mules, Robert Dudley on horseback just behind it. Elizabeth's maids had brushed out her hair until it gleamed, letting it flow loose and long over her shoulders.

She would move slowly, halting within the City for various pageants put on by the guilds of London, each of which would be symbolic of their support of her and hopes for her reign.

I did not join the procession, but Colby, newly knighted in the Tower, marched with Elizabeth's guards. He was dressed in white trimmed with green, his back straight, his crooked arm hidden by the fine silks of the queen's livery. Aunt Kat rode with Elizabeth's train of ladies, she exalted by her new position, Uncle John with Elizabeth's gentlemen.

I slipped from the Tower and mingled with passers-by on the streets, where I shouted and waved with the rest of the joyful Londoners. Conduits had been set up so that free wine from wine shops and barrels could flow, spigots allowing us to fill our cups again and again. I lost myself in the frenzy and didn't find my bed until well into the night.

The next day, though my head ached and my tongue was thick from my overindulgence, I stalwartly attended the coronation banquet and waited on Elizabeth.

I never came close to her place at the table, being far less highborn than her other ladies. I passed wine and cloths to baronesses, who handed them to duchesses, who handed them to Elizabeth. I minded not at all.

My heart was light. After so much darkness and so much fear, my Lady Elizabeth was queen at last.

A QUEEN, ELIZABETH'S PRIVY COUNCILORS ANNOUNCED ONCE THE coronation was done, needed a husband.

As with Mary, they felt that a woman could not rule without guidance from a man—had not Mary made disastrous decisions once Philip had left her, such as reinstating the heresy laws, not to mention losing Calais?

I longed to point out that it had been Mary's *husband* who'd gone and lost us Calais, but the council would not have listened to me. They fondly believed that the correct marriage would make all the difference in Elizabeth's case.

What followed was a string of suitors who courted the queen one by one: Philip of Spain himself; Archduke Charles, another son of the Holy Roman Emperor; Sir William Pickering, one of Thomas Wyatt's conspirators; Eric, the new king of Sweden, and many more. Every eligible bachelor in Europe wanted to pair himself with Elizabeth, England being the jewel each prince wanted to add to his crown.

I knew, however, as did Colby, that while Elizabeth let these gentlemen of the Continent woo her, only one man in the world existed whom she could envision as her husband, and that man was Lord Robert Dudley.

As Elizabeth's Master of Horse, Robert saw to it that she had the best horseflesh in Europe made available to her. Philip had brought lovely Spanish horses to England, where they'd remained, and now Robert ordered horses from Flanders and Ireland to add to the English stock.

He'd also quickly became Elizabeth's most trusted confidant and her closest friend. This friendship grew and twined into something strange and complex, and by the time Elizabeth's reign was less than a year old, every person in the kingdom hated Lord Robert.

"Is he so very terrible?" I asked my husband one evening in the first August of Elizabeth's reign.

I lounged by the fire as the day had grown cool, stretching my legs as I stifled a yawn. I was easily tired these days, as only a week before I had given birth to our daughter, who slept in a cradle at my feet.

Before I had pushed her out into the world—I wailing loudly no matter how the midwife had tried to shush me—I'd had no idea how profoundly I could love one small person.

Equally as profound was my fear for the mite who struggled to live, especially after my experience the first time I'd found myself with child. She'd been born a little too early, and Colby, Aunt Kat, and I hovered over her, taking turns sleeping, terrified that we'd watch our Catherine Elizabeth drift into her final sleep.

"Dudley?" James's eyes remained closed, his long legs beside mine. "Well, he *is* arrogant, and he makes no bones about using people to get what he wants. He flirts with every wife but his own and has the queen dancing in his hand. Do you consider that terrible?"

"A bit," I admitted.

Colby shrugged, his shoulder rubbing mine. "While his wife lives, Elizabeth can have only a flirtation with him. At worst, an affair. Our friend Dudley is not likely to become king."

"Yes, but I hear Amy is often ill," I said glumly. "And tongues wag that the queen would not be sorry if she died and set Robert free."

"'Tis rumor only, Eloise. Have you heard Elizabeth say this yourself?"

"No," I answered. "But when Elizabeth becomes impetuous and imprudent, she endangers herself. We must stop her."

James opened his eyes, his red brows rising. "We must, must we? Elizabeth is queen, twenty-six years old, and has ceased listening to the likes of us. She is no longer the little princess so careful of how she comports herself. Remember that she can now send you to the Tower for twitting her about her behavior."

I pursed my lips, refusing to see this in an amusing light. "Perhaps she would not listen to you or me," I said. "But I know someone she might."

James caught my thoughts as he so often did and nodded. "I believe you are right. Shall you ask her?"

"Indeed." I yawned again. "But in the morning."

Colby grinned at me and pulled me close, erasing my worries with his tenderness.

The next day, after a much-needed sleep, and leaving my daughter safely in the arms of my husband, I went in search of Aunt Kat.

ELIZABETH AND WILLIAM CECIL HAD THEIR HEADS TOGETHER, speaking softly and rapidly, but these days this was a usual sight. Cecil had begun working not an hour after Elizabeth had received word of Mary's death, and since then he'd labored almost ceaselessly.

Together they would face Parliament to revoke Mary's return of the Church to Rome and end the persecution of heretics. Elizabeth and Cecil had already had to fight against the bishops in the House of Lords, many of whom had prospered under Mary and were reluctant to return church supremacy to the monarch.

The Lords tried to dance around her demands, but Elizabeth was firm—she was of the reformed religion, and that was that. No more answering to the Pope and no more persecution of heretics.

I wish I could say that the instant Elizabeth put the crown on her head England became a smoothly running kingdom of peace and prosperity, but of course I cannot.

At the time of Mary's death, influenza had run rampant. I'd come down with it myself soon after reveling at Elizabeth's coronation, one reason my babe came early, or so the midwife claimed. I suppose my illness had made the child ill too, though at the time I'd had no idea she was inside me.

So, with half her kingdom sick, Philip's war in France continuing, and the bevy of eager suitors constantly besieging her, Elizabeth spent most of her time at the business of ruling.

Not all of it, however. Aunt Kat and I had come today to confront her about her private life.

Cecil gave us a courtly, if preoccupied, bow when we entered. He only nodded when Elizabeth said she would withdraw to speak to us, clearly wishing to return to the task at hand. Cecil ever enjoyed his labors.

"You look well, Eloise," Elizabeth said after we'd made obeisance to her, and she had kissed our cheeks. "Motherhood agrees with you."

"I have become fond of its state," I answered neutrally. In truth I adored my little daughter, but I knew Elizabeth did not like mothers gushing about babies.

"One day, I too may sample it," Elizabeth said briskly, as though she did not care one way or the other. "What is this important matter, Kat?"

Aunt Kat creaked to her knees, and I knelt beside her. "Lord Robert Dudley," Aunt Kat said without preamble. "You must leave off."

Elizabeth stilled, the silk of her dress rippling like silent water. Her mind had obviously been elsewhere, and she'd only indulged us with this private audience because she was fond of Aunt Kat. Now she focused on her, eyes narrowing.

"Oh, must I?" Imperious frost entered her voice. "Who are you to tell me I *must*?"

"Your old governess," Aunt Kat returned. "I have looked after you these twenty years and longer. And never more than now have you needed me to chide you about your behavior."

"Chide me?" Elizabeth laughed, the sound cold and shrill. "There is no need for your chiding, Katherine Ashley. I have been friends with his lordship nearly the twenty years you have been looking after me, as you well recall. We were children together, as close as—nay, closer than—brother and sister."

Aunt Kat fixed her with a disapproving frown. "Your flirting, dancing, laughing, and kissing have nothing to do with being brother and sister."

Elizabeth reddened, the daughter of Henry working herself into a fine rage. "And you, Eloise Colby." She turned her hard stare on me. "Do you agree with my aging governess?"

I nodded, bravely meeting that unforgiving gaze. "I am afraid I do. It was I who persuaded Aunt Kat to seek you today. I, who insisted she speak."

Aunt Kat sent me an offended glance. "I certainly know my own mind, Eloise. I speak as I please."

Elizabeth regarded us for a moment longer, then she balled her fists in fury. "My friendship with Lord Robert is none of your concern," she snapped. "It is friendship only—mind that."

Aunt Kat barely winced at her temper. "Rumor says otherwise. They say you enter his chamber as you please, day and night, and that you might well be carrying his child. These things are discussed at the courts of Paris and Spain. I'd not be surprised, at this rate, if it has reached the Saracen lands. Take a husband quickly, Your Grace, I implore you, and stifle these stories."

Elizabeth stormed to Aunt Kat and slapped her. The red imprint of her hand was stark on Aunt Kat's face, but Aunt Kat set her mouth in stubborn lines.

She'd said far more than I would ever have dared, but Aunt Kat knew she'd needed to say it. Or rather, she knew Elizabeth needed to hear it, bluntly and without diplomacy.

Elizabeth lowered her arm and stepped back, her breath coming fast. A muscle in her jaw moved as she strove to master herself.

"I know that you are devoted to me." Elizabeth's fire dispersed and the ice returned. "Because of that devotion, you see fit to speak to me of this. But I cannot simply take a husband because *you* wish it, or because you think it will be good for me. Such things need to be weighed carefully, because I must marry for the good of the realm and nothing more."

"If ever you marry *him*," Aunt Kat said, not daring to say Dudley's name again. "I believe your realm will oppose it."

Elizabeth's smile was brittle and terrible. "How lucky for me then that Lord Robert is married. Your concern is noted. Now, go from my side, and never speak to me of this again."

Aunt Kat firmed her mouth and made no move to rise. "I will take any punishment you choose to give me."

Elizabeth scowled. "I do not wish to punish you. That is, unless you do not *get out.*"

Aunt Kat did not flinch at her command. "Help me to my feet, Eloise. It is difficult for me to rise these days."

I sprang up and assisted Aunt Kat, and then, under Elizabeth's incandescent glare, we took ourselves out of the room.

Cecil, still scribbling away in the outer chamber, pretended to have heard nothing through the door, but his quick glance at us revealed he had. He, too, disapproved of Elizabeth's excessive flirtation with Dudley, and I noticed a small smile hovering about his rather pompous mouth.

CHAPTER 27

I'd hoped Aunt Kat's cautionary words would sink into Elizabeth's very sensible head, and that would be the end of the matter. But alas, it was not to be.

August merged into a blustery September, which gave way to winter, before spring came once more. My daughter grew plumper, and against the odds, became robust and strong, for which Colby and I fervently thanked God.

As Elizabeth expected us all to work with the same dedication as Cecil, I didn't see as much of my husband and daughter as I could have wished, but I still managed to enjoy my domestic bliss.

Elizabeth, vivacious and a natural coquette, teased the gentlemen who pursued domestic bliss with *her*, and drove her council mad with her prevarications. Ambassadors and go-betweens continued to parade their masters before her, and English hopefuls flirted with her at court. Elizabeth pretended to consider each one, some a longer time than others, before saying either *no* or a provocative *maybe.*

And all the while, Dudley was at Elizabeth's side, especially when she rode the hard-to-handle horses she favored, as spirited and reckless as the horses themselves. As Master of Horse, this was Robert's job, of course, but few mentioned that when they criticized him.

Whenever Elizabeth invited me to ride with her, a coveted and much-sought-after position, she would gallop into the woods and bid me act as lookout while she and Robert kissed each other in the shadows.

When Cecil went north to Scotland with an army to help the Scots noblemen tame the French there, Robert stayed behind with the queen.

Colby stayed behind as well—now the captain of the queen's personal guard, he was with Elizabeth at all times. My husband did not want to leave me or our child, either, but I could see he'd prefer a clean and simple confrontation with an angry French soldier to the complex intrigues of court.

Elizabeth's dalliances with Robert, if anything, increased. The two were not often out of each other's company. Robert was at her side when she received ambassadors, and he teased them along with her.

Robert lounged on barges she took down the river when in London or to sun herself in the country, and ran his fingers through the satin, velvet, bejeweled skirts I sewed for Elizabeth. He pulled ribbons from her gowns and tied them around his wrists and, some whispered, around more intimate parts.

In short, almost everyone at court muttered that Elizabeth was a wanton. Such was to be expected from a wanton's daughter, they whispered, although no one dared mention the name *Anne Boleyn*.

Elizabeth never mentioned her mother, either, but I knew she wore a locket with her mother's portrait inside it, and was rarely without it.

"I hear that your wife has sickened," I said to Lord Robert one day when I'd ridden out with Elizabeth, Robert's presence inevitable. Elizabeth had galloped a little ahead, her guards fanning out to keep watch over her, but Robert dropped back to spell his horse.

"Indeed, the poor lady," Robert replied in earnestness. "A sickness in her breast that she has had for some time now. It makes her weak and wretched. I send her gifts and hope they cheer her."

Charming, smiling, handsome Robert was playing the devoted husband. I restrained myself from making a skeptical comment. "Please convey to her my hope for her swift recovery, my lord."

"I will. You are kind, Lady Colby. Your daughter does well?"

My immediate smile blossomed in spite of myself. "She grows by the day. We are most pleased with her."

I was unable to keep the pride from my voice, and Robert laughed at me. "A fine hit by my friend, Sir James Colby," he said, and sent me a bawdy wink. "My felicitations."

I flushed, which only made Robert laugh the harder. "Thank you, my lord," I said stiffly.

Elizabeth galloped back, her hair glowing like fire in the sunshine, her smile wide. Robert immediately forgot all about me, and rode after her, she laughing as he followed in hard pursuit.

WILLIAM CECIL WAS A HARD-WORKING MAN. HE HAD A WIFE, AN intelligent woman who loved book-learning as much as her husband, and he enjoyed gardening when he had an hour to himself, which was rare these days.

Cecil dove into the business of running Elizabeth's kingdom with dedication, helping her restore the church in her own way —doing away with the elaborate ceremony of Catholicism but not paring it down to the austere Protestantism of John Calvin. Elizabeth wished her priests to retain their costly vestments and some of their ritual, though she frowned coldly at excessive ornamentation, hordes of candles, and blanketing clouds of incense.

Cecil had had to persuade her to take the possibility of the French gaining a foothold in Scotland seriously, and to commit troops. He'd resorted to threatening to resign if she continued to dismiss his advice on this score.

In addition to all this, he had to contend with a queen who not only was evasive on the question of marriage but put off her council when asked to name a successor.

"Marriage is a dangerous undertaking," Elizabeth had declared. "Naming a successor is equally dangerous, if not more so. See how many plots and intrigues revolved around me—without my approval, of course—when Mary was queen?"

She'd never *condemned* the plots to elevate her to the throne, I remembered. She'd pretended not to know about them but had quietly provisioned her estates while the conspirators planned to raise armies against Mary.

All in all, Cecil had a difficult job, steering the queen without incurring her displeasure. Elizabeth was generally reasonable and intelligent, but she had her blind spots, and Robert Dudley was one of them.

"He makes me laugh," Elizabeth said when she learned of more complaints about her flirtation with him. "He understands me better than anyone, and raises my spirit high. Why should I not have that?"

"I cannot blame her," I told Colby after she'd said this to me. "She spent years alone, keeping quiet and never putting a foot out of line. Why should she not enjoy herself in the light after such a long darkness?"

"No one minds that she enjoys herself," Colby said patiently. "Her entertainments are becoming legendary, and I am pestered every day to use my position to finagle invitations to them. But she stirs anger and disgust with her favor to Dudley.

She will divide the kingdom over him as surely as Mary did with Philip."

"I remember *that* well." I shivered. "I spent the winter in horrible rooms at Woodstock and had to meet you in a ruined house if I wished to speak to you."

Colby sent me a grin. "You loved the duplicity."

"Of conspiring under Mary's nose?" I smiled in return, reflecting that it was easy to romanticize hardship in a comfortable chamber before a warm fire, with one's beloved husband and cooing child nearby. "Of course, I did. If I'd sat meekly sewing, I should have been wretched."

He nuzzled my hair. "You ever like to meddle, Lady Colby."

"Uncle John says that about Aunt Kat."

"It must be a trait of the Champernownes, then." Colby became serious once more. "But you do see, don't you, Eloise? If Elizabeth has an affair with Dudley—or God help us, marries him—she will divide her council and Parliament as much as Mary did. More, because Dudley is widely despised. He is too …" Colby went silent, groping for words.

"Handsome and charming?" I supplied.

I did understand. Dudley was the sort of man susceptible ladies swooned over but whom other gentlemen did not like. Add to that his father, the Duke of Northumberland, had been executed as a traitor, and King Henry had executed Robert's grandfather, citing the same reason.

"No one wants Dudley to charm the queen into molding England into what he wants." Colby leaned to me, the firelight catching on his red hair and somber expression. "I say this not because I don't wish happiness for Elizabeth, but because I fear she will ruin all she has begun. There will be rebellion and evil once more. At the moment, Elizabeth is the sun to England, the golden princess who became their beloved queen. But if that opinion ever changes, England will be plunged into chaos."

I knew he spoke the truth, and I heaved a sigh. "What a

shame she does not love a stodgy, ugly gentleman who would give her many children, make friends of her advisors, and fade into the woodwork."

Colby laughed out loud. "Is that your description of a perfect husband?"

"For a queen," I said without mirth. "For a queen as radiant as Elizabeth. She is a Tudor, and *she* will rule, not her husband. Make no mistake about that. Not even Lord Robert would be able to tell her what to do against her own wishes."

"I agree with you," Colby said. "And if he should rise up against her? He obediently rose against Mary for Jane Grey and then supported conspiracies against Mary, even while trying to keep his own nose clean. What if Dudley decided he should have more from his wife the queen than her smiles? What if he wanted her kingdom?"

A qualm touched me. "She would have to fight him."

Colby nodded. "England will not be stable if Dudley becomes its king. Too many do not trust him. We cannot let that happen, Eloise."

His voice rang with determination. I had seen that determination before—in Elizabeth, in Mary, in Henry himself.

I'd speculated ere this that Henry's descendants seemed to possess his temper and unwavering belief in themselves in pure form, undiluted by their mothers' blood.

"What are you going to do, James?" I asked with some trepidation.

Colby subsided. "Nothing, for now. But if she makes a foolish mistake, I will have to act."

"On that day, I will have to decide where my own loyalties lie," I said quietly.

"Yes." Colby leaned closer to me, a watchful look in his blue eyes. "You will."

I sat silently for a long time. I wanted my life to continue as it was at the moment—in a privileged position with the new queen, working with fabrics I never dreamed I'd be able to touch: costly cloth of gold and gold tissue, velvets so fine they were like rippling silk.

The clothes I designed for Elizabeth's portraits, her balls, her entertainments, and her progresses had already begun to become famous. Great ladies of the world wrote to me begging for my advice or trying to tempt me from Elizabeth's service, which of course I would not leave.

I wished to remain here with my husband by my side, for my daughter to grow up unharmed and happy. I wanted this, and I wanted Colby to be an ordinary man, son of another ordinary gentleman of Shropshire.

But he was James Colby, ever driven to act for England. Colby had once told me he worked for the greater good, and I had not believed him. I believed him now.

Colby wanted England to prosper as much as did Elizabeth. He'd always known Elizabeth would make a great queen and had worked hard to install her. I realized now that if Colby ever considered Elizabeth bad for England, he would not hesitate to remove her. He'd told me he did not want the crown for himself, but he might decide he had no other choice.

"Oh, James," I said, heartfelt.

Colby sent me a faint smile. "Perhaps you should have married the dull gentleman your stepfather offered you."

"No." I surged to my feet, gazing down on him where he lounged on his chair. "I pledged myself to *you*. I love you, James Colby."

Instead of answering, Colby pulled me down into his lap. I buried my face in his neck, my heart thumping. I'd never believed I would one day have to make a choice between my husband and my queen, and I would be heartbroken no matter which way I went.

ELIZABETH CONTINUED TO PLAY WITH LORD ROBERT. I SAW courtiers grit their teeth when she and Robert made them the butt of their jokes. The pair were shameless, whispering, heads together, smiling as one at the baffled courtiers, and teasing them unmercifully.

She would play the lute and shoot fond glances at Robert as he watched her, in view of everyone at court. But she'd turn a dangerous glare on anyone who even appeared as though they might rebuke her.

I ceased trying. Not because I was afraid of her retaliation, but because I knew she would not listen. If she would not listen to Aunt Kat and Cecil, she would certainly not heed me.

Cecil speculated in early September of 1560 that if things continued as they were he would have to resign. "Even if the queen were to lock me in the Tower for the rest of my life," he sighed. "I cannot stay."

If Cecil went, I asked Colby in panic, how long would it be before the entire council followed suit, and Colby's fears of civil war came to pass?

These decisions were taken away from all of us.

On September 8 Amy Dudley was found dead at the bottom of a staircase in Cumnor Manor in Oxfordshire, her neck broken.

CHAPTER 28

The uproar of Amy's death drowned out all else.

Had she killed herself in despair, many wondered? Because her husband was the queen's lover? Amy's servants reported that she had been ill and depressed, and expressed hope that her end would come soon.

Or, had Lord Robert had her murdered so he could be free to marry the queen?

Amy had been alone in the house, the other inhabitants having walked to a local fair. Amy had sent them away, they said, claiming the need to remain quietly at home. Did that point to an intention to end her own life?

On the other hand, the staircase she fell from apparently was not steep. That the fall alone had killed her was unlikely. More probably, someone had broken her neck elsewhere and arranged her at the bottom of the staircase in an attempt to make it appear an accident.

Rumor put it that Robert and Elizabeth had discussed poisoning Amy—perhaps she'd been weak with poison when she fell.

Tongues wagged, gossip soared. The scandal spread across

the Channel to the courts of Paris and beyond, royals across Europe shaking their heads at the English queen's folly.

Elizabeth, to my amazement, remained oblivious of the rumors, or at least she pretended to be. Both she and Robert made certain that Amy's tragic end was investigated, and a jury was sent to examine the nature of her demise.

The investigators decided Amy's death had indeed been an accident, but this did not dampen the speculation. The uproar continued.

My husband said nothing of the matter. He did nothing, until the day he learned that Elizabeth had told Cecil she would wait a short interval and then let Robert begin courting her.

Colby took me with him when he requested an audience with the queen. Elizabeth was at Whitehall, in the very chamber from which Mary had watched the men of Thomas Wyatt's army swoop down the street, coming for her.

It spoke much of my trusted position with the queen, as well as Colby's character, that Elizabeth agreed to speak with us alone. She dismissed Cecil and her other ladies and led us to a smaller chamber where we were by ourselves.

She glanced about the little room with a pointed look, as though to invite us to see that no screens were positioned for the convenience of eavesdroppers, no doors behind which conspirators could hide. I recalled how Philip had whispered instructions to Mary. Elizabeth would allow herself no such trickery.

Elizabeth positioned herself in the exact center of the chamber, and Colby and I stood in before her, me right next to my husband. After we had exchanged the requisite greetings and inquiries into the health of our daughter, Colby began.

"Your Grace, you will not marry Lord Robert Dudley and make him king."

Elizabeth's eyes, already hard—because she must have

known what this requested interview was about—grew still more granite-like. "This is your command, is it, Sir James?"

"Mary made a husband of Philip, against all opposition," Colby went on firmly. "She decided that she knew, better than her council, better than her government, better than the English people themselves, which man would be good for the nation. Her choice divided England and created rebellions against her. You know this—you were at the heart of those rebellions. I recall how you remarked upon her obtuseness, how you declared her arrogance in the matter was her downfall. And now you hurry to repeat the terrible mistake she made."

Elizabeth listened in absolute silence, her face like chiseled marble. When Colby had finished, she turned and walked a few steps toward the window.

The lovely gown she wore today, silver fleur-de-lis embroidered on a black surcoat over a gold skirt, shimmered in the sunlight. I made certain her clothes always caught the light, to ensure that she was brighter than anyone else in the room.

"And will you begin this rebelling?" she asked in a quiet voice, her gaze on the passageway below the window. Not far from there, Wyatt's army had battered on the palace gates. "Will you recruit your adventurers and rise against *me*?"

Colby said nothing, wise never to admit anything to a Tudor.

"You will not." Elizabeth swung back to us. "You are mine, James Colby, and you always have been."

Colby gave her a bow. "I've never made any pretense otherwise. I work for *you*, Your Majesty, which is why I advise you thus. Though you do not like to hear it."

I relaxed a little, but I knew that our mission had been for naught. Elizabeth would not listen to Aunt Kat, she would not listen to her trusted Cecil, and she'd not listen to James.

"I am more careful than my sister," Elizabeth said briskly. "There is no one to take my place, no second person in the realm to rally around. Who is left to take the crown? Jane Grey's sisters? They are a pathetic pair, and all of England preferred Mary to Jane. No, the Greys will never do. There are a few more of the blood, but much removed. My father did his best to rid us of all our relatives and rivals. Courtenay, the last of the Yorkists, died in Padua a few years ago. Mary of Scotland? Would anyone dare bring about such an obvious tie with France?" She lifted her chin. "You have no one, Sir James, and the people of England would quickly see through a pretender."

Colby moved a step closer to her. Elizabeth had to look up at him—she was tall, but Colby was taller.

"There is someone," he said in his rumbling baritone. "One other person who would—reluctantly—step into your shoes."

"Who?" Elizabeth scoffed.

Colby said nothing. He simply looked at her.

"James," I said in alarm.

Elizabeth gazed steadily at Colby, then her eyes, which were so like his, flickered. "I see," she said at last.

I held my breath, expecting her to call for her guards, to command that Colby be arrested and dragged to a prison. He'd be tried and condemned for treason, because he bore her blood.

Henry would have done so without hesitation. Mary might have done so, perhaps hesitating a little. With Elizabeth, I could only watch and wait for her choice.

"Would the English people rally around a bastard?" Elizabeth asked softly.

Colby did not relent. "I mean no offense, but there were those who said the same about you."

Elizabeth's indignation rose. "My mother was a queen and a noble lady."

"So many claimed otherwise," Colby reminded her. "And yet, they adore you."

Rage poured into Elizabeth's eyes, fury so strong that I knew we were both doomed. Colby's head and mine would adorn pikes on London Bridge, and my poor child would be left all alone.

"You are a bold and brave man, James Colby." Elizabeth emphasized his name.

"I want what is best for England, as do you," Colby returned. "It is in my blood to wish our land to be great. *You* will make it great. I know this." He paused to draw a breath. "But if Dudley is your husband, all will come tumbling down."

Elizabeth faced him in silence, carefully masking the thoughts that raced through her head.

I knew this woman well. She might fly into rages, and her tart tongue could strip a man's flesh from his bones. Ever since the Seymour affair, however, she'd done nothing without thinking through every possible outcome. Her flirtation with Robert had been the exception, and as we stood in this small chamber, I saw her realize that.

I will never know what it cost Elizabeth to draw her conclusions and agree that Colby was right. I saw in her eyes furious anger, deep sadness, and the draining of hope for her personal happiness. And with all that, loneliness. She would always be lonely.

But I also witnessed her vast determination and the need for her kingdom. I recognized the strength of will that had carried her through her disgrace during the Seymour scandal, through her imprisonment in the Tower, and throughout the cold days at Woodstock, when she'd feared every day that assassins would dispatch her in secret.

This fortitude had let her sail through the dangers of Mary's reign without falling. Jane Grey had fainted when she'd been handed England. Elizabeth had taken it and raised it high.

After a long, chill silence, Elizabeth gave Colby a nod, albeit a frosty one.

"I will not marry him," she said in a quiet voice. "I will never marry, Robert Dudley least of all. You have my word on it."

Colby nodded, his tension easing. He bowed to her then, a deep courtier's bow, acknowledging her as his superior.

Elizabeth sent him a cool glance, accepting his obeisance, then she transferred her sharp gaze to me. "You keep secrets well, Eloise. All these years I have watched you, and you never once revealed this knowledge, not in word, look, or deed. I commend you."

I drew a quick breath. I'd never said aught of it to anyone, not even Aunt Kat, in all this time. "You knew? You knew about James?"

She huffed a laugh, Elizabeth the confident. "Of course I knew, my dear. I knew when I saw him at Robert's wedding. I spied him across the room and understood exactly where I'd seen that look, that stance, that bearing before. I admired my father, and studied him much." She smiled tightly. "A favor, Eloise. Bear him only daughters."

"If I can," I said doubtfully.

"You can, do you but put your mind to it. I will assist you with my prayers." Elizabeth sent me a wintry smile. "Leave me now. I would be alone." As she turned from us, her face to the window and gray autumn sky, she added softly, "I will always be alone."

A beam of sunlight fell on her golden-red hair and gleamed on the threads of her gown, the jewels on her bodice. Elizabeth was a piece of the sun, a new light for England.

An idea for another gown sprang to mind as I gazed upon her, one studded with pearls, glistening and glowing in patterns to highlight her purity and her power. Her headdress too would be covered in pearls, and the entire ensemble would portray her mastery of her court and of the world, Elizabeth, our great monarch.

We would do it, she and I, she the ruler, and I and Colby her conscience.

Colby took my hand. He led me from the room and through

the outer chamber, past the curious Cecil and creaky William Paulet, who was now Elizabeth's treasurer.

We moved through the winding pile of Whitehall Palace and up the stairs to our chamber under the eaves where our daughter waited. Aunt Kat held Catherine on her plump lap, and both my aunt and child looked up when we entered.

Catherine held out her arms for me, laughing in her joyous way. Aunt Kat rose as I scooped up my girl.

"Well?" Aunt Kat asked abruptly. "Did she listen to reason?"

"I believe so," Colby answered.

He slid his arm around me and our babe and laid a soft kiss on my cheek. My James, so gentle, when minutes ago he had been ready to face down his queen, with force if necessary.

"Good." Aunt Kat sniffed. "Elizabeth has ever had a wise head on her shoulders, never mind how impetuous she can be, or how silly about men. She'll make England the best queen it ever saw, before or after." Aunt Kat gave us a decided nod. "I have always said so."

AUTHOR'S NOTE

Thank you for reading! I began this book after I'd written one about Anne Boleyn, called *A Lady Raised High*. *A Lady Raised High* was to be part of a six-book series about the wives of Henry VIII, each written by a different author but published collectively under the name Laurien Gardner. I was thrilled to be chosen to write about Anne, the intriguing woman who was mother to Elizabeth I.

The series was sadly cancelled after three books (Henry only got to have three wives), but I'd learned so much about the Tudor period while researching the book, that I wanted to continue writing about the era.

I have done extensive reading and research on Elizabeth and her times since then, though I needed to put everything aside for a while, as I had many other books to write!

Recently I pulled out this manuscript (which had a brief life years ago as *The Queen's Handmaiden*), and began to extensively revise and rewrite it. Much new scholarship has been published since then, viewing Elizabeth's reign from different angles and with new historical and archeological information. All my current research has encouraged me to delve deeper into Elizabeth's life, and I plan to continue the saga with Eloise and Colby interacting with the queen throughout her reign.

I have included in this edition questions for discussion for book clubs or groups who wish to discuss aspects of the novel, and also a cast of characters as a reference to the many historical figures important to Elizabeth's story.

I hope you have enjoyed my version of Elizabeth's young life, as told through Eloise's eyes.

All my best,

Jennifer Ashley

QUESTIONS FOR DISCUSSION

Suggestions for Book Club / Book Group Discussions:

1) How possibly did Elizabeth's attraction to Seymour in her young years, and his subsequent actions as she grew older, color Elizabeth's outlook on marriage for the rest of her life and reign. Or did it at all?

2) Women in Tudor society were forced to put aside any sort of personal happiness in order to survive or be successful. Contrast Catherine Parr's decision to marry Seymour with Mary's decision to marry Phillip and with Elizabeth's decision not to marry at all.

3) How does the fictional character Eloise bring a different perspective to Elizabeth's young years? In what ways are their lives parallel and how do they diverge? How were Eloise's choices in her life influenced by Elizabeth's choices in hers?

4) Elizabeth was the third of her siblings in the succession laid out by Henry VIII. Speculate on what her life would have been

had Edward lived to have (male) children, or if Mary had produced a few children of her own.

5) What would Jane Grey have been like as queen, if Mary had not prevailed?

6) Much has been made of the relationship between Robert Dudley and Elizabeth. Everything from them being nothing but close friends to secret lovers and having several children has been speculated on. What do you think that relationship was?

CAST OF CHARACTERS

Historical characters
(alphabetical order by surname or title)

- **Roger Ascham:** Tutor to princess Elizabeth, later to her as queen. Wrote a book advocating using kindness and persuasion to teach instead of harsh discipline.
- **Katherine Ashley** (sometimes rendered Astley): Governess to Elizabeth from 1537, made First Lady of the Bedchamber (highest honor) at Elizabeth's accession.
- **John Ashley** (or Astley): Husband to Kat Ashley. Became master of the jewel house at Elizabeth's accession.
- **Sir Christopher Ashton**: A conspirator late in Mary's reign who wanted to put Elizabeth on the throne
- **Sir Henry Bedingfield**: Jailor to Elizabeth at the Tower and then Woodstock. A staunch supporter of Mary.

- **Anny Boleyn:** Second wife to Henry VIII and mother to Elizabeth I. Executed by Henry on trumped-up charges of adultery, so Henry could marry Jane Seymour.
- **Susan Clarencieux**: Lady in waiting to Mary I since Mary's childhood.
- **Edward Courtenay** (Earl of Devonshire): Son of Marquis of Exeter, who was son of Edward IV's sister, so had a Yorkist claim on the throne. Father was executed in 1538 by Henry VIII. Courtenay imprisoned in the Tower from then until released by Mary in 1553. He was a strong contender to marry Mary I.
- **John Dee:** Astrologer, alchemist, geographer, and mathematician. Imprisoned by Mary on charges of plotting against her, but brought back to court by Elizabeth I. He supported world exploration including the search for Antarctica.
- **Sir Anthony Denny:** Companion to Henry VIII, appointed as Elizabeth's watchdog after the Thomas Seymour scandal. Married the sister of Kat Ashley.
- **Lady Denny:** Wife to Sir Anthony and sister to Kat Ashley. Appointed Elizabeth's governess after the Thomas Seymour scandal.
- **Jane Dormer:** close friend and lady-in-waiting to Mary. Married Gomez Suarez de Feria, ambassador from Spain and moved with him to Spain at Elizabeth's accession. Died in 1612.
- **Margaret Douglas:** Daughter of Margaret Tudor, Henry VIII's oldest sister. Served and became close to young Mary. Barred from inheritance by Henry VIII, married off to Matthew Stuart, Earl of Lennox in 1544.

- **Guildford Dudley:** Brother to Robert Dudley, son of the Duke of Northumberland. Married to Jane Grey in Northumberland's efforts to put Jane on the throne.
- **Robert Dudley:** Fifth son of the Duke of Northumberland. Childhood friend of Elizabeth. Married Amy Robsart in 1550. Imprisoned in the Tower for Jane Grey uprising, pardoned by Mary in 1554. Appointed Elizabeth's master of horse at her accession. Was rumored to be trying to marry Elizabeth even before his wife's death in 1560. (Was made Earl of Leicester in 1563.)
- **Sir Henry Dudley:** Cousin to Robert, leader of failed uprising against Mary
- **Edward VI:** Only surviving son of Henry VIII, mother Jane Seymour. Ruled from 1547 (at nine years old) to 1553. Named Jane Grey as his successor, fearing Mary's rule as a Catholic.
- **Elizabeth I:** Daughter of Anne Boleyn and Henry VIII. Was declared illegitimate when her mother was executed but later was restored as heir when Henry married Catherine Parr. Became queen at age 25 in 1558.
- **Bishop Gardiner:** Lord Chancellor under Mary. Sent to the Tower by Henry VIII for supporting Catherine of Aragon, released by Mary. Mentor to Edward Courtenay.
- **Jane Grey:** Daughter of Duchess of Suffolk, who was daughter of Henry VIII's sister, Mary. Center of a plot to cut Mary and Elizabeth from the succession, married to Guildford Dudley. Was queen of England for nine days.
- **Henri II of France** :(r. 1547-1559), offered to help Elizabeth plot against Mary then changed his mine.

Married to Catherine de Medici (Diane de Poitiers was his mistress)

- **Henry VIII:** King of England (later of England and Ireland) 1509-1547. Father of Mary, Elizabeth, and Edward. Married to Catherine of Aragon, Anne Boleyn, Jane Seymour, Anne of Cleves, Catherine Howard, and Catherine Parr.
- **Mary I:** Daughter of Henry VIII and Catherine of Aragon. Ruled 1554-1558.
- **Mary, Queen of Scots**: Daughter of James V of Scotland and Marie de Guise of France. Queen of Scotland from 1542. Married heir to French throne in 1558.
- **John Dudley, Duke of Northumberland**: Earl of Warwick and Lord Great Chamberlain to Edward VI from from 1547; made Duke of Northumberland in 1550. Father of five sons, including Robert Dudley and Guildford Dudley.
- **Mistress Norwich:** Lady-in-waiting to Elizabeth, accompanied Elizabeth to the Tower when arrested by Mary
- **Blanche Parry:** Appointed attendant to Elizabeth in 1536, remained with her until death in 1590.
- **Sir Thomas Parry** (no relation to Blanche): Comptroller of Elizabeth's household from 1530s.
- **Philip of Spain**: son of Charles V, Holy Roman Emperor. Husband of Mary (his second wife of four). Also a suitor to Elizabeth at her accession.
- **Cardinal Pole:** Exiled for supporting Catherine of Aragon, restored by Mary, brought edict from the Pope forgiving England for its heresy.
- **Simon Renard:** Ambassador from the Holy Roman Empire, advisor to Philip of Spain.

- **Elizabeth Sandes:** Lady-in-waiting to Elizabeth, exiled to Geneva under Mary.
- **Philibert Emmanual, Duke of Savoy:** Inherited Duchy of Savoy (more or less in northern Italy) that was then occupied by French. Served Phillip II and was governor of Netherlands. Led Hapsburg troops to victory over French in 1557 (and restored to Savoy). Put forth as possible bridegroom to Elizabeth.
- **Edward Seymour:** Earl of Hertford until 1547, then Duke of Somerset, Lord High Protector of England. Brother to: Jane Seymour (mother of Edward VI) and Thomas Seymour. Executed 1552.
- **Thomas Seymour:** First Baron Sudeley, Lord High Admiral of England. Brother to Jane Seymour and Edmond Seymour, Uncle to Edward VI. Executed 1549.
- **Henry Grey, Duke of Suffolk:** Father to Jane Grey.
- **Frances Grey, Duchess of Suffolk**: daughter of Henry VIII's youngest sister, Mary, mother of Jane Grey.
- **Henry Radclyffe, Earl of Sussex:** Mary's supporter, arrested Elizabeth and took her to Tower
- **Anne Calthorpe, Countess of Sussex:** wife of Earl of Sussex, once arrested for witchcraft, very strongly reformist
- **Sir Robert Tyrwhitt:** Master of Horse for Catherine Parr, sheriff of Lincolnshire and then of Cambridgeshire. Placed in charge of Elizabeth after Thomas Seymour's arrest.
- **Lady Tyrwhitt (Elizabeth):** Married to Sir Robert Tyrwhitt, made Elizabeth's governess after Thomas Seymour's arrest. Served in the households of Jane Seymour and Catherine Howard, became close friend of Catherine Parr.

- **Edmund and Francis Verney:** Brothers, leaders of failed uprising against Mary
- **Thomas Wyatt:** Son of poet Sir Thomas Wyatt, raised rebellion against Mary, 1554, arrested and executed, 1554.

Fictional Characters

(alphabetical order by surname or title)

- **Sir Philip Baldwin:** Eloise's stepfather
- **Margaret Champernowne:** Eloise's mother. Became Margaret Roussel (marriage 1) and Lady Baldwin (marriage 2).
- **Grandmother Champernowne:** Mother to Kat Ashley, Lady Denny, and Margaret Baldwin (Eloise's mother).
- **James Colby:** adopted son of the Colbys of Shropshire
- **Eloise Rousell:** Raised by Kat Ashley and seamstress to Princess Elizabeth, later First Seamstress to Elizabeth I
- **Thomas Rousell:** Eloise's father, a strolling player, deceased

ABOUT THE AUTHOR

New York Times, USA Today, and *Wall Street Journal* bestselling author Jennifer Ashley has more than 100 published novels and novellas in mystery, romance, historical fiction, and urban fantasy under the names Jennifer Ashley, Allyson James, and Ashley Gardner. Jennifer's books have been translated into more than a dozen languages and have earned starred reviews in *Publisher's Weekly* and *Booklist.* When she isn't writing, Jennifer enjoys playing music (guitar, piano, flute), reading, knitting, hiking, cooking, and building dollhouse miniatures.

More about Jennifer's books can be found at
http://www.jenniferashley.com

To keep up to date on her new releases, join her newsletter here:
http://eepurl.com/47kLL